THE REIGNING QUEEN of the "cruise of a lifetime" industry, the *Palace of the Dolphins*, is preparing to embark on one of its most successful waterborne milk runs: a seven-day Caribbean cruise beginning and ending in San Juan.

Exhaustion, energy and tension swirl together between the embarking passengers, the stressed out crew and the entertainment staff. This is a true Ship of Fools, a large cast of enticing, complex characters who are about to set off into the Puerto Rican sunset on a journey that will push everyone to their human limits and take the reader on a seven-day journey of hilarity, tragedy, riveting suspense, keen social satire and a plot laid out like a Chinese box, stacking piece on piece from the first page to the shocking and impossible-to-predict climax.

The burned out and partied out cruise director, Derrick Doolittle; the aging, but still popular star of their musical productions, Flora Frampton; the wise-cracking, but tormented head show writer, Rory Riley; the billionaire owners, the Talbotts and their spoiled party girl daughter Twinkle; their guests, Mimsie Von Essen the "Countess" from Texas and her grandson Ian; Leah, Walter and Clarissa Worth, the "perfect" family, who don't quite belong in the Talbotts' world; Poe Evanoff, the brilliant psychiatrist and guest lecturer and Elonzito, the newly promoted Portuguese butler, assigned to serve the VIPs, none of whom have any idea what this voyage will reveal.

Seasick

a novel

Also by the Author

Virgin Kisses

Unapparent Wounds

Natural Selections

Radio Blues

House in the Hamptons

Looking for Leo

Marriage

The Beauty

The Wizard Who Wanted To Be Santa

SeaSick

a novel

by

Gloria Nagy

Jorge Pinto Books Inc.
New York

Seasick

Published by Jorge Pinto Books Inc., website: www.pintobooks.com

Cover design © 2009 by Nigel Holmes, website: www.nigelholmes.com

Book design and editing by Charles King, website: www.ckmm.com

ISBN 1-934978-13-2
978-1-934978-13-9

For Tony Wurman

There are no words
for what my heart holds.

Contents

Acknowledgments

My deepest thanks to my friends, children and grandchildren for providing me with the Space Mountain Ride that has given me the experience, wisdom, agony and ecstasy that love brings and without which I would have nothing to say. I would also like to thank Françoise Brun-Cotton, who has been on this part of the ride since the first book and whose support, insights and brilliant notes were as invaluable as she is; Dr. Frank Sullivan for keeping it and me honest; Wendy Hyland, for being on this journey with me since the very beginning and for her belief in me and this joyful madness we call our work; Melissa Ford for putting it all together and making it possible to actually read it at all; Nigel Holmes for his brilliant cover and gentle genius; Jorge Pinto, a gentleman publisher who has renewed my faith in the process; Charles King for his elegant and meticulous edit and Richard Saul Wurman, my hand in the dark.

"Take me for a trip upon your magic, swirlin' ship, my senses
Have been stripped, my hands can't feel to grip, my toes too numb
To step, wait only for my boot heels to go wanderin' . . ."

—Bob Dylan
Mr. Tambourine Man

⌁

cruise, n. **1.** a pleasure voyage on a ship. —v.i., **2.** to sail about,
as a warship patrolling a body of water. **3.** to travel without
a particular purpose or destination. **4.** to travel slowly, looking for customers or for something demanding attention.
5. to move slowly through in search of a sexual partner. **6.** to
travel at a moderately fast, easily controllable speed.

—*Random House Dictionary*

⌁

". . . She had found the pointless conversation of
Mr. Ned Plymdale perfectly wearisome; but to most
mortals there is a stupidity which is unendurable and a
stupidity which is altogether acceptable—else, indeed,
what would become of social bonds?"

—George Eliot
Middlemarch

⌁

"People live now in a way I don't comprehend"
—Anthony Trollope
The Way We Live Now

Prologue

IT WAS NOT HAPPENING, not happening. She was dreaming, drunk dreaming; too many Cosmos in the disco, whirling around and around. She would wake up any second now, had to wake up, get up, tell someone . . . hands all over her, pushing, pulling, so dark; a moonless sky . . . silent night blackness, stars boogying all over the universe. Up, up they were holding her up . . . No! Don't do that! Up, pushing against something cold and hard. Oh my god! I'm on the side of the ship! It must be a dream . . . that can't-scream-dream . . . wake up . . . have to wake up . . .

SOMETHING FALLING PAST the windows, shiny in the darkness. A golden, shimmery something—a falling star. A falling angel. A sparkler sizzling and then snuffed. An absence where the flame was. Blown out. Fizzled. Only the stars, not even the moon as witness.

The ship seemed not to notice, to blink, to hesitate, as calm and steady as all mammoth things are, slicing through the water, onward. Always moving forward, no matter what. The ship took no notice, but notice would be taken.

ROY ROGERS, the Head of Security for the *Palace of the Dolphins* sat in his office making figure eights with the maple syrup pitcher in great flourishing swirls across the top of his buttermilk pancakes, calming himself down. Why he felt the need to calm himself down in such a, well, child-comfort way, he was not sure. Something had his sniffer up. Something didn't feel right.

He put down the maple syrup, and filled in the center of the figure eights with pats of softened butter, watching it melt and pondering his unease. Another Saturday, another cruise soon to begin. He was still struggling to figure out all the bells and whistles on his new security system. State of the Art or major pain in the ass—overkill is how it felt. So much technology and so little understanding of how humans used the damn stuff.

First the Overboard Groom and then the piracy scare and then those drunken fools from somewhere or other, falling off their terrace and floating around for hours, and the entire cruise industry had turned into paranoiac over-reaction mode. Plus, of course the daily wacko terrorism threats.

Trying to secure one of these babies was a whole other level of head-scratching.

He cut the properly congealing mound of his favorite breakfast into eights and devoured it, chewing fast and smacking his lips. Not like his Mom made, only Southern women really knew how to make pancakes, but not bad.

Roy finished in fast forward, pushed back his plate, and picked up his coffee, slurping it down with gusto. Now the unease. He turned back to his computer and pulled up the manifest, scrolling down the endless list of new passengers who would soon be arriving.

He did his best to check out any suspicious types, but nothing could find the loose cannons or time bombs or fake I.D.ers or God only knew who or what. Crazy stuff can always happen. He'd seen enough in homicide to find little left to surprise him about the behavior of his fellow man, but this pleasure business, these floating human deep fryers were a whole different deal.

He set down his cup and squinted into the screen. Hot damn, he was twitchy. Call it hunter's instinct. Call it too much caffeine, too early in the a.m. but he had a bad feeling about this cruise. He blinked and then he blinked again and then again. A nervous habit, he hadn't had since he retired from the force and began this new career. Almost as if he was fighting to see something, not yet available in the present. And it wasn't just this cruise, he'd been feeling it for months. There was something wrong on this ship.

He burped, the cakes supporting his anxiety. It was already messing with his digestion. And he had a hunch this new cruise was going to tip it over at least enough for him to stop burping and blinking and start seeing what the hell it was.

Chapter One: Day One

LATITUDE

Your Daily At Sea Newspaper

WELCOME ABOARD! A MANDATORY LIFEBOAT DRILL WILL BE HELD at 4:30 p.m. Please find your muster station by viewing our safety film on your en-suite T.V. Also, please note that luggage delivery is a lengthy process. We thank you for your patience and we invite you to join your Cruise Director, Derrick Doolittle, and the entire *Palace of the Dolphins* crew for our Willkommen Grand Esplanade Parade and Departure dinner. And don't miss our Lost at Sea (just kidding!) show featuring the entire cast plus important cruise information. SUGGGESTED ATTIRE TONIGHT IS CASUAL. Ships Ahoy!!!

DERRICK DOOLITLE, the former Dwayne Druel of Norman, Oklahoma, stood at the top of the entrance tunnel in his perfectly cut, startlingly white uniform with the over-size name plate, identifying himself to the emerging dazed, anxious, confused, overwhelmed, already inebriated, already exhausted, over-energized, barely walking, almost skipping, hardly moving, video-cam recording, animal cracker box assortment of new passengers, now flopping onto the deck reminding him of barrels of freshly caught fish, each flipping and thrashing and jerking about in various states of final confusion.

Lambs to the slaughter, Noahans to the Ark, termites to the mound, ants to the mother of all hills; these were the images gliding across the inside of his head, while the outside featured a wider than a rictus headed smile, exposing most of his cosmetic bonding and the cause of all those crow's feet that he now had Collie in the spa botox out of his head every couple of months.

Showtime. He smiled even more broadly, hoping the sweat already forming on his also botoxed brow wouldn't make those disgusting ridges in-between his hair transplants. Fifty-five hundred old passengers departed at 9:00. Fifty-five hundred new passengers arriving at 2:00. And his job, all their jobs really, but especially the hands on-staff, was to make it all new again every seven days.

This was a milestone for him, one that would undoubtedly be pointed out by the captain himself, the new captain from Naples was it? Capt. Salmetti or, Sal-ami? Another in the long and seemingly endless supply of short, strutting Napoleonic little greaseballs who really saw the ship as their cock.

Well, he *was* the captain, but in a ship like this, the biggest, fanciest passenger cruiser afloat (for the moment), he was such a remote being, no one really knew what he actually did besides meet and greet, hold forth at the Captain's table, seduce members of the crew and the occasional passenger.

This was his 600th cruise and from the thoughts floating across his brain, maybe he was getting close to the checkout line. Dead fish and termites? How would he ever get it up for another week of shipboard Bingo and The Newlywed Game ("So — now after 40 years, I bet you just talk to keep the dog from getting bored!") and all those unbelievable questions.

He'd even thought of writing a book after he retired: *The Stupidest Cruise Questions Ever Asked, by Anonymous.* "Does the elevator go to the front of the boat?" "Does the crew live on board?" "Is the water in the pool so choppy because it's sea water?" "Why isn't there a bowling alley?" "Do you generate you own electricity?" "No, we're connected to San Juan by a very long cord."

It did make him sad, though. It was not how he had started, not how he had felt for the first twenty years. Why now, when he'd reached his pinnacle as the cruise director of the biggest ship in the world? How ironic.

Bigger was certainly not better. Bigger would be the end of civilization. The American Dream morphed into the ultimate horror movie. More, more, more. Money, people, things, a demon-driven (oh those Baptist roots) need to out-do.

He saw it as a symbol of the despair of the twenty-first century; nothing was enough. Has the world grown that tired? Have we over stimulated ourselves into a kind of joy deadened torpor, a TOP THIS need with everything in our lives? Now it takes a cruise "city" hurling 220,000 tons of ice skating rinks, rock-climbing walls, discos, casinos, theaters, spas, fitness centers, pools, basketball courts, man-made surfing waves, full scale shopping arcades, movie complexes, activities for every imaginable (and unimaginable) interest and enough to eat, drink and keep one entertained to see the entire population of Kabul through a very long winter.

If the ships got much bigger and the at-sea condo developments everyone in the water-based travel biz was buzzing about were built, it might not be long before people could simply walk from ship to ship without ever dealing with what might be left of the ocean.

What an awful thought, he thought watching the cattle-slightly-prodded look of the streams of new arrivals, many of whom were asking where the ship was, having no sense that the beast on which they were standing could possibly move, let alone whiz them across the Caribbean for seven unforgettable days of sensory and gastronomic overload.

He stretched his smile, glad no one had asked him, *yet*. But the truth was Americans *loved* big. They staggered forth, full of once-in-a-lifetime expectations, thrilled by the new. Blow those whistles, ring those bells. Where would it end? Well, it might just end with the O Man in the White House and the economy in the latrine. Everyone in travel was too unnerved to even talk much about it. But, on the spin side, so far, cruising was a bargain and business was still booming.

On they poured, types and archetypes. He gazed out at the mass of humans moving his way, looking for anyone interesting. The rare few, he could spot by day two, and so could most of his crewmates. Amazing how fast they could sort—a kind of psychological triage they all did to save their energy.

He took the manifest out of his pocket and scanned the group lists. The groups, of course, were their bread and butter, and they also came with their own tour guides who, if they were not total jerks, made his job far easier. They soothed the entry process. He let his smile slip. One hundred black Baptist church women from Mobile; 75 Downs Syndrome singles from Buffalo; a Holistic Healers tour from Sedona; 230 honeymooners; 20 weddings and their bridal parties; the usual array of family reunions and 50th anniversaries. He could *make up* a manifest and stack it against a real one.

The dipsos who use the cruise to drink without standing out and the four-hundred-pounders who use the cruise to eat without standing out and the compulsive gamblers who use the cruise to bet without standing out; the swingers who use the cruise to swap without standing out; the bickerers who use the cruise to fight without standing out and the other side of the quarter; the plastic surgery couples and the aging beauties who use the cruise *to Stand Out*; the exhibitionists who use the cruise to flaunt their lavish jewelry or designer duds; the spinster schoolteachers and overweight manicurists who have saved for this since high school; the doubled-up "Cof-bin" dwellers, cheerfully crammed into the cheapest cabins with blasting ACs and mirrors designed to deflect the fact that they *have no windows.*

The elderly who cruise compulsively to stop time; the Love-to-Dancers who cruise to re-create their Fred and Ginger fantasies "Nightly in the Sky Lounge"; the spoiled rich kids who want to play and "slum" away from Momsey and Popsey's private yachts. And the most annoying of all, the "Isn't-This-the-Most-Fantasticers" who spend the entire trip behind their snap-and-clicks or video cams, recording everything and seeing nothing, the whole trip being an elaborate photo shoot for the Less Fortunates back home, who will endure hours of railing shots and drink trays being carried, rope-pulling contests, and Mom on the first rung of the Rock Wall, looking excited, terrified and bloated from the midnight buffet. *Oh boy, Derrick, get a grip. You have fifty more to go before you can retire.*

Where are we going anyway? He re-checked his notes. Depart San Juan; then St. Thomas; St. John's, Antigua; Bridgetown, Barbados; Castries, St. Lucia; Philipsburg, St. Maarten; at sea and back here.

He hadn't divided up the fun and sun duties for his staff. Not that 99% of the passengers would know the difference. They could probably take the boat in a big circle, docking at various parts of the same island.

How different is surfside volleyball or a steel drum picnic on the beach or a kayak ride down a mangrove estuary from island to island? Who would know or care? More and more of the passengers never even got off the ship. Why risk getting mugged or sick or sunburned or lost or hawked by endless and aggressive locals proffering cheesy baskets and bras made out of coconut husks, when onboard they had more than enough to keep them entertained.

He re-stretched his smile, straining his cheeks. People were starting to make eye contact, and his last moments of reverie were about to end. Risk-free, now there's a hooter. Little did they know. Well, they knew a lot more now, since the stomach flu nightmare that had various cruise crews scrubbing down entire fleets as they were operating suites at the Mayo Clinic. So ridiculous. As if they could really stop anything from spreading or anyone from falling off one of these floating city states.

Food poisoning? The only thing that surprised him was that hundreds of people weren't puking their guts out all the time. They provisioned 90,000 pounds of pork alone every week. They went through a half ton of bananas and ice cream every day. How could anyone think it was all really safe? Just last week the captain of one of their sister ships came in too fast, made a very quick, hard turn and almost flipped 160,000 tons like a buttermilk pancake.

There were rapes and assaults of crewmembers and guests; a coffin-equipped morgue hidden discreetly beneath the clinic to deal with the average of three or so anticipated deaths on every trip; the racism beneath the pecking order (Italians or Caucasians at the top, Filipinos usually on the bottom). Everyone finding someone beneath them to push around, so Darwinian it all was.

Plus, the legal and illegal dumping of sewage which was growing out of control with the ever-expanding numbers of new ships. The solid waste produced by each passenger each day was, what had he read? 7.5 pounds? BIGGER must be better! 60,000 gallons of raw sewage alone every day just from their ship? And the exhaust equaled about what 13,000 cars spewed out. Ah, the sea air!

Derrick caught his reflection in one of the stainless steel panels and sucked in his stomach. When had he turned into this middle-aged person with the thick gut and the soft chin? Horrifying. No hint of the former college fencer or John Wayne look-alike. All that remained was his height; at least he was still tall. Tall and employed. One of the lucky ones.

But he was so tired. This was new; tired had not been one of his things. Low energy types did not become Cruise Directors. Cruise Directors were like permanent Game Show hosts, like that movie with that really annoying guy with too many teeth, whose entire life was being filmed and he was the only one not in on it. That's what his job was like. Only he *was* in on it!

Terror was being tired. Tired meant resting. Resting meant being alone. Terror was closing that cabin door at night. *Gotta get down to the infirmary and get some B-12 shots.* Besides, he had three more cruises before he could take a break. Break from what? To do what? To go where? Where do floaters go when they hit land? His *life* was like a continual vacation, so what exactly would be the point in taking "time off?" Don't want to think about that. Do not need to think about that. Think about what lies ahead. Think about the Esplanade reception. Think about the champagne party and the Captain's table seating for tonight. Think about cutting down on the mashed potatoes and hitting the gym, that would be helpful. Don't think about the sublet in Key West with no pictures on the wall.

"We've been on board for two hours, and we do not have our luggage, buddy. Do you know who I am?"

Derrick turned, glad to be out of range. A muscley little man with a dark, hawky face and a nervous, equally hawky wife, was pushing his thumb into a cabin steward's chest. The cords on his birdy neck were strained. Ah, his first "Do-you-know-who-I-amer" of the new manifest.

Yes, Derrick did. *I do know, sir. You, sir, are nobody. If you, sir, were somebody, you wouldn't be caught in a coma on the same pier with the* Palace of the Dolphins, *sir. If you were anybody, you'd be on your own yacht with your luggage being laid out by your personal valet, or chartering one of the Big Boys for more per week than you, sir, probably make in a very good year. And you would certainly know, sir, that except in rare exceptions — like the suites on B-Deck — if serious money cruises commercial, they go small. Ah, small. Smaller is all the rich have left these days to protect them from the likes of you, dear sir. Small cruise ship. Big bucks. Privacy costs, sir. Keep those guys in the khaki shorts and baseball caps AWAY from me!! Is how they see you, sir.*

Whoa. Was this him? This was more than tired. What was happening to him? He *loved* people! He was easygoing and accepting and accommodating. That was his job, to charm and disarm. Anger at the passengers was not his thing. *Difficult people are my specialty.* In four languages!!

Breathing, heavy breathing, hot heavy breathing moving closer. The Downs Syndrome group encircled him, pushing against him, warm and soft and smushy. They patted him and touched him, leaving moist prints on his uniform. Mucous dripped onto his arm. He put his hand up, fending, a fending gesture as if he had been overrun by a herd of friendly beasts, playful but menacing.

"Are you the captain?" They fondled him, invading, too close, too close. He wanted to run. He had been taken by surprise. "Captain! Captain!" They patted him; he could smell sweat and saliva. They were gleeful as if Christ had been lowered down among them.

Joyful, innocent with excitement. "Captain Cruise!! You're Captain Cruise!! Very nice!! Very handsome! Will you take a picture!! Take a picture with us!!!"

He fought the urge to push them off. "No, no. I'm not the Captain. I'm the Cruise Director! I'm going to make sure you have fun every day!"

He felt panicky searching for their guides. Waving above his head. Trapped.

"Now, now, let's move on. Come, come!" Rescue. A better person than himself. A kind, unafraid, person. A person who would choose such a job transporting mongoloids (Was that politically correct? Could you say that?) and be responsible for 75 childlike people with special needs and no sense of boundaries or danger?

Who then was he? Behind all the bonhomie? Not a brave or nice man at all. He was stained. Stained with snot and sweat of others, not his own, which was repelling enough. He stunk. Thousands of trips and nothing like this had ever happened to him before.

Everyone was on board now. He could feel the tension of departure moving across the reception area. Deck hands were whizzing by. He had to get to the Cruise Desk. No time to change. He reeked. *Jesus.* He turned and caught sight of himself in the reflecting panels and saw something in his face he had never seen before. Doubt.

And so the ship moved on, out of San Juan Harbor and into the open sea. The sun lowering slowly, shooting streaks of orange and lavender across the spring sky, the warm wind blowing the cumulus clouds, pushing against their sharpened edges, relaxing their outlines.

Off she went, provisioned for any event, enough for a small army, one that served and was served, but fighting only for space at the pool or a place up front for the Ice show.

She was serene in the setting sun. Opaque and revealing nothing but power and purpose. A mask, an illusion, a lie, if you will. Inside, the ship was anything but serene. A churning, giant cauldron of clanging parts; steam and fire and hissing pipes.

Techno-turmoil and banging gizmos. A vast mass of noise and energy from the machine and its managers and an even vaster combustion from the compression of its emotional human cargo. A juggernaut or a joy ride or both, many times a minute.

Of course the truth was that no matter how thorough and thought out the voyage, how well trained and prepared the crew, how well behaved and enthusiastic the guests, two things could never be anticipated. Mother nature and human nature. Acts of man and God, which would alter the course of some of those aboard and change their journeys, forever.

✒

THE ELEVATOR OPENED and Vera and Solly Russolini, of Great Neck, Long Island, cautiously moved forward as if approaching the side of the Grand Canyon, Niagara Falls, the Eiffel Tower or any other exhilarating but potentially life-threatening experience.

"Solly, I am frozen. I am frozen with fear. Do not let go of me. Do not even think about letting go of me."

"I don't have to think about it, since you are holding on to me. Your nails have cut through three layers of cashmere and are entering flesh, now. I'd need a saw to get you off."

"Don't joke. This is so not funny, Solly. What was I thinking? What could I have been thinking? Showing off, I was showing off for my sister. 'We're goin' on a cruise on the world's biggest ship.' God is getting even, big time."

"Vera, if God continues to focus on paying you back for every little thing you do, what will happen to the rest of the planet? You are not his only concern."

"Don't move so fast. The floor is so shiny. I can't see where I'm going. Shiny floor, and everything else is dim. Like I'm going blind. What's this deck? Why are there Cowboy things everywhere?"

"I'm checking the map. We're on the Promenade deck in the Cowgirl Lounge. Everything has a theme. This is the Western Bar. See, the bar stools are saddles. It's cute."

"It was cute at Camp Coyote when I was nine. I didn't stand on line at the Manolo Blahnik sale for three hours and the Versace pantsuit sample sale for an entire Saturday to sit on a saddle. Keep moving."

"You just told me not to move so fast."

"I changed my mind. I didn't know we were going to be in Frontierland."

"The ship hasn't left yet. We can still get off."

"See? See? That's what you do! That's what the counselor said! You're playing me, Solly! You know I'm not leaving. Do you not know that? If we end up sitting in the goddamn cabin for the entire week, I am not getting off this thing and leaving my money here!

"I packed for this, did I not pack for this? Two hundred sheets of tissue paper, I used. I saved for this! Who am I? Do you even know? Who I am, Solly? Am I a someone who would face her relatives and say, 'We got off the cruise of a lifetime before the friggin' boat left?' Am I that woman? I will do this. I have drugs to take. I will be fine. Just don't let go of me and keep moving. What's this, this looks better?"

"I'm reading. It's hard to see, the lights got pink all of a sudden. Oh, sure, Pink like Flamingos. This is the Pink Flamingo lounge. See, everything looks like birds, it's a motif. Every 30 feet, it's an entire different décor. Like that little fruitie-tootie who decorated your brother's house. Every room with a theme. Only on a grand scale. So first, cowgirls, now flamingos."

"Don't stop. I want something like old movies. Shipboard romance. Something nice and normal."

"Okay. Okay. Alright, we're going to go up that staircase and, I see something called, the Sinatra Room. See? See? The glass is half full? Alright, Vera?"

"OHMIGAWD. Look at that staircase! What is that, crystal? The steps are rare crystal or something. Can you walk on that? What if it's just for show? It must be ten stories high! My Manolos will slice right through there and we'll end up lying in a pool of blood. You go first, check it out."

"I'll be glad to, but you have to let go of my friggin' arm. The circulation is going. I'm getting tingles up and down."

"I can't. I told you, I'm frozen with fear."

"Okay, we'll go together. They wouldn't put something like that here for show. Wait, look, there! Two kids are running up. See. See? Just kids and they're not scared."

"Yeah, they're not scared because they're just kids—fearless and clueless. What do they know. Our kids are still fearless and clueless and they're in college!"

"Okay, Vera. You gotta let go, so you can hold on to the rail. Just hold on and I'm right behind you. If you fall, I'll break your fall. Now go. Take a deep breath, like they taught you in the class, and just go one step at a time. On the count of three. One, two . . . Three!"

"Ohmigawd. I'm doing it. Solly. I can tell them I walked up

crystal stairs on my way to the Sinatra lounge. I'm going to have a Manhattan. I'm doing it. I'm going up."

"That's my girl. Doing fine, just don't look down. Oh, Christ! . . . I looked down! I'm getting a little clammy. Vera, I think I'm going to faint. Gotta sit for a minute."

"Here, take a sip of my water. It's okay, Solly, I'm right here. Just sit until you get through it. Just a panic attack. It's the height thing. You'll be fine."

"Okay, I'm better. I think I can move again. Are you okay?"

"I'm okay. Let's try again. Slowly. We're doing it. Think of Frank. Solly. Think of Frank."

～

Dames at Sea, by the Sea, one of them is me, have a cup of tea, then you're gonna pee, My Country 'tis of thee, longing to be free, That's how it's gotta be, Swinging from a tree, swimming cross the sea—can't say sea twice—swimming to Galilee; ski, pee, tree, me, key, If I could only see, The worst song yet to be.

Rory Riley Saltz lowered herself into the Jacuzzi in the De Milo spa and closed her eyes. The songwriter's curse, ritualistic rhyming. *Drain that mind, babe. Drain all the lousy lyrics right out of there.* Something was not working. The writing on command something. She was blanking; couldn't get it going in the same way. Menopausey? Was that it? Just couldn't seem to work with people hovering, only at home on her terms. Some sort of infantile regression? When *I'm* fucking ready, pal! Whatever it was . . . oh, maybe it was just THE SHIP deal. *How about keeping it simple, Ror? Too much stuff to filter. It always takes you a day or so. You always choke the first rehearsal. Flora knows it. The director knows it. Just settle down.*

She sunk deeper, trying a visualization exercise. She was floating in some pure, clear, bubbling mountain hot pot. Somewhere in Iceland, pure mineral water bubbling up out of the ground from deep, deep down in the center of the earth where the world began, from the dormant craters and steaming, boiling crevasses, building up, up, waiting for the right moment to explode out of all those blowholes and steamy, salty pools, bam! Blowing their antediluvian lids off of the fucking planet. Pow.

Billions of years of discreet gurgling with only an occasional gigantic volcanic eruption now and again to keep the whole thing kosher, but steaming underneath, forgetting nothing, biding their time until the right opportunity to let all that passion and disgust and anguish and need not-to-try-and-behave-the-way-the-world-on-top-expected-them-to; while the world soaked and dunked and oohhhhhed and ahhhhhed at their relaxing, soothing, calming effects. All the while, lying in wait as it were, until they'd had enough. Enough! No more going with the flow or curing arthritis or being generally therapeutic and whatever else steaming, mineral pools were supposed to be. One fine day, *bam*.

Hmmm. This was interesting. Projecting onto hot pots in Iceland were we now.

"Stacy, the jets are sta-rong!"

Pool people. She was no longer alone. *Shit*. So much for Iceland, for a perfect little mineral pond in a meadow just for her. She opened her eyes behind her sunglasses, checking out the intruders while maintaining no outward signs of noticing. Two twenty-somethings, who seemed to be the same person except one had fat little feet with bright red polish and one had long skinny feet with silverish polish. The fat little-footed one seemed to be the un-Stacy.

"I'm so stressed. The entire bridal party has to be done by 2:00 tomorrow and Paul and I had a fight last night about, so ridiculous! . . . about where to put the nanny's room in the house when we build it."

"Hello? You haven't even gotten married, yet."

"You have to plan for everything, Stacy. You don't just let major decisions like this happen to you. You don't just someday build a house and then realize you have no room for kids or a nanny."

"So, you mean a live-in?"

"Absolutely. I really want to be a good Mom, and I know I'll be far better if I'm not overburdened."

Rory sunk deeper into the non-Icelandic water. She imagined those fat, smug-about life, in that before-life-has-fucked-with-you, pre-Bridal-way-toes being sucked into the bubble suction cup and plucked out one at a time and how that would affect the way the un-Stacy thought.

Stop now, she told the inside of her head once again. More people were approaching. Maybe all 5,000 or so passengers might decide this was exactly the right moment to soak and it would turn into some Guinness Book record of Jacuzzi submergers.

She flicked her hidden eyes around, the way she did at the pool, stunned by the endless variety. Too tan, too pale; tiny tits, huge tits, pot-bellies, washboard abs, ingrown toenails, and twisted veins and thighs full of cellulite and skinny and flabby and centerfold-perfect, thick curling body hairs sprouting all over and shiny and hairless, swollen ankles and yellowed heels, and wizened old women, sucked dry by seventy years of sun worship, wobbling toward the tub in Hawaiian flowered swimming skirts. How they would all end up. Withered and puckered and hobbling toward a hot tub. *Rory!*

A man with black snagged toenails was lowering himself in beside her. YUCK. She moved a bit to her left, trying not to be obvious. Of course if he was a sensitive person or maybe even just a normally self-conscious person, he wouldn't appear barefoot with toes like that, now would he. He would at least cover them up until the very last moment when he had to slip out of his shoes and sink in.

She felt slightly nauseous. The thought of being squished in with strangers and all their secretions and pubic hairs and chest hairs, and urine dribbles and funguses and sweat and god only knew what was lurking under their bathing suits or flaking off, peeling away and swirling around under the fake bubbles; not pure pre-historic evolutionary bubbles fighting their way up from the center of the earth. No. A phony marble manmade tub.

And there *she* was, soaking away, no right to scorn. Earning her keep. Singing for her suppah, or writing the songs to be sung for the suppah. Writing the patter-chatter and cruising around. *Judge not less ye be, oh fuck that.*

"Rory Saltz to the Spa reception desk, please." Rory climbed out, carefully avoiding contact with the fungusy foot next to her and moving quickly away avoiding eye contact with the other tub dwellers.

"Hi, I'm Rory Saltz. Do I have time for a quick shower before my massage?"

"Absolutely, your esthetician is running late," the receptionist smiled, revealing gummy lipstick-smeared teeth. She never knew what the protocol was about whether to tell the innocent smiler about the lipstick, piece of meat, or whatever. She made a gesture with her finger and her own teeth which was met with distinct coldness around the receptionist's eyes.

The shower room was filled with naked and semi-naked women. How was this possible? They were already strolling around as if they lived on the ship, as if this was their neighborhood spa and they'd barely finished the life boat drill, which had further convinced her that in an "at-sea emergency," she wouldn't even try to find-her muster station but simply fling herself overboard and hope some kindly crew member would pull her into the closest lifeboat.

She always dreaded the drills; marching up and down surrounded by thousands of other life-vestees; dehumanized, depersonalized, lemming-like, all trudging in chipper collusion like some Christo event, like draping the fucking Reichstag: Wherever the eye traveled stood a moving, undulating wall of red-vested silly-looking people. A large hive had popped out above her left eye, a sudden violent reaction to being herded.

An older naked woman with no visible eyelids waddled by and smiled, her lips bulging with some injectable substance, giving her mouth a Simpsons quality.

Rory tried to be nonchalant and not gape at her high, hard breasts. The breasts were looking north; from the waist up, she was heading north for sure, but from the waist down, she was losing the battle, headed for the equator, for Quito at least.

She soaped up, avoiding eye contact with the drain, and keeping her pool slippers on. What were these women thinking? Did they not know that we *knew*? And if everyone knew it was fake, what exactly was the point?

Rory patted herself dry and returned to the desk. "I'm back," she announced to the gummy smiler, who had wiped off her teeth, but refused to look at her.

"Take a seat. I'll call you."

She sat. A glass wall separated the gym from the spa. A bank of treadmills was already filled with fellow life-vest drillers, all huffing away, their faces pulled into that tight little picklish look all joggers and treadmill users share.

The fake walking she did not get. "Hey, I just had a terrific, two-hour fake walk on a big noisy, ugly metal machine. Went nowhere, saw nothing."

Right above their heads was a huge empty deck with a walking-running path. "So here's your choice, people. A lovely walk around the deck with the ocean splashing all around you and the sky warm and blue and pelicans and sea gulls and maybe some frigates or what have you above, heading out of San Juan into the Southern Caribbean, the seeing of which you have paid a pretty penny for—OR, a fake walk next to sweaty, squeezed-faced strangers. NO CONTEST!"

Well, the goal was the thing. And the goal was being thin. "I lost 100 pounds in six weeks without dieting . . ." "Being fat is not your fault! It's the result of the stress hormone cortisol building up in your system . . ." Yackata yackata. "Diet Tips of Drug-addicted Former Child Stars!" "Diet Tips of Death Row Serial Killers," "Diet Tips of Africa Famine Victims." Well, why not. If television was any guideline, only two things seemed to be necessary for becoming famous without possessing a shred of talent or skill of any kind. You had to be thin ("Diet Tips of Coal Miners Trapped for Long Periods Under Ground") and you had to have straight hair that could be cut in jagged sharp strips. That was about it. If you had those two things and were willing to let deadly snakes and tarantulas crawl all over you, or eat someone else's vomit or a scoopful of maggots or discuss your sex life with 20 million strangers or marry some volunteer part-time fireman with one brain cell and nice eyebrows, you could be rich and famous.

Or, you could be very unattractive and allow yourself to be publicly humiliated and then surgically mutilated into a slightly less seriously unattractive person who has gone through unimaginable pain and loss of privacy, that was a way.

It was no longer necessary even to give the President a blowjob to have your own line of designer purses and march into roped-off VIP rooms in snarky, drug-infested nightclubs in Miami. Just thin . . . ("Diet Tips of Swedish Bi-Polars Living Outside Their Native Land") . . . and with the right hair style. Was it true? Did she really believe that it was true? She did.

Jesus H. Christ. And what was *that* about? Why, Jesus *H*? Did anybody ever ask what the H. was? Was it even a Jeopardy question? A Trivial Pursuit tile? She had her suspicions. Jesus Hymie. Jesus Herbie. He was Jewish after all. Unlikely it stood for something Roman, Jesus Heraclites or such.

If her brain kept this up much longer her head was going to blow off. A nice quiet massage. In a nice dark room. *You are not a guest, this is work, Rory. This is le rent, Rory.* No time for an attack of xenophobia, claustrophobia, agoraphobia or even hydrophobia, though that would certainly thin out the spa crowd . . . "Woman werewolf spotted on cruise ship. Captain says, 'No cause for alarm' " . . . (Diet tips from the cruise ship Werewolf who will undergo an Extreme-Makeover and have her hair straightened on camera before launching her new line of hirsute beach bags and hosting her own talk show!) *Go lie down Rory.*

Oh, the simple joys. A candlelit little massage room. Warm, and dark and smelling of oils from rare plants, clean sheets and Yanni music and quiet, unless the inside of your brain wouldn't shut up, but eventually, even a brain like hers, feverish and hard to control, would succumb to the kneading and stroking and the eight-bar refrain chanted over and over and over until the disc ran out. How did they record that stuff? Did they really sing the same line for forty-five minutes or just once and then they cheated it out?

She took a deep breath waiting for the pretty little Irish girl Flora had introduced her to. Collie was it? A lovely little lass from the Emerald Isle. Plump as a Christmas pudding, soft and sexy and straining at the creases of her uniform. Ripe, that was the look. Ripe and lickable. Coppery curls, no T.V. reality bullshit for her.

Oh, this was nice, like a sweet, sensual womb. Were wombs sensual? Doesn't sound right. A sweet, *safe* womb. Safe, yes.

Tears. Lots of them. Oozing. *God*, she was going to melt down in the massage room. Room, Womb. *I want my fucking mother.*

Warm, soft hands attached to sweet, soft ladies in tight pink uniforms, caressing her in candlelit comfort, as close as she could ever get. *Think of something else. Think of, a nice glass of chardonnay and Harvey, dogs are good. Picture Harvey and his big brown eyes. I need some mother to show up here right now.*

Gentle spa-level knocking noises. "Come in." *Wipe the evidence away.*

"Hi, Rory. Are you ready?" Any mother, even one young enough to be her daughter or, her son . . . *don't think about that. Don't do this now.* A daughter-mother. A fresh peach-perfect-bursting-at-the-seams-with life-and-sex-and-hope-ginger-smelling momma, nothing like her own; dead so long. So hazy, marshmallowy, a smudged photo image, without odor or feel. How *had* she felt? This would have to do. Better than nothing. Safe for an hour, like men who paid for sex, this was like that. She paid every week for an hour of pretend mothering. Womb-time for a motherless, middle-aged woman.

"Yes, all ready."

"Any particular problems?"

"A vast array, where should I start."

The soft, ripe gingery mother laughed. "Flora told me about you. She says you're a riot."

"Uh, oh, now there's expectations. Well, I'm only funny before. I never say a word during."

"Very important. Your muscles need to be quiet. When people talk, they don't relax. How's your body today?"

"Well, I was having just such a conversation with her before you came in and she said she was knotted as tight as a headful of corn rows and would probably need a stick of plutonium to unkink, so feel free to use torture if necessary."

The mother of the moment touched her stomach. "Oh, yes, I can feel it. Take a deep breath."

How much sadness can you bear before you disappear forever. The hands on her stomach, her womb. Tears gushing now, pouring forth. Too unprotected. Not a safe place to touch.

The young motherer stopped. "Are you okay?"

"No, actually. No. Wow. I didn't expect that."

"No problem, happens all the time. It's your center. For women, it's right there. If you're feeling vulnerable, it can just pop the feelings out. It's good. 'Spring rain for the soul,' we say in Ireland. Tears are spring rain for the soul.' "

"I like that. That's a very comforting thought." She took a breath. "Okay, storm's over."

Comfort. That is what it was, that is what she couldn't face needing. Comfort. Someone to pat her and stroke her back and kiss her cheeks and wipe the tears away. *There, there, now, Rory darling. There, there. Momma's here. Momma loves you. Everything's going to be fine.*

A shoulder to lean into. A breast to rest her head against, someone who would never go away, would stay forever, always right there with a pat, when the world went wrong; when she was frightened. *There, there, Rory darling.*

This was a good fake mother, she had the touch. Strong and sure; pressing hard, knowing what she was doing. She let go, the spring rain releasing some of the anger snapping in her brain today, fear traveling with it, sidling up and shaking its hand. She thought of her spring rain drowning the two little fuckers, leaving her in peace, while her fake Mommy in the pretend womb with the healing smells and the synthetic music carried her away for a while.

⤸

My darling Maria,

This is my first letter to you from my new job and my new ship. I wish you and the boys were here to see me. I think you would be proud and they would be proud of their poppa. I will try to write a little every day and then, like always, send one big letter every week, but I have been so busy and there is so much to learn that it may not be such a big letter as usual.

Where should I start? Let me start where I will end. I miss you very much. I kiss your picture and the picture of Pablito and Jaime and momma and poppa every night no matter how tired I am. I long to hold you so we can dream about the future. I love you with all my heart and it is that love for you and the family that gives me the strength to do this work and live without you for so long. I know it is harder for you, but be brave.

Now, I am a "Butler". I have a special uniform and I have been given the honor of being assigned to the suites on Deck B where the owners and their friends and the VIPs stay. If I do a very good job (and I promise that I will for you. I will work so hard, I will be the very best butler the Empire Cruise Company has ever had!) if I do, then I may even someday be assigned to be the Captain's personal valet, which is the highest job, better hours and more pay. I do not know how the gratuities work then, but I'm sure it is generous. So, by serving the most exclusive and wealthy passengers, I do hope to save more in gratuities for our future, for our little shop with the café in Estoril. For the boys.

I will send you more photos of this ship. I thought the Palace of Neptune was so huge and grand but this one is more so. I walk so many miles every day! I am getting quite trim, you will be surprised.

The suites I am in charge of this week are very beautiful. The suite of the owners even has a piano in the living room! Can you imagine? I am a little nervous because the head of the hotel Mr. Hensler, himself, (remember I told you that the cabins and dining rooms are run as a separate hotel and have their own boss?) Well he called me into his office to inform me that this week, one of the real owners (many other people rent the suite and we are never sure who is who) and his wife and daughter are aboard and he wants me to "be flawless" is what he said. Well, you know better than anyone that I am not that! So don't laugh too hard, but I will try.

The family's name is Talbott, and their daughter has the very pretty and unusual name of Twinkle. She is very tall and has beautiful blond hair. Her mother looks somewhat the same only smaller and much older, I think rather too old to have a daughter of maybe twenty-two. She is very tan and she is very well mannered but not friendly. I have been warned that that is the way wealthy people behave and I must be very careful to not be in any way informal or talk too much and only provide information on request. This is very important.

The Mr. Talbott is also very tall and he walks in a stiff way with his head very high and he has a bald sunburned head and a long neck and an adam's apple that bobs up and down when he talks. He is more cheerful and seems to like to think he is outgoing and at ease, but I don't think he really is.

The daughter, I must say, though I hope to find out that I am not correct, but on first encounter, I must say I do not think her to be a very nice person. She was quite rude not only to me, but to her parents and even to their guests. She seems very spoiled and disrespectful and her eyes are cold. I know you will be clucking your tongue and saying, "Oh, Elonzito, you are just like an old woman, so full of intrigue and drama."

The other family is not like them at all. They are a handsome family named Worth. They were so friendly and pleasant to me, that I had to remind myself of what my job is and not laugh too much or talk beyond the appropriate amount.

The Mrs. Worth is as beautiful as an actress, one of the older (but not old) stars from films with bright red hair like Maureen O'Hara, who Momma liked. Their daughter is named Clarissa and I think she looks like what her mother must have looked like as a girl. She is the friend of Twinkle, which seems odd to me because she is very polite and has beautiful sparkling green eyes and a big hearty laugh and seems to find humor and happiness in everything, not at all like her friend.

They also have two other guests, another friend of Miss Twinkle's, a young man who it seems comes from a very prominent family in Europe and his grandmother, who they call "The Countess" though I do not know if this is what she really is.

She has a little dog, a tiny strange skinny thing with big pop eyes, which she carries strapped onto her chest, but with its little paws sticking out toward the world! It is a very unusual and peculiar sight and she never seems to take him off. She is wearing all varieties of jewels. The boy is very handsome and educated, but he is also like the Twinkle daughter, with his nose up above.

I do not think that these children have ever worked or struggled in any way, they live their lives in a velvet box with no windows, just sky above. They do not have a real picture of anything. I have a feeling that Mr. and Mrs. Worth are not rich like the others, but somehow are part of their lives.

I know all of this is none of my business and I should be thinking about bringing the right champagne and hors d'oeuvres and making sure the Countess has the little crib (with silk sheets which she has brought herself from New York) for the little dog and stocking the bar with all of their special requests, but I do find people so intriguing and I have never talked to such illustrious persons before.

I know what you would say to that, "Elonzito, they are just like anyone else, no better, do not be impressed by anything as silly as money," but it is quite fascinating to see how different they act and talk and think from the regular passengers, especially the people in the very cheapest rooms with not even a porthole. So very different! Those guests are so happy and excited about everything and never complain and have looked forward to this vacation for years sometimes and now I see this other world of people who complain about everything . . .

not enough ice in the bucket . . . the pillows are too soft, the towel rack heater (yes, Maria, the towel rack has a heater that keeps the towels warm!) isn't hot enough. This is just another trip for them. They talk as if they go on vacations like this or far grander than this all the time! I am very confused by all of this and find it stirring in my thoughts, so I must get over this and clear my mind.

One more thing about this new ship is my new boss. I regret to say Mr. Hensler, also, is not a very friendly person. He has this way of looking at us. (I have discussed this with Jo Jo my friend of whom I've told you before.) It is harder for Jo Jo because he is Filipino and he is the only Filipino on board who has become a steward, and so there is also much jealousy about Jo Jo for being promoted.

Sometimes I think they promoted him to pick on, but he takes it all lightly. "I think of my fishing boat, what she will look like and I don't give a damn," he tells me. Jo Jo has a very positive attitude and I am lucky to have found him for a friend.

Mr. Hensler looks at us in this very stern way, piercing is how it feels, like we were bad little children, lying about taking candy and had been caught. I feel so nervous before him it is hard for me to concentrate and be myself.

He is from Germany I believe and he talks with an accent that is quite harsh, so maybe that is part of it and as I get to know him a little more, I will understand him better. Not that I have much contact with the Boss, but if I continue to serve the VIP suites, I will have more than the other stewards, so I will have to overcome my fear.

Well, Maria, my life, my soul! I must say good-bye for now. The Talbotts are having a small cocktail reception in their suite (the star of the shows, Miss Flora Frampton is going to sing!) I believe the new captain is also attending, so I must prepare for this.

One last thing to make you laugh. The little dog of the Countess, whose name is Tou Tou, only eats fresh frois gras, which has been specially shipped and must be served rare with mashed potatoes! And he is put to bed in the crib with a diaper on, like a baby! So you can see why this is so interesting to me! I will have lots of stories to tell you and the family when I come home. I kiss

you and the children a thousand times,
Your husband

⟨⟨

TWINKLE TALBOTT dropped her copy of *In Style* onto the marble floor and sat up. "Sidney Poitier puts *water* on his granola. Can you like deal with that? Imagine him like as a father? So totally rigid, I mean not even fat-free milk? I bet he's one of those parents who give little inspirational talks to his children and they all have to totally stand in formation or something and no one can smile or make eye contact until he's done."

"Twinkle, he's an actor. An *actor*, playing a 'fine man' all the time. He's not Alexander the Great! He lives in Los Angeles of his own free will. Who would care if he put pony piss on his corn flakes, he's an actor on or off camera."

"Not pony pee Ian, it has like estrogen in it! He could grow breasts or his voice might go up and he'd lose his moral authority, he'd be more Dennis Rodman than Mr. 'I-am-a-disciplined-and-serious-person.' How about, bird plop. At least it looks like milk. We could gather a bucket while we're on board, add like a little honey and send it to him 'as a token from your fans for your delicious breakfast.' "

"You are so hopelessly American! Twinkle Talbott, the Jamesian wannabe heroine of her own novella. Obviously you have a thing about celebrity or maybe it's a Paris Hilton envy issue. If that's the subtext, I have a friend who can make you a star, and all you have to do is stay your own bitchy, ignorant, narcissistic self and make sure your parents don't lose any capital."

"You are such a snob, Ian. Just because you went to some school in Switzerland for hopeless fuck-ups whose own families can't stand them hardly makes you the judge of me. I'm merely pointing out a little known fact about a sacred cow of our culture. And I've actually met Paris Hilton and her sister and their whole click and they're like really very nice to hang out with and at least they know how to have fun, unlike Sidney Poitier."

"*Who* is this man, anyway? Why are we talking about this old has-been actor? What has he done in the last twenty years? This is very sad. Have we run our course? We're not even married and we've run our course. This is too boring. What to do? Okay. . . . Give me a word from this conversation, any word you can remember and I'll give you a fact about the word."

"Fine. Birds, from the bird plop idea."

"Perfect. Did you know that Audubon had to kill the birds before he could paint them? All of those exquisite drawings, so reverent and authentic and capturing nature in such delicate detail, a true lover and observer of the natural world, you would say. An environmentalist of the first order, but in order to capture them artistically, he had to murder them first."

"Cool! That is like, major, Ian! My parents have like this entire collection all framed and hanging in this gigantic hallway in their Santa Fe house. They are going to turn a corner of their flat little brains about this. Promise you'll let me tell it, like I thought of it. Promise?"

"Amazing, how much you trust me. How do you know I didn't make it up? Why would you believe me?"

"Did you? Ian, did you?"

"No, but it really isn't such a great way to approach daily life, dearie, to take everything anyone says, especially a perverse sort like *moi* at his word."

"I only take *you* at your word. Well, and Clarissa, but for like entirely different reasons. Clarissa can only tell the truth and be honest or she actually breaks out in blotches all over her body and you, well you I trust because you lie so much about everything to everyone. I'm like your little satin-pill-pill, your little cozy baby place where you don't have to play all those games all the time."

"How you flatter your self. You're right though, it is tiring to have to be cunning all the time. But the game of figuring out the chinks, drawing people out and then playing with them is my mission, raison d'être as it is. If I'm never going to work (God Forbid) and if I want to live a life as close to De Sade as possible in intellectual pursuit of my truth without being corrupted by the need to please or conform or be a productive member of the community or any of it, then my calling is to fuck with their little minds as research, as science.

"Here's what I wrote watching passengers chat one another up when the ship was pulling out of San Juan Harbor. *Thought for the day: Whatever anyone tells you, believe the opposite. Examples, 'I love my wife,' 'I have a fabulous, close family,' 'I have incredible, devoted friends,' 'I love my job.' Just think of the opposite as being true and you can figure them out.*"

"Or like if a guy tells you how great in bed he is or one of your friends goes on and on about how men can't get enough of her, like that?"

"Primitive, but yes."

"Well, maybe I am primitive but at least I don't intend to be like a totally rich bitch and never work or like do anything except read and make fun of everyone else."

"Are you not the very same 'Rich Bitch' who did a rousing depiction of a group of Downs Syndrome passengers working out in the gym so short a time ago? The same 'Rich Bitch' who has never worked one single day in her twenty-three years on the planet or even gone to college? I guess I missed your Career Day epiphany. What will it be? Neurosurgery or, possibly a Peace Corps stint?"

"That is so low, Ian. I'm going into P.R. and design. Daddy's going to help me."

"Oh, well then. Of course. Far better for mankind than READING and THINKING! 'The meaning of life, and the meaning of death . . . the feeling of existential dispossession, the thing people feel when they go from room to room for no reason and then they go back from room to room for no reason and then they go out for no reason and come back in for no reason' . . . Tennessee Williams."

"I have meaning and that is so totally depressing. It's like whatever, Ian."

"My poor little pinhead. It doesn't make any difference; it's all just bloody distraction from the absurdity of life. So American! All those happy endings and pop psychology. Your movies either destroyed your culture or your culture was so naïve and unable to deal with reality that your art forms just reflect that fatal flaw. No one in this country wants to tell the truth! Cough it up, Twinkle Talbott, you want to loll and live like a lazy, lithe, luscious lovely, sleep till noon and party till dawn while pretending to be 'on the verge of seriousness.'"

"I hate you, Ian. You won't be happy until you see me crack into a million tiny pieces like one of those trays of teeny little ice cubes, crack, crack, crack. Okay, so maybe you're right. Maybe I want to have my cake and eat it, too."

"You are the cake, dearie."

"Oh, Ian, you're so totally bad."

" 'I'm a man — nothing human is foreign to me.' Terrance, one of those ancients I waste my time reading."

"That's so cool. If I use that on my parents, do not say anything. They only think I read like *People* and *W*. Terrance? Way cool. I could like name a puppy that."

"Oh, he's perfect for you, Twinks. He came to Rome as a slave and won his freedom because he was so intelligent and handsome. He wrote comedies of manners about people like us."

"Like us? It was like thousands of years ago?"

"Human nature doesn't change. Have you gained nothing from our talks? In one of his plays, a character says that if you want to win friends, agree with everything said to you because the truth is unpopular. He'd figured that out a century and a half before little Jesus sprung forth. Might as well be on this ship of folly."

"I'm using that, too! Very cool. Okay, I'm remembering why I thought I liked you. Let's call that little Mexican man, what's his name? Elozo? Have him bring us some Dirty Martinis, if he like even knows what they are. Let's have some fun, this is already getting old."

"Elonzito and he's Portuguese."

"Whatever."

✑

CLARISSA rolled onto her stomach and pulled the overstuffed feather pillow over her head. *Five more minutes and if they don't stop talking and Ian's grandmother's dog doesn't stop barking, I'll give up.*

A nap had seemed like such a fine idea. She couldn't even remember her last nap. School and work, work and school. Not that she was complaining. She loved graduate school! Loved it! And she loved her job. So lucky. She was so lucky! None of her friends seemed to even like anything they were doing and there she was just rolling in clover and covered with joy.

Sometimes it was all she could do to keep it all inside. Sometimes she just wanted to grab her friends and hug them hard and shout into them. "Life is so amazing! Be happy. Be kind! Don't be afraid!" Not that they'd listen. She'd tried enough times, but she still had so much hope, even for Twinkle and Ian.

It wasn't like she was just a blubbering fool, and she certainly could be a lazy slob and a bitch with the best of them (well maybe not a bitch, that never had been her style), and if she tried she usually got macerated by the other person, but she *was* a big sleeper and a big eater and she liked to dance and drink and have fun. She wasn't just some Pollyanna with no bad days or excesses. But she couldn't help it if she was happy more than unhappy even if most of her friends thought she was a dork or a phony or both.

What was that article she'd read about depressed people actually seeing reality and themselves more clearly and happy people being kind of delusive about themselves and thinking they were prettier and smarter and more interesting than they really were? *That* was scary! She certainly didn't want to overdo her value, then she'd stop growing and learning. She didn't think she was like that, but she was paying more attention to how she looked at things.

What if the alternative was looking at life the way Ian and Twinkle did? What a horrible conversation they were having! She was still trying to be optimistic; after all, she and Twinkle had been friends since Marymount, since eighth grade, but it was getting harder and harder to be around her. It was giving her headaches and making her angry and when Twinkle was with Ian, she was completely horrible.

What was she even doing here? She should have stayed in New York and earned some extra money during her break. It really had been one of those offers she couldn't refuse. A cruise! In a suite with her best friend and both their families. Well, that part was kind of weird. All those years she and Twinkle had been friends, their parents had hardly spoken to one another and then all of a sudden, her dad and Twinkle's dad are doing business together and going out and about? Talk about opposites attracting!

Well, maybe not opposites. Her parents could get along with any-body. The "perfect couple"—everyone who met them called them that. And they were, they really were, though no one believed her, especially not Twinkle and evil Ian. Oh God, did she really think that? He wasn't evil, just spoiled. Hurt in some way; inside there was good in him. She kept hoping he'd open up to her more and she could like him and maybe even really get to be his friend.

Good in everyone, just like Ann Frank said, that was how she chose to look at the world. It was how her mother did. Beautiful inside and out. How many times had she heard that line!

She rolled over and threw the pillow off. Well, no sleep but at least a little time out from all that competitive chatter. Why had she come, really?

Well, her parents had been traveling so much she'd hardly seen them in months, and this was a way to be together as a family. She missed them so much, and she knew it made her mom really sad when they weren't in close touch. Her mom did seem sad, sort of. No one else could probably tell, but she could. Being an only child maybe does that, makes you more sensitive to their moods. Maybe her mother felt that she had pulled away and didn't know how to mention it. Had she?

Okay, Clarissa, be honest, don't take the easy way out. She had. It was all so confusing lately. Her mother's beauty, her mother's goodness just felt so, so what? Oppressive. Oh God, it was! Her entire life she'd had people stare at them. "Oh, you look just like your mother!" "What a lucky little girl, you're going to be a beauty like your mother!" "What a lucky young lady to look like your mother, are you as good inside as outside, like your mother?"

Her mother always acted very modest about it all, but underneath she knew her mom enjoyed it and expected it. She'd never say that to her, but she did. If someone didn't say anything about her looks, she got a little funny look in her eyes and afterward she'd be more quiet.

Kids pick up on that kind of stuff, and she certainly remembered feeling the tension when it didn't happen and then either she or her dad would brown nose it up and make sure they said something about how great her mom looked just to make that look leave her face and have her cheerful again. God, she hated that! Hated it! So, she wasn't just positive about everything.

Her parents and everyone else were always telling her she looked just like her mom and how beautiful she was, but she didn't believe it. They did look alike. Same red curly hair, same pale skin and green eyes, and they both had big boobs, but not huge; nice figures, but on her mom it was all gorgeous and delicate and on her it was more hearty and earthy and just shifted a little, mixed with her dad enough so it wasn't beauty. Attractive, but not show-stopping. Thank God! Her mother was fine porcelain china and she was everyday stoneware, and that was okay with her.

Being beautiful like that made it impossible for people to really see you and it became all you were. Things were expected and things were shut down. She sighed and put the pillow under her head. This was a new line of thought. What was shut down in her mom? Just thinking like this made her feel really nervous and guilty, but she did want to see clearly and not just spend her life in reaction against being like Twinkle and Ian. So, she'd try and tell the truth about this.

Well, everyone expected her mom to be kind and sweet and ladylike and friendly and gracious because that's the way we think delicate, gorgeous women should be—unless they're celebrities or models or rock stars. Then they can be witches or maybe that was wrong, maybe that was just the way her mom felt she should be, part of her image? Good-hearted. She had never heard her swear or say a jealous, mean thing about anyone. Was *that* normal?

Well, whatever it was, it was hard to live up to, even for her, and unlike her mom, she hated all that attention. Most of the time she wore her glasses instead of her contacts, no make-up and a baseball cap so no one would bother her or single her out for any attention. Most of the time, she only had to deal with it when she was with her mom, anyway.

Why was that? If they really did look so much alike, (which she didn't believe, but if they did) was it the aura around her mom? All the grooming and perfect clothes and make-up and stuff certainly added to it, but maybe people sensed her mom craved it. So, *there* was a sort of flaw. Her mom was vain about her beauty, though she never talked about herself like that. She was used to being the center of attention and having men ogle her and help her carry things and open doors and stuff; that might be part of her mom's sadness. She wasn't getting that kind of attention as much, sometimes not at all, anymore.

Well, she was fifty-two now. It has to wane sometime. She had changed, aged, though she still looked fantastic. Things shift around and she was a little heavier, but for someone as perfect as her mom, it must be hard. It did seem her dad was doing double duty with the compliments, so maybe that was why she seemed sad.

Oh boy, that was not going to happen to her! No way! How scary, to rely on something you had to lose! Everyone got older. Her mom had never really worked and now her daughter was grown and her beauty was fading (just a little, but still) and even though they never talked about it, she knew money was a big issue.

She sat up; her chest felt tight. No wonder she tried to look on the bright side! *This feels really weird, thinking about my family like this.* She looked over at the clock. Ten more minutes and she'd get up and start getting ready for the party the Talbotts were having before dinner.

Money sure wasn't the Talbotts' problem! They had too much and her family didn't have enough. Well, enough for most people, but not for the kind of life they tried to live. New York City and private schools for her and traveling and private clubs and everything. And socializing with people like the Talbotts. They were billionaires, probably.

Well, to be fair, it was business, at least partly. But it seemed to her all of their friendships were about business opportunities for her dad. He struggled so hard! She loved him so much. He was everything any girl could want a father to be. Handsome, wise, funny. He always took time for her and made her feel so special. He worked *so* hard! But nothing seemed to ever work out. And he was so brilliant, really a visionary. If he had just stayed being a research scientist, he at least would have had some security, but he had such big dreams and ideas for inventing medical devices and surgical aids, but they all took huge investments of capital to bring to market and that part was always letting him down.

So, as much as she hated all their phony socializing and going off here and there with one dreadful rich couple or another, it was always about finding investors. Which was why her mom was such an asset. Both of them, really, were like the perfect houseguests or ship guests or whatever.

They were interested in others and fun to talk to—her dad particularly—who was up on everything and always had some hilarious story to tell. They played bridge and golf and tennis and ate just enough and drank just enough to be enjoyable company but never overdid anything or said something politically incorrect or were too loud or ill mannered or hurt anyone's feelings or . . . Was *that* normal? No one was really like that, were they?

Even *she* wasn't as cheerful and friendly as she thought she was. But they were like that with her, too. Mostly. They were really private; even she got left out of their intimate conversations. Even if she thought they were fighting or heard raised voices or whatever, when they came out of their room, they were always back to normal. Was *THAT* normal?

When they told her that they were having trouble paying for graduate school and she would have to help more and get some student loans, she realized things were getting serious. Her mom had even cut out some of her massage and grooming rituals, and her dad gave up their car. "We don't need a car in the city; it's a waste of money," he'd said. But she knew he'd never do that unless things were really tough. So, enter the Talbotts. Too strange.

They'd always been pleasant enough to her, but she knew (and she'd even told her parents) that they were really snobby and anti-Semitic and sort of anti-everyone who wasn't a Park Avenue WASP with old money. Whatever that meant. How ridiculous! She'd never understood how some people could think they were better than other people just because their immigrant riffraff ancestors had bought real estate in the "New World" a hundred years before someone else's immigrant riffraff ancestors. You didn't have to be a big brain like her dad to figure out that anyone who left France or Ireland, or England or Sweden or wherever to come to America, was not doing so great at home.

She had never seen any Jewish or black or even catholic guests at the Talbotts' parties, and even though they were always polite and friendly to her, or at least Mr. Talbott, Mrs. Talbott was not really friendly to anyone; not that she was rude, she was just, what was the word? Reserved. Really reserved or as her friend Andre said, "She doesn't have a pole up her ass, she's got a nuclear warhead in there and it's probably set to detonate if she so much as farts."

Boy, did she wish Andre was here now! Not that he'd be caught anywhere near this group. He loathed Twinkle and had since junior high school. He'd met Ian one night when they were all at some bar and he'd imitated him for weeks. "That dude gives the term 'Eurotrash' a bad name."

"Well, what about that? Ian's grandmother was a Countess but she was from Texas! She'd just married some Eurotrash type with a title and no money (or so Twinkle had told her); his father was from Austria but his mother was as American as his grandmother, so what was all of that, 'You Americans' stuff?"

Well Andre had his own prejudices, since he'd never get across the threshold of the Talbotts. If her family was okay Jewish, he was not okay Jewish—a scholarship student from Brooklyn! No way. She was always trying to bring her friends together and help them see the good in one other, but maybe she was the one who was wrong. Where were her values anyway?

"Ohmigawd, this is like the weirdest Dirty Martini I've ever had! What is that gross taste? Hey you, what's wrong with this?"

"I'm so very sorry if you do not like it. I make it a special way with a jalapeño pepper in it. It gives it a less salty and strong flavor than the olive, but I will bring another immediately, Miss Talbott. I am very sorry."

"It's really quite good, Twinks. Your palate is just too violated by all that trendy bullshit you consume. I'll take hers, Elonzito, my man."

"Oh, no, Mr. Von Essen, I will bring you a fresh one. It will be much more chilled."

Clarissa crossed her arms over her face. Her chest still felt so tight and her head was pounding. She never felt like this. Five more minutes and she'd give up, get up and take a nice hot bath.

"Yip yip yip. Yip yip yip. Yip yip yip."

Oh great. Tou Tou was at it again. She'd never sleep tonight unless she slept in Twinkle's room, which presented other challenges depending on how wasted Twinkle got. Where was the Countess? She couldn't possibly be sleeping through that? Maybe she was so used to it, she just tuned out.

She'd been so excited when she heard Ian's grandmother had a puppy coming with them. She loved animals completely, even if she'd never been able to have one of her own because her mom was allergic. Sometimes she'd just walk around New York and pet every pup she passed and think about having a little house in the country with a horse and lots of dogs and a great big fat short-haired Persian cat. But this Tou Tou was really a challenge. He was so bony she couldn't cuddle him; she was afraid she'd snap him in two (not that he'd let her, anyway); he bared his little sharp teeth and growled, really growled, every time she came near him. Boy, this trip really was a test of her positive approach to her fellow beings! And it was only the first day!

How had her dad gotten friendly with Mr. Talbott in the first place? It must have been after graduation at that huge party they had for Twinkle at their mansion in Southampton. Of course her dad knew all about the illustrious Teddy Talbott. His family company was involved in everything from cruise lines to computers to appliances to pharmaceuticals and medical devices, which was what her father chatted him up about—and from that party on, they were on the guest list.

One thing she knew about the Talbotts and their friends: none of them liked to be alone or even alone together. They always had at least another couple with them and houseguests galore.

Sometimes she felt bad for her parents because so much of their going off to someone's fancy house or on a yacht trip, was sort of like they were being paid (not with money but with hospitality) for being companions of the rich and lonely.

She wanted everyone she cared about to be happy and loving one another and having great relationships. Poor Twinkle. One of the reasons she'd tried so hard to keep being her friend was she knew how unreal her home life was. Twinkle almost never even had a nice quiet family dinner with just her parents. They didn't seem to really know her or have much interest in her life.

Well, not that her life was the kind of life parents would really want to know about! Shopping and partying and trashing all your friends in text messages wasn't the kind of conversation the Talbotts would enjoy.

So, now she was a part of her parents' performance. Did she really think that's what they were doing with the Talbotts, performing? They were certainly less Jewish around them. Not that they were very Jewish, anyway; pretty secular, but she could see where they acted more WASPY around "Teddy and Sissy." "Leah and Walter" were hardly cut from the same cloth. Sort of linen versus cotton. It made her really uncomfortable, and she knew Twinkle and Ian were onto it and probably made fun of them behind their backs. Oh, God, this was her best friend she was talking about!

But that wasn't really true anymore, either. Now she was being as fake as the rest of them. She had pulled away from Twinkle. She loved her and wanted her to be happy with herself and find something that had some purpose, but she didn't like her very much. Most of what she said and did made her sick inside, and Twinkle just didn't seem to feel anything for anyone, not even her parents.

And she was mean, too. The way she talked to the people who worked for them and to that sweet man, Elonzito—so horrible! At least Twinkle's parents had good manners and treated their servers and workers politely, even if it was with a kind of patronizing tone. Her own mother would say, "Very low rent to talk to help like that, Twinkle Talbott." Too funny the way Twinkle's mom used both her names when she was upset with her.

Twinkle called her parents "the Ungrateful Dead," which was kind of funny, but not really. They never touched one another. None of them. *Ever.* She and her parents were always hugging and kissing and saying "I love you" even when they were just hanging up the phone. That was really awful, to not be touched and kissed.

Maybe that's why Twinkle slept around so much. There she was, after all, twenty-three, with her own trust fund and an apartment off Madison and a car and no responsibility at all. She knew her parents didn't approve of Twinkle, but because of her dad's trying to put this company together with Mr. Talbott to produce some of his inventions and all, her mom was being pretty quiet about Twinkle these days.

Was that sort of like a betrayal of her? Her poor mom. She was so much the kind of woman who should have everything like Mrs. Talbott and not have to worry about finances all the time and also being around all those successful people but not being one of them. It must be hard for her even if she never let on and always seemed to see the best in everyone. Like her? Was she like that? . . . Was *that* normal? Was it being an optimist and happy-go-lucky or was it being delusive like that article said? Maybe it was both.

Time to get up. She yawned and stretched, feeling the tightness in her chest release. So many things to think about. What was that line in that really bad Sci Fi movie she'd seen on cable before she left? "There are no answers, only choices." Well, she had chosen to come and she couldn't complain or blame anyone if she wasn't liking it much.

A hot bath and a new outfit and a nice glass of champagne and lots of delicious hors d'oeuvres would do the trick! Maybe she'd try again with Ian. Maybe he was just insecure and underneath he was really a good soul. After all, being shipped off to boarding school at five! Imagine how awful that would be. Apparently the Countess was the only one who paid any real attention to him. She was more his mother than grandmother, and she was pretty out there.

"Yip. Yip. Yip. Yip Yip Yip."

Clarissa laughed. Well at the very least, she'd have lots of funny stories to tell Andre.

ᴄᴍ

"ʀᴏʀʏ ʜᴏɴᴇʏ, it's Flora."

"Hi, y'all."

"Boy, you sound mellow. Musta been some massage."

"Amazing, thanks for telling me about her."

"She's a real peach pie, that one; I even forgive her for sleepin' with the enemy."

"A new enemy or one of your perennials?"

"Yew know what they say honey lamb: even paranoids have enemies, this ship is crawlin' with saboteurs, the cast is like one big *Survivor* episode."

"Collie of the healing hands is sleeping with someone in the cast? They're all gay."

"Did I say it was a man?"

"No way."

"You're right, just havin' a tease. No one in the cast, just that Nazi swine who runs the hotel and everything. Heinrich, sounds like just what he is, a fascist pig. Really awful to all my little buds from housekeepin'."

"She's so sweet. Please do not tell me it's just another phony façade and underneath she's a bad person."

"Not at all. She's the real deal. Just young and of course he isn't a sick, bigoted pig when he's wooin' her; he's turnin' on the charm and the Dom and caviar. She's a little Irish village lass and he's the big, bad wolf in Italian clothing."

"Shouldn't you warn her? Boy I'd want someone to warn me. How much grief would be saved the women of the world if warners warned and *we* listened. I hate charm. Charm is the devil, it really is."

"That's the point, though darlin'. She's in that awe phase. The guy is oozing the stuff and obviously the humpin' is sumthin'. She's only a kid, ya know. I'm watchin' it. She'll figure it out, especially since she's a real Union Organizer type, and always gettin' upset over the way the Filipinos are treated.

"Sounds far too risky and subtle. I'm more the Fools Rush In and Shoot Off Their Big Fat Mouths type of friend, which is probably why my friends list is so short these days. If only people came with instructions, how grand it would be."

"Yeah, well, dream on, honey lamb. Did she tell yew what happened to her roommate?"

"No—it was one of those, touch-me-and-the-damn-bursts deals; we didn't talk much."

"Well, her roomie, another masseuse, got stuck working a double—twelve hours straight, thanks to Herr Hensler and her hands froze up. Just locked like rigor mortis. She's been in the clinic for two days getting shot up with cortisone and muscle relaxants and heat treatments, and she still can't bend her fingers."

"That's horrible. How does she eat?"

"You're a trip, Ror! That's your first thought?"

"I'm highly oral. If you can't move your fingers you can't really eat or pick up a glass or wipe your ass. I'm rhyming again, can't stop it today. Imagine having to have someone feed you; that would kill. How can they work them like that, anyway?"

"You need a tad of my paranoia, honey. They can do what they like; no unions for these folks. We got ours, but that's 'cause we're booked outa New York and we're U.S. of Aers, They got jack."

"Well, I can now safely say most of the effects of the massage have been dulled, so tell me the real reason for the call. Something's wrong with the new material?"

"No, no, I love the new stuff. In fact that's the favor I need. I'm supposed to sing for Teddy Talbott, one of the owners, and some guests in his suite tonight before dinner and I wanna try some of the new stuff yew wrote. I need yew there to hear it and give me feedback and see how the audience reacts. Also, I can introduce yew to the Talbotts. Not bad for the big Kahuna to meet ya. I know yew hate these things, but pretty please?"

"Well, the knot in my neck just re-formed. I could have saved my money. I'm tired and my hair's greasy and I'm already in my nightgown. Please don't make me do this."

"It's not for me, it's for the show . . . your show. Yew gotta hear it before rehearsal tomorrow, and I really need the support. I promise, yew can come just before and leave right after. Besides, yew might even meet someone interesting."

"Please, spare me. I'd be more likely to meet someone interesting at a Trekkie convention. Besides, I don't want to meet someone, interesting or otherwise. Ever."

"Liar."

"Whatever I may be, I am not a liar. I mean it. I don't even have a sex drive anymore, anyway, so what would be the point."

"It's just bidin' its little ol' time, until The One comes."

"Tell me you didn't actually say 'The One.'"

"I did and I truly believe it."

"This is noteworthy. Have you recently met such a person? Is that why you're kicking over your head again?"

"Maybe, but I can't reveal the identify if it is true."

"Oh, shit. He's married. Guess what. I don't want to know. Promise you won't be slithering around with that cat and canaryesque pussy-faced look at rehearsal. Women are so fucked. Truly, utterly, completely fucked."

"I'll try, but I'm sure it'll show a bit. It's been a long, long time, Rory. And the rest of my fading little life is not lookin' so hot right about now. Let me have my little bright spot."

"Flora, I'm sorry. I just don't want to see you get racked up. Married is so, hard."

"Oh, yes, he is, honey. Really hard."

"Okay, I give up. So what's the other stuff?"

"I have that creepin' feelin' they're gettin' ready to dump me. I can tell; lots of averted eye contact. I'm the oldest headliner in the entire industry; forty-five is ancient for this job. I've got chorus boys who could be my sons, doin' love duets with me, and I'm kind of losin' it. Not a lot, just a bit. I've been at this for thirty years, darlin'. I thought I'd be ready to go, but go where. Don't have a dime or a home. Soooo, let me have my little ol' romance."

"Flora, you're still the best there is; maybe it's true but maybe it's the P word. So, okay, I'll come. But this better not be some Southern Gothic ploy to make me worry about you so I'll go to the party. Shit. I have no clothes. What time?"

"I'm set to start at 7:00. Just a few songs and you're free."

"I'll be there. I just hope they have nice dark corners and nice cold chardonnay."

"Thanks, honey. I owe ya."

"No, you don't."

ᴄᴍ

PARTIES. Rooms full of masked creatures. Grinning and spinning. Yacking, backslapping, Venus flytrapping. The social contract in action. How we behave in groups. How we behave in big groups. How we behave in smaller groups (about the same). How we behave at home alone in the bathroom (not about the same).

What works at parties: Beauty, always. Fame, OF COURSE! Have someone famous at a party and just watch the acquiring of insect-like peripheral vision, the looking without staring, the sidling without actually approaching. Energy pops, the very nearness to the bigger-than-life being, crackles through the room. Power and money. The appearance of power and money. YES! Wit and charm, ESSENTIAL.

No wit, no beauty, no charm, no fame, no power, no money, never fear! Brown Nosers have their place. Brown Nosing is great at parties. Flattery and the fanning of narcissism works. In fact, it is a necessity. It is required. Sycophants add balance and provide audiences for the others.

What doesn't work? Self-absorbed, bad smelling and boring, unless also powerful, rich or beautiful. No serious party-giver invites such people anyway (how would it look to the others?), even if they are blood relatives; they do not appear. They are saved for strictly family occasions when the illustrious hosts of wonderful, fabulous parties are less glowing; re-tied to their roots, the exception being a few rare people like the Talbotts who are always the same, most likely even alone in the bathroom.

Well-bred, over-bred, a new shallower breed—bred like good pets. Purebred to remove all annoying individual characteristics, bred for manners and predictability in all situations, bred for social success. Bred to be unflappable, never at a loss, no flicker of humanness, rudeness, spontaneity or opinions of any kind that could in any way affect their social grace. Bred bloodless and without irony, prickliness or passion. Bred to fit in with others of their kind in a seamless way.

Bred to golf and sail and like small lamb chops on the bone and look good in white slacks and play doubles tennis and garden and love charitable works and boards and committees and Episcopalian Churches on occasional Sundays and to wear suits and pearls and be polite and punctual and write thank you notes immediately after attending a PARTY and to always be appropriate.

But bred, most of all, to love social events of all kinds: lunches and brunches and teas and ribbon cuttings and weddings and christenings and funerals and swearing-in ceremonies and retirement dinners and charity balls; endless, glorious charity balls ("for all those precious little Leukemia victims"), for any cause, for any reason.

Garden shows and horse shows and Kicking-off-the-Season-in-Palm Beach galas and Ending-the-Season-in-Saratoga galas and every conceivable kind of birthday, anniversary or holiday party (Easter Egg Hunts and Coaching Weekends). Bred to love, love, love all activities involving lots of other people like themselves. Yacht club barbeques, croquet and cocktails.

Purebreds. Best in Show were the Talbotts. This was hardly even a party by their standards, a little teeny "do" to smudge any real intimacy that might be expected by their suitemates. Bring others in, just in case the Worths or the kids or the Countess might let their hair down or expect something more from them. They were not bred for that. If they were, they would have been weaned out of the litter long ago.

This was, however, a rather unexciting event, really a party for the help, as it were—except for the Countess, who were these people? The Worths, after all, as attractive and enjoyable as they were to be with, were Jews! And he was a business associate! Highly unusual to begin with! The Captain? The guest lecturers for the week! Well, Poe Evanoff did have some celebrity, but again, a Jew—however well his book had sold or popular his talks were; who did things like that, anyway?

The Cruise Director? Well-mannered and delightful company (but certainly not their crowd), and the Performer, well, she was clearly there as decoration and entertainment, not really a guest at all.

They had left the rest to Doolittle, for him to choose a few "suitable passengers" to fill out the room, to make it at least a party, and it was, of course, their duty as Owners to be charming and extend every courtesy.

Good food and good drink and music and a couple of provocative, exotic guests to titillate, but not fit, that's what a good party had. One could just do their best and move on to the next, always another opportunity to shine. Always another party to plan. The purebred Talbotts, poised at the edge of the ring, ready to show their stuff, to do what they were born to do, Best in Breed, at least.

Sucko, sucko, sucko. I hate parties. Rory Saltz slid inside, grabbing a glass of wine and heading for the first corner she saw, feeling as if she had been suddenly shoved from the womb into the world. She had never actually been in one of the fancy suites before. *Unfucking believable!* She saw Flora leaning against a piano. A baby grand piano in a boat cabin! Man, oh man, this was worth seeing.

If only she were invisible, she'd probably love parties. Wandering around, snacking and snooping without having to engage in banter and small talk. What did that really mean anyway? Small talk. Was it one step up from baby talk? She would have to think about this more, maybe a song.

She waved, catching Flora's eye, doing her duty. Flora waved back and gave her watch a tap, meaning, she supposed, that it wouldn't be too long, now. She spotted Doolittle chatting up a couple who could be the hosts; they looked like the Talbotts type. God, Doolittle really gave her the willies. All that fey elitism, as if he were one of the guests. Too hearty the laugh, too enthusiastic the reportage.

Why was it that people who were too cheerful made her feel so lonely? Maybe because it never gave her anything real to connect to? His voice boomed over the room. Poor Derrick, if he could only be gay, but he was one of those got-too-hurt-by-somone-and-could-never-again-risk-any-form-of-intimacy types. So here he was, natty and chatty, still good-looking, but thickening up.

He was always on, always. Or at least as far as she had seen, even when he was piss-eyed. He freaked if anyone thought he was gay, which was all the time. What *was* his deal? Nothing was more fascinating than other people, at least in the abstract. Now who had intimacy issues?

She swallowed, letting that first sip of wine warmth trickle down into her stomach, greasing the social wheels. *Jesus, the room is twice the size of my entire apartment.* Shapes were starting to define. She put on her glasses, bringing a deeper level of reality to the scene.

Thirty or so overdressed people, blabbing away as if they had known one another forever. Nothing worse than silence at a party. Fill those cracks! Who did she know? She saw Elonzito, her cabin steward from the last trip, passing trays, looking very serious and slightly stressed. She saw Flora chatting up the, Captain? Must be the captain, that little swagger thing all the captains seem to have.

The problem with her corner position was that none of the servers were aware of her suddenly serious need for sustenance, and the hors d'oeuvre table was across the room, and the tray passers were whizzing down through the middle.

Shit. The Fray, I'll have to travel or starve. The Fray? Why did she use it like that? It really meant "a noisy fight" or "something rubbed away, or ragged." Hmmm, must think about that. Was that what parties felt like to her, a ragged fight of some kind? Fight for what? To hold onto herself, her values, who had said that?

Virginia Woolf. No, her paramour, Katherine Mansfield? Gotta look that up. Maybe it was Virginia's sister; sounds like something she would have said. Vanessa was the one who stopped going to parties where she and Clive "had to dress up." Not ol' Virginia . . . never solved the conflict, solitude or society.

*She had. Sort of. Mostly. "In my solitude, I see you...." Billie
Holiday ... "If I take a notion to jump into the ocean, Ain't nobody's
business if I do.... If I get beat up by my poppa and I don't call no
coppa, Ain't nobody's business...." Oh Rory, what a stream of consciousness thought bank you have. Feminist Woolf segues to Billie
the Victim, love as battery, a bad man is better than no man. No
man is what she told Flora she wanted. Wonder what kind Flora's
found. She certainly is radiating, looking great. Sexy. Well, Flora
always looked sexy. She was one of those sexy ladies, always a little
bit of slink, lowered eyes, flirty Gerty stuff, southern belle shit. So
not like me.*

*I like Flora, but I don't necessarily trust Flora. Who do I trust,
anymore? What would it take for me to trust someone now? Don't
think about that. Think about shrimp. Think about brie with toasted
almonds on top. Thank God for glasses! I can see the details. Do
I want to see the details? Do I really need the Brie with Almonds?
Everything magnifies, wrinkles and flaws, mine and theirs; do I like
it all smudged more, less visible? Yes. Except when I'm in my corner,
then I like it clear and clean. Pristine. I want to see out but I don't
want them to see in. Move, Rory. Think smoked salmon. Keep your
eyes on the prize.*

She glided, listening to the sounds, the voices of the small talk,
tinkling in her ears, accompanied by Maurice on the piano, like
a scene from Stephen Sondheim, "So I bought a little condomin-
ium.... These are the movers, these are the shakers...."

"Well, I am a foodie, I admit it, and I love Caribbean food because the colors are so bright, especially when they're served on
very white plates."

"On our last cruise, my nephew kept trying to convince me to
dance with him to that awful rap music, and finally I said, 'I will
not dance to that! That's the music black teenagers get pregnant
to, and that's why we have welfare.' "

"First thing I tell my executive trainees, 'if you're gonna be a
leader, when you go into a new company to fix a problem, find the
person who's made himself indispensable and fire him.' "

"Well, you know how impossible it is to get an appointment
with any of the really good dermatologists anymore. I wanted to
see Fleisher, because he is really the Botox genius, and they said I'd
have to wait six months! Can you believe it? So I went online and
found out he does cosmetics to support his pro bono work with

advanced skin cancer patients, and I had the most brilliant idea. I called back, put on my most pathetic, teary voice and told the receptionist that I'd just been diagnosed with advanced malignant melanoma, and she got me in the next day!"

"I didn't believe in all the Life Coach hype either, but my psychic moved to New Mexico and I thought what the hell and now I'm hooked! She'll say, 'take a walk. No magazines in the bathtub! Don't let anything negative into your vocabulary. Don't say loser. Say, Jelly Bean.' "

Get a plate, Rory, get a shrimp; skip the brie. What's that green stuff? Eggplant? Yuck. "Why can't you love me for who I am, where I am? 'Cause that's not the way the world is, baby." Paul Simon? Who are these people? People who nobody loves for who they are, where they are. "Who will be my role model, now that my role model's gone?" Move now as quickly as possible back to your corner. Go. Go.

How do I do this? Glass and plate. No place to put anything down. What if I put my glass on the floor? Totally tacky? Probably, what the hell. I'll put my glass down and gobble really fast. Maybe, I can sit down on a chair? No, too likely to be seen and have to talk to someone. Don't flatter yourself; what makes you think anyone is the least bit interested in talking to you? Look around. You're a real sore thumb, kiddo. Where did that come from? Sore thumb? All these words we use, sayings, and we have no clue what they mean. God, I do love words. I trust words. Why is that? Words are used for unbelievable bullshit, mendacity and pain. Not my own words. Oh, a clarification. You love your words. Eat. Good, now you can bend down and get your glass. Ah, better. Don't want to drink on an empty stomach, sore thumb that I am, anyway.

Back to the Woolf thoughts, no her sister, her sister's thought; if being in groups is a betrayal of our true selves, why is that? Because to fit in, you have to give up parts of your identity? Yes! That's what it is. People want to fit in so badly, they get so scared of being alone, they pick out identities like, clothes. Squeeze themselves into the nearest size. Hmmm, well, I guess I'm somewhere between a 6 and an 8, so I'll go for the 8, easier fit. They schmoosh themselves into a lifestyle, an identity wardrobe complete with almost-fitting politics and religious beliefs and hobbies, and settle for something outside themselves to define them, give them a safe place from which to launch a life. YES!

So when does anyone change or grow or claim themselves? Ah, well, you know something about that. Well, maybe, except you never fit in, period. Nothing about your life ever fit. Oh, God. It's coming back. Why now? Something weird is going on again. Focus back on this idea. So why does anyone change? The fit is really bad? Yes! It's a shoe, not a dress, and you're forcing a size 7 foot into a size 5 and sooner or later, it hurts so bad you can't walk, can't pretend it fits, and you have to take them off, then you can begin to sort, to find yourself, your true identify, what really fits, but who wants to do that?

Being barefoot and bunioned and in pain and alone, unprotected, without illusions and delusions, not a big line for that! So we hobble on, not comfortable, but we can manage and even if we can't, we grimace on in agony, blistered and miserable rather than face the terror of surrendering the false identity . . . leaving us without a peer group.

Are you just being smug, because you never had one to begin with? You never had to take off the toe-crunchers, because you were barefoot to begin with. Are you jealous? Do you have fitting-in envy again? Is that why parties are so hard for you, now? You long for this, underneath? You didn't hate parties before. . . .

Oh shit, I am not going to cry, here. Breathe. . . . Billy, Billy, Billy. . . . Not now. Put the plate down. Put the glass down. Move, Ror, find the bathroom. Go.

"Rory, honey bun, what's goin' on, I saw yew bobbin' up and down in that corner like a little ol' Jack in the Box. Are yew all right?"

"Fine. I just had a little Muppet moment, and I'm going to repair myself in the loo. How much longer until show time?"

"Sorry, but it looks like another fifteen or so. They're all havin' such a good ol' time! Derrick's in his glory 'cause he chose the guests, and I sure don't wanna start until they're sauced up enough to love me. Want me to ask Elonzito to bring you some aspirin or sumthin'?"

"Nope. I'll be fine. I just need a time-out. It's the remnants of the massage catharsis; I feel like fucking Humpty Dumpty."

"Well, yew sure don't look like him. Lookin' good, girlfriend. That hair is so wild. Everyone asks me how you get it all white and slutty like that, and no one believes me when I tell them you're like some genetic mistake and it's natural. I was chattin' with this couple the owners brought along, and the wife asked me about yew, 'cause of your hair. She wants to meet yew. Oh, Lord, she's movin' this way. Better go quick, fix up."

"Rory? Is that you? Rory Riley?"

Rory turned. She was trapped. The sore thumb with someone's ill-fitted stiletto digging into her palm. A face in focus. Too focused. The past. A face from the past. A uniquely singular face from the past. A Fairfax High School face. An unforgettable, hauntingly beautiful face. A face attached to heartbreak and envy.

Impossible. Was this possible? Could this really be happening? Maybe all of this stuff bubbling up at her today was hooked to this moment. This about-to-be reunion. Her body knew first. Her heart knew first. Where are the Hot-Line Psychics and the Life Coaches when you need them? No escape ever, is there? Life will make sure eventually that every dropped stitch, every cut corner, skipped step and loose end in every fucking one of even the worst-fitting lives will have to be reckoned with. *Leah.* Shit.

"Leah Frankel!"

"Well, it's Leah Worth. You remember Walter?"

"How could anyone forget Walter. You *married* Walter?"

"High school romance that never ended. Thirty-four years!"

"Wow. That's a lot of Seven Year itching. Congratulations."

"Oh, Rory, still the same. Such a special girl! Actually, not a single itch. It's really so boring. We're still like honeymooners, like swans, I suppose. We beat all the odds. How about you? Where did you go? You just disappeared after graduation. I heard your grandparents died and I tried to call you, but your Aunt, when she finally called me back, she said you'd just 'picked up and left town' and I never heard from you again."

"Yeah, well, it was kind of a rough time and there was really no reason to stay, so I went to New York."

"We live in New York now! How wild that we've never run into one another."

"I can go years and not run into people who live in my building. I bet you live uptown."

"Yes, East Eighties. You, too?"

"Hello? Leah? Do I look like East Eighties to you? Lower East Side between Mott and Mulberry."

"Oh, Rory. It seems like yesterday. Now, I realize how much I've missed you. You look exactly the same. The hair is what I first saw.

"Remember? We had a sleep-over, you were at my house and you woke up in the morning and your hair was white? It was like a fairy tale! I remember my mother and I were horrified, and you just shrugged and you said the funniest thing, I've never forgotten it, you said, 'The only thing my mother left me, a defective gene.'

"It made me so sad for you. I cried in my mother's arms after you left. 'Poor Rory, she's a orphan!' I wanted my parents to adopt you, so we could be sisters but, of course, you had your grandparents. Are you here alone? Flora told me you write all the special material for the show, just like high school. You wrote everything!"

"Yes. I do and yes, I'm alone. And my name is Saltz now."

"Oh, you're married."

"Not anymore."

"Any children? I want you to meet my daughter, Clarissa. She's our shining light."

Why is this happening? Someone get this spike heel off my hand. "I'd love to meet your daughter, but I've really gotta pee and then, I think Flora's going to sing, so maybe later."

"Oh, of course. We'll find you. This is unbelievable! I'd just been introduced to Flora and I saw her wave to someone and I looked across and saw that hair, and it was as if it was still 1970. Oh, Rory, what a treat. Walter is going to faint!"

"I would think that highly unlikely, but it's an interesting visual. Leah, you still are the most beautiful girl in the world. I'll see you after."

"Oh, Rory. Wait till you see Clarissa!"

Moving through, moving fast, a hall, gotta be down the hall, hold on, babe, almost home, breathe, breathe . . . what the fuck is that? A woman draped in emeralds with . . . what IS that? A ferret? A dog? Some ugly, horrible creature attached to her chest, like Alien. Alien with Emeralds . . . move, up ahead, gotta be a bathroom. Excuse me . . . sorry, thank you . . . close the door, lock the door. Oh god, I'm cracking, I am Humpty Dumpty. Sit down, Rory. Wipe your face. Put your head down. Cry. You've got to cry. Get it out. Don't know why. Just cry. Bill . . . Billy she's going to ask me again. Oh God, why can't I just die . . . can't die, have to stick around in case . . .

She looked up. Her face had melted. So much for waterproof mascara. Her mask had been ripped off, her social façade, such as it were. All she saw was wound. Gaping, eviscerating sorrow. Shrouded in a white spiky helmet. A haunted face in a ghostly frame. Hair.

*What a joke! Betrayed again by all she had as a legacy. A freak in
nature. Sticking out like a, guess what! A sore fucking thumb. That's
how Leah had spotted her after thirty-four years!*

She stood up and reached for a towel. How could she put herself
back together? She wet the towel and wiped the steaks of mascara
away. She hadn't even taken a purse, as if by that very gesture she
could ensure the shortness of her stay. She opened a drawer. Whoa!
Stocked with every conceivable guest amenity. Everything! Lipstick,
mascara, powder. Cotton balls. Vaseline, Visine, Listerine . . .
rhymes everywhere. *Do what you can. Do it quick.*

The wave had passed, like food poisoning. Emotional projectile
vomiting. It hits and if expelled, a respite, a release of tension, a
reprieve, if you will, until the next bout. She felt calm. She patted
and powdered. Did the best she could with her 52-year-old unal-
tered face—her non-Leah face. Leah Frankel! Oh God, the past was
going to push right up into her throat like a bad shrimp. Spasms
of it clenched at her, gnawing at her insides, like small convulsions
of memory.

Curson Street and the smell of boiled cabbage, of wilted lettuce
soaking in lemon juice, what passed for a salad. Smells of tea bags
and mothballs, Vicks VapoRub and corned beef. Cheracol cough
syrup and Irish whiskey. Fried potatoes. Ivory soap.

Her grandparents, sitting in their chairs, side by side, the plastic
covers squeaking when they moved. Glued to the small black and
white television. Roller Derby and wrestling, hour after hour. Old,
so old, they were always old. Two sour-smelling old Irish people
in the middle of an Orthodox Jewish neighborhood.

Why were they there? Her slutty, drunken stupid aunt, swaggering around in her bathrobe. "Don't call me Auntie, call me Maddie.
I'm telling my men friends I'm your older sister . . ." Click, click,
click. Her mother's high heels above her sounding angry, always
sounding angry, though her mother never acted angry, never looked
angry. But her feet were angry.

She trusted those feet, felt the anger, stayed away. Click, click,
click. Her father was tall? Was he tall or was she just so small?
Spiffy dresser. Hard worker, on his way up. Her mother was pretty
and not on her way up. What did her mother do up there? She was
always downstairs at her grandparents, handed off. Handed off to
people who were too old to read to her, or walk her to school or pay
attention. Too old to care, anymore. People who ate boiled things

on trays in front of the T.V. People who watched Roller Derby of their own free will.

Bloody bodies of Christ hanging on the walls, scaring her to death. No explanation. No one went to church, just the bleeding naked man, hanging everywhere. Click, click, click. What *did* she do up there? Her mother stayed at home, tended to the apartment, living free in her grandparents' Four-Plex while her father, who may have been tall, worked on his way to being wealthy.

She would hear him tell her mother, "Next year, we'll have enough and we'll build a house." Her mother would smile. Her mother would make something nice for dinner. Her mother would act attentive to her when her father was home—that seemed to be her job, a mother and wife to an on-the-road-to-successful father—but when he was gone, she couldn't be bothered with her.

What did she do up there? Click, click, click. Her mother with the snow white hair, when it was fashionable, in the years of the big blondes. Marilyn and Jayne and Mamie. Not that her mother was like that. She was, shy? Quiet. At least with her. No interest in talking to her, except when she fought with her father—then she would rush downstairs and get her. Take her in the car for ice cream. Take "a little drive" and "pour out her heart." As if Rory could help.

How old was she? Five? Eight? By ten, she had it mastered. If she wanted a mother, she had to be a good listener and always tell her what she wanted to hear. Her father was bad. Her mother was good. He "had affairs," whatever that meant. "She suffered," whatever that meant to grown-ups. Click, click, click. When they were getting along, she forgot all about Rory. Rory was in her way. Rory's father preferred Rory's company to hers, she would yell at him. "You never want to be alone with me!"

They were moving up in the world, though. He was building their "Dream House." They were going to move out of her grandparents' house, away from "Jewville," her father said. On weekends they would drive to the lot where the house would be. What did he do? She never really knew. She was just getting to the point where she would start asking questions like that and being entitled to an answer. Old enough to participate.

And then they were dead. Dead. No warning. Smashed up. Crashed into. Dead. No more click, click, click. No more Sunday drives to the dream house. Dead. And she never found out what he did or if he was really tall or why her mother didn't love her.

Rory stiffened, the cramping inside her head, the squeezing up in her throat, the truth. *Her mother didn't love her.* What Leah remembered. Leah Frankel! Here. Now? Bringing that smack of truth. That slap upside her head, that bad shrimp. No one had ever loved her. And the one person she had loved was gone.

Lettuce soaking in lemon juice. Roller Derby and Gorgeous George. Click. Click. Click. The scrapbook of her childhood. She moved downstairs for good. Her Aunt moved upstairs, replacing the click, click, click, with grunts and groans, drunken lust sounds, moans in her head. Her heart convulsed with longing for the gone thing, the never-had thing, the lost hope of comfort—of mother love.

Fairfax High School. What *was* she doing there? The Catholic kids went to Catholic school, even the poor ones. She spoke Yiddish and ate bagels and cream cheese before anyone who wasn't Jewish ate them. She hung out at Cantor's Delicatessen and ate matzo balls and cheesecake and hamantashen. She said "Oy Veh" and "schmuck" and "plotz."

High school is no place for a Sore Thumb. She was always alone except when the school plays were going on, when a poem or song was needed. She was always entertaining; she had a "smart mouth," her aunt said. Voted Most Talented in her Class, but no one ever invited her home but Leah. Leah was her best friend. Leah was her only friend. Leah Frankel, whose parents owned the nicest house of anyone, nice for the Fairfax area, where not that many kids even lived in houses.

Leah the Prom Queen. Leah the cheerleader. Leah the Best Dressed and the Most Popular and Best Figure with real parents and a real brother and sister and normal relatives and a wardrobe of party dresses. Leah, whose mother adored her. "My Hope," she called her. Leah would "marry well." Leah would lift them from the Fairfax District to Beverly Hills, to Brentwood, to Malibu. Leah, who had a drawer full of cards from agents and talent scouts who spotted her here and there. Leah, who was so kind to her, so accepting, so sweet—the guilt of her envy festering like a cut that never healed, never stopped oozing and cracking and bleeding. She would pray for the pain of it to end, the jealousy to stop, a scab to form so she could love Leah with abandon and be grateful for her friendship—without that throbbing thing in the way. Leah had everything she longed for, a longing for something indefinable, unimaginable.

She had one thing Leah didn't have. She had Walter Worth. Walter Worth liked her. Walter Worth, the male equivalent of Leah Frankel. Captain of the Football Team. Student body President. Best Looking, Best Dressed. Most likely to Succeed. Walter liked her. Walter took her out in his car and told her what he dreamed of. Walter was going to be a doctor. (A Jewish Doctor! Mazel Tov!) Walter put his minty tongue in her mouth and touched her boobs and made noises in her ear, and she made noises like her Aunt. (Was she like that? Would she end up like that? A drunken slag living in the Four-Plex forever smelling of cheap perfume and cheap whiskey? No, she would marry Walter Worth and live near the ocean and write poetry for her children.)

Walter was her secret. She never told Leah or anyone else. It was private; it was just between them. After school, in his car, his own car! *"No, no, Walter. Don't touch me there . . . Don't do that . . . Not, yet . . . I'm not ready. Please, no. Oh, Walter, I do love you . . . I do . . . I want to, oh so much, but I just, I . . ."*

What a joke, as if she would win, as if she even wanted to win, as if No really meant No. As if the night wouldn't come when her Aunt would spring forth from within her closed-down, virginal little Sore Thumb self, rip right past her fear, leap over her numbness—slutty, grunty, messy little niece of Maddie Riley. *Yes, Yes, Yes! Oh, Walter. I love you so. Oh, Walter, gentle. Please be . . .*

Everything would be all right now, no visions of smashed-up parents, no more shame and loneliness: Walter Worth's secret lover. She would compose songs for him. She would sing them while they made love on the Beach near their home.

How could she not have known better? Not have known that Sore Thumbs in high school do not end up with the Captains of Football Teams, the Presidents of Student Bodies—only in those fucking movies that screw everyone up, telling them lies about life, selling the endless summer, the Sore Thumb finds Prince Charming and lives happily ever after.

Sore Thumbs have their place, even as the second Mrs. Charmings, but never the first, not in real life, not in any life she'd ever seen. Leah and Walter. Wasn't it inevitable? The king and queen finally worked their way around to one another and that was that.

She never told Leah about him. She ran away, holding her scabby broken heart, nothing left for her there. Biding time until the diploma, freedom in a piece of paper. Graduation, like a band-aid for her wound.

"Miss Rory? It's Elonzito, are you okay?"

"Yes, yes I am." She opened the door. A shiny, smiling face. A lively, good face with big brown eyes, Harvey's eyes, her mutt's eyes, eager for everything, watching her every mood. She resisted the urge to fling herself against his starched white chest. "Elonzito, look at you! You look like the Captain, very impressive."

"I'm a butler, now, Miss Rory. Miss Flora sent me to see if you needed anything and to tell you she's going to start in a couple of minutes."

"Great, the sooner she starts, the sooner I can boogie out of here. One favor, tell me if I look weird or smeared, before I head back in there."

"Miss Rory, I do not know this word, 'smeared,' but you do not look weird."

"Oh, sorry, I'm embarrassing you. You're blushing; you are too cute, Elonzito. It means, messed up, like my makeup being, well, smeared! Sorry, I'm out of vocabulary selections right now."

"Oh, no. You look very fine. Would you like some water or anything?"

"Well, actually I lost my chardonnay somewhere. That would be nice. Come on, I'll walk back with you. How is your beautiful family?"

"They are well. Thank you so much for asking."

"They must be very proud of you."

"I hope so. I will get your wine and bring it in to you."

"Great, look for me in the back corner, by the door."

"No problem, and I'll tell Miss Flora you're okay."

He left her at the end of the hall and she hugged the wall, moving back toward what now felt like her place, her centering space. Everything had changed. She had started out to find the safety of the bathroom to sort out her feelings, and en route her mission had collided with an entirely new set of emotions: a kaleidoscope of new shapes and forms and colors of loss and confusion. Life in its full metal jacket, never any preparation for a grenade suddenly lobbed at your illusion of control.

"Ladies and gentlemen, good evening. For those of you I haven't met, yet, my name is Derrick Doolittle, and I have the double honor of being the Cruise Director of the greatest cruise ship in the world and introducing you to the star of the greatest at-sea show in the world, who is going to give you a sampling of our newest show, which premieres on the last night of your cruise. We are also honored to have the creator of the show, Miss Rory Saltz, here with us tonight. Rory, where are you hiding? Oh, there you are! Rory Saltz, ladies and gentlemen. And now, the one and only, Flora Frampton!"

"Thank yew, Derrick, and thank yew, Mr. and Mrs. Talbott, for havin' us up for this lovely party. Us, meanin' Rory, Maurice, my wonderful accompanist, and myself. I'm goin' to sing three numbers for y'all from our new cabaret show. I think the songs will speak for themselves. So, Maurice darlin', if yew please . . ."

"There are worse things than being alone
Just to name two . . . there is being with you,
There are worse things than breakfast for one,
Or days without sun, you'll agree
So though scared as I am
At having no plan
But dinner in bed with T.V.,
There are much worse things
Than phones that don't ring
Than being alone with me . . ."

People were looking back at her, and she put on her own mask, a slight, tight little smile, unreadable and pleasant she hoped, though it might really look like a grimace.

No place to hide now. She had been forced from her hideout like a master criminal cornered by a SWAT team, her own little SWAT team. *Don't think, just listen. The song, listen to the song.* She tried to focus, sip her wine, let the wine do what wine was invented to do, but her mind had a mind of its very own—impossible to control despite all the meditation and Yoga and chanting and the other bullshit she had tried: her brain still tripped along from image to image and if she was strong enough it eventually led her right to the truth.

The room had shifted, like a virtual reality cap had been shoved onto her head. Everything was moving slower. *Flora was On, Flora was super On, she had that look, that "Look of Love Is in Your Eyes" look; would I know this if she hadn't told me? Probably not. Could he be here? Unlikely.*

Keep your eyes off them. Don't do it, Rory. Of course I'm going to do it, how can I not do it. Oh, shit, there he is! Walter Worth. Jesus Herbie. He's still gorgeous. Better. All that silver wavy hair. Kept the hair. Kept the tan. Kept the waistline. Look at them. Darby and Joan, Jack and Jill, what did Leah say? Swans. Fucking swans, together forever. Regal and perfect, smiling side by side since twelfth grade.

He never even told her, never called her and said, "It's over. I'm in love with Leah Frankel." He just stopped waiting for her in his Buick convertible in front of her house after school. Fools Rush In, Where Irish Idiots Fear to Tread; it had never occurred to her that he waited in front of her house so no one he knew ever saw him drive away from school with her!

His dirty little secret. The little Catholic Albino orphan. Oh God, who's that next to Leah? Got to be her daughter. What was the name? Clara? Clar something. Talk about déjà vu! Leah and Walter, the super gene combo. More character than either of them! Not so pretty—pretty, but not so China Doll pretty. More hearty. More approachable. She looks like a good kid.

"They wait at the bus stops,
Batting at the haze
And stare out their windows
In the earthquake of their days. . . ."

That's what she did. Stood at the bus stop, earthquakes every-where. Walter's car never pulled up in front of the Four-Plex, ever again. Graduation Day, the prom . . . didn't go near the prom, drank too much beer with other Sore Thumbs, parked somewhere in Linda Levinsky's mother's station wagon . . . free, she was free . . . heartbroken, deflowered but free to go . . . working to save up, to go to New York, just dying to go to New York and write musicals. Why was that? How did she even dream such a thing?

Bussing at Cantor's for the summer. Double shifts and so tired every night, eating deli and passing out, listening to Auntie Dearest, moaning and groaning, "Do it to me. . . . give it to me," knowing what that meant. Got to get out of there or I'll end up like her.

Fourth of July, so hot, no fan in her room, going down the hall in the dark, going for water . . . a shape in the dark, huddled on the floor, crying: old man's crying, a sound she'd never heard; Grandpa was crying, "No, no, God, don't take her first, take me first, don't leave me here alone!"

What about her? Was she nothing? Not even a reason to stick around? "Grandpa? Grandpa, please, let me help!"

"Too late, too late, go away girl, go away."

Running upstairs, banging on the stupid slut's door, banging forever, "Maddie, call an ambulance, Grandma's sick! We need help. Help!"

Slow, so slow, seemed like forever, like slow motion, everything suspended. Waiting for her to finish, sexed out, left me waiting while she came or whatever she did. Drunken swaying, smelling vile, smelling a smell she knew now.

"You call. I'm not feeling well."

Down, down, hands shaking, so hot and sweaty, fingers sticking on the phone. Everything taking forever. The old man screaming at God, "Take me, first!"

Men in uniforms, lights flashing, neighbors peering out. "Let me go, too, Grandpa! Please, let me go, too!"

He didn't hear her, didn't see her, the ambulance doors closed in her face. Where were they going? Racing behind. Terror chasing her. "Please, someone, take me, too!" Into the police car. No shoes, no money, no one to turn to.

"Sit down, young lady, and have some water. The doctor wants to speak with you. Come this way." Kind, they were being kind. Having pity on what she must have looked liked. A ghost, a ravaged ghost, pale and white from head to toe.

Shaking in terror, first time in a hospital, all alone, even for a Sore Thumb. Someone standing over her, bringing the news, terrible news, no way to prepare for it, no way to absorb it. Her grandparents were both dead. "He stroked in the ambulance miss."

God heard him. God kept his promise. Was that the way death worked, always in twos? Pairs of loss. Starting to slip off the bench, everything going black . . . my own grandpa would rather be dead than left with just me.

Who could she be? All alone, but free. "Freedom is another word for nothing left to lose . . ." She had that, nothing left to lose. Everyone was gone. No one cared about her, so she could go. Lucky, she was lucky. If someone would be there to feel bad, to miss her, maybe it would be too hard. She left Walter and Leah to one another (who would have believed it was forever!) and she left Curson St. behind.

"And watch out their windows
In the earthquake of their days. . . ."

Walter fucking Worth, Leah fucking Frankel and Clar- fucking something, NOW! What was this about? The New Agers would say this was in her Karmic destiny, that they appeared now because she had unfinished work to do. No shit! Maybe this was what they meant by her Third Eye opening? Well, as long as she didn't have to put mascara on it, let it open the fuck up.

Can't run forever; even The Fugitive got tired. Take a long look, but don't be obvious. You can't be obvious, their backs are to you! Well, their sides. Oh, God, she's whispering into his ear. Maybe she hates the songs. No Leah never hated anything, never had a nega-tive, impolite word or probably even a thought. What was inside Leah's head? Were other people's heads all revved up and full of the same junk hers was? Not junk, don't call it junk. If only she could eavesdrop inside other people's heads, how completely great that would be!

Oh, God, he's turning around, get that smile back on, he's turn-ing around to look at her! Of all nights! Her face looked like she'd walked into a water balloon. Splayed with sadness. Smeared. She was probably all smeared. Elonzito was just trying to make her feel better. At least she was right by the door. People were clapping and looking back at her. The criminal after the teargas attack, waiting for the police backup, handcuffed to a fence, no escape possible. Two songs down, two to go and then she could just shimmy along the wall and out the door.

"It was Marilyn Monroe
A long time ago who said,
"Diamonds are a girl's best friend."
But now that I've had
A canine or two
I've developed a
Different point of view . . .

A Dog is a girl's
Best friend
Loyal and loving and
Committed end to end.
A dog is a great amigo
Protective, accepting and
Perfect for her ego . . ."

Who are these people? How did Derrick round up this group? Think about that, look around, keep your mind off the Worths for a while, save it for a sleepless night of humming along to No-Thanks-for-the-Memories. There's that bizarre woman with the emeralds and that Thing hanging off her. She's next to Leah. What is she wearing? A sari and a turban? What is that thing? Must be a dog. Harvey could swallow it in one bite. God, I miss Harvey. Maybe next time they'll let me bring my dog. Probably not. You probably need to be a guest of "THE TALBOTTS" for that.

There they are in the flesh. They look like an ad from one of those magazines selling condos on golf courses to rich retirees. Who's that flippy girl, their daughter? Could be their granddaughter. They're not smiling. Shit, they'll hate this song. Why did Flora do this one? Maybe she knows better. Put in a little risqué number to liven things up.

"Diamonds are expensive but hard
They won't scamper around you in the yard
You can't walk them in the park on a leash
You can't run happily beside them down the beach . . ."

Who's that with Derrick? Is that Collie from the spa? How does she qualify for this gig? The guy next to her looks like a recruiting poster for the Third Reich. That must be the one Flora told me about, Herr somebody—don't call him that; that was Flora-speak. Boy, he really does look cold and steely and pointy. She's so round and warm and cuddly. That must be the draw. It would be like sleeping with an ice pick. They're not smiling either. Well she is, but that may just be because she's on the guest list.

Must be a lot of lust floating around this ship. Remember lust, Ror? Not really. How long has it been since I wanted anyone? How long has it been since I slept with anyone, whether or not I wanted them? Oh God, Billy my. . . . Stop it. Shift that thought right now; no more public displays, not now, now they're on to you, looking at you.

> "So roll over Rover and give me a hug
> Scratch me and sniff me
> All over the rug. . . ."

Oh shit, I hope she knows what she's doing. If Mrs. Talbott's lips get any tighter, her chin's going to fall off. How old is she? She could be forty or she could be sixty. Talk about buttoned down; talk about stiff. Embalmed. She looks like a taxidermist has had a go. What could Leah and Walter possibly see in those people?

What's Mr.'s deal? Oh, he's easy, he's one of those carrot dudes, just scrape a little off the top and he's all set. As deep as an omelet pan, not even a wok. Where did that come from? Imagine sleeping with him? Like being mounted by an egret. Rory, you are bad, okay, stay with this, this is good, think about sleeping with the people in this room; that'll keep you occupied for one more song.

Derrick. Is he or isn't he? He's a self-abuser, for sure. Probably whacks off looking in the mirror. I want you, Derrick, Oh, Yes! Bet he doesn't like to be touched. Virtual sex for him. Internet, porno or fantasy. The way he looks at Flora, though, there's some juice there, maybe he's not really gay and repressed, maybe he's just, REALLY FUCKED UP. Never talks about his background, tries to convey something hoity toity, but what did Flora say? He grew up in the Bible Belt; that would do it. Is there anyone hoity toity that ever grew up in the Bible Belt?

Oh, hmmmm, there's a hunk Young enough to be your, NO, Rory. Who is that? Gorgeous but he really looks snooty. Oh, he's with the Sari-Swami Hat dame. Boy toy? Yuck. Maybe she's his mother or grandmother; no, you are not going to think about them having sex, move on.

Hmmm, oh, too hilarious, a matching set of plastic surgery couples. His and hers facelifts and eyelifts and everything. Matching outfits? A small break here! They are wearing matching outfits, only hers has a skirt—or maybe it's his; he looks more feminine than she does.

Uh oh, Walter's back in view, smiling at someone in the corner. Who is that? He's laughing at the song! What a great face he has, horn rims and everything. What a nice smile. He looks so, real. Wonder who he is. Rory, stop it. Hmmm. Walter's motioning him over. He probably has a wife with him. He really has a very unusually nice look to him. Big shiny bald head. Smart. He looks smart, like he has a lot of big thoughts whizzing around up there. Big talk as opposed to small talk. Who does he remind me of? An actor? Hmm. See, you're doing it, keeping your mind busy. Almost home. One more song.

"I was a Roadie at the end of the road
I was a groupie at the back of the pack
A trendie at the end of the trend
I wasn't moving forward
And I wasn't looking back . . ."

Okay, keep tripping around the room. Hmm, the egret is looking at Flora like she was a delicious little minnow. Could it be him? No way, not enough money in the world. Flora isn't a Big Ticket Type anyway, she's more Blanche-ish, the kindness of studly losers, more Billy Holiday ("I'd rather my man just hit me—than for him to up and quit me"). Virginia just rolled over in her little Sussex grave.

Wonder how Walter knows the guy with the bald head. . . . "Your Majesty, shall I tell you what I think of you? You're spoiled!" —Yul Brynner, that's who he looks like! King and I. . . . Wonder how I'd look in a hoop skirt. Rory, stop it. Move it along. Maybe he's a doctor, too. . . . maybe they treaded on the mill in the fitness club: that carrot thing, that Male Pattern Bonding—didn't take much for men to buddy up. Not like women. If men were carrots, what were women?

Onions. Layers upon layers. Deceptive, lots of tight, bright, succulent layers, taking all that peeling time, and burning, teary eyes and so often the cores were rotten and shriveled. What you see is usually not what you get—so much harder to tell with women. A carrot, scrape a little, you know. A man "Up and Hits me" YOU KNOW, maybe you stay, maybe you bullshit yourself for awhile but you—know.

Onions take forever. Female friendship. Leah. What was her core like? The layers were so luscious, never got that far down. Maybe there was no core, rotten or otherwise, just endless layers and then, nothing.

Where did her daughter go? Oy, she's with the Hair Flipper and the snooty male model type by the Talbotts. Now, Leah's kid has a delicious core. How can I know that? How rare to say that right off about someone you haven't even spoken to? Now that's good, Ror. That's trusting yourself. I just know. What about Yul? No, Rory. Carrots don't have cores, do they? No. They need onions, thrust that long stalk into that bulb (it even has hair-like stuff at the end you're supposed to cut first—how metaphorically perfect!)

Gotta write this down, maybe there's a song in here somewhere. Okay, now what? The icy guy has a wandering eye, got his hand practically on Collie's ass and his beady blues are scanning, ogle eyes. Men are Pigs, who said that? Who didn't! Listen to the song. You're hardly listening to your own stuff. Stop thinking and listen. . . .

How do I stop thinking? "Women over think and that's why we have more depression." Where did that come from? Oh, of course, the New York Times. *How can you "Over think"? Do men then "Under think"? Maybe we over because they under. Why would we have all that thinking apparatus up there if we weren't supposed to use it? It would have been Darwined out of us by now, replaced by—Oh, maybe an always-open Third Eye or a nice little shelf to keep things on.*

Maybe it's more what women think about, what I think about that gets us down. Maybe if I thought about bigger, more important things like, hmmmm . . . like that new planet they've found beyond Pluto, or about the meteor that smashed into earth hundreds of millions of years ago and killed 90% of everything alive.

Big thoughts, manly thoughts. New York Times *thoughts. Gotta stop reading the* New York Times, *too schizoid and pompous and phony. All those ads for Bulgari watches and Cartier diamonds right next to stories about massacres in Darfur villages and bombings by Rawandan rebels and starving children in Haiti. At least the* Post *isn't so hypocritical; at least their horrible stories, babies thrown out of tenement windows and crack head moms being stabbed to death by ex-con, drug-dealer boyfriends are next to ads for liposuction clinics and patio furniture. Real cut-to-the-chase ads.*

All that over thinking is just part of the female deal. We figured something out, going all the way back to Paleolithic life. Who decided that the ladies would stay in the nice warm cave by the food and the fire, with the cooing little babies and the cute little pet wolves

*and the comfy fur throws for winter nap times while the assholes
with the spears went on out there to beat the shit out of each other
trying to get first crack at some horrifying wild animal? Not a carrot
sort of choice. An onion was behind that decision for sure. Probably
one with a stinky black core. "Oh, Grunt, you big, strong lug, you!
What would we do without you? We'd never survive the winter. Look
at those muscles! You were born to thrust a spear. . . ." Okay she's
almost done. . . .*

> "The Millennium was a pendulum
> Moving quick, moving slow
> Ticking off the past
> Ticking off the present
> Never telling me
> What I really need to know . . ."

*Over. It was over. People were clapping, real clapping, not polite
clapping. Good, that was good. Okay, keep the smile on and move out
now, don't make eye contact, just keep moving toward the door.*

*"Mrs. Saltz?" A hand on her back, no way out without a shredding
of the norm—what would happen if she just kept moving or shrugged
the hand off or whirled around and shoved the person attached to
the hand backward and ran, Or . . .*

She turned around, already knowing who it was, anyway. "You
must be Leah's daughter."

"Clarissa. How did you know?"

"My Third Eye just opened up."

"Sorry?"

"Just a little New Age humor. But better than 'A little bird told
me.' I saw you talking to your parents, and since you look a lot like
them, it did lower the odds."

"Of course. That was lame of me. Everyone always thinks I look
like my mom anyway, even if they see us separately."

"Well you do, but you also look like your dad, and then there's
that little thing called yourself, which you also look a lot like."

"You think? That's such a nice thing to say! No one's ever said
anything like that to me before. Thank you."

"You're very welcome. I was watching you during the performance and I decided that you were a great kid."

"Really? How could you know that just by looking at me?

"I'm not sure. I just did. Now don't prove me wrong by making me schlep back into the party and do old acquaintances with your parents because I'm really not in the mood. Tell your mom, she'll understand and I hope we'll have some time to talk later, okay?"

"Absolutely. I hate these things, too, but I have to be here because we're sort of like houseguests of the hosts. I'll tell Mom, but—can I just walk out with you—I just wanted you to know that I've heard about you all my life and I've seen pictures and I've read stuff you wrote and everything and I loved your songs. It's really great to actually meet you in person, and I'd really love to talk to you sometimes, maybe even back in the City. You just seem to know so much about life and all. Anyway, I just wanted to say hello."

They were at the door. Could she leave without thanking the hosts? Was that really rude? *I don't think I can do it.*

"Clarissa, meeting you was the highlight of this evening and I'd be honored to talk more with you, but I've gotta get out of here now. I'm in the middle of some sort of hormone hell or something and I'm trying to behave myself and not embarrass Flora or get fired or anything. Let me ask you something. If I don't go back in and thank the Talbotts, will they be offended? Could I just send up a note tomorrow? Please say yes."

"No problem, Mrs. Saltz."

"Rory. Mrs. Saltz sounds like someone on a baking soda tin."

"*Rory*, you are too much. I'll take care of it. I'll tell them you weren't feeling well and you told me to thank them, but a note would be good. They're very big on thank you notes and stuff, and I'll tell my mom, but you haven't seen the last of us. I can promise you that."

"I know. I just need a little time out right now. But before I go, I want to give you a hug because I think you're swell."

"Swell! You've made my night. Thanks, Rory."

Rory held her, smelling cherry blossoms and youth, Leah's child's silky red hair tickling her nose. She had to force herself to let her go and keep the tears up inside her eyes. *Jesus Hymie . . . go, Rory.*

She was out the door, moving down the hall to where? Where was she? Where was the elevator? No one else had left, so there was no one to follow. There had to be a stairway somewhere, all those emergency exits from the Muster Station drills, all those 'in case of a fire, do not use the elevators' escape routes. She felt dizzy with sadness.

"If you're looking for a way out, follow me." A soothing, slightly

British voice, commanding obedience. A deck officer, waiting calmly to lead her to safety. She turned around.

Yul! It was the bald guy with the horn rims. "No fucking way!"

Oh God, she was losing it. She'd said it out loud! This did not happen in real life. This was some Hollywood meet cute set-up deal. This was a joke. This was really funny. Why was it so funny? She was laughing in his face, doubling over in hysterics. Out of control once again tonight. Maybe someone had slipped something into her chardonnay.

"I'm sorry, I know, ha, ha, ha, I know, you must think I'm insane, ha ha ha ha, I can't tell, I, you, oh please, forgive me. . . . I just can't stop. . . ."

"Well, don't apologize. Having any effect at all is always a plus, so unless something's caught in my fly, I'll consider it a huge compliment."

"No, oh, nothing like that . . . It's just . . . hilarious . . . for you . . . to be . . . out here . . . and there I was . . . scoping you out in there . . . and I never . . . do that . . . and I thought you had such a. . . . Great face . . . you looked so. . . . Ha . . . ha, so SMART, I thought and . . . what are you doing here?"

"Well, my oh my. Now I know what I'm doing here. I followed you because I wanted to tell you how much I liked your work and because I saw you in the back corner in there jerking up and down and laughing to yourself or whatever you were doing and you looked so smart, yourself — different, you see, not usual, which you certainly are not, at least so far, and I thought I'd ask if you wanted to have a drink or something and . . ."

"Oh, Shit. Yes! Ha, ha, ha. Yes! I'm fucking falling completely apart right before your eyes, I don't even know your name, and YES I would. Even though you probably noticed me because of my hair and the only men who are attracted to me because of my hair are men who wear white patent leather loafers all year round and you don't, do you? And you certainly don't wear a toupee — ha . . . usually goes with the white loafer types . . . no you certainly don't, unless you have one helluva funny toupee adviser. . . . Ha, ha. . . . Oh shit. I'm going to pull it together now. I'm going to take a deep breath. So, okay I'm calming down. Who are you, anyway?"

"I'm Poe Evanoff and I already know who you are."

"Yes, I'm the albino nut bag, with really bad social skills."

"Well, then, follow me."

⌁

"Good Evening."

"Good Evening. Is this the Fountainsblow Dining Room?"

"Fontainebleau, yes, sir, it is. Your name and cabin number please."

"Russolini, like Musso only with a Russo. G-6302."

"Oh, yes, right this way, please."

"Ohmigawd, Solly, look at this! Wait a minute, I wanna take a picture. It looks like something from a museum in France. Gold and blue velvet, just like Donald Trump's penthouse, only huge. Gorgeous! It's like a movie set!"

"Vera, not now with the pictures. It took us forty minutes to find the friggin' place. First we eat, then we'll photograph."

"Okay, party pooper, but watch your tone; there's that edge in your voice. Remember what the counselor said? Oh, god, Solly, look over there! Is that ice? And what is that? A porpoise made out of ice? Look at the shrimp! To die! Enough shrimp for an army."

"Well, eat up, 'cause all the chow's included and I want my money's worth. We're gonna gorge, even if we gain, even if we spend every a.m. in the fitness center. We're eating up!"

"I hope we like our tablemates. My cousin said if you don't like your tablemates, it's hell. How do I look? Do I look okay? Everyone's so fancy. Maybe I should of worn the gold lamé pant suit."

"You look beautiful. No one here can hold a candle to you. Still have the best boobies in the world. Where the hell is he going—we've been walking for ten minutes? There must be 2,000 people in here. We're almost at the kitchen."

"He's turning off to the side. Behind those columns. Are those real marble?"

"Here we are. Enjoy your meal."

"Solly, Solly, Ohmigawd. What is this? What's wrong, something's weird about these people?"

"Hello, we're the Russolinis. Solly and Vera from the *great* Great Neck, Long Island, New York."

"Solly, wait, I need to whisper something."

"Not now, Vera, sit."

"Hello, nice to meet you, I'm Vera."

"Hi. Hi. Vera. Hi, Hi, Great Neck. Vera of Great Neck. Nice to meetcha. Nice. Very nice. Nice. Nice of you to join us. Very good food. Very good. You're pretty. You smell very good."

"Why, thank you. So . . . (Solly, I need a word. Solly, I'm whispering, put your ear right here. Something is wrong with these people. Are they drunk?)"

"Shhh. Vera, they're like Aunt Florencia's niece. You know. Birth defects. Downs Syndrome."

"Ohmigawd, Solly, I am not doing this. I am not a bad person. I feel terrible, but I didn't spend all this money and wait on line at all those sales to sit at a table with people who I have nothing in common with! We are outsiders here, and we're talking about seven days! This is not romantic, Solly. I want to move."

"Vera! We can't. How will that look? We'll hurt their feelings. We have to make the best of it. Just talk to me. Just look at me. One dinner and then I'll slip that Maitre'D a few bucks and we'll have a better table tomorrow, doll. Be my girl, now. Look at the menu. They have oysters Rockefeller, your favorite."

"Okay. Okay, Solly. I'm just disappointed. I'm not unfeeling. How many Saturdays did I spend with Florencia's niece at the park? I took her to the mall. I was very fond of her niece. I'll think of something to say."

"Is this your first cruise? This is our first cruise."

"My, too. First cruise."

"Are these all your friends?"

"Yes, all my friends. And our teachers. We go together."

"How nice. What do you enjoy doing?"

"We enjoy doing dancing in the disco. Drinking and dancing. Beer. We like to dance and drink beer."

"Oh, I hear they have a very good band there."

"Very loud. We can kiss and rub, rub, rub. We like that. Very nice. Kiss. Kiss. Kiss. Aaaaachooo. Aaaaachooo. Have a cold. Sorry."

"Oh, I have a tissue, somewhere, oh. (Ohmigawd, Solly, a word—Solly, he just blew his nose with my lace sleeve. My sale Escada sleeve! I can't do this. I'm getting a migraine. Solly, we're going now.)"

"Excuse us, please. My wife is feeling a little seasick. So nice to meet you all."

"Nice to meet you all, too. Vera from Great Neck. Bye bye."

"I need water. Solly, I have to wipe my sleeve. He's sick and his snot is all over my Escada."

"Okay. You find the bathroom. I'll find the bastard who put us at that table. He must think we're a couple of gumbas."

"No, Solly, I can't go alone! I'll get lost forever! I'll wait until after. I'll just keep my arm loose."

"Okay, there he is, bringing some other poor schmuckolas in. 'Excuse me, sir. We would like another table please.' (I'll slip him something. It's gonna be okay.)"

"I'm sorry, is there a problem?"

"Yeah, and I think you know what it is. Look, we don't want to be difficult, but we were looking forward to a nice romantic dinner; we don't mind meeting new people, but we would like a table where we can have some conversation with peers. Here's a little something for your trouble."

"Well, we're totally full. Let me see what I can do. I'll be right back."

"Everyone's staring at us, Solly. Are we making a scene? Oh good, he's motioning for us to follow him. Let's go, act casual."

"I have room at this table or the one over in the corner."

"Ohmigawd, Solly! Everyone's a hundred years old! Look, they all have walkers or wheelchairs! Look at that man in the middle! I swear he's dead. His mouth is wide open and his eyes are closed. There's a nurse at the table! Do we look like that! We're not even over fifty! I am not sitting there for a week. Tell him."

"Now, I'm getting hot. He thinks we're a couple of fools or he wants more money."

"Give him more. Give him anything! I won't have a massage tomorrow. See if there's a table for two. Give him fifty dollars. Give him my wedding ring; I am not sitting with dead people!"

"Hey, what is going on here? We filled out our questionnaire. You people are supposed to match people up with like-minded guests. Why ask us all of those questions about interests and hobbies and then pull a number like this? Do we look stupid to you? We are not sitting here. Try again and I'll make it worth your while."

"Good, Solly, that was perfect."

"People have to be flexible, sir. We have thousands of people to tend to."

"How about a little table for two, anywhere?"

"Not a chance. All of those went early. If you want one you have to make a special request."

"Well, we want one for tomorrow. For now, do what you can."

"I only have two tables left with any room at them, and we stop serving in thirty minutes."

"Let's see what you've got."

"Right this way."

"Ohmigawd, Solly. They're all Black women and they're reading the Bible. Look at them! They're praying at the table and some of them are humming! Humming Baptists! I am not sitting there. What could we possibly talk about? We're Italian lapsed Catholics for Christ's sake! No."

"Show us the other table, okay pal?"

"Very well. It's way over to the side, so the air conditioning can blast, but it's your choice."

"Solly, I think we're okay. They look normal. They're laughing. They're drinking wine and talking normal. You did good, honey."

"Okay. We'll sit here. Here's a little something for that table for two tomorrow. Remember, Russolini, like Musso with . . ."

"An R. Yes, I'll remember. Thank you, sir."

"Hello. Hello, we're the Russolinis from Great Neck, Long Island, New York."

"Cool! We're Sunshine and Starlight and Dragonfly and Ray Beam, and over on the other side of the table is Amber, Cicada, Meadowlark, Sage, Clover and Larkspur. Welcome!"

"Are those your names? How unique! What original mothers you all must have had. What a coincidence to put you all together! Solly, isn't that something!"

"We're a group. We came together from Sedona. These are our chosen names. We discarded our birth names and picked the names that our spirit guides wanted us to have."

"Well, our kids are gonna be stuck with the names *we* wanted them to have or the car keys go back in the drawer, right Vera? Ha. Imagine trying to pass something like this off. "Hi, Dad, I'm not going by Solly, Jr. no more. Now I'm what was that? Ray Ban? Ha, ha. Hilarious."

"Ray *Beam*. And you think like that, the way our families did, because you haven't gone far enough on your path to enlightenment. Come to our seminar tomorrow. You might change your mind."

"Right now, I'm too hungry to change anything. What's good? I saw Oysters Rockefeller and a piece of Prime Rib go by that looked pretty nice. What's that you have there, Daffodil?"

"Dragonfly. We're vegans. This is tempeh and tofu."

"What? Temple? Is that kosher food?"

"No, macrobiotics."

"Oh, Solly, I read about this. Like putting antibiotics in chicken feed? This is like the opposite of that. Very healthy."

"We eat no living creature."

"Oh, I see." (Solly, a word. Solly, how can we eat shrimp and meat and oysters here? They'll get upset. They looked normal. They are not normal.)"

"Your order, please, Sir."

"Uh, yes, well, we'll uh, have whatever our tablemates are having, the Tempy and stuff and two very dry Beefeater Martinis—don't panic, it's not really made with beef, ha, ha, straight up. Make those doubles, pal."

"Brr, it's freezing back here. The air conditioning is terribly cold. Look at you girls, little skinny straps. Aren't you freezing?"

"No, we mediate and our body temperature stays constant. We control our bodies with our minds. We chose this table because the biorhythms over the ship are better on this side. If you close your eyes, you'll feel the power of the positive energy. It's very strong, here."

"No kidding? You're gonna be great at menopause, hear that Solly? Controls her temperature with her mind, no less. Solly, a word. (Solly, I've got to get the snot off my sleeve. I can't eat with this on there. It's giving me the creeps. You stay. I'm going to try to find the ladies'.)"

"I'm gonna get our drinks and I'm going to find you and we're going to get drunk and go down to that little pizza place in the arcade. Enough of this shit, Vera. I'm not going to sit here with these fruitcakes and eat that crap just to be polite."

"Oh, Solly, I love you. Edge or no edge. I'm going to cry. Thank you. I'm not a bad person, Solly. I'm not."

"Vera, you're a saint. A friggin' saint. With the best tits in the place. You go. I'll cross fire to find you."

↬

THE SHIP MOVED steadily south, heading deeper into the open sea, toward the Virgin Islands. It was only one of many such ships—larger and grander—but one of a fleet. A freighter, really, under all the trimmings: a freighter of humans on one of the endless Caribbean milk runs, re-tracing with invisible ink the route of pirates and explorers who would no doubt have looked through their spyglasses in horrified amazement at this use of their treacherous, unconquerable ocean.

Cruise ships, glittering in the darkness like enormous fireflies, carrying their cargo. And who were these people who used the sea for amusement? The same sea that their forbearers fought and died on, where they battled through storms and battled one another: the sea they used to survive, to conquer, to claim.

Land was their goal. Land was safety and freedom. How odd this would be for the spectres of those earlier voyagers to watch: human cargo, traveling of their own free will, using the sea for pleasure, for release from their land lives and from themselves.

Travelers are questers whether they know it or not, and no matter how tame the journey, it still involves an alteration, an opening of a porthole into themselves. The person who leaves is not quite the same person who returns.

Chapter Two: Day Two

LATITUDE

Your Daily At Sea Newspaper

Good Morning, Cruisers! Welcome to the historic island of St. Thomas, formerly the bustling Eighteenth Century center of the pirate trade and now the equally bustling center of shopping and sightseeing bounty! We will be at anchor in the charming, bargain-lovers paradise of Charlotte Amalie from 8 a.m. until 6 p.m. sharp.

Please take one of our fabulous shore excursions, or simply wander the quaint streets of town. But do remember that "all aboard" means just that! The ship departs on time, without exception.

For those of you who prefer to stay onboard or return early, we will keep you as busy as you desire. Check out our Better Bodies classes on the Sports Deck: Work off that midnight buffet with our Eat More, Weigh Less clinic or practice your golf swing with our simulator. Whoops! In case anyone forgot their tux—tonight is formal and tuxedo rentals are available on the Promenade Deck. And remember to check out your welcome aboard photos in the Portrait Gallery! For you singles, don't miss our Singles Mingle midnight tonight in the Dolphin Disco!

All today's events and lectures are listed in the *Latitudes at Leisure Guide*. Tonight's enticements will begin with a chance to have your photo taken with our Captain, Guido Salmetti, after his Welcome to the Palace speech on the Piazza of the Porpoises sky bridge, followed by the spectacular Captain's Gala Dinner, and then at our acclaimed "Broadway Babies" revue staring the one and only Flora Frampton and the Dolphin singers and dancers!

Have a great day in port! See you tonight in your glitter and glam!

"THE WAY I see it, Walter, the Republicans are in the pack of wolves and the Democrats are in the flock of sheep, but if we're going to live in a war zone, we're better off with a wolf than a sheep."

"Well, I see it a bit differently, Teddy. I think the Democrats want to make an omelette without breaking any eggs and the Republicans just like breaking eggs and don't really give a damn what happens to the mess they make."

Sissy Talbott lowered her lounge chair a notch, as if leaning further back would help her concentrate better. Teddy was getting ready for his civics lesson; George Washington would appear any moment. She should have gone up to the spa pool VIP section instead of staying on their terrace, but she was still waiting for that damn Dr. Padma.

And the CD player was too loud for her to read her magazine. "Walking around, some kind of lonely clown, rainy days and Mondays always get me down." *Oh my, the Carpenters. What was her name? Karen. She died of something awful. Self-destructive. Always loved that music. Now it just makes me sad. Lost love always makes me sad. Try to concentrate, Sissy. Where was I? Oh yes, a new trend in design.*

"More and more of our clients are asking us to copy the look of hotel rooms they've stayed in. They're looking for a place that doesn't make them feel at home."

Unbelievable! Beyond nouveau. What a shocking idea. A home that feels like a hotel room? Ye gads.

"One client I had brought in dozens of photos and said, 'Make the house look just like the Delano Hotel lobby in Miami.'"

I bet they're on this cruise. I don't think I've ever seen so many tacky overdone people in one place in my life. Teddy has got to come to his senses and sell off this business. How did he ever move from sailing yachts to this nonsense?

That awful woman in the gym this morning who talked my ear off. She'd do something like that. One of those Phoenix transplants, so proud of "Moving West." So loathsome, all of those created places, without any history or traditions or water! They destroyed a living desert to put up a bunch of Home Depots and fancy car dealerships. Phoenix made me so twitchy. All the overdone houses and overdone hostesses competing with bad jewelry and bad Chanel wardrobes. Well, most of them are probably broke by now.

And Twinkle hated it, too. One of our rare moments of agreement. "Mom, I'm like totally dehydrated. I mean it, Mom, I'm like Lizard *Girl. The insides of my eyes and nose are like scabby. I can barely swallow and my vagina, Mom, is like totally shriveled up! I'm like an old granny. I have got to get out of here!"*

Sissy smiled. Crude and certainly slovenly grammar-wise, but she had laughed. They had laughed together and gone directly to the Spa for hydrating treatments. So few moments now to connect at all. Of course, what could she expect? After all those years of barely phoning in motherhood. Not that she'd known better. She had no basis of comparison. It was how she'd been raised and Twinkle had come so late it was such a huge adjustment. By the time she'd even begun to sort it all out, it was too late.

Oh, this is rich. "VIP isn't what it used to be." *No surprise there.* Anyone with an extra fifty bucks could push their way in just about anywhere now. First class on a commercial flight, a joke! Well at least that wasn't anything she had to worry about, yet. One reason to stay in the shipping industry: they did still have use of the plane whenever they wanted, even with all the cutbacks.

She looked inside at her daughter and Clarissa and Ian playing Scrabble with the Countess. Smoking away and drinking champagne, and it wasn't even noon. Oh well, they were young. She'd done the same, though it wasn't enough anymore. God, she was feeling so itchy. Too restless. Too down. Where the hell was the damn doctor?

" 'Charybdis,' oh Ian, just did it! What a word! Damned if you aren't my grandson! Such a brilliant boy!"

"Like, hello? What does it mean? You can't just pass that off. It doesn't even look like a real word in English. 'bdis.' I don't think so, Ian."

"My dear little tadpole. Would I cheat at Scrabble in front of my beloved Grams? I can fetch the dictionary, but it means, 'caught between two perils or evils, neither of which can be avoided without risking the other.' It's an ocean metaphor, so apt, don't you think? The Greeks again, dear. 'Between Scylla and Charybdis.' Charybdis is actually in the straits of Messina. Female monsters, forming a whirlpool effect, I believe."

"How do you like, know that?"

"He reads the Greeks all the time, Twink. It is a word. I remember it from one of my mythology classes."

"Bummer. But if Clarissa backs you up, I concede. Way too complex for a sunny day. Let's go swimming. We missed the morning tour. Want to go ashore?"

"I was going to take a yoga class with my mom at eleven, but she's been having an allergy attack so I guess it's okay."

"Ian? Want to wade in?"

"By all means. Let's buy some cheap emeralds and have one of those insulin-resistive rum drinks the brochures keep pushing. Want to come with us, Grams?"

"I'll do the emerald part. Never met any kind of emerald I didn't like. Sissy, want to come?"

"No thanks. My back's in spasm. I'm waiting for the doctor to give me something."

"Later then, Momsey."

Sissy watched them go. What was the Countess's secret? Must be all that Texas grit, the woman never slowed down and genuinely enjoyed being with them.

She had never found young people interesting, not even now, let alone when Twinkle was a child. And Teddy—he was absolutely hopeless! If it wasn't polo or tennis or one of his clubs or causes, he couldn't be bothered. Well, why should he be any different with his daughter than he was with his wife?

Now Walter Worth—there was a man who treated his family with consideration. But she'd always heard that Jewish men were like that. Her own mother had even once told her, "Sissy, I never said this, but if you found some spectacular Jewish man, even if everyone is horrified, you'll have a better life."

Well, God knows I certainly missed the boat on that possibility. The very idea of my mother suggesting such a thing was shocking enough. Imagine trotting Walter Worth into the Maidstone in the Seventies! Well, he at least would have passed. Certainly doesn't look Jewish, quite handsome really and very refined. Leah, too. Well, feminine beauty is a whole other thing, and she does use it. Can't quite decide about that one.

Oh, God, this is such a bore! Now I have these people in my head! What are we doing with them, anyway! So unlike Teddy, snob that he is. It's almost as if Walter and he had some secret pact or something. Teddy seems like a little boy around him. Wanting to show off for his new friend. They are fun, but fun is so overrated.

Dear me, that's a funny thing to think! I'm just out of sorts because of my damn back. If that doctor would just get here, I'd be fine.

Everything is such a bore lately . . . can't concentrate on anything. People are making me prickly, even the Countess. Now there's a life! Wouldn't give someone like that the time of day if she didn't come with that title. Certainly not because of all that widow's wealth. Can't even remember how many husbands she's had. Five? Good grief. Just imagine that. And a child with each one! Or was it three with one and then one each? Too complicated.

All those houses all over the place and then getting stuck with Ian. Too smart and handsome for his own good . . . perfect for Twinkle, though. Cut from the same cloth . . . or maybe not. Maybe he brings out the worst in her—not that she'd listen.

We've ruined them. Too much too soon. Wasn't that the name of a movie? Susan Hayward. She looked like Leah Worth, except she was rather coarse, had a funny smirky thing she did with her mouth. Leah is nothing if not a lady. Wonder what she really thinks of us. Probably not much, though they both do seem to "aspire." Don't think they have much. Too bad. Some women are meant to be rich, and she's one if I've ever seen one. Men just want to take care of her. Wonder what that's like. God knows, it's not Teddy's style. Never was. The perfect couple. What a laugh! Oh, come on, Sissy, read something. Don't think so much it isn't good for you. Hmmm. Smart Houses. What on earth is that?

Some 7.5 million American homes are currently equipped with a degree of computer networking that automates security, entertainment and lighting, mechanical systems and climate control. The most advanced homes can coordinate heating and air conditioning, security, lighting, home entertainment, Internet and email, even from afar. Appliances like window shades or even vacuum cleaners can be taught to monitor themselves. "Think of them as test labs with décor." An entire industry of experts has been created to help overwhelmed Smart Home owners deal with the complexity of these systems. "Some people haven't even figured out how to control the thermostat. . . . It's scary that people haven't asked themselves why they really need to open the front door for the plumber by remote."

Maybe I'm just tired of being alive. Maybe I do hold too tight to tradition and the past, but if this is the future, 'Stop the World, I want to Get Off.' Good heavens, I'm really on a roll here. Carpenter songs, Susan Hayward, and now old musicals. Who was that actor? Anthony Newly. He was adorable. Very cute. British, but Jewish. Now if I'd met someone like that . . . oh, that's a hoot! Imagine Anthony Newly, the skinny little cockney Hebrew Theater Person at the Knickerbocker Club! My mother would have rued the day she'd made her little off-the-cuff suggestion. A house with controls for shades! Roll me out in my Scalamandre curtains, thank you very much!

I need that doctor, damn it! Think about something else. Where was I? Oh, the Countess. She certainly took a shine to Derrick Doolittle. I'm sure he's light on his feet, but she doesn't seem to care. Maybe that's what she likes about him. God knows she's had enough sex! Not that that's a problem I'd know much about.

Reminds me of that New Yorker *cartoon Muffy Mavins gave me. The man on the couch at his psychiatrist's office. "Well, I've finally gotten in touch with my sexuality—it's disgusting." Oh, that tickled me. Teddy didn't even chuckle. Sore spot, for sure. Probably our attraction to each other besides all the merging of two sets of good human horseflesh. Neither of us could ever really stand being touched. No wonder it took twenty years for Twinkle to pop out.*

Uh oh, he's standing up. That means it's time for his Washington speech. I'm going to call that damn little quack.

"Did you know, Walter, that in one of our current high school textbooks, there are but 33 lines on George Washington and 213 lines on Marilyn Monroe? A disgrace! Now there was a true leader. If your fellow scientists had been able to clone Washington, we wouldn't be in the despicable mess we're in today.

"American college students know nothing of our own history, and that's a big part of the problem—why we're stuck with the liars and fools we've got.

"Did you know that Washington was 6 feet 3 inches tall? Very impressive for the time. He was a superb horseback rider, a wonderful dancer, an intellectual as well as a successful entrepreneur, and perhaps the most inventive farmer in America! No one else could have won the Revolutionary War or held the Constitutional Convention together because he was the only man respected by the North and South, by the farmers and merchants.

"But the most important and unique thing he did, what no other politician has ever willingly done, is to leave office—an office, mind you, created with only one man in mind . . . created for him! At the height of his power, he resigns and steps down. This was astounding in 1783 and it is more astounding now. None of today's power maniacs would make such a choice! That's what we need in government today. We need another George Washington."

"You're right, of course, Teddy, but with all due respect, if we had cloned him and he were to rise up right now and try to be elected, he would fail. Either because, at some point, he'd say, 'forget this insanity—I'm going back to my farm,' or because he'd lack the ruthlessness and egomania, not to mention the ability to lie (remember ye olde cherry tree) that's now required to be elected game warden, let alone President. I'm afraid that time has passed.

"A bit of trivia maybe you haven't heard. When Napoleon was defeated and in exile, he was bemoaning his fate, and he said, 'They expected me to be another Washington.' Fascinating, isn't it? From Napoleon, who certainly didn't go willingly or stay put once he went."

"Walter, my man, you never fail to surprise me. What a delight to converse with someone who knows his history. I'll have to write that down. Good show!"

"Teddy?"

"Yes, my dear? Were we too loud?"

"No, no. Sorry to interrupt such a stirring discussion. I'm going to lie down. I've called for the doctor again. Please listen for the door or have Elonzito come up. I've called the clinic again, and they said Dr. Padma is on his way."

"Sissy, can I bring you something? I'm on nurse duty for Leah. I may have to take her back to the clinic so I'll be here all morning."

"That's very kind of you, Walter. My, we're a sorry lot today. No, I'm fine. I just need something for the pain. If Leah wakes up, give her my sympathy."

"I will, of course."

✒

"MRS. TALBOTT?"

"Dr. Padma?"

"Yes, yes, may I enter?"

"Yes, and close the door behind you, please."

"I am so very sorry. I was on my way right after I saw Mrs. Worth and then Mr. Hensler called and informed me of a terrible situation, of which I can only speak to you and your husband as the owners, but must be kept very quiet, very quiet until we can ascertain the extent of the damage to the victim and find the perpetrator. Very serious situation. I am deeply sorry for the delay. Deeply sorry."

"What on earth are you babbling on about? What happened?"

"I apologize. I am the father of three daughters. This has caused me very deep distress. Very deep."

"What has? Please get to the point. I've waited more than two hours in spasm, and I'm not in the mood for guessing games."

"A young woman on the spa staff was sexually assaulted and very badly beaten about last night. She was quite hysterical. Very distressed and frightened, and I was paged on my way to see you. Terrible thing to happen and, of course, Mr. Hensler is quite agitated, concerned that it be kept a secret, not to alarm the passengers. I have just informed your husband, and he has gone to see Mr. Hensler. Mr. Rogers, the head of Security is with the young lady now. Quite an upsetting event."

"Good grief! What a nightmare! Have they found the man? This is terrible! No one must find out about this. This would be disastrous and extremely embarrassing to us personally!"

"They have not found the fellow. The young woman says she did not see him. It was dark and very late. He came up behind her in the hall and put something over her head and shoved her into her room and knocked her unconscious. She has quite a large hematoma on her forehead. She did not see him. Her roommate has been a patient in the clinic or it could not have happened. Her hands were injured doing too many massage treatments. This man must have known she was alone. A very sweet young woman. Terrible thing. Terrible."

"Well, we will have to warn our daughters. They're all out in the discos till all hours. Was the woman drunk?"

"I do not know. I think not. She seemed to be alert. She said she had had some champagne at your party but was not drunk. She is being a bit mysterious. We are hoping Mr. Rogers can find more facts from her. I think she is very shamed by this."

"Dear God! She was at *our* party! How on earth did that come about?"

"I believe she was the guest of Mr. Hensler. They are friends."

"Outrageous. He has some nerve bringing someone like that uninvited."

"I'm afraid I do not comprehend. Someone like what?"

"A *spa* employee! What could he be thinking? One, he's fraternizing, which I believe is against the rules and two, she was most certainly not on Mr. Doolittle's list."

"I do not know of any of this. Maybe I misunderstood. She was very upset."

"Well, we'll find out soon enough. That's the trouble with this whole cruise business. Thousands of people and God only knows who they are. The crew alone come from 52 different countries, and the passengers – quite a mixed bag. Anyone can book passage. Anyone! It's not like a private yacht where you have control! And even then, the crewmembers do all kinds of disreputable things. Quite a world we're living in, Doctor."

"Oh, yes, ma'am. I am from the part of Pakistan near the Indian border where all the fighting has been going on for decades. So violence and (what was the word) disreputable people are familiar to me. So, now, how may I be of use to you?"

"Yes, well after all that, it seems a bit silly, but I have a very bad back, Doctor. And I have muscle spasms that are extremely painful and for which I have regular injections of pain medication, and I also take pills for it. Needless to say, my regular doctor is not on board and, alas, my back is acting up, so I would like you to give me an injection of Buprenex. I have the exact dosage on this prescription pad given to me by my physician for emergencies like this. And I would like you or your nurse to come twice a day for the duration of the cruise and inject me. It usually takes about a week for any relief, and I have guests and my family to see to. I can't afford to be laid up."

"Yes, yes. I understand, Mrs. Talbott. I do have this medication, but this is a very strong remedy. Very strong. Are you certain that this is what you were given at home?"

"My dear man, do I look like a fool? I see the best doctors in the world. I know what I'm given and what I need to control the pain. Now if you would be so kind, I have been waiting in considerable pain for a long time."

"Yes, yes. I do regret. And I thank you for your patience and for being so thoughtful of the young lady. If this is what you wish,

I will prepare this, and I will arrange for my best nurse to come this evening and give the second injection. But if you feel too, too medicated, we will cut down the dose at once."

"I doubt that will be necessary. But I will certainly let her know."

"Yes, of course. If you would be so kind as to turn over, I will try not to cause you more discomfort."

"Thank you, Doctor. I am very grateful, and I will show my gratitude before we leave the ship."

"No, no. I am doing my profession. No need. This will sting a bit."

⁓

"MIMSIE? What on earth are you doing?" Sissy, eyes glittering and miraculously recovered stood in the Countess's open doorway.

"What the hell does it look like I'm doing? I'm changing Tou Tou's diaper. I can't just leave him running around while I go ashore, and I don't dare ask Elonzito to do this. I thought you were out of commission?"

"Yes, well, I thought so, too, but the doctor gave me something for the pain and I'm feeling so much better, I thought I might just tag along and do some emerald damage with you and Twinkle."

"Wonderful! I'm almost ready, just got to find my sun hat and that damn I.D. thing for getting back on the boat. I'll meet you at the departure door in fifteen minutes."

"Fine. I'll grab my bag and round everyone up. You are not going to believe the dish I've got to share."

"Oh no, Sissy, I don't do dish. I'm from Texas, remember. If I gossiped, I wouldn't have enough time left over to breathe!"

"Oh, this is quick and important. It involves our personal safety. You won't mind a bit."

"As long as it doesn't feature any of my friends or relatives, I'll open an ear."

"Not likely. I'll be waiting."

⁓

BELLS WERE RINGING, ringing, louder and louder, forcing him awake. Derrick thrashed around in the blackness of his cabin searching for the culprit. Opening his eyes was not yet a possibility. He grabbed at the alarm and pushed the button in. Sweet savior, what *had* he been thinking? His head felt like the inside of a cantaloupe, dense and pulpy at the same time.

Drunkenness and gluttony, two deadly sins, to which could be added avarice (how often does a guy like him get to hang out with a Countess until the wee hours, swilling Dom Perignon and ninety-dollars-a-shot French brandy?) . . . must have been at least one other sin in there somewhere? Oh sure, envy, and how about lying? He certainly did not regale her with his life story, skipping right over the Norman, Oklahoma childhood, even though she herself was being so candid—which was probably what shut him up.

Candor from a Countess, even one who had bought her title by marrying it. (How could she have told him something so, personal?) The booze or maybe she was just like that. Texas and all. Not refined, not quite up to the Talbotts' class, but so refreshing. He opened his eyes one at a time. *Gracious sakes, does anyone really open their eyes one at a time except in the movies? If I sit up too quickly, I'm going to either vomit or pass out.*

Now his head had turned from melon into explosive device. Throbbing, squeezing pain shooting from back to front. He risked a look at the clock. 6:30. He had a staff meeting at 7:30 and he was leading the Around the Island tour at 9:00. Well, at least he'd be on a bus with a driver/guide to do the spiel.

This was very bad form. So unprofessional of him! Maybe he needed to accept the fact that 49 was not 30 and no matter how great his capacity or stamina, he could no longer burn the wick this way.

Up, Dwayne, UP. Oh no! What had he said? Even in his sleep, he was Derrick. He never made a slip like that! It was the Countess; all those stories of life in Dallas on the wrong side of town pulled at his roots. Well, actually, his family was far up from her family! Aspirers they were, but his father had been a professor at the University and his mother was a sort of socialite, always striving for inclusion in Norman society, whatever that meant. They had "help" and entertained "nicely," so why was he so mute with Mimsie?

Oh Lord, they had gotten to the "Mimsie" stage! He hadn't wanted that. Calling her "Countess" was far more enticing, but what could he have said? "Sorry, but I'm not really very good at up close and personal, so if we could just keep it at the Countess Von Essen level, I'd be greatly obliged."

The last thing he'd planned on when Teddy Talbott asked him to "escort the Countess" for the evening was having her turn out to be a real person and not some prefab *poseur* who would keep her acquired "airs" on and give him a chance to show off his language skills and knowledge of European watering holes and Impressionist Art.

Did they dance? Oh my, they did. Twirled and dipped. She'd even changed out of that god-awful Arabian Nights outfit into a very chic little Dior dinner dress. Great legs, too, for "an old broad," as she'd said herself.

Take a look, Derrick. Be brave. He switched on the bathroom light. He'd replaced the horrific yellow florescent bulb with a less horrific pink one, but nothing could soften the puffy, blotchy sight before him. His comb-over was lying on his neck, looking like some straggly dying creature. Lord, he had to do something about it. Maybe he'd finally let Buddy from the show buzz cut him.

He splashed his face over and over, clearing his head. *What do I need? Mega aspirin for starters. Wonder if I have time to get to the clinic for a B-12 shot and a huge whiff of oxygen. Quick shower, and I may make it. I can't give up the comb-over. I'm too big for a buzz cut; I'll look like the Jolly Green Giant.*

He turned on the shower and spread paste on his electric toothbrush. His comb-over now looked like the hair on Mimsie's dog. Oh my, he was calling her that in private, like they were friends! Like they knew one another. Well, he knew her or at least a lot about her. It was all starting to slip back into his memory, the entire evening.

So, stimulating! Even Hensler's eyebrows had risen when he saw them together. What an intimidating man he was. Always watching with those X-ray eyes, scorning, judging. If he could see me now!

He's not your mother, Dwayne. Oh God! I did it again! That woman really affected me. Was she really honest? Or was the "Country Countess," just her disguise?

Now he wasn't sure, but he was glad he'd held back, just in case. No one on the ship knew anything about him except that he'd been in the Diplomatic Corps and lived all over the world before his life at sea.

Who else made him feel threatened like that? Rory Saltz. The same thing. She just said whatever was on her mind. She was unnerving because she really *was* honest. Not that she was mean or said impolite things — she was just so, daring. It was just not the way people talked to one another. At least in his world where being subtle and diplomatic and always putting a pleasant spin and a smiling face on everything was essential. One put their best foot forward in as perfectly presentable a package as possible. Was he trying to impress? Yes, but most people were trying to make a good impression.

Well, the Countess was so rich and old enough (probably 75, even with the plastic surgery) to risk it, but Rory was no Countess, and she was just herself, anyway.

Was it admirable or a terrible flaw in her character and socialization? It must certainly limit her circle. Well, she didn't seem to have or need a circle. Not that he should talk. Who was his circle these days? Chorus boys and maître d's? Flora Frampton and Dr. Padma from the Clinic?

Well, if he'd conducted himself as well as he thought he had (at least before that third shot of brandy) and if the Talbotts and their guests—(Oh for Walter Worth's hair!) approved—maybe things were looking up. Who knew where this could lead.

He toweled off and checked himself again in the pink steamy light. Better. *A little face bronzer and a hit of oxygen and I might just pull this off.*

THE MEDICAL CLINIC on a cruise ship is always below the passenger decks, near the bowels, which is an appropriate metaphor, since it is the last thing the marketing agents and public relations and advertising agencies who spend millions of dollars a year extolling the romance, exotic adventure, hedonistic and healing benefits of cruising want their guests to visualize. They want you to visualize the spa, the pool, the decor—the pretty face, not the rectum, as it were.

Management will allow select passengers a tour of the wheel room and the main kitchen, but not the boiler room, the crew quarters or the O.R. Yes, the O.R. Not just the usual cheerfully attended outpatient clinic, geared to the treatment of sunburns, turista tummies and hangovers. The O.R. and morgue are the unadvertised necessities.

People on cruises overdose on drugs, commit suicide, have strokes and heart attacks and on a ship as large as the *Palace of the Dolphins*, people may die on every journey. Not such a pleasant thought, especially considering that the doctors who man the clinic are more likely than not to have been trained in one of the Third World medical schools and whose English, not to mention skill, is probably more than a tad less stellar than would create a high sense of inner peace for the potential patient.

But there it is. Real life getting in the way of the press releases and fantasies. And of course, there was the crew itself. Another sixteen hundred or so human beings from all over the world subject to the same range of minor to life-threatening ailments, and with enough frequency to keep two doctors, a nurse practitioner and two nurses fully employed.

Most passengers, however, never venture down below the wall-to-wall carpeting to the other ship, the backstage of the cruise show, where the floors are linoleum and the walls are whitewashed metal, and the perky, energetic, smiling faces on view continuously two decks up are few and far between. Exhaustion is more the look here. And passengers are as welcome in these halls as cockroaches at Christmas dinner. Here, they are intruders.

Derrick was a straddler of both onstage and backstage, and he knew his way around the clinic both from his regular visits for B-12 shots and oxygen and to chat with Dr. Padma, the Pakistani doctor whose English and personality were passably pleasant.

But the real power behind the clinic was Peggy, a retired Army nurse with the brisk, humorless efficiency that seems to be *de rigueur* for all medical receptionists; land or sea, a form of paranoia reserved exclusively for sick people; as if they were all con artists with nothing better to do on their hard-earned vacation than extort something from her clinic.

She viewed each new arrival with a barely concealed hostility that worked for management's benefit (you'd better really be sick) but led to numerous complaints from passengers and crew. Nurse Peggy didn't like anyone—but she liked Derrick.

"Nurse Peggy, what a sight for my swollen little eyes. I like your hair like that, dear, hate to barge in so early, but I need a double of my usual, ASAP. I've got a tour to do, and I was a very bad boy last night."

"So I heard. I've got everything ready for you. I had a feeling you'd be in."

"Dear Lord, that's fast even for this gang. What exactly did you hear?"

"Sit down and roll up your sleeve. Bebopping around with a Countess old enough to be your mother. Shame on you."

"We weren't bebopping. I don't remember any bebopping, though I'm not exactly sure what bebopping really is. We did dip though. Want me to show you how?"

"No and remember I have a great big needle in my hand and my day is already off to a rotten start. Got an emergency in with Padma, came in before I had my coffee. Much to do about nothing, if you ask me."

"What is it?"

"Allergy attack. One of the Talbotts' friends. A real drama queen is my opinion. He's been in there with them for almost half an hour. Here, hook this on and take some extra deep breaths. You look like hell. I gotta check on them."

Derrick breathed, fighting a wave of nausea. *Oh God, it must be the Worths. Can't have them see me like this. They'll tell Teddy Talbott I'm a degenerate or a lush.* The door swung open just as Derrick set down the oxygen mask, the telltale canister resting guiltily beside him. Leah Worth, looking very pale, with huge blistery blotches covering her arms but still managing to convey elegantly ethereal beauty, stopped before him leaning on her husband's arm.

"Mr. Doolittle, are you all right?" She smiled at him, filling him with an overwhelming desire to evaporate into thin air. Something like shame was how it felt, as if she had uncovered a secret, ripped open the door to his bathroom and found him soggy and puffy, with paste on his teeth and his hair on his shoulder: a sinner for sure, cowering before the Virgin Mother herself.

"So like my wife! She's the one who's been wheezing and breaking out in hives all night, and the first thing she asks is if you're all right." Walter Worth extended his hand to Derrick, who was now on his feet and making a valiant effort to appear quite a bit more than just all right.

"Walter, Mrs. Worth . . ."

"Leah, please."

"*Leah.* I'm right as rain. You've caught me at my little recharging ritual. A nice deep inhalation of oxygen does wonders at the start of a new cruise. Is there anything I can do for you, Mrs. Wor . . . , Leah? You should have called me. I would have guided you down here."

"Oh, that's so sweet of you, but you know, Walter consults to the Empire Line on all the hospital design and equipment; he knows his way around so well. I didn't want to cause a fuss. I'm just so allergic, and we never know what will set it off. But I'm fine now. Dr. Padma was a darling."

"And a great chess player to boot."

"Oh, you are too kind, my friend. I am not so good as all that. You are just not used to much challenge. I must get back now. Mrs. Worth, please do not hesitate if you have more problem. Nurse Peggy will supply you with the proper medications. Now I advise a little nap and you will be soon better."

Derrick checked his watch. If he sprinted, he would be on time. "Well, duty calls. If you're sure there's nothing I can do?"

"No, we're fine. I'll just take Leah back up to the suite. Oh, one thing. If you see our daughter Clarissa on shore, will you tell her we won't be joining her?"

"Absolutely. Have a wonderful day." His smile was hurting his face, but he held on to it, until he was at the steps. No time for the elevator.

"Derrick, wait up, I'll race you." Nurse Peggy, carrying her little medic bag, huffed up next to him.

"I'm late for a staff meeting, but every stair feels like Everest. Where are you going?"

"The B-12 will kick in in a couple of minutes. I could use one myself. There's an anxiety attack or something on F Deck (pray it isn't a heart attack)! One of the guest lecturers. Uri Something. He's on for the Jews since this is their Passwhatever week. Calls himself a 'Charismatic Rabbi,' but I call him a pushy little Christ killer. I can set my watch by them. Every psychosomatic illness allergics, panic attacks, always the Jews."

"Peggy, shush! You can't say things like that!"

"Why not? You're not one of them. I see who you pal around with, don't see you seeking out any of them as buddies. You like your Talbotts and Countesses as Christian as possible."

Derrick stopped to catch his breath. "Well, in fact the Worths are guests of the Talbotts. I may be a snob, but I'm hardly a bigot."

"Scratch one, you're sure to find the other, is how I see it. But I'm sorry if I offended you. It's been that kind of a morning. One of my nurses is sick, so I get stuck with this creep."

"You go on ahead. I need to wait for my head to stop pounding, but I strongly suggest you get a hold of yourself before you see Rabbi Dayan. He's a very prominent man and a pet of the Head of Marketing, who is also Jewish."

"Just venting to a friend."

Derrick waited, his heart beating fast while someone he thought he knew bustled around him and up the service stairs, her heavily muscled legs flexing with the effort.

Another wave of nausea hit, but this one caused by something other than French brandy after midnight. He sat down on the stairs and lowered his head between his legs until it crested and released him.

He had liked her brisk, no-nonsense competency which reminded him of those dour, bristly female relatives from his childhood, who buried their frustration and long-submerged rage somewhere far beneath their powdery, dry demeanor: but he had missed her cruelty, the warping of fear into hate.

Dear Lord, did he *seem* like that? What had made her feel comfortable to voice such a risky, not to mention revolting, thought to him? "Scratch a snob and . . ." Derrick patted his self-bronzed face and rising slowly, he smoothed his uniform and re-fixed his Upper Deck smile.

URI DAYAN was pacing. *Like a shark, like a shark, keep moving, moving, moving. If I keep moving, I won't sink. Don't want to sink; if I sink, I'll fall into blackness, move, move. Don't stop, think like a shark . . . you have the power, you are not helpless . . . bare your teeth at the enemy, the enemy is your own fear, help is coming. Help is coming, you are not dying, it's just fear, just panic, sharks don't panic; you're okay, Uri. You're okay. You're a shark. Not a salmon, not a schmucky little salmon, swimming upstream, thrashing and pushing against the natural force, pushing against yourself. . . . You are in control, in control . . .*

The bell rang.

Help. Help is here.

"Oh, Please, please come in! I think, I'm having, some sort of a panic attack! I think I need something to calm me down . . . very agitated . . . can't catch my breath—but I'm in sound health, very sound. I run marathons, have regular check-ups. I just need something to calm me. Are you the doctor? I'm Uri Dayan. I have a lecture to give and a prayer to lead and I must have something. . . ."

"First, sit down. I have to take your blood pressure and listen to your heart, Mr. Dan, then we'll discuss what to do."

"Day-an. Rabbi Dayan. And you are?"

"I'm Peggy. I'm the nurse practitioner, and I'm qualified to do what the doctor would do in this situation. I spent twenty years in the Army, so trust me, I've seen panic attacks and every other kind. Take off your shirt, please."

"Yes, yes. I'm having a lot of trouble breathing . . . my heart's racing. . . ."

"Your pulse is fast, but not alarming. Try to take some steady breaths so I can hear."

"Of course. Of course, I will try."

"Shhh. Please. Turn around, now."

"Oh, God, I feel faint. Very faint."

"Come on, sir. Get a grip. Be a man here. You can snap out of this. Your vitals are good."

"I beg your pardon. I need some help, and you're being extremely rude."

"I'm not rude. I'm just very busy, and it does seem that you people have an excess of hysterical symptoms that always need immediate attention and take us away from others who may really be sick."

"You people? I see. You mean Jews, don't you, Nurse whoever you are. If you can give me something for the panic, I will follow up later with the Doctor."

"Very well. Pull down your pants, sir. This will sting and you'll probably sleep awhile, so if you have a prayer session or whatever you do, you may want to set an alarm."

"You are appalling! Do not think this will go unreported!"

"And what exactly can you report? I did my job. And I called you no names. I don't have to like everybody I treat. You'll just look foolish, but do what you want. I need some air."

Nurse Peggy put her equipment back into her bag and walked out, leaving him stunned. He could sit now. The medicine was working some kind of miracle within him. The panic so real and terrifying only moments ago already seemed like a silly indulgence. How could he not have been stronger than that? How was God working through him, sending this hideous woman to him? What had triggered his anxiety in the first place?

Well, that part wasn't too hard. It was his breakfast encounter with Poe Evanoff. What an unbelievable start to what he had hoped would be a day of peace and harmony!

Everything in his career was going so well. So amazingly well! He closed his eyes. How could he have let Evanoff push his buttons like that! Jealous, the man was clearly jealous. How had he allowed it to escalate like that? God, he felt wonderful! Euphoric and utterly relaxed. Now he understood what it was that made people seek out drugs.

So this is how it feels! I should lie down and rest for an hour. Reconstruct what happened. Think it through, troll the event with steady, non-emotional searching. I have too much at stake for another episode like this. Go back to the beginning, to the gym.

IT WAS A GLORIOUS morning. He'd done five miles on the treadmill in the fitness center, had a steam and a shower and was looking forward to a nice breakfast.

Evanoff didn't see him. He was sitting across from a woman with short white hair, and he'd assumed she was old, but when she got up to leave, he saw that she was quite attractive. She resembled that actress his father had had a crush on: Doris Day. What had ever happened to her? The woman left and Evanoff was bent over some papers, and he'd taken his tray and started over there.

Why? A colleague of sorts. Evanoff had a name in behavioral psychology, and he'd been on many of these cruises. Evanoff was represented by the speakers' bureau that he was just now going to sign with. A good connection and he'd written several books. Of course it made perfect sense to join him for a friendly breakfast. One never knew.

But when he'd approached and said, "Good morning," Evanoff had not asked him to sit down, had seemed in fact not very eager for company, and he should have been more sensitive to that. He wasn't used to such a response. Most people were a bit uncomfortable with representatives of religion and went out of their way to be inclusive and polite. How had it started? He'd asked if he could join him.

"You're welcome to sit here, but I must warn you, I've been very lazy, and I do have to prepare a little for my morning Dog and Pony Show, so I may seem preoccupied."

"I do understand. We can be preoccupied together. I have a 'Dog and Pony Show' of my own later, and this is my first cruise lecture, and I'm not at all sure what to expect."

"I thought you were going to conduct a 'Seder at Sea?' "

"Yes, yes, of course. But I am also going to give a talk. I don't know if you know anything about my work, but I am really more of a spiritual philosopher than a rabbi. I consult and advise many corporations and prominent business leaders, and celebrities, and I'm more concerned with how the use of Talmudic principles combined with the best of other spiritual doctrines can help us heal and live better lives.

"In fact, I'm about to join you in the book business; I've sold a book on my work. There's even talk of a television series and a 'Center for Moral Meditation', that's my working title. Quite exciting, really. So, I agreed to lead the Seder as a courtesy, but I'm really here to talk about other things to a broader audience."

"Is that so? A budding Deepak Chopra are we, now?"

"Actually, I'm trying to meet with Dr. Chopra in Los Angeles next month. I want to interest him in a project I've started with a group of very wealthy philanthropic business leaders. We get together once a month in Palm Beach to discuss how to reinvent Talmudic principles for highly successful people.

"We all share the belief that you must be powerful to have choices, to take risks. We've set an entry-level net worth for the group of eighty million dollars, so you can see they are serious and can effect change, not just talk and volunteer for things, but shape policy. They are all seeking something more in their lives and as they gain power, they gain conscience."

"Oh, I see. So you're the Charismatic Rabbi to the Filthy Rich and Spiritually Deprived. Now I understand why Chopra might find you of interest. He's the guy who spread the seeds of that notion: 'People who have achieved an enormous amount of success are inherently very spiritual . . . affluence is our natural state.' He is also now adding new seductions, a 'Center for Well-Being' based on the insanity that people grow old and die because they have seen other people grow old and die . . . aging is simply leaned behavior. Well, that ought to bring in the masses."

"Are you being sarcastic, Poe, if I may call you that? I detect a lack of genuineness in your remarks."

"Really?" Well, I'll have to work on that because I was hoping to convey contempt and revulsion."

"Dr. Evanoff. I am a man of God, and I try to find the good in all and view my fellow man with tolerance, but such hostility from a colleague whom I scarcely know, cannot be about me. If you are in pain and need to share your feelings with someone, I would be glad to try and help."

"Very good, Rabbi! An almost flawless narcissistic response. I talked to you in an aggressive and nasty way and your face is telling me that you are very angry and frightened by what I've said, but your response is full of fake solicitousness and concern for my emotional state.

"What *I* mainly do now Rabbi, is read faces. That is *my* work. I read faces for a living. I show the police, the FBI, the CIA and other psychiatrists how to tell if someone is lying, if someone is dangerous. It's work that certainly alters the way I see the world, and it does make it much harder for people to mislead me.

"One of the great pioneers in this work, besides Darwin who really started it all, was a brilliant, flamboyant scientist named Silvan Tompkins. You would have liked him, Rabbi, because he was not just one of us sloggers; he used his insights to become a rich man. He made a fortune handicapping horses by watching them for hours through binoculars and predicting who would win based on the horses' emotional relationships to the horses on either side of them.

"He absolutely believed that emotion was the code to life and the human face was the way to break into the code. He could walk into a post office and just by looking at the Most Wanted posters, he could tell the FBI what the criminal had done.

"Tompkins once said, 'The face is like a penis'—a perfect metaphor for the idea that it has a will of its own that could not be controlled. And there is a very serious system for reading the micro expressions, astonishingly complex and rigorous science done by a Tompkins acolyte named Paul Ekman, who coded the face, spent years and years traveling the world, Japan, the jungles of New Guinea . . . found stunning things about the universality of expressions, of what you could learn from the face if you knew where to look. What could be unmasked: the false friend, the liar. Evil. Instinct coupled with science.

"He and his colleague spent seven years in a small room making faces at one another and documenting every conceivable muscle movement—over 10,000, in case you're curious.

"So, you and I are both Dick Heads, Rabbi. The difference is you couldn't read my face or you wouldn't have put your tray down and intruded on my privacy and I, having the advantage, could see that your smile of greeting was not warm and spontaneous, in which case you would flex your zygomatic muscles and your orbicularis oculi, the muscle which encircles the eye and is all but impossible to control. You, Rabbi, used only your zygomatic major, revealing another agenda, say, opportunism and egoism, and then I insulted you and you lied again."

"My, god, you're right."

"Well now, that's a surprise. I was expecting more lying. So now, I apologize. I've learned something more about you. Now your response is honest and your face reveals distress, anguish of a sort, A.U. 1, if you want to be technical, and fear, some sadness and embarrassment. Your frontalis pars medialis plus frontalis pars lateralis, your inner and outer brows A.U. 1, 2, 4, 5 and 20. A very expressive face you have. So, I am sorry. I usually have better control than that.

"You pushed my buttons, Rabbi. I basically loathe everything you've just told me, not you personally, but what you represent, the way the world works now. I know I sound self-righteous, but I'm just as hard on myself. I'm here, too, after all. But this is my last public appearance, as it were, so I guess I don't much give a damn about professional protocol anymore."

"I don't understand. Are you retiring? You seem too young."

"By Dr. Chopra's standards, I'm a mere tot. I'm 59, but I'm not retiring from my life, I'm just retiring from the world of Well-Being Centers and networking and speaking engagements and book deals and cruise lectures and showing off to 'colleagues' and the entire business of Career Maintenance, which you are so eagerly embracing. Of course, so did I—twenty years ago.

"I don't believe in experts anymore. The arrogance of thinking that 'Your Way' (whatever the 'Your Way' is) is *the* way or using the power of fame or religion or expertise or wealth as a reason others should follow 'Your' map is devious and destructive, and when you mix such ambition with God or whatever his new moniker of the moment is, you've got trouble in River City, Rabbi."

"I don't understand what that is?"

It's from a song in a musical called, *The Music Man*. He's a con man who comes into the town of River City and seduces everyone with their own longings. So American! That's what we want—fairy tales and Santa Claus. Heroes! We'll deny any reality to create them.

"We yell about politicians not telling the truth, but all we really want is a better liar—one we won't see through, one who won't get caught. So we collude in our own misery and line up at Centers like yours and keep the Longing Industry booming."

"Why do you see it so harshly? How can it not work for humanity and for the heritage of the Jewish people to incorporate Talmudic principles into all of society? And who can effect change but the wealthy and powerful? How much good can I do standing in a suburb of Illinois when I can reach millions this way?"

"And I was starting to like you better. Can't you hear yourself? From what Mount did you give your sermon? You were called, like Jesus? Like Abraham? Like bloody Joan of Arc?

"This is about power for yourself. Personal power and glory and your own television show. Is that human? You betcha, and American all the way. But it corrupts. It can't help itself. In five years, you will stop knowing yourself, and then you will stop looking in any mirror that reminds you. I saw fear and anguish because I shocked you with your doubt, your conscience, which you still seem to have.

"I don't know why I'm getting into all this, but it's too late now, so let me show you something I wear around my neck. It's a piece of silver with two bits of rubble welded into it. One from Buchenwald and one from Dachau. My father was at Buchenwald and my mother was at Dachau. I wear two bits of rubble so that I never forget what is under all the pretense and bullshit of human nature. The beast of life, as well as the beauty, must be grappled with every day, if we are to stay human. It can't be shoveled over with three choruses of 'We are the World' and a week of spa therapy."

"Now I understand. I had no idea you were the child of survivors."

"No, now you do not understand. I have not told you anything that would make you understand. *I* don't bloody understand."

"Please, I am not your enemy here. We are landsmen."

"Have you been to Dachau?"

"No, no. I have not been to the camps. I want to take my children when they are older."

"Well, frankly, I think you should go before you *have* children, let alone practice as a rabbi, but I'm rather prejudiced about things like this. Let me tell you just a little about Dachau and Buchenwald.

"Buchenwald looks like what you think a concentration camp would look like. It's buried in the woods, like a secret, hidden — supporting the old German rubric that no one knew what was going on.

"Except for a couple of facts, not talked about. The apartment block where the SS officers, camp commanders, doctors, and their families lived sat on the edge of the camp, in *sight* of the crematorium. The *fraus* cooked their meals and played with their children, right beside the atrocities. Do you really think they told no one? And that no one came to visit?

"But that's only shameful. Evil is *today* at Buchenwald, the tourist museum, the 'solemn reminder' as they say, complete with the former SS housing which has been converted into *apartments* for East German families.

"If you should visit on a weekend in the summer, you will see them hauling their picnic baskets and beer coolers right past the tourist buses, back to their cozy little condos with wonderful views of the chimneys: never read that little factoid, did you, Rabbi?"

"No. No, my God. This is horrible! But this is exactly the kind of thing my group can address because it is powerful."

"Please spare me the self-serving rationalizations, and just listen. Dachau is not set deep in the woods in a hidden place where people could pretend not to know anything. The monstrousness of Dachau is that it is located right on the main road.

"It was a munitions factory converted to a camp, and so it was placed where the citizens of the quaint medieval town of Dachau as well as the burghers from Munich, could walk or bicycle or take public transport to work. Right there, chimneys smoking for all the townsfolk to see. Today there is a Burger King or something and a car rental agency and a few other examples of indifference right across the street. The 'Banality of Evil' in action."

"I am ashamed not to know this. I must go there. I must speak about this."

"There you go again! That is ego, Rabbi! I'm telling you this for a different purpose. You need a bit of tripping. You are too sure of your path. Very dangerous in potential message carriers. You don't know shit. Neither does anyone else. Some of us are just more willing to live with the realities of life and human nature and separate from the tribes of pretenders. But if you really want to teach anything, you at least have to start with humility."

"I can't be held responsible for being born here, for being younger and further away from the Holocaust."

"True! My parents didn't hold the hate, either. My parents were doctors and they believed in healing, and when they married and immigrated to England, they still had hope enough. But my father's heart was broken and his body was weak. When he died, my mother stayed in England until I finished school. She wanted me to go to America; she didn't trust Europe, any of it, though England was the best of it."

"When I was accepted at Yale, she sent me off and moved to Israel that very week. She didn't tell me because she was afraid I'd go with her. She knew that meant the army, and she couldn't bear the thought of that. She told me if I came to live there, she would kill herself, and I believed her. Well, she didn't even have to. All she had to do was get on her usual bus one day, and a Hamas teenager did it for her.

"Nothing is over, Rabbi. Write as many self-help books and do as many T.V. shows as you need to make you rich and sought-after. Join Elie Weisel on the Great Men circuit—hobnob to beat the band to raise shekels for your 'Non-Profit Foundation.' Another lie. *Everything* is about profit of some kind, it's just a matter of degree and honesty about why we do what we do. And that is the button you pushed in me and one, I think, you may need to push in yourself."

"This is a lot to think about. I wish I could have recorded this exchange. I am hurt, I will be honest, but I have leaned something important. I hope you have learned something, too."

"Yes. But really this conversation is the end of something for me—the end of an extraordinary night that I spent with someone who actually lives her truth in a braver way than either of us or anyone else I've ever known. You were really dessert, rather than breakfast. I'll come hear your talk. I've got to go now."

They stood and shook hands. A ritual of male courtesy neither of them was quite ready to discard.

⁓

URI PULLED A BLANKET up over his chest. The cabin was cold. *My God!* What an amazing experience he was having! He had just relived one of the most unsettling and disturbing conversations he'd ever had with another human being, and he felt completely calm. Serene and so, powerful! Yes! Powerful.

This was what they meant by being "centered". He had talked so much about it, but now realized he was only pretending, because he had never felt this way. Well, a moment here and there, in between the way he usually felt, as if he were, what? Floating in his life, pitched somewhere between terror, doubt and always a ratchet away from serenity. Was it possible to feel this way *without* drugs?

Did Chopra? Or, what had he just read about Maharishi Mahesh Yogi? He'd thought he was dead! Once you stop reading about someone who's been so famous, they cease to have any reality, become dead in a way.

I feel so relaxed, so pleasant! Where was I? He kept drifting off ... *Oh yes, Maharishi ... transcendental meditation, and who? Someone in the movie business? Twin Peaks! Yes, the Twin Peaks fellow ... going into business together to build "peace palaces" all over the world ... movie stars ... "Oceans of Bliss," the movie man said ... the man who directed Eraserhead and Blue Velvet! David someone and the Maharishi. "Oceans of Bliss."... Yogi flying ... meditations ... sending positive vibrations into the world.*

He'd been envious, cynical. He'd made fun of it. Why didn't he tell Evanoff? Evanoff would have understood that. He would have felt a connection. Did the movie director and the Maharishi reach this state he was in now?

Three thousand Centers in urban areas! They had announced it at a press conference at some ritzy hotel, and he hadn't even seen the irony! He'd thought of where to announce *his* Center! They were raising a billion dollars! A "vast network" ... "It's kind of important to have peace on earth," the movie guy said.

Evanoff thought he was a fool. Why did that matter? Why had he stayed? He'd been shocked beyond belief, offended, but he sat there. *He saw something in me I don't want to face.... Was he bringing God's message? Do I even believe in God? Is everything I'm doing a lie? This is amazing! Whatever she injected into me is letting me see something I would never let myself see. I wanted him to approve of me.... I want them all to love me. Revere me. I'm used*

*to it. Crave it. I do. Oh God. . . . Holy Moly . . . it's so big! . . . What
was that? On my Email . . . Viagra pitches. Sickness, sin. Opposite
of peace and bliss? The minute something becomes commercial, can
it maintain? Why am I only attracted to rich and powerful people?
Why don't I want to be a real rabbi?*

*The world stinks. Oh God, do I think that? What did I say to that
woman at dinner last night at the Captain's table? The beautiful
red-haired woman who was a guest of the owner? I said something
horrible. She was talking about her wonderful childhood in Los
Angeles, a close and loving family, and I was drinking too much,
showing off. What did I say? Something about, "If you have a bad
childhood, you're fucked." And she was shocked.*

*A rabbi was not supposed to talk like that! A rabbi was sup-
posed to have faith in his fellow man, believe in the power to heal,
to overcome! She was shocked, and I was shocked. What a thing to
say in public! What a thing for someone like me to think! Evanoff
saw right through me!! God. What does this mean?*

*Drifting again. . . . It's so powerful to not be afraid of myself.
All great men have doubts. Abraham. Moses. . . . Pesach, "passing
over" protection, it means protection . . . leading on faith, believing
the sea will open . . . believing God would not abandon them. . . .
Locusts, frogs, boils, hail, vermin, blight, blood, darkness, slaying
of the firstborns; he trusted the word of God. He could have been a
Prince of Egypt and he turned away from it all.*

Abraham, seventy-five and childless, who better to test? Two
sons so late in life . . . one a bastard, sent off into the desert . . . tied
to Hagar. Isaac, son of Sarah, his only hope and God commands
him. I have never been tested at all. . . . Until Evanoff! No sacrificial
child! No taking on the Pharaoh! Just a disgruntled, bald behavior-
ist at a buffet breakfast table and I quiver and fall into panic and
tremble with doubt!

How will I do Seder? And thou shalt tell thy son . . . what can I
tell my son? The story of the Haggadah, the Exodus? The innocence
of children asking the question . . . "Why do we eat bitter herbs at
our Seder?" "To remind us of the cruel way the Pharaoh treated
the Jewish people in Egypt."

*Eyes trusting that I care . . . that I believe. . . . Seders for the rich. I
have only done Seders for famous families. Movie people . . . spoiled
children . . . that dreadful four-year old girl last year. "What pretty
red shoes! They look like the red slippers from The Wizard of Oz."*

"They're not Wizard shoes, they're my Prada shoes." Four years old. God.

Can't stay awake. . . . What if my life is all a lie? I was so excited by my accomplishments and he swept them away! Why did I sit down there? Why didn't I read him better? Maybe I did. Maybe I was looking for what he gave me?

The Nazis. . . . H's—so many H's . . . Hitler, Himmler, Hess, Heyderick. Did they feel peace and bliss? Did they believe they were right? No doubt? Yes! Evil has no doubt. No shame. . . . On the road. . . . Dachau is on the road! Burger King or something? Eating a hamburger and looking across at Dachau! Living in a condo in view of the chimneys!

Peace palaces. . . . Insanity. That is insanity.

Peace on Earth. Three thousand years ago . . . Ramses II torturing the Jews, three thousand Peace Centers . . . ironic . . . where can there be peace in human nature? There has never been peace in any nature. How can I not deal with this? I am a liar. He saw right into me!

What had the woman at dinner said? "You can't really believe that. Rabbi? People overcome all kinds of terrible things and have good lives. Why, I ran into someone tonight that I haven't seen since high school. She was my dearest friend, and she had the most horrific and tragic childhood, and now she's a successful songwriter. She writes the material for the cruise shows, actually. She pulled herself out of terrible loss: no money, no family. You can't *really* believe that?"

He had seen the sheen in her eyes change, her ardor toward him, the ardor he was used to seeing in lovely, decent women looking for heroes, for father figures, for leaders to lead them to something they didn't have within themselves; he saw it shift. He wanted it back. He needed it back, and so he'd lied.

"I'm so sorry. I was being sarcastic—trying to imitate the way cynics I have counseled think—but I'm afraid I'm not very good at mimicry."

Instantly, she was back. The veil lifted, and he was safe again.

But Evanoff wore no veil. No place to hide with someone who could actually read the lies in your face! He'd been overwhelmed and their positions had shifted. It was he who wanted Evanoff to lead him.

Drifting off again . . . that woman, that bigot with the needle. Maybe the whole thing is a dream. I'll wake up and find that it's dawn and I can go on as if nothing has happened. Yes. . . . Turn it all back. . . . No doubt . . . no fear here . . . peace. Just a little more peace. . . .

⸻

RORY ROLLED ONTO her back and adjusted her pool lounge. *Woe. Foe. Low. Bow. Poe. Toe. Go. Sow. "Why This Feeling, Why This glow? Why this thrill when you say hello? . . . Rory, Rory, Rory, this is not good. You only have a half an hour break and you've had two hours sleep. You must squeeze that brain shut. . . . How can I rest? I'm in a frenzy! I need to process, but it's too loud here.*

Yaka YaKa YaKa. Is everyone at the pool speaking Italian? Why does everything always seem more interesting in Italian? They're probably talking about hemorrhoid ointments or how dry the Vongole was last night but it always sounds so impressive.

Oh, God, that old geezer is giving me the little eye winky thing. Amazing, when your antennae goes up, men just sniff it; they KNOW your switch is on. . . . So much for my rant to Flora. She was right. I'm vibrating with, with what? Oy.

Yaka, yaka , yaka. I love Italians in the sun; they're all twelve years old. Look at them! The papas in their speedos, with their little pot bellies and little saddlebags and their skinny legs and their original wives with their saggy topless boobies, turning over and over like a rack of rotisserie chickens, smoking and searing, splashing and strutting, totally unselfconscious about their stomachs creasing into their nipples; side by side with their gorgeous half naked daughters; butts and boobies bobbing around, scalded like carpaccio, puffing and squinting into that sun. So free! They must think we're so silly with all our rules and sun-blocks and smoking bans and eating bans and expectations. Taking ourselves so seriously, we stress and they stroll . . . uh oh . . . non-Italians approaching pool ladder . . .

"Uganda! Get out of the pool, sweetie."

"But, I want to swim more, Mummy, please."

"Not now dear. Come on, we have to meet Poppy. Please don't step on that nice man next to you. Come now."

"You have a very brown head."

"Uganda! That's not a nice thing to say."

"Why? He does have a very brown head. A very big brown head. Don't you?"

"Yes, I suppose I do and you have a small brown head."

"I do! You're funny. Mummy, I have a brown head, too!"

"Yes, you do, darling. Now, please."

"My mummy has a big white head and my Poppy has a huge fat white head!!"

"That's nice, too."

Oh, this is good. Yuppie mom has turned as red as the Italian teenagers. Black Man in pool is being a very good sport while probably as freaked out as I am, even though, God only knows, I'm not black. . . . Talk about a big white head; imagine naming an adopted trophy kid Uganda . . . especially when the closest she's ever likely to get to her birthplace is Safariland. . . . Poe would love this. Did you hear what you just said? Rory, Rory, Rory. . . . 'Poe would love this!' One long night and an hour in a lecture hall and it's 'Poe would love this' time? Rory you're scaring me. "I took one look at you, that's all I meant to do. . . ." Oh my, oh, oh, my . . .

How much time left? Twenty minutes. Sort now or you'll never be able to handle rehearsal. He took your arm and led you to the elevator and away from Leah and Walter and into a ten-hour fairy tale. "And then my heart stood still. . . ."

He was leading her, holding her under her elbow, so gently but sure, knew where he was going, she hated to be led, never liked not to know where she was going, but she liked this, up and down round and round, through the casino, past married couples, husbands holding other elbows, wives used to it, not like her. No man had ever quite held her elbow like this, like she was important to them, worthy of guiding.

All these couples suddenly everywhere, going to eat or to drink or to gamble, inside and outside, hundreds of them and she was now sort of one of them, one of the elbow guided, over-dressed middle-aged women wobbling around the passageways on too high heels, holding their wraps and shawls around them like furled flags, that's how they looked, like furled flags.

The husbands seemed so protective, the women always looked so unsure, guarding their hair-dos and their make-up. So carefully prepared, so much time invested in their public presences; any rain drop or gust of wind a threat to the effect; that's the look of long term marriage, husbands guiding their furled wives toward their destinations. It is their responsibility to get them to the party unscathed—so fragile, so crackable, any outside element a potential assault that could unfurl them, desecrate their image, and the husbands take this on as a sacred trust—to guide them through, out of harm's way. Yes, she'd never seen it before, only watched with disdain or envy or both, but now that this man had her elbow, she understood how moving it was, that guiding, tenderness; that's what tenderness is, keeping those ladies from cracking as they wobble forth to make their entrances. *Oh Rory, now, really, is that what you want? To be a Wobbler Forther?*

"There's a quiet little bar in back of the casino if you'd like to have a drink and then we can have supper if you haven't had enough of me." When he smiled his eyes twinkled, more Mr. Clean than Yul when he smiled.

"Sounds great as long as there's no theme and no mimes or magicians roaming around."

"No, which is why no one goes to it except the strays like me."

Strays like me, he said. A fellow "stray". Another sore thumb, maybe. No, Rory, don't start that . . . how many years of therapy have you had? Up it pops, fucking jack-in-the-box . . . unmet needs, un-held hand, unheard prayer, longing for contact, connection, compassion, comfort . . . oh, comfort . . . "there, there Rory. . . . I know, I know you're scared . . . I know it hurts, there, there." . . . Longing for the gone thing . . . no one can fill it; that was HER job—only one mother, only one chance.

Hours passing, time standing still while moving quickly, silently slipping away: oblivious, they were oblivious. Drinks came. Food somehow was brought in from somewhere, just enough to keep them going without having to stop; without moving out of the magic space, even to pee, the energy crackling between them; not like any other meeting either of them had ever had; a truth current, connecting them to something precious, something that felt pure. Freeing themselves, the reverse process of the couples they had passed, unfurling before one another without fear of what could result! The goal, both egoless and guileless: to be real to another soul.

How had they started? She'd asked him a stupid question. A Dating Game level question, a set-up of sorts—a way of testing and keeping her distance. Maybe she just didn't know what else to do.

There she was, leaving the party, escaping from the shock of Leah and Walter Worth, limping off to the safety of her cabin to recover from her emotional tsunami event in the powder room and there *he* was, the man with the cute head, appearing from nowhere and now here *she* was in a dimly lit lounge up close and personal.

She needed to control something, ask the first question and get her luminal lamp ready. Scan the man for signs of psychic blood splatter, phoniness, pretentiousness, sleaziness anything that would allow her to remove herself from the danger of the opposite possibility.

"So, Poe, how do you feel about golf?"

And he'd smiled that Mr. Clean smile and looked right through her. "I see, we're going right for the, 'Now I'll be able to eliminate him and get the hell out of here' question. So, Rory, how do *you* feel about golf?"

"Wow, that was, unexpected. Didn't even bounce that one. Lobbed it right the fuck back. Okay. Fair enough. I have nothing against the *idea* of golf. I find it to be a very civilized and strangely relaxing sport to watch on television and I'm convinced it requires great skill but I would personally never want to be involved with a man who actually plays golf because they're rarely individualists or loners and I'm pretty certain golf has become a mega cultural necessity to keep a serious number of upper-income middle-aged retired men from committing mass suicide.

"Even the fact that they play it on fields of grass—the male human equivalent of being 'put out to pasture.' All those little carts filled with all those red-faced smug white men with their 'clubs' (ah, hunter-gatherer) and their competition disguised as play. It sort of revolts me and so, I was setting you up, because if you'd gotten that glazed, 'Oh man, I love to play' look I'd be, well, safer.

"Gee, this is horrible . . . I'm way too out of practice to be here at all. But at least I didn't ask you how you got the name Poe—not that I wouldn't have gotten to that next. Maybe we could go back to our cabins and do this by E-mail. I'm much better at E-mail relationships."

He took her hand and held it between his. And he was very quiet, something usually very scary for her and yet it made her feel peaceful and calm. She wondered if she would ever need to speak or think again.

"I have never played golf. I do not participate in any team activities. I do not have buddies. I do not belong to any clubs or even professional organizations. I take strong exception to elitism, to any door that isn't open to all. Golf is a bastion of exclusion, so on principle if nothing else I wouldn't play it. Private clubs, private courses. 'I'm better than you because I can go through that door.'

"The gospel of Thomas, a little known Coptic Christian tract, says that God is manifest in self-knowledge, and is within each individual and that journey to the self which Goethe and others have also written about, is the God Head.

"I believe that in holding our individuality is our holiness. The art is to be able to contribute to society which would otherwise crumble and still keep that journey active. Quite difficult. Maybe impossible. So we become a species of golfers or loners and we do need both to survive, but the price can become too high. They pay, too, Rory Saltz. Everyone pays."

Tears dropping from the sides of her eyes like raindrops on glass. A small voice unlike her own, not quite connected to herself.

"At this moment all I want from the world for the rest of my life is to put my head on your shoulder and sob my guts out, to have you hold onto me and let me cry. So you may want to let go of my hand and run for your life."

"Well, you may want to run, too, because I feel exactly the same way."

"No shit."

"No shit."

·"Have you ever read an Icelandic novelist named Halldor Laxness?"

"Oy. Maybe I should reconsider my stand on golfers. I think I may be way over my educational head here. We're talking Fairfax High School and then the N.Y.C. theater world school of hard knocks with a lot of New School audited courses, so my shoulder may not be smart enough for you to cry on."

"Don't tell me in addition to everything else, you're Jewish?"

"No, from that lost tribe of Israel, the Irish. It's a long story which I'm sure I'll tell you after another glass of wine unless we do the sobbing thing first."

"Halldor Laxness was not to put you off and I'd rather not start on the difference between education and intelligence so don't be coy, you know how smart you are . . ."

"I'm never coy. I'm an uncoy goy who says oy. Rhyming is part of the songwriting disease. I know I'm smart in my way but I'm not an intellectual and I didn't even know there were novelists in

Iceland. I barely knew there were people there. I only know about their bubbling mineral pools. I love a good soak."

"It's very mystical and primordially beautiful. I'll take you there if you'd like."

"You will? You're going to break me open, Doc. Don't say things like that."

"Why not? I mean it. Let me tell you why I brought him up. He wrote a dauntingly strange book called *World Light* and what we were saying to one another a moment ago reminded me of a passage. 'When one is born one only knows how to cry. It's only very gradually that one learns to smile.'

"Really a fascinating truth about being human, is it not? I'd never heard of him either and I'm not such an intellectual, don't let my accent fool you. I do have the education, that I do. Both my parents were doctors: Jewish, European and concentration camp survivors. Education was essential. I heard about Laxness through my work reading faces. Which is also a long story."

"Woah. Too much to process. I'm still on the Laxass. . . ."

"Laxness."

"I know, couldn't stop myself. Anyway, *now* we add the Holocaust and 'Face Reading'? What the hell is Face Reading? Some sort of New Age alternative medicine? Like palm reading for the Boomers? 'I like his face. I can read it like a book.' 'Yuck, that's an ugly face, must be a bad guy.' 'Nice eyes, I can see your soul.' What?"

He laughed. She had made him laugh. He had a big hearty laugh and he threw his head back when he did it, in a nice lusty, free way. *Oh boy.*

"Oh, Rory Saltz I owe you an apology. A colleague of mine calls what I just did the 'disease of familiarity' you get too close to something and you forget how it sounds to someone not involved in it. How, well, *elitist* of me to throw that out like that.

"I bet you think it's your way out of here, that I'm some sort of faith healer, but it's not like that. It's a form of behavioral psychology. I study the muscles of the face as a way of telling when someone is lying or to see danger, even evil. I do it to help the police and also to help other psychiatrists and psychologists better evaluate their patients. It's very effective, especially with sociopaths, people who are very seductive and clever at manipulating, but hard to read or see through."

"No shit. What did you read in my face?"

"I didn't do it with you. Funny, I usually do it without even think-ing about it, but I didn't."

"Is that good?"

"I think it is."

"Boy, would you have been a great 'What's My Line' contestant. No way anyone would figure that out. How about an application at the Department of Unemployment. Profession. 'Face Reader'—lots of demand for those. Before this the most unusual the day job I'd ever encountered was the free-loading daughter of a singer I know who works for Gillette as a 'Professional Leg Shaver.' They pay her twenty dollars an hour to shave her legs with various razors. Where were you twenty years ago? What a lot of bullshit I could have saved myself, with all those sociopaths lined up in my life. How did you become interested in this?"

"Now that is a long story."

"Well, if we're not going to sob right now, I have time."

Tumbling, they were tumbling . "Down and down I go, round and round I go, that old Black Magic called . . ." Words and feel-ings, life stories. She was free-falling, fearless, everything, she told him everything.

Aunt Maddie's sun-bathing rituals, lying on the cement driveway of the Four-Plex with band-aids over her nipples and Iodine and baby oil slathered from toe to dyed yellow head, little pink eye cups which left white circles around her cheeks.

Fairfax High and her hatred of team sports, praying in the line not to be chosen last, "please God, just don't let me be last," her relief if she was second or third from the last even if she was "last for the normal kids, the ones not having an impairment of the permanent nurses excuse level"—her parents, her grandparents, and all the deaths. Walter Worth and her broken heart. Leah and her jealousy. Cantor's Deli and her escape from L.A. Her struggle in New York and then Jesse. Jesus Hymie! She'd told him about Jesse! . . . Her husband, the live-in liar, the promise and the fantasy—composer and lyricist, the beautiful music they would make together. So much charm, he had so much charm. Out it poured, as if she had never talked to anyone before in her entire fifty-two years. Well, had she? Really?

Maybe it was because he was listening. Truly listening, not just waiting to jump in with his own story. He was so calm, as if there was no rush, no need to control where the conversation was going, no impatience: *listening* to her. She never talked about herself like this, too big a risk, too much chance for something unbearable to fall out. Billy. Oh God, she wanted to tell him about Billy, but that was too much, too hard, too sudden. How could she tell about Jesse and skip over Billy?

Oh God, how she wanted to tell this man everything! She felt an almost compulsive need to tell him what had happened to her little boy. She stopped though, her bladder making the decision for her and then she needed something else, she needed to listen, needed to know him. The man part of him, she wanted to know and didn't, jealous already, another Leah would take him away, but she asked him anyway. She had to.

"So Doc, is there or was there a Mrs. Face Reader?" So dumb, impossible to do it straight and he had hesitated, for the first time, paused and her heart was pounding, banging around in her chest from that pause.

"This is harder than the Holocaust, but here goes. I had a wife and a wonderful little girl. My daughter died. She was five years old. She was very ill and we couldn't save her and my wife blamed herself. Nothing more could be done, but she thought she hadn't been careful enough during her pregnancy and the guilt destroyed her. She killed herself. And after, I couldn't do regular therapy anymore and I started reading Darwin that led me to the research on what the human face can reveal. I thought if I had seen more clearly my wife couldn't have fooled me about how ill she was and I could have saved her.

"So, that's how I started doing what I do. It was all a long time ago, almost twenty years, but I've not really moved on. I know how that sounds, but at least I knew when a psychiatrist loses hope, he shouldn't be treating patients and so I stopped. Holding my dead with me has been necessary until tonight. Until I saw your lovely white head bobbing up and down in the corner of that awful party and heard your songs and something shot me forward as if I'd been physically shoved back into life. So there it is."

He had given her himself. She could see his family, feel the agony, the pride, the courage, feel the magnitude of the losses, what he carried, mirroring her own.

Tumbling faster. "Round and Round we go" . . . or they were still, absolutely still and the world was spinning round them, more like that. They were at the center of something and she believed him.

People came in, jarring them. Young people, pretty young people, drinks in hand, mocking someone, laughing and loud. They moved slightly, instinctively, away from one another.

She'd seen the young people before. Red hair, Leah's daughter and her friends, the Barbie set of tall blondes from the party.

"Do you mind if we go somewhere else?" She'd asked and he'd already signed the check. "That's Leah Worth's daughter and her friends, I'd rather not, you know . . ."

He'd taken her elbow again and steered her out and she'd followed, trancelike, floating almost and somehow they were in another lounge and they were dancing. Dancing! He was holding her and she could sniff him, like a puppy with a new shoe, sniffing in his smell, soapy, with something lemony and crisp and under that, a bit of cedar, and he was warm. . . .

How long had it been since she had danced with a man cheek to cheek and they were dancing *to* "Cheek to Cheek"! . . . "Heaven, I'm in Heaven, and my heart beats so . . ." no, her heart was standing still.

They kept tumbling, wandering, drifting; outside on the deck he said something about Leah's daughter?

"The young woman with the red hair, isn't happy with her friends; she was pretending, but she wasn't enjoying herself. She's right about them, but she doesn't want to be. They're both sociopaths. I watched them at the party for a bit."

"You could see that?"

"Absolutely. Their faces don't express the way normal faces do. Leah's daughter should find new friends. Soon."

"Can I take you to rehearsal with me tomorrow?"

He'd smiled and they wandered around on the deck. The air was warm and the sky was filled with stars and they stood at the side and looked down into the water, sliced by the moonlight, and the force of the ship slashing through the sea.

The two of them alone in the universe, feeling both enormous and infinitesimal; giants of uniqueness and antlike in the vast indifference of existence.

They stood there looking down, not speaking or needing to protect themselves in any way from the power of their emotion or their helplessness and when he turned her toward him and kissed her, it was an alliance. It was the acceptance of love.

Nothing more was required. They went to her cabin and ordered a pizza and fell asleep in one another's arms. No sex. No need, yet. Perfect. Harmony.

⌒

THE COUNTESS MATILDA (Mimsie) Von Essen of Dallas, Upper Fifth Avenue, West Palm Beach, The 15th Arrondissement and Monticantini sat regally posed under an umbrella on a crowded beach somewhere outside of Charlotte Amalie feeding her long-haired toy Chihuahua Tou Tou the remainders of her filet mignon lunch. Tou Tou was making due, but was clearly less than pleased at the absence of his foie gras.

"Come on now, bukie, bukie, Momma grew up on grits and beans, you can choke down a prime piece of beef once in awhile."

Tou Tou was not impressed with her rough and tumble early years. Well, why the hell should he be? She'd spoiled him rotten. Same reason none of her children or grandchildren were impressed. What a mess she'd made.

She looked out to the water where her grandson Ian was wind-surfing with Twinkle Talbott. A pulsing throb of envy shot through her, leaving her breathless for a moment. *God damn. How young they are. How gorgeous and thoughtless of it.* It was unimaginable to them that someday they would turn into her. The eccentric old "hoot" who used to be a stunner. She could feel their eyes rolling behind her back whenever she told them a tale from her misspent youth. Was it misspent?

The Countess licked the steak off her fingers and gave Tou Tou his baby bottle filled with Evian. *Really Mimsie, this is getting to be a little extreme.* She never even did *that* for her grandchildren! Tou Tou sucked cheerfully. She probably would have breast-fed the little bugger if she could.

How ironic that with four living children and five grandchildren, her Chihuahua was the only being she really felt loved her, needed her and who she loved back fearlessly.

Hot damn, that was scary! One thing she was more and more sure of as her seventy-fifth birthday beat down on her: it really was far more painful to admit what you didn't feel than what you did.

Like regrets. All of that nonsense about only regretting what you don't do. She'd never quite understood what that meant. Then, of course, there wasn't much she hadn't done. *Five* husbands—more lovers than she could now even remember. Thousands of friends. In the end, if she mushed all of them up into one huge person, she might eke out a single absolutely swell human. Lots of nice bits and pieces, but no soul mate. Not even one truly special and irreplaceable comrade, not since her first husband.

Well, she was picky and hard to please. Her mother had always told her she set her sights too high and she'd never be satisfied with anyone or anything the world could offer and that was probably true, but the alternative had looked to her, the young her, the Ian and Twinkle young her, as too horrifying to contemplate. Namely, her mother. To end up bitter and poor and sick and sucked clean of all life force, all hope. Far better to set your sights too high than give up without a fight.

Of course she did have beauty and brains on her side, not to mention a hugely lusty libido and an iron will. She's flung herself forth and look at her now. Alone, yes. A kooky eccentric with too much money and not enough love in her life, but better than her momma! Maybe that's all most women of her generation had wanted anyway. To just not end up like their mothers.

Men were where she misspent. She had always been a lousy picker. Bums, but at least three of them were *rich* bums, and not psychotic. When she left or they left, she had done fine. Not like so many of her women friends, deserted, old and running out of money, sticking their heads into their fancy restaurant-quality ovens or flinging themselves off balconies in the South of France.

The truth be told, with all the romance and wild sex and flowing champagne and whizzing around, she'd always believed her purpose on earth was as a mother. (Not that she'd been any good at it.) But she loved them and at least she never shipped them off to boarding schools like her daughter had done to Ian.

Tou Tou had fallen asleep in her arms and she lifted him as gently as she could and eased him back into his Hermes traveling kennel. She smiled. Tou Tou slept in something that cost ten times what her parents' first house cost!

What would her mother think if she could see her now? Would she be proud of her or horrified? Envious or ashamed? Probably all of it and incredulous that she'd had all those children, a real pumpkin eater she was, even if they were scattered all over the world. One drunk. One prescription drug addict, one cross-dresser, and Ian's mother, an anorexic socialite with the brain of a mollusk and the heart of a toad (no offense to toads). Her daughter had ruined him. He was probably already a goner before she'd retrieved him. Amazing how much damage can be done before a kid is ready for kindergarten and he was almost ten when she rescued him, which is what she called it, anyway.

The one wonderful child, Louis, her gift (not that she hadn't loved all of them, but Louis was special). Her wise souled first born and the only child conceived with anyone she really loved, was the one she lost. She lost him and she lost his father. One to the war and the other to cancer. Why Louis? Well, God knows if anyone does.

She hardly saw her grandchildren anymore. Once a year or so and then only because she compromised herself and made a huge effort. And Louis hadn't lived long enough to have a child. Ah, sweet mystery of life.

Sadness flowed through her like warm wine, stroking her insides into surrender. She wiped her eyes. *No crying on a public beach for Godsakes.*

Ian hit a wave and bounced off his board and she jumped up, mother instinct always first no matter what other feelings were involved. She'd moved too fast and she reached for the umbrella to steady herself. The sun was too much. She felt dizzy and frightened. Where was he?

A bright splash of blond hair and muscle popped up in the sea, flooding her with relief. She sat down again and took a long sip from Tou Tou's bottle. Ian. Grief moved into the sadness and then rage covered all the rest.

Motherhood. She had started so impassioned, so innocent in her desire and confidence that she would be the best mother ever: cheerful and fun, not prissy and rigid and sour like her mother—fiercely protective, loyal, and honest with them, and there through thick and thin. But she'd been blinded by too much hope and illusion, too many women's magazines and phony T.V. mothers.

All those fakes: Mrs. Lassie and Mrs. Cleaver and Mrs. Walton and Mrs. Brady, whose lives began and ended standing in the kitchen or waiting at the front door. Smiling, serene and bloated with patience and wisdom; without doubts, needs, feelings or bathroom habits, just waiting with cookies and homilies; distant, well-groomed and slightly out of reach. She certainly hadn't pulled that off, not the apron or the homilies or the one befuddled Dad, but she'd stood beside them, got them through, told them the truth and loved the hell out of them.

And in return, she was "allowed" to participate in their lives on their terms, kept at arm's length unless they really screwed up, needed more money, a shoulder, a contact or a maternal Rock "Wall" like the one on the ship, one with slightly spongy foot holes, to climb over, bash into, blame and mock and bully as a way of fleeing their own demons, their own truth.

The more delusional they were the worse they were to her. "It's all your fault that I'm so unhappy. It has nothing to do with me!" The way they saw it everything bad about them and their lives was her fault and everything good about them or their lives came solely from within as if they had not only been conceived in a petri dish, but raised in one as well. Talk about your no-win situation. She sighed and wiped another tear. *Wallowing in the pity pond today aren't we Mims?*

Well, sometimes we just do. So what were the rewards for parenting grown-up children? Few. Far between, and the next great myth takes hold. The last greatest rationalization, one she heard continually sputtered with just a tad of desperation by all the grandparents she watched trotting around family-friendly resorts like the *Palace of the Dolphins*, looking frazzled, exhausted and often, disappointed.

What they all said was, "these grandchildren make it all worth-while." That line always made her laugh. Was it shorthand for, "These grandchildren make all the crap I have to put up with from their parents somewhat bearable."

Who wants to see life head on like that? Was the entire struggle from the birth of those precious, beloved beings to the hearthurting, disappointing, spoiled self-centered middle-aged miserables her children had become, made worthy of a life's work by a few crayon drawings and an occasional "I love you, Grandma?" The jury was still out. She sighed. *Whoa Nelly, where did all that come from?*

Of course she knew. Where it came from was back on his wind-surfer whizzing through the waves like the Adonis he was. Ian. Her last chance. Her final attempt to make good by taking this one child with a deadbeat father and an uncaring mother and loving him back to health.

Oh dear God. Was it her fault?

"She shuddered, remembering Sissy Talbott regaling her and

Twinkle and Ian with the horrifying tale of the poor Irish girl who'd been attacked last night. Sissy was telling the story in that patronizing uppity way that made Mimsie want to smack her and her grandson was *laughing*. Ian was enjoying it. *What a horrible man!* The thought had shot forward before she could control it.

Tou Tou whimpered and she opened the little doggy door so the fresh air could reach him. *Please Lord. Let me be wrong about him.*

Tou Tou stuck his little pointy head out of his case and cocked his ears and she laughed, pulling him back onto her lap and covering his bony little body with kisses. "Bukie, bukie, bukie. Momma's little funny face . . . make a tinkle for Mommie, right here on the sand. Good boy. What a good boy." These little creatures just crawled up into your heart with such enormous force.

She watched the little pooch make his pee pee. God, he was an ugly little thing. She'd always liked big, hearty dogs with big heads and some meat on them, but now she couldn't keep up with them and she traveled so much

This one was like warm, breathing worry beads that she could keep close 24–7, a living teddy bear or security blanket. He was always eager for a pat, a kiss. Always ready to lick, to cuddle, never wanting anyone or anything but her. No wonder they hooked you so hard!

Well, at least he wasn't a cat. She'd always been terrified of ending up in a big empty decaying villa somewhere with old newspapers piled in front of the windows and twenty cats slithering around. She shuddered. *NO, no, Mimsie, we are not going there. Ian is bad enough.*

A child was crying. She reached over and pulled Tou Tou back onto her lap. A little boy, no more than three, was running away from a bigger boy toward what must be his mother. "What's the matter, honey?" The Must-Be mother asked, the way millions of mothers do everywhere, every day.

"I'm mad at Joey," said the crying child.

"Why is that?" Said the Must-be Mother.

"He messed up my feelings." The little boy replied.

The Countess smiled, resisting the urge to grab the little yummykin and smother him with kisses. "He messed up my feelings." So perfect. That is what people do, now don't they.

Derrick Doolittle's face popped up, distracting her from darker thoughts. Speaking of people "messing up your feelings". She hadn't had so much fun with anyone in years. Dancing and drinking the night away, speaking French and Italian and God only knows what else. Making fun of people. Not nice, Mimsie, but the cruisers were quite an assortment. What had she called the boat? "Wal Mart with Rudders." Really naughty, considering he was Cruise Director! But he'd laughed the hardest.

So who was he, anyway? Well, she saw the obvious. She'd known enough of the type. "Derricks" were the lot of aging, rich, single women the world over. Most of her friends found one they could stand and trust with the "Emeralds" and made some companionship for cash deal with the devil—feebly hoping "the Derrick," would stick around until the end without putting a pillow over their heads or running off with the butler.

Not for her. Alone was much better. But, this one was rather nice and more manly than the usual. Vain and pretentious and all that—loved her title and the status, but then who was she to talk? She'd married the Neo-Nazi swine with a secret captioned picture of that psychopath Himmler hidden in his closet: "If 10,000 Russian women collapse in exhaustion and die digging a ditch, I only care about how the ditch will be completed." Finding that was the last straw, but the signs were there for her to read any time she chose and she chose not to until *after* she was a Countess.

She shuddered in shame. Fear. Pure and simple. She was still more afraid of being nobody and not being part of the social whirl than she was of rotting in hell for the sins of avarice and status-seeking.

And who did she choose to carouse with? A social-climbing closet-case, a snob for sure, who was twenty years younger at least and very impressed with her title?

You get what you pay for girl. And you never learn. You do have choices, you know, it's one thing money buys. You could dump the title and the phony friends and get off the merry-go-round before all the horses crumble under you. Wasn't that you blabbing on in the bar about, "if you look to the world to fill you up, you're gonna die empty." How about putting your you know what where your big Texas trap is?

So, okay, Derrick fit the prototype, but there was something better about him. Something kind of sweet and lost and vulnerable. Maybe under all the showboating, there was a nice man as lonely and fed up as she was?

Of course there was the age thing. But even if he wasn't gay, which was a big *even*, she still liked younger men. What, after all, was the alternative? An older man would have to be NINETY. Or ONE HUNDRED. *Jimminy crickets.*

Except when she looked in the mirror, she felt as young as she had when all those babies were sliding out of her and she could run around the world without a trace of lag, energy to spare and heels to kick up.

What in hell would she do with some ancient geezer, who wouldn't want anyone her age, anyway. They felt the same way she did!! What a joke. So, okay, maybe the Title and the money worked for her the way the same things worked for the geezers. Wasn't that the way of the world? Or at least the world she knew? Use whatever you've got.

The Must Be Mother was holding the little boy on her lap, unmessing up his feelings. She smiled. What irony the Lord gave us. We start out crying and helpless and in diapers, needy and frightened of not being fed, and cared for, and if we live long enough we end up the exact same way!

The Countess plopped Tou Tou back into his carrying case and got to her feet, more slowly this time. She waved to Ian, the sun making her new emerald ring sparkle. Enough of this, her head was spinning—time to go back to the ship and have a nap.

Well maybe God wouldn't forgive her for Von Essen, but she was damn well going to forgive herself. Life was getting shorter by the minute and Ian was going to cause her enough grief in what time she had left. She was not going to waste a precious second with a past she couldn't change.

And if in the end she was just a shallow, foolish old woman of less than sterling character, who had failed at the thing she wanted to be good at most, then so be it. She might pay in Hell, but in what she had left of time on earth she was going to try and have some joy.

✦

CLARISSA WORTH SLOWLY opened the door to her mother's room and peeked in. It was after three and she was still sleeping. Loneliness engulfed her. All day she'd had an almost overwhelming need to be with her mother. She felt like a little kid with a boo boo.

Obviously whatever they'd given her Mom for her allergy attack had totally knocked her out and she probably hadn't slept all night and she should just back out and let her be, but she tiptoed in and waited, hoping her mother would stir.

She was being really selfish. She eased herself into the chair by the bed, willing her mother awake. Guilt and anger flashed through her. Her mother was such a fragile flower. Sometimes she just wanted to punch her, do something ungentle to her. *That is a really, really horrible thought, Clarissa.*

It wasn't so great to have a mother who was almost saint-like and also delicate; her Dad always treated her like she would disintegrate if she felt any stress or worked too hard or had to endure any bad news. It was getting to be a bit much. Why hadn't she ever realized how much she resented her mother before? This trip was like one big consciousness-raising session. Had she just been living in total denial for her entire childhood?

Maybe it was because she'd been living away and hadn't seen much of her parents in the last year, or at least not much for *them*, the Constant Togetherness Family. She couldn't bear feeling so confused and cut off from her, but, she had to tell herself the truth, she was angry.

, She was supposed to be hearty and strong and able to "handle" the world and her mother got to be protected and pampered. Well, that was a little harsh, her Mom protected and comforted her, but there were so many episodes of "delicate doll" stuff. Allergies and migraines. Too many dark rooms with Clarissa standing in the corner trying to be seen.

I want to go home. What was happening to her? Where was that always upbeat, always able to have a good time and see the best in everyone person she'd always been or thought she was, anyway?

Tears covered her face and she wiped them away with her tee shirt. It must be Twinkle and Ian and all of that meanness and negativity. One thing she was certainly starting to face, she couldn't be friends with them anymore. They were unbearable! The way they'd made a joke of the attack on that poor girl from the spa! Even Mrs. Talbott was disgusted with them.

She couldn't believe what Twinkle said. "Oh the little pudgeball with the bad foil job. I saw her at the party, and I was like, 'no way' my parents invited '*That*'. She was like hanging out of her *tarty* dress—like! Tarty! instead of 'party' I am totally funny, admit it,

Ian. She was probably prowling around, waddling her big butt and she got what she deserved."

"I thought the damsel was quite Rubenesque, all that doughy Irishness to sink one's teeth into. Certain macho types love those milk maids, the boys with the testosterone overloads, the ones you read about in your precious *Post* everyday who are always slitting the throats of their common-law wives and blowing their longsuffering-recently-escaped spouses away on the playgrounds of their children's pre-schools.

"To be crude, she shimmied up the wrong shaft, and some Neolith let her have it. Could have been you, dear, you were shaking it up with that fireman from Chicago, teasing the poor beast all over that disco. I'd think you'd have a tad of empathy or at least, fear for your own hot buns. They haven't caught him, yet, Twinks."

Mrs. Talbott was not pleased but all she said was, "Now, now. You two, don't be vulgar and do be careful." But the Countess had shut them down, Thank God! She was clearly revolted and Clarissa had been so grateful that *a* parent had spoken up. "One more word and you're both getting a smack, grown-up or not! You should wash your mouths. Shame on you!" She'd reached over and taken hold of the Countess's hand, which wasn't easy with all the jewels on her fingers.

Even if it hurt her Dad's business relationship with Mr. Talbott, she had to pull away from them. And she really needed to tell her Mom and for her Mom to understand and, what? Give her permission? Tell her it was alright, that she felt the same way. What if she didn't? What if she got mad and told her she was being childish and her father had worked too hard and this would be terribly embarrassing and would probably end his business relationship with Mr. Talbott?

She couldn't really believe that her Mom would do that or her Dad, either; they loved her too much and they'd always told her to trust herself and do the right thing. Not for what anyone else would think or whether anyone would understand or agree or thank her or whatever, but to do what in your heart you knew was right because of how that made you feel about yourself. "Your opinion is the only one that matters," her Dad told her whenever she was in some sort of moral quandary and had to make some changes.

Hopefully, she could just sort of slip away. Twinkle had tons of friends and was so self-absorbed it shouldn't be too hard. She could blame school and work. But she had always been some sort of pacifier for Twinkle. Twinkle liked to have her available, on her terms, of course.

She sighed. Every year life got more complicated. She couldn't even imagine what it must be like for her parents! She must try and see things through their eyes, like St. Francis. "It is better to understand than to be understood. It is better to love than to be loved." Well, okay, she'd try even if she was Jewish and not a saint, she'd still try.

Her mother turned toward her and opened her eyes. "Issa?"

Her mother hadn't called her that in awhile. Her baby name, what she'd called herself before she could say her full name. She smiled and love filled her heart, taking away all the other feelings. Just hearing her mother's voice could do that, hearing her concern, the question always in her voice, the unsaid 'are you okay?'. She should be so grateful to have parents who loved her and cared about her so much.

"Hi, momma, are you feeling better? I was starting to get worried. It's after 3."

Her mother pulled herself up onto the pillows and yawned. "Oh my heavens! I've slept the whole day away! I have no idea what the doctor put into that shot, but I was out cold. Oh, honey, I missed Yoga. I'm so sorry!"

"Don't be silly. I went ashore with Ian and Twinkle and the Countess and Tou Tou instead. We were quite a sight, like right out of *Death on the Nile*. Ian insisted that his grandmother put Tou Tou in a carrying case instead of strapping him onto her chest.

"We went emerald shopping. Well, I mean they did. Oh my God, Mom, I have never seen people spend money like that! They knew about this one store that apparently has the best ones and they just loaded up. The Countess even tried to buy *me* an emerald bracelet! It was unbelievable. Then we had lunch and went to the beach. I just got back."

"It sounds like fun. I'm sure they'll be wearing the loot at dinner tonight. Sorry I couldn't go with you for moral support, anyway."

"Pa-leese, I thought the whole thing was *too* Marie Antoinette. I don't get the jewel thing. They all look like fakes to me. Are you okay, now?"

"A little dopey, but I think I'm fine. I just need a shower and some fresh air. All the hives are gone. Miraculous!"

"Mom, something really terrible happened on the ship last night and Mrs. Talbott said she had to warn us, but not to tell anyone because it would start a panic, but I've got to tell you, of course."

Leah sat up and switched on the light by her bed. Her mother looked pale and drawn and the lines in her face that were mostly hidden when she was feeling well and had her make-up on, were more noticeable. "What is it darling?"

"Remember that sweet Irish girl who gave us facials yesterday?"

"Yes, Collie. She's lovely. She was at the party last night for a bit."

"Well someone attacked her when she was going back to her room. They beat her up really bad and raped her and really hurt her and they don't know who it was, because he came up behind her and pushed her into her room and she didn't see his face."

"Oh my God! That's horrible. It could have been you or Twinkle or anyone. How can they not warn all the passengers! Does your father know?"

"I don't know, I haven't seen him but I'm pretty sure Mr. Talbott would have told him. Mrs. Talbott said they were having a lot of emergency staff meetings and beefing up security. Apparently this entire ship is like one big maximum-security prison. They've got hidden cameras everywhere and lots of plain-clothes officers and stuff. But still, it's pretty creepy."

"Well as soon as I find your father, I'm going to make sure they assign someone to stay with you girls tonight and no more of this getting home at all hours."

"Mom, don't get all hysterical now. That's why it's hard to tell you stuff. We're New York City kids, we're cool and besides, Ian's always with us, but I'll certainly be more careful. We think we're just floating around out here in some unreal little fantasyland, not on the Mean Streets, so it's easy to turn your antennae off. Do you want me to wait and we can go for a walk on the jogging deck? It's really pretty up there and no one seems to use it."

"Absolutely. I'll just jump in the shower and throw on some sweats."

"You? I've never seen you in sweats."

"Well, something casual. Why don't you just lie down and take a little rest, yourself. I can't imagine you've had much sleep."

Clarissa looked at her mother's nice warm bed, smelling of her, cozy and dark and safe. "Sounds good. I'll just zone while you get ready."

"Good." Her mother stood up and walked across to her and put her soft, rose-smelling hand on her cheek. "Like old times, Issa. Having you curl up in my bed. I love you so, baby girl."

"Me, too, Momma," she said feeling guilty and safe at the same time.

✕

"Solly! Thank God, I need to talk, Solly. I just had a traumatic experience. I'm very unnerved, unnerved. Let's sit by the pool. I need a little something. A snack, maybe, my blood sugar's too low. I need carbs. That's what I learned in the seminar this morning. I think it affects my emotions. Oh, I'm crying, here. Solly sit."

"Vera, what the hell happened to you? You were supposed to meet me half an hour ago?"

"I know. I know. I had a traumatic experience and I was filing a complaint with the Spa Director."

"You had a traumatic experience in the place you went to get over traumatic experiences?"

"Don't take that tone. That's that little put down tone. Yes, that's exactly right. And if you're my friend, you need to support me and listen with an open heart, like the counselor said."

"Vera, sweetheart. I do. I'm not putting you down. But it is, you know, kind of funny."

"Solly, it was *so* not funny! I'm hypoglycemia here. My heart's pounding. I was very upset."

"Wait a minute honey, I'll get a waiter."

"Look, Solly, that one has a tray with fruit drinks. Get me one of those."

"Sir, can we have one of those drinks over here, please?"

"You want one of the Dolphin Delights?"

"We'll take two of them. Can we sign?"

"But of course. I just need to see your room card."

"Here, Vera, drink."

"Oh, good. Solly, it's delicious. Has a nice kick to it."

"That's the rum, Ma'am. Jamaica's finest."

"Oh, God, Solly, it's alcohol. They said not to have alcohol and fruit together. Bad carbs."

"Vera, enough. Drink up. The friggin things cost fifteen bucks apiece. You're drinking it."

"Oh Mi Gawd! Robbery!"

"So what the hell happened in there?"

"Okay. I'm calmer now. So, I went in for my massage and they were very nice and I was relaxing and feeling good, thinking about this trip and all the fascinating things we heard this morning. Doctor Evanoff picking me out of the audience and saying what an honest face I had and all. And the Spa cuisine class and what a nice time we had last night after we left those New Agers and everything. Nice.

"So I soaked in the Jacuzzi and chatted with a very lovely young lady who sells jewelry in Atlanta and she told me she has clients who spend over $200,000 dollars on a watch! Could you die! And she told me about another client who is one of those later life mothers and she had the umbilical cord from her baby saved and rushed over to a special lab so she could harvest it for collagen injections into her laugh lines! Can you imagine this! And then . . ."

"Vera, alright already!"

"Okay, I'm getting there. So they call my name and this guy named Craig or Greg, comes out and I must say, I had a gut feeling, 'My knower knew' like your mother used to say, God rest her—he looked kind of creepy, too skinny, a little weird, but I figured, a ship like this, they choose the best and off we went."

"And he started the massage, and I was, like I said, feeling good and then when he touched my stomach, he sighed. Solly, I mean like a big, deep sigh. And then he did it again, you know like my Aunt used to do when she wanted attention, she'd sigh until you asked her what was wrong? So of course, stupid me, like a spider to the frying pan, I say, 'Is something wrong?' "

And this Craig, Greg person, he does it again and then he says to me, "Do you have trouble being on this planet?"

"What the hell does that mean?"

"Well, Solly, Hello? Exactly! He was saying it like he'd felt something inside me that was sick or diseased or something, like I was going to die!

"And I was stunned. Stunned! And I said, 'Look, I'm a human, of course I have trouble being on this planet, me and every other person, so what are you saying?'

"And he sighed again! Like he could see into me or something and I said, 'look Craig or Greg or whatever, that's a very upsetting thing to say to a total stranger. You don't know me and whatever the hell you felt it was probably just gas from the cooking class salads I ate, all that fiber I'm not used to, but I feel my privacy has been invaded.'"

"You said that? I'm impressed."

"Thanks, Solly. That was in that talk we went to after the cooking class. 'How to set your boundaries and find your truth.' Anyway, I think that got him, he didn't expect me to say anything like that. I bet he was going to try and scare me into buying all those vitamins they sell there and whatever. 'Manipulate my fear' that's what they said in the talk, but I sat up and I said, 'I do not wish to continue. I'm not feeling safe here.'

"And then Solly, it was like, Jekyll and Hyde or something. He got very angry and he clenched his fists and I thought he might hurt me. He said, 'What's your problem, Lady, I'm trying to heal you, you fool.'

"So, I wrapped the sheet around me, got up and moved past him out of that room and called for help. And then the manager came and I had her get him out and then I went back to get dressed and OhmiGawd, Solly, I was shaking like a leaf and I couldn't stop crying. I felt terrible. He frightened me and I made a scene. I thought, maybe he's like those New Agers, maybe he does see into me and I'm riddled with cancer like your mother was and it was horrible. But I pulled myself together and went and made a complaint and they were very nice. They offered me another massage for free and gave me some bath oils and so, that's why I'm late."

"Jesus. What a thing. Don't you let him get to you. I'm telling you Vera, they're all a bunch of loonies, like the people last night. I talked to a guy on line for coffee this morning, he said there's a group on board who believe they're regularly abducted by Aliens and I think they were our tablemates. It's like a cult all those types think like that. Come over here and give me a hug. I'm gonna track that sonuvabitch down and tell him something and I'm gonna get his friggin ass fired."

"No, Solly, enough. I filed the complaint, let's go forward. It's not worth the stress. Move forward, that's what they told us in the class. I'm feeling so much better, what did he call this? Dolphin's Devil?"

"Delight".

"Exactly. I'm proud of myself, I stood my ground. So, enough about my trauma. What have you been doing? Did you go to that business talk?"

" 'How to Protect your Assets in a Bad Economy and a Post-Madoff Market.' Very informative. The guy giving the thing is one of those natural salesman types—the kind of guy who'd 'convince Eskimos they needed an ice-maker'—he said that. He was a funny guy. A Brooklyn guy, no bullshit. And he's written a book, which I bought, about how everybody, your ordinary people and your fancy people, everybody gets sold a bill of goods."

"Like if the Craig or Greg guy was trying to scare me so I'd buy all the herbal remedies?"

"Exactly right." He told this really hilarious story about how it works at the higher end of the deal. All these Boomers like us who finally have some dough and are trying to protect it, but make it grow, you know, whadda ya do now that's safe but you don't end up like my father, too scared to invest anything and you work your entire life and end up with zippo.

"Then he says, 'so after you all settle in and he's let you know he's a trustworthy guy with at least as much money as you have, the pitch begins and the pitch is very tricky, because he's gotta at the same time, make himself look like an expert without who your hard-earned cash will shrivel, but he can't treat you like a friggin idiot, because after all, he's sitting there because you were smart enough to make some fairly big bucks to begin with and nobody trusts these guys anymore, since Bernie, so he's gotta really work it. Then, 'at some point the couple, usually the wife, right?' "

"Oh Mi Gawd, It was me wasn't it?"

"That's my girl. The wife, who he says has a better antennae or maybe she's just worried about the husband buying a load of baloney and her ending up with him croaked and being pawned off on the Sisters of Mercy."

"So not funny, Solly!"

"Actually, it was funny. All the guys cracked up. Anyway, the wives usually start to ask a few polite but no bullshit questions about risk and then the guy, who never really answers any direct question, shifts into the finale, where he starts giving the success stories of his other clients, who are far wealthier than you; he'll throw in a couple of billionaires who trust him so much they want to give him more and more of their money, but he won't let them, looking out for their interests so he never lets clients invest more than a safe amount with the smallest possible risk (not that there really is any risk). Remember? We started to feel like he was gonna do us a great big favor to let us give him our money!"

"I think I even said, 'we'd be honored to invest with him!' "

"You did, but I was right there too, shaking my head yes."

"But we snapped out of it, thank the Virgin! We came to in time."

"We did. So anyway, after the talk I was schmoozing with a couple of guys at the coffee and pastry deal."

"How was that?"

"Very tasty. Lots of Danish and those little fruitie things with cream in them your sister always has."

"That's nice, a little extra touch. They could have just served coffee."

"Oh yeah, they don't skimp. I'll give them that. Anyway, we were talking, and it was enlightening, because I realized, like a flash of insight, that this is the way the whole world works now. Look at your average day. Almost everything we do involves some one conning us one way or another.

"We're buying a new car, a new house, a boat, a T.V., a cell phone, a friggin appliance, shoes, gym equipment, and then there's the spa deal or the doctor deal or the dentist deal; everyone's selling or being sold, hustling or being hustled. And most of the time, not all, there's some good people out there, but most of the time it's bullshit.

"Look who's telling us the thing is great? The jerkowitz who's selling it! And then we even do it to one another, to impress our friends or co-workers or bosses or whatever. We play ourselves and each other all the time. I'm telling you Vera, it made me very upset. Made me want to call up our kids and tell them, 'we gotta do better.' We do."

"Oh Solly, that was beautiful. So deep the way you think! You are so smart, Solly. Do you see a kind of theme going on here? We started with Dr. Evanoff talking about the face revealing the truth and those scientists deciding to, what did he call it, 'Unpack the face.'

"And afterward I told you I wanted to take that course and learn the 'Facial Action Coding System' at least a little bit so I wouldn't be such an easy touch and get hurt so much? And then the Craig/Greg person and then this?

"We are having some sort of big opening in our consciousness,

Solly. No one in our family ever opened their minds up like this. I'm very proud of us. This is life-changing."

"Yeah, you know. It is. And what did that big brain say about my Doll? Whose face did he choose? Do I have pictures of you up there to show your sister? Whose beautiful puss did he pick from all those people?"

"I'm blushing now, enough. I'm getting embarrassed. It was nice though, that he thought I was an honest person. That cute lady with the platinum hair sitting next to me, she said he was a genius and I should be flattered because he wouldn't say it if he didn't mean it."

"That's my girl. Come on, let's go eat something and then I wanna try and find the photo gallery, so we can see if any of the pictures that lady took of us last night are worth buying."

"Only if I'm holding my stomach in."

✍

My darling Maria,

I have been working hard and there is still so much to learn. The first day is always quite exhausting and it is now almost time for the passengers to return from the town. We leave in an hour and so I only have a moment, but I must tell you things are very peculiar and I do not quite understand what is happening, but I am getting a very odd feeling about this trip.

I do not want to alarm you, I will be fine, but I think dark things are going on. My friend Jo Jo for example is behaving strangely.

I saw him coming out of the boss's office and he seemed quite upset. Mr. Hensler as I told you, is not very pleasant and going in there is always difficult, but Jo Jo wouldn't look me in the eyes and then he said, "Elonzito my friend, bad vibes, be careful" and I said, "What do you mean, Jo Jo" and he said, "Look, don't ask me anything, but be cool."

This made no sense to me and I took his arm and asked if he was okay. And then he told me something very disturbing. He said our friend Collie had been assaulted last night and no one was supposed to know this, but of course on a ship, everyone knows everything at once. I asked him why he was in

Mr. Hensler's office and he said, "Don't ask, my friend, don't make my mistakes" and then he started to cry! I tried to offer comfort but he pushed me away and ran off.

This is not like Jo Jo. He is always so cheerful. And then later I saw him again coming out of the Talbotts' suite! This is most unusual, I am the butler for them and Jo Jo works on a different deck. He did not see me and I did not try to stop him.

Well, maybe it is just my active imagination as you always say, but I am having very strange feelings about this voyage. I think I am pleasing the Talbotts and their guests, though they do not say anything to me. I am finding the Countess to be a kind woman and I am even liking her little dog. I think she is just very lonely and this dog is to her what our babies are to us.

Mrs. Worth has been quite ill from allergies and the others have been out most of the day, but now everyone will be back and there is much to do to prepare for cocktail hour and refresh their rooms and re-stock. It is the young people though, the grandson of the Countess and the daughter of the Talbotts who are the most difficult to please, but I am getting better with them.

So, now we are moving into the second phase. The passengers always start to relax a little after the first day and it becomes a bit less frantic.

I would like to offer comfort to Collie, but since we are not supposed to know, I do not know what to do. I only pray it was not someone in the crew! So this is the mystery of this afternoon. It makes me miss you and the family even more but I will try to "be cool" as Jo Jo said.

One thing that happened that will make you laugh. They have quite an amazing laundry on this ship. It is a real Chinese laundry run entirely by Chinese people from Taiwan. You would be impressed. They clean 8 to 9,000 sheets every day and 12–15,000 table clothes and napkins, this is just a part of what they must do. It is very hot down there and they work very long hours and Miss Twinkle came to me this morning, very angry because a baseball cap which she loves had gotten a stain, which looked to me like lipstick, but of course I did not say this, and she demanded it go to the *laundry and be brought back within the hour so she could wear it to the beach.*

Well, this was most difficult to ask of the laundry and I told her I would take it down personally and do my best, but they were always very busy and it might take longer. This was not acceptable to her, so I ran all the way down and told the story to the laundry manager, who does not speak English very well and she laughed at me, until I told her that the father of the passenger was the owner of the ship and then she took it and brought it back in 10 minutes and it looked like a brand new hat to my eyes and then I ran all the way back up feeling quite proud. But Miss Twinkle threw it down on the floor and screamed at me, "You call this clean? I want it to look white as snow. Take it back! This is my favorite cap and I spent $100 to have it cleaned in New York, so I know what it can look like."

Well I did something very crazy, Maria, I went out and then I just waited for ten minutes, because I thought she was just doing it to push me about and I had to even chuckle because I don't think the hat cost more than $20, so why did she not just go out and buy many more white caps! So then I ran back, huffing and puffing and told her they had put their boss on the job and she took it and smiled and said, "Now, that's better." So, I am not being such a chicken as I was. I'm starting to understand a little more.

Your loving husband, Elonzito

⌒

CLARISSA AND LEAH WORTH, red hair blowing gently in the late afternoon breeze, strode around the huge, empty running track.

"Issa, this is such a good idea. I never would have come up here. It feels so great to move! This is much better than the fitness center. It's too crowded, and I just can't make myself climb onto those machines and my hips are showing it."

"Mom, you look great. I came up here yesterday and there were a few people, but hardly any."

"Look at the sky, how clear it is and what a beautiful shade of blue!"

"Momma, look at two o'clock! I think it's a frigate bird. Ian told me the most fascinating thing about them. They have forty-inch wing spans and during migration they can fly for 30 days without landing! They have to because their wings are so big that if they drop down into the ocean to rest and their wings get wet, they drown because the wings become too heavy for them to fly. And they can sleep in the air by slowing down parts of their bodies, heart rate, respiration, kidney function — they sort of glide for long periods. Isn't that cool?"

"Incredible. I had no idea. But then, I'm always watching Lifetime for Women while your father's watching the Discovery channel, so what I know about nature you could put in my pocket."

"I love stuff like that. I'm thinking more and more of switching to Marine Biology even if I lose some credits."

"Well then do it! Choose something you love because knowing what you love is a gift."

"I know. I'm lucky. So many of my friends have no clue. I think that's why Andre and I are so close. We both love science and nature and we know we want to spend our lives doing it."

Leah slowed down and sighed, "Can't keep your pace honey, your legs are much longer and I'm still a little woozy."

"Oh, sorry, Momma, I get carried away once I start moving."

Leah leaned over and kissed her cheek. "That's a 'connahora' kiss. You're like your father, you both have that passion for learning and ideas and you're never bored or unsure. It's a blessing Issa. I envy you both."

"Why? It's not like a big deal, you have things like that, too."

"No, I don't. I didn't ever really think much about it when I was your age. I fell madly in love with your father and all I wanted was to marry him and help him become a doctor. Remember I never even went to college."

"But you worked to help put him through medical school. You modeled and did commercials and you worked at Bullocks Wilshire when it was the fanciest Department store in L.A. You have lots of talents and things you love to do."

"Well, you're so sweet to say so, but it never seemed very important. It certainly wasn't a calling or anything. What I really wanted was to have lots of babies and stay home cooking and sewing little outfits for all my adorable children so . . ."

Now it was Clarissa's turn to slow down. "I never knew that! I always thought you guys didn't really want any kids and that's why it took so long to have me. I thought you were just too in love to want an intruder."

"Oh, Issa no! I couldn't hold the babies. I had several miscarriages and then they told me to stop trying or I could end up having a hysterectomy and then several years later, my miracle happened."

"I never knew this! How weird is that? We're so close and talk about everything and I never knew this."

"Well, you're a woman now, so there are probably lots of things that weren't important or appropriate to talk about, that will start coming up from now on."

"I like that idea, like meeting Rory Riley last night after hearing about her forever. That was really wild."

"I haven't stopped thinking about it! I was going to call her first thing this morning, but instead I was in the clinic getting shot up with drugs."

"She's really terrific Mom. She hugged me and said she knew I was a great kid just by watching me at the party and then, she was really funny; she wanted to get out of there—it was obvious she was hating it and she asked me if the Talbotts were the kind of people who would freak out if she didn't say good-bye or if she could send a note and I said that would be okay. And she was *so* relieved. She practically flew out the door."

"Leah laughed. "That's Rory. She was like that in high school. She hated all command performance kinds of things and she hated big parties. Did you happen to see her today?"

"Nope. I think she was going to rehearsal. I mean she's here working, she's not a guest. But I even talked to her about seeing her back in New York."

"Really? Should I be jealous?"

"Mom, don't be ridiculous! It's nice to have mentors. She seems really wise about life and I just thought it might be a great experience. Her life is so different than ours."

"Well, that's certainly true. Don't be surprised or disappointed if she doesn't follow through. She certainly vanished from my life without a trace."

"I totally spaced that Mom! It must have really hurt a lot to have a best friend just abandon you. You're such a giving person and a good friend."

"It did, for a long time. But I forgave her and I do understand. She'd lost everyone and I think I probably was too much for her then and I always thought she had a crush on your father, so that didn't help."

"No way! You never told me that part."

"Woman's intuition."

"The Countess said something really smart on the beach today about intuition, or sort of about it. Ian and Twinkle were making fun of people from the bus tour walking by with the Cruise Director, Mr. Doolittle and the Countess and he were kind of flirting with one another and he was telling her about some passenger who was driving everyone on the bus crazy, being really demanding and rude and she said, 'What I have found in my long and sordid life is, if everyone thinks someone is a crumbag, then it's probably true, however, if *everyone* thinks someone is wonderful, they're also probably a crumbag.'

"So I asked her how she figured that out about someone, if they really seemed nice and she said, 'wonderful people are never nice, they're real, and you just get better at seeing through, but you have to live longer.'

"She's quite a character, isn't she. And Ian certainly is brilliant."

"Yes, he is but," Clarissa stopped and walked over to the railing and took a long deep breath. The wind dried the perspiration on her cheeks and caressed her fear. She loved the wind.

Leah came over and put her arm around her daughter. "What is it, honey?"

"Momma, I've got to talk to you about something. About Ian and Twinkle."

"Of course. Let's go sit down and have some tea. I thought something was wrong. I could see it in your eyes."

"Mom, I'm wearing sunglasses."

"I can see it, anyway. Let's go."

"Mom, I don't want to sit and have tea or anything, someone might come by; this is really hard to tell you, but I have to say it, the longer I wait the weirder I feel, like I'm losing connection with you and Daddy. I can't stand to feel so isolated, so I just want to say it right here and now. I can't be friends with Twinkle any more. I don't want to see her or Ian after we leave the cruise.

"They're horrible, Mom, really mean and they make me feel terrible. I'm not myself when I'm with them, I mean I don't like myself and I feel so uncomfortable, uneasy and fake and angry and I'm not like that! I mean not usually. I know you guys are really close to the Talbotts right now and I know Daddy is trying to put a deal together with him and I don't want to do anything to mess that up, but I really have to get away from her. I'm not having a good time at all. I wish I'd never come."

She thought her mother would put her arms around her and wipe her tears and hold her and comfort her and tell her it was all okay and she felt the same way. That is what she was used to, that is what her mother always did when she was upset—but she didn't. She just stood there looking out at the horizon and sort of shaking her head which scared her. She felt worse, not relieved as she usually did when she blurted something out to her mother or her father and they patted it away.

"Mom! Say something. Why are you being like this?"

Leah leaned into the railing and closed her eyes, letting the wind whip her hair back.

"Mom!" Please, what are you doing?"

"I don't know what to say, Clarissa. I'm speechless."

"So, now I'm 'Clarissa', now you're mad at me? Like you don't know how mean and spoiled they are? Like you didn't raise me to not be like that?"

"She's been your friend since you were kids and friends tolerate one another's frailties. That's called loyalty. Of course I know Twinkle can be hard going, but I do think your friendship means the world to her and this would be a deeply upsetting thing for her and her family. I just think you may be overreacting and maybe you should take some time and once the cruise is over, you can discreetly make some space, but ending the friendship seems a little, well, emotional, honey. A good friend is a rare thing."

"Mom! You think I don't know that? Do you even have any idea how I've struggled with this? She's *not* a good friend, Mom. She just uses me for her needs. You can't not know this! Why aren't you supporting me? I can't believe you don't know me well enough to know I'd never do something like this easily.

"Twinkle has dozens of friends like me. I don't have a click or a group like she does, it's a much bigger loss for me, but she makes me sick. Literally sick and I can't go on pretending. It's a betrayal of myself. How can you not want what's best for me?"

"Of course I want what's best for you! Of course I don't want you to have a relationship that makes you unhappy. All I'm saying is, you have so much history, you should take more time, because this is a huge decision and . . ."

"And, maybe it's because your best friend abandoned you and you never got over it or maybe, it's because Twinkles' parents are billionaires and you and Daddy need their money and their contacts so you want to use me for your own purposes and you don't want to know if something is really not okay, so *you* won't have to deal with it and you're selling me out so the Talbotts will fund Daddy's project!"

Her mother's hand flew across her cheek, that soft rose-smelling hand that had caressed her just an hour ago, that same hand that represented everything loving and safe in her world. This couldn't be happening. It wasn't possible. Her mother had never, ever, ever hit her before!

She stumbled backward and so did her mother. They faced one another, staggered by the words and the act, like two frigate birds who had fallen into the sea and lay stunned, useless wings growing heavy and immovable, confused and unable to re-gain their momentum.

"Oh God, Issa, I'm so sorry. I didn't mean to, it, what you said was so, soo . . ."

"True? So true. Look at us, Momma. That's what Twinkle and her family have done. That's the price."

She turned and ran, no longer striding forward in healthy sea-air-sprayed hopefulness, but running away from something unbearable, running away from the person she had always run toward, her cheek stinging from the blow, still inhaling the smell of her mother's hand.

ᴄᴍᴄ

"CLARIE?" Can I come in?"

"Sure." Clarissa rolled over onto her back. Her father had found her. He always found her—the man in the family, the referee, the unemotional, male figure, the one who provided her and her mother with balance and logic and perspective. She had hoped he would come. He would fix it, fix the unbearable break, bring her and her mother back from this terrible place.

He was always so steady, so sure of himself, not hormonal like them. "Their rock," her mother called him. He closed the door behind him and walked toward her, the smell of him, lemony and cool and his presence, overfilling the small space. She did not want to look at him.

He sat down on her bed and waited for her. She loved that about him, the way he could just be silent and wait for her when she was in turmoil, the way he didn't have to storm into anything and fill the space with talk.

It was like what she imagined a shrink would do, and he often seemed to her to be that way, even though it wasn't his field. Maybe all good doctors learn how to wait like that, check out the situation and listen before they start pronouncing. She tried to do the same thing, but she wasn't so good at it, or maybe things would have turned out differently with her Mom.

"Daddy, I messed up. We had a horrible fight. She hit me. I don't know what to do."

"Well, your mother's in her room feeling probably as terrible as you're feeling, so let's see if I can broker a truce."

"Daddy, it isn't funny. It was really awful. Did she tell you what happened?"

"She did. Would you like my opinion?"

"I don't know. I'm still really angry and hurt and confused. I don't want to be ganged up on."

She lifted her head, feeling slightly defiant and looked at him. He was so handsome, not like any of the other fathers she'd ever seen. He looked like a movie star, even handsomer, at least to her. She couldn't even imagine him ever growing old or being ordinary in any way. When he walked into a room, everyone looked at him, even more than her Mom.

"I wouldn't do that, baby. But if it's any comfort, I agree with you and I do think your mother does too; in her own way, she was trying to protect you, give you some balance and I think she's been so worried about me and our finances that she was trying to steady you and it backfired.

"We try not to burden you, but I think we've made a mistake. You're a woman now and we're a family."

Clarissa sat up straighter, the seriousness of his tone and the slight shifting of adult responsibility onto her shoulders, sharpening her attention. Something was changing here, something she had never anticipated.

"Is something wrong. Are we in trouble?"

Her father slouched forward slightly and took a deep breath. She had never seen him do either thing before. He was always pretty vain about having been a star athlete and he always held himself as if he still was.

"Look, Clarie, this is tricky. What I just said, about making a mistake by over-protecting you, I think we have, but I can't march in here and bang your brain into 'now you're an adult so deal with it' mode. Let me talk for a few minutes and then, you can ask me any questions you want to."

"Okay," she said solemnly, her heart beating faster, trying to look worthy of his confidence but not at all sure she wanted to hear any of it, wishing fiercely that she could turn the clock back and she was lying on her mother's warm, comfy bed, dozing and waiting for their walk.

"Clarie, You know if someone puts you on a pedestal, the problem is there's only one way to go. You and your mother have put me on one and I let you. I loved being revered by my 'girls', but the truth is, I'm not who you want me to be. I'm a failure, honey. Great ideas, lots of charm, and I'm a hard worker, but I've pretty much blown my life, not much to show for it or we wouldn't be here going through this right now. . . ."

"Daddy, no! That's not true. You're a genius and you've taken such good care of us, we have a wonderful life!"

"Well, that's nice to hear, but it's come at a big price Clarie and your mother, well, she's the kind of woman who should have had better. She loved me and she's never complained, but money has always eluded me and since you went away to grad school, a lot of the borrowing and over-spending finally caught up with me.

"I'm not like you and your mother, I'm not so pure and idealistic. I'm a flat out opportunist and I've justified it by rationalizing my motives, the old 'end justifies the means' routine, but I've done some things I'm not proud of and hob-nobbing around with the Talbotts is one of them."

"But, Daddy, that's just the cost of living in the world. All successful people have to do stuff like that even missionaries and people who do legal aide, everyone. . . ."

"Honey, don't stick up for me, just listen to me. I'm okay with this, I'm not asking for sympathy, I'm just trying to level with you and give you credit for being a very smart and together young woman."

"Your daughter. You raised me."

"I'm a doctor, remember? Part us, part a whole lot of DNA. Anyway, the point is, Teddy Talbott came into our lives in the nick of time and by the end of this cruise we will actually sign an agreement with him and two of his companies, his pharmaceutical division and his cruise line to license two of my patents that will change our future and finally give us some security and we should be able to make sure you never have to go through the sleepless nights and knots in the stomach we've gone through.

"I think your mother just panicked, thought you might run downstairs and confront Twinkle or whatever, certainly not the way you behave, but it's been pretty rough on her. I'm not minimizing how hurt you were or the bad choice she made, but what you said was pretty hurtful, even if it was at least partly, true.

"We would never be here if you and Twinkle hadn't been best friends, that's a fact. And I have used that to ingratiate myself and your mother and I have spent far more time with them than we would have chosen to and we're neither of us proud of that, but that's the truth. It's a great big carrot, Clarie. A Bugs Bunny caliber treat. Let's hope it isn't attached to a stick."

"I had no idea things were that grim, Daddy. I've been so involved with my own stuff, I've been very selfish."

"No, you've been a 23 year old in a big tough world and if the fault for it lies anywhere, it's with us, treating you like a kid and shutting you out.

"So, now comes the end of the mea culpa. The truth I owe you is, I can't stand Twinkle Talbott or her little punk pal Ian. I worry about you every time you're with them and I've felt that way about Twinkle since you first brought her home when you were fifth graders or whatever the hell you were. She's bad news and you're making the right decision.

"But I gotta tell you, baby, she's a tricky one, she'll make trouble and she'll play with your head. She's not the kind of girl who lets go of anything until she's through with it. She rejects, she doesn't get dumped. If you can get through the next five days and I can pull this off, I promise you, your mother and I will plan a strategy and 'psyche her out' as your friend Andre would say. Can you hang on until then?"

"Oh, Daddy, I can wait forever now! How could you have never told me this? All those years. It would have helped if I'd known how you felt."

"Yeah, well hindsight is grand. If she'd pulled you into harm's way, drugs or anything, I would have. I guess your mother and I, well, she opened up a pretty seductive world to you and I think we kind of voyeured through it. See why pedestals are tricky? Also, you worshipped her and we didn't want to be too controlling about your friends. So, we kept our mouths shut. We trusted you to use good judgment."

"Oh, boy, Daddy, now who's being naïve! I haven't been such an angel and I've been pretty close to some really depraved stuff."

"Jesus. Clarie. We really let you down."

"No, no. I didn't do any of it! I mean a little drug stuff, but everyone does that. No, I'm just saying, now that I'm not defending her anymore, she was always trying to get me to do more. I think she hated me for being a goodie-goodie, she wanted me to be like her but she also kind of liked that I wasn't, I think it made her feel safer. Good old Clarissa always there to hold her head or dry her tears and drive her home. Sort of like a mini mother. Because it was so impossible to bond with her own mother."

"Super glue couldn't bond with her mother."

"Oh, Daddy, you're too funny. I love you so much."

She put her arms around her father's lemony neck, feeling the softness of his hair and the strongness of his shoulders, sinking against him like a little girl, just once more, in between her new role as a responsible adult daughter, the need for the other, the Daddy's Darling, the little princess, the protected and adored, conflicting needs, fighting for position.

"I love you, too, baby." He held her for a moment and then she felt him shift, stiffen and move her back. . . . He faced her, holding onto her arms, but holding her away, eye to eye, father to daughter but without the comfort.

"One more thing, Clarie. I want you to know, that whatever happens in our lives now because of this deal or anything else, that my love for you will never change. Never, forever. Never doubt it and call it up to get you through any tough times.

"Life doesn't always give us what we want or expect, things change, people change, but the love we have for one another will never change."

Her heart was beating fast again and tears splashed down her face. "Daddy, you're scaring me. You're not sick are you? Is Mom sick? Is there something else?"

"No, no. I guess, I'm on edge about what's at stake and when we get off the ship, your life moves forward and ours does too, but once a kid leaves home, well, it's a whole new play-off. So, I wanted to address it."

"Okay. I think I understand. I haven't been around much this year. And I know we all have to let go, I guess. . . . It's so hard to know what that means. So, what do we do now?"

Her father smiled his movie star smile and ruffled her hair, the way he always did when he was going to tease her out of a mood.

"Now, I'm going to be the quarterback. The Talbotts have a guest coming up, some fancy novelist from Boston who's giving a talk this week and Ian is probably going to give him a hard time. Anyway, cocktails are being served. Your mother is attempting to de-swell her eyes and I suggest you do the same and let's do our best to do what we do so well, be wonderful guests and have as pleasant an evening as we can. You and your mother can sort out the rest, later."

"I'm not upset anymore. I see what happened. Will you tell her that I'm sorry?"

"Yep. And for the record, I'm telling you that she's sorry and I think something good came out of it, so let's move forward."

"I won't let you down, Daddy. I promise. I never would have acted out all over the Talbotts, anyway. No way would I ever do that! I just wanted to tell Mom how I was feeling. But I guess I was too wobbly and defensive. I'm fine now. I can handle it."

"That's my girl. Class and character, like your mother."

"No way, she's perfect. I don't even want to try and live up to that."

Walter Worth stood up and under his smile, Clarissa thought she saw something angry in his eyes, maybe it was just the way the light hit or maybe it was because she didn't have her glasses on, but it was not a look she had ever seen before.

"Clarie, no one is perfect and nothing is ever what it seems."

✐

ELONZITO MOVED QUICKLY back and forth between the small kitchen in the Talbotts' suite and the living room delivering drinks and bringing the hors d'oeuvres while trying to remain as invisible as possible. He had asked Jo Jo to help, thinking this might give him an opportunity to uncover the cause of his friend's distress, but the Talbotts had changed the time and Jo Jo wasn't due for another twenty minutes.

He found the ritual of inviting people to have cocktails and then not eating with them, quite unusual. It seemed to be something only wealthy people did.

The guests always seemed to understand and no one ever seemed slighted at the abruptness with which the host would announce that it was time to leave. In fact, most of the guests sensed this and made their departure before the host had to say a word, but the entire event made him feel nervous and slightly guilty, as if he were in some way responsible for the abrupt ending of the hospitality. In his family, it would have been a source of shame. But everyone at these occasions seemed very pleased to be invited at all.

He placed the tray of salmon and caviar canapés on the table and handed Miss Twinkle her Dirty Martini, which he had now perfected. Cosmo for the Countess. Champagne for Miss Clarissa, Merlot for Dr. Worth, Chardonnay for Mrs. Worth, Gin and Tonic for Mr. Talbott. Dry Gin Martini for Mrs. Talbott. Single malt scotch for Mr. Ian. It was difficult for him to concentrate at parties, because he was curious and found himself listening in when he should not be thinking of anything but his duties.

Jo Jo waved to him from the kitchen doorway and he felt for a moment as if he might cry with relief.

He motioned to Jo Jo and quickly moved back toward the kitchen. "Jo Jo, they have begun early. I've gotten the first drinks for the family, but not the guests. I need two glasses of champagne, one bourbon and water and a, a, oh, my mind! . . . Wait, the man in the black leather jacket with the beard, Oh . . . a, vodka martini with a twist, on the rocks. And please take the quiche out of the oven and cut it into slices. I'll be right back, I have to get the door."

"No problemo." Jo Jo flashed his big white smile, which confused

Elonzito and made him doubt himself. Had he been wrong? Was it just his overactive imagination again? He crossed the marble entry to the door.

Mr. Hensler his boss and Mr. Doolittle stood together, looking slightly uncomfortable with one another. They seemed relieved to be released from the awkwardness of waiting on the other side. They were impressive men, he thought. Both so tall and beautifully dressed and perfectly mannered.

"Good evening, Elonzito, you're looking very fit. I guess your new job is keeping you on your toes. It looks like better exercise than I've been getting." Mr. Doolittle patted his mid-section and smiled at him, which seemed to displease Mr. Hensler who merely nodded and moved past him into the room, saving his smile for the owners and their friends.

He had not had time to take their drink requests, which meant that he would now have to re-enter the main room and try to do this without interrupting Mr. Ian who had begun what sounded like a long discourse on literature directed at the man in the leather jacket, who had gotten his vodka martini with a twist on the rocks from Jo Jo and was looking at Mr. Ian over the rim of his glass with what Elonzito thought was contempt—but if he had been wrong about Jo Jo, maybe he was wrong about all of these looks and behaviors.

He tiptoed around behind Mr. Hensler and whispered into his ear and Mr. Hensler raised his hand as if to swat him back and snapped his request, "Kir Royal." Mr. Derrick he knew would have brandy and soda so he could retreat without further intrusion, even though he was fascinated by Mr. Ian. This very young man was so sure of himself, so confident and smart that he could command the entire room and, from the way it sounded, insult the guest, a famous writer of some sort who was older, though still young, but who had certainly accomplished far more in his life than Mr. Ian. He tried to overhear, while he helped Jo Jo arrange the hot hors d'oeuvres for passing.

"All set," Jo Jo finished and Elonzito picked up the tray and the little napkins with the ship's logo and the Talbotts' personal initials on them and returned to the party, checking drinks and passing the delectables, almost ghostlike in his discretion—an invisible man, a silent witness to all manner of revelation—like a pet, like Tou Tou on the Countess's lap, no one noticed or thought of either of them as observers of what was underneath the social costumes, but they were.

"Of course I read your book, when the *Times* and the *Review of Books* carries on, I always take the bait. I know you were short-listed for the PEN/Faulkner and the National; two of my classmates at Oxford took your seminar at Iowa. But I'm not referring to your work specifically; I'm talking about an entire œuvre of fiction. No offense to you, Mr. Wortowsky, but I find this post-modern fiction well, ridiculous.

"I'm far in the minority, in fact, I may be alone in my view, certainly all the critics applaud the kind of work you and your peers do. Actually I did part of my dissertation about it, a satire on what was required to write literary fiction in the current climate and I published it in England, where, the viciousness of the literary world makes New York look meek."

"Really? Well, now, I'm curious Mr. Von Essen."

"Ian, you're not going to give your poor old Grannie palpitations, now, are you?"

"Thanks for your concern, Countess, but I grew up in Brooklyn. I enjoy a good bout. Excuse me waiter, may I have another one of these, please?"

"It's not a serious piece, just a folly—my faux rules for creating a literary sensation, meaning a work that is gushed over by the right critics and leads to invitations to participate in prestigious writer's conclaves, PEN events and the receiving of nominations for coveted awards."

"I could have used this ten years ago. Okay, sock it to me."

"First rule: No plot. Nothing can really happen. Things can almost happen. Someone can seem to be missing, or suffering from a horrible disease, or committing murder, but in the end, they are not.

"Two. No imagination. The story such as it is must be based at least loosely on the writer's own life and experience.

"Three. The characters cannot develop nor radically change during the course of the narrative. They also must not be physically too unusual or memorable.

"Four. If the protagonist (the narrative is usually in the first person anyway) but if it's a female, the 'voice' should have a sort of waifish, innocent but wry, 'New to the Planet quality'. Never shrill, edgy or angry. If it's a male 'voice', he may be pugnacious, edgy and angry, but it must be restrained inside a sensitive, loner posturing.

"Five. The story should take place in either a small American suburb, town or slightly rural but not hickish locale or somewhere foreign and exotic where the main character is either visiting or living temporarily, but not permanently.

"Six. The tale must be peppered with a second language. French is highly preferable because most of the fancy critics, editors, etc. speak it and so they feel smart and in on the joke and recognize one of their own. If the language is German or (God Forbid, Japanese) while impressive, it could intimidate the powers that be, leading to jealousy, and or, insecurity, the hint of possibility that the writer might conceivably be more intellectual or worldly than the critic. Italian is also good, but not Spanish which is considered too common, what the dumb kids who flunked out of French took in high school.

"Seven. The work must be either very slim or voluminous. Anything in the middle smacks of commercial fiction, which means it was written with the reader in mind, who might want enough heft to justify the almost $30 dollar price tag, but still be packable in a carry-on, so anyone crass enough to think of 'bang for the buck' or to be unwilling to commit the rest of his year to thwacking through the book is unworthy of the experience.

"Eight. It must never have a discernable beginning, middle and never an obvious ending and lastly, if the author is either fourteen years old or the first generation born in America or England of foreign (preferably Indian or Arabic-speaking parents) you are almost guaranteed the short-list to the Booker Prize and a reading at the Ninety-Second Street Y."

Elonzito had made another entire round during Mr. Ian's speech, the guests were finishing their second and in the case of the author, the object of Mr. Ian's dialogue, their third drink. Miss Twinkle was fidgeting with her pearl necklace and sighing, while swinging her foot, the way his little daughter did when forced to sit still too long.

Miss Clarissa, who seemed unusually solemn was shaking her head and holding onto her mother's hand. Mrs. Worth seemed to be thinking about something else, smiling politely but not really listening.

Mr. and Mrs. Talbott looked as if their bodies would at any moment break in half from tension, the other guests were nodding politely, seeming slightly intimidated and bewildered by the subject and the break from drinks invitation protocol.

Dr. Worth seemed to be amused and disgusted simultaneously and the Countess had excused herself to put Tou Tou to bed or at least so she said.

Everyone seemed to be slightly holding their breath waiting to see the response of the author, Mr. Wortowsky and, Elonzito imagined, praying there would not be a scene, on their second night as the ship moved further into the journey with a soft caressing wind and everyone so nicely dressed and looking forward to a long evening of pleasure and relaxation.

Mr. Wortowsky, who looked confident and a bit vain, drained his drink and set the glass down beside him, a little too quickly or so Elonzito thought. His hand seemed tense but he was laughing. This laughter was a great relief to Elonzito and to the entire assembly, everyone laughed then, especially Mr. Hensler, who seemed to find Mr. Ian captivating.

Mr. Wortowsky began to clap. This was a very good choice and Mrs. Talbott actually began breathing again. "Bravo! How old are you?"

"Twenty-three."

"Well, I sure as hell hope you choose something other than literary criticism as a career or me and my pals are toast. You got it, dude. A fresh point of view. Funny, too. This is what makes the juices flow, you know. Young people who aren't afraid to express their opinions. Obviously I don't agree with you, but I like your malice, kid."

Elonzito dared a look at Mr. Ian, his mouth was smiling but his eyes looked filled with rage, as if he wanted to slash at the author, who had somehow in his compliments, demeaned and dismissed him without saying anything but "kid" that could be taken the wrong way. His eyes were filled with hate.

Elonzito was moving toward Mr. Ian to take his empty glass but his instinct told him to go the other way around. He was afraid of the look in his eyes. And as if Mrs. Talbott could read his mind or had seen the look too, she stood up.

"Oh my goodness, everyone, we've forgotten the time! We promised Miss Frampton, we'd see her early show. Come along Ian, get your grandmother. We're late."

Everyone stood up abruptly and the author, Mr. Wortowsky seemed to find this quite amusing and he smiled at Mr. Ian as if, Elonzito thought, to show he had not been humiliated which seemed to be what Mr. Ian had hoped to accomplish. Miss Clarissa went over to the author and said kind things about his book and everyone very quickly departed.

Elonzito stood quietly in the remains of the gathering. It was always a little sad after people left, so much anticipation and effort to prepare, the room filling with lively, sweet-smelling handsome people looking forward to the event and then, it was so quickly over, so much beautiful food was uneaten, the ice melting, the tables filled with crumbs and fingerprints and the silence, the emptiness. He sighed, not moving for a moment—feeling discarded, like the canapés and the cocktail peanuts and went the kitchen to find Jo Jo and pick up his tray.

As he passed the Countess's door Elonzito heard voices and he realized that she and Mr. Ian hadn't left with the others. He lingered, feeling guilty to be eavesdropping, but wanting to hear what the Countess was saying to her grandson.

"Mr. Doolittle is waiting for me and I want you to take Tou Tou up on deck to do his business and let him have a breath of air. I cannot ask Elonzito to do one more thing, he's been running non-stop."

"The damn little runt is your responsibility. I invited some friends I know from the Hamptons to meet me at the show. Doolittle's an employee, he can wait; get that other little man who's helping to do it. If you insist on dragging that creature everywhere, it isn't fair to expect me to enable you. He's not a child, Gramms, or a husband, no matter how fervently you might wish, otherwise."

"Now you listen here, Ian, grandson or not, after all I've done for you, don't you dare speak to me like that! I can snap my fingers and your trust stops flowing faster than Odessa crude. Now, do it and make sure he's diapered and put to bed properly. I may be late."

"Oh, alright. I apologize for being prickly. No need to make idle threats, my Countess."

"Nothing idle about it, Ian. I should have made it years ago. I'm sick of your attitude. I left the room rather than hear you pounce on that man. If he gotcha, good! Even you can't win 'em all. You're a bully, Ian. I love you to death, but I see who you are. When this trip is over, we're going to have a talk. Here's the leash."

The door opened and Elonzito jumped back, pretending to occupy himself tidying up the table beside the door. The Countess marched out, her head high and right behind her came Mr. Ian with little Tou Tou scampering to keep up and looking none too happy about his reluctant companion. His eyes following his owner all the way to the door, the way a child's would.

Elonzito felt sorry for the funny little doggie, and he almost offered to take over, but he knew that would rob the Countess of her moment of maternal triumph.

He ran to get his tray, thinking of what he would write his wife and whether she could even imagine such a conversation with one's grandmother. Jo Jo was carefully cleaning the table. Now they would be able to talk. It would mean he would not have a break until bedtime, but he wouldn't rest anyway without trying to help his friend.

~

"WHY THIS FEELING, why this glow... there she was, not curled up in her cabin with a DVD and a burger, no... no... she was sitting in a theatre next to a man she barely knew, a man she was now totally mad for, "Crazy about you, I know I'm crazy"... a song Flora was singing.

The show was so sucko. How many ways can they destroy the greatest songs ever written. Who'd done these arrangements? Cole Porter to disco rhythm? He was next to her, holding her hand, dropping down into her nomad life, nomad, no man mad, no nothing life like a tiny meteor blistering her defenses.

Okay Rory, now, settle down, look around, enjoy the moment... Shit! There's Leah, and Walter and their daughter and the Egret couple she'd forgotten to send a note. Taylors? No Talbott, Talbotts, like the dress store for dumpy housewives in New England. There's Doolittle with that crazy old chick with the rat on her chest and the turban. Hmm, maybe she was feelin' the glow herself, lookin' good, no rat, no turban.... "Time After Time, I tell myself that I'm, so lucky to be loving you...." Flora was looking the love look, too, what was this? An epidemic? Maybe her fella was here.

Couldn't be all the usual suspects, a passenger maybe? Where would she have met him? Oh, Jesus Herschel, he's putting my hand to his lips!... can't be real... this whole day... the entire last night... waking up beside A MAN. How long, not since Jesse, too pathetic, never thought it could... that I would feel... "There's a strange, exciting magic you do, Mr. Wonderful I...." Chorus boys on; Flora off . . . God this show was really looking tired, but maybe it was because she'd seen it too many times. Well, at least her stuff was holding up . . . The funny stuff. She wanted him to laugh, to like it, what could she do that compared to . . .

That talk of his! Eight a.m. She had gone to an 8 a.m. lecture of her own free will! His brain was . . . so fast, so smart, so out there. She should have taped it, taken notes, so she could remember . . . ask questions, but she was riveted, even her mind behaved, not wandering all around, listening, focusing, no idea a face could tell all that! Aborigines in the Jungles of New Guinea or axe murderers in solitary confinement or nice Long Island housewives like the woman next to her, Vera? Yes, all the expressions in the face can be read the same way. . . . Oh, Oh. . . . the story about the cop who didn't fire at the creep racing toward him with a gun because his instinct said he wouldn't shoot, the maniac's face told that!!!

And the way he spoke, with that touch of irony, that little private mirthful twinkly deal in his eyes and the sorrow, too, so much loss, and he liked her . . . this was not possibly happening.

Uh oh, Leah's trying to get my eye. They're going to want to have dinner or something. I'm being so rude. Don't wanna go there, no, not yet, but I've gotta do something. I'll ask him . . . what is it with you Rory? Can't say his name? Too intimate to say his actual name? Makes it too real? Say it, Rory, one, two, three. . . . Poe, (oy), Poe, I'll ask him if he wants to.

Don't think so, think he wants to be alone . . . uh, oh, oh, that means, S-E-X, probably. I'm so rusty I probably need a lube job to make the attempt. God, my stomach just knotted into a solid ball, terror, pure and simple. What if he can't or I freak or leak or there are unsavory smells or diseases disclosed at the last minute or . . . Stop, it Rory! Go back to room scanning. The photographer is snapping couples . . . aiming everywhere, coming this way. A couple, I'm sitting here, like part of a couple, an elbow holdee. . . .

She's snapping the Worths, don't want a picture up there in that gallery with everyone browsing around looking for their moment, posed in finery, posed over pork chops, posed in the nightclubs, all with that, smiling arm-around-your-lady-people-on-vacation-wanting-a-memory-look . . . leaning on tables cluttered with dining debris or men standing slightly up on heels, look taller, women with best angles, look like they're arriving at a premiere . . .

The Captain's dinner . . . hate the whole deal . . . posing . . . talk about Face Reading! Talk about the mouth smiling but the eye muscles, what the hell were they called, occululus? How did he remember all that stuff? He's is stroking my palm and the Worths are looking . . . Leah's whispering to Walter . . . brings back memories! Walter you schmuck. . . . Oh no, Ricky Romano and that horrible siliconed wife of his are on. . . . Bad magic tricks . . . wish we could leave . . . such a nice hand, strong with fine golden hairs and perfectly shaped fingers stroking my fingers . . . that might be stroking other things later. . . . "Those fingers up my spine . . ." don't go there Rory. . . . Just be happy for a minute.

✐

LEAH WORTH ROLLED away from her husband and looked at the clock. 3:10 a.m. and she was wide-awake. She turned back and looked at her husband sleeping so peacefully beside her. How did he do that, just fall asleep so quickly and solidly as if they hadn't a care in the world? His face looked so seamlessly serene, lying there he could have been 30. Unfair. She envied him so many things.

She sighed and turned over. *I slept too much today. I might as well give up.* She rolled onto her back, thoughts crisscrossing her mind like one of those old hand-cranked moviolas her grandfather had. What a day! Horrible from start to finish. Her allergy attack, the fight with Clarissa, that terrible drinks thing with Ian and that writer, having Rory avoid eye contact with her at that show. Tears poured down her face. Even Walter was acting strange. Almost disinterested in her, detached. Well he had enough on his mind but still, what a terrible day!

At least she and Clarissa had made up. So much to think about. The worst of it was, Issa was right on the money. Oh God, they had to talk about all of this! Well, maybe not, if the deal with Teddy went through. Would it be truly disgusting to sign the deal and then stop seeing them?

Almost unthinkable for them, not for Clarissa, she could withdraw, kids were kids. Certainly Sissy wouldn't give a damn, it was more than clear she just tolerated her and Clarissa, but Teddy adored Walter and Teddy wrote the checks and Sissy had a yen for him, she could tell. It would all be alright, things did work out for the best. She must be positive and stop this fretting.

A door slammed. Loud footsteps clicking across the marble entry. The kids coming home? *Please God.* The door had opened and closed several times since midnight. She'd heard Sissy walking around and she'd peeked out and that nurse from the clinic was following her to her room with her doctor's bag. Must be an injection for her back, but what was she doing there in the middle of the night?

Sissy had certainly been lively at dinner. Maybe she was all drugged up. It was always impossible for her to tell things like that. Walter would see it and Issa, "Mom, pa-leese she was totally loaded," she'd say about one of their friends, but she was usually oblivious unless someone was falling down or slurring or completely manic. She just didn't have their insights. Rory, was like that. She'd loved that about her. Another pang, anger this time. And she was hurt. Maybe in the morning she would call her and try to get together.

She sat up, straining to hear the voices. *Please let it be the kids.* They still didn't know who had attacked that poor woman and the girls had promised they would stay with Ian and come home reasonably early. She sighed, kids, nothing frightened them, well not that kind of thing.

She swung her legs over the side and tiptoed to the door to hear better. *Damn.* It was the Countess and Mr. Doolittle. How did someone her age keep such hours! She was always ready for bed by 10 even if she'd slept in.

Laughter, tipsy late night laughter. She crept back to the bed and crawled in beside her handsome, peaceful husband. *Maybe if I curl up next to him, I'll be able to relax.* She edged closer and put her arms around him. He was murmuring something in his sleep. A word, what was it? *Soon.* Soon?

Someone was screaming. She sat up again. Walter did not move. She shook him. "Walter, wake up!"

The Countess was shrieking, agonizing sounds piercing the quiet. Leah jumped out of bed, feeling slightly dizzy and grabbed for her robe. The awful day wasn't over yet.

✐

THE SHIP HEADED south, a glowing white leviathan, steady in the sea-light, sure of its course, not bothered or bumped by the complexity within. Night screams were not its nature; it was free to stay its course, follow the instructions implanted in its mechanized heart.

Not that it was immune, like its seemingly invincible forbearers *Titanic*, *Andrea Doria* and *Lusitania* who had left their rusting remains beneath the same oceans. Nothing was immune, despite the cleverly designed brochures touting the state-of-the-art-safety-features and cutting-edge technology. The ship and the sea accepted the truth, accepted the reality escaping their guests, and proceeded as usual transporting and allowing illusion to smudge reality for one week at a time.

LATITUDE

Your Daily At Sea Newspaper

Good Morning Dolphiners! Welcome to the luscious island of Antigua's historically charming town of St. John's. Even if you partied the night away in the Grotto or boogied to the Blues Brigade in the Pelican Lounge or just overindulged at the Midnight buffet, you won't want to miss one moment of the fun-and-sun excursions we have planned for you. Unless, you prefer to laze and linger in the Spa or attend any of the twenty events or lectures in our state of the art 500 seat Neptune Lecture Hall, or in-line skate, ice skate, swim, miniature golf, need we go on?

St. John's, for those of you who missed the indoctrination lecture given by our Cruise Director Derrick Doolittle in the Orientation hall or on your en suite T.V. last evening and every evening at 5:30, was discovered by Christopher Columbus on his second voyage to the New World, even though the island was not officially established for another 150 years. Today it is a popular tourist destination known for its balmy climate and 366 postcard perfect beaches!! Please check your activities schedule for the numerous shore excursions we have available on this legendary paradise!

Oh, and don't forget, sign-ups for the adult talent show are being held today at 4 p.m. in the Mother of Pearl Theater. This is your chance to strut your stuff and who knows . . . maybe a star will shine!

Now for today's special events. Wedding of the Day! This week we are thrilled to announce the *Palace of the Dolphins* all time Weddings record. . . . Twenty separate ceremonies will be held! Eat your heart out *Love Boat*, wherever you are!

Each day we will try to feature one of the couples. So Today's couple (see photo below) hails from San Diego, California. The lovely Tiffany (Summer Rain) Goldenburger will be wed to Stormy (Blueberry) Boronski at a high noon ceremony conducted by White Moon, a Native American of the Navajo tribe. Ms. Goldenburger is an animal rights activist and the owner of an Earth Friendly clothing boutique in La Jolla, California. Mr. Boronski is a professional surfer and lifeguard. Congratulations to the happy couple!

Today's Trivia Facts: Did you know that: The term "Booze Cruise" was coined during prohibition, when New Yorkers would board cruise ships and sail beyond New York waters where hooch could legally be served!

The acronym SOLAS, which you will find in various ship's documents stands for Safety of Life at Sea and is our commitment to you above all else.

The World's Largest Floating Slot Machine, is right here in our Conch Casino!

And for those who want it all: Don't miss our Grand Fine Art Auction where hundreds of Rare Masters will be sold at the lowest prices available. And bets are being taken for our Horse racing Daily Double. Race starts promptly at 1 p.m. Winners (or losers) can proceed to Jackpot Bingo where thousands of dollars can be won!

Also today for our Jewish passengers, the eminent rabbi and motivational speaker, Uri Dayan will be conducting a Passover Seder in the Pirate's Cove private dining room at sundown. Seating is limited, so please reserve now.

And Don't forget for you lounge potatoes, The Belly Flop Contest, main Pool at 2. Right after lunch! Ouch!

A further reminder about departures. Today is a short day. We leave promptly at 4:30 p. m. No exceptions. So, set your watches and have a blast!

THE COUNTESS VON ESSEN's naked thrusting body lay beside him moaning in ecstasy. More, give me more . . . she whispered, her large, loose, but remarkably well-preserved breasts flapping against his side. He reached over to stroke her mound, but something was in the way. Charlton Heston, his penis throbbing with lust, pushed into her, leaving Derrick to watch. "Hey, I'm not into this, Mr. Heston and besides, you're dead!"

Charlton ignored him and thrust harder and the Countess screamed, "I'm coming! Oh God!! I'm coming!" Derrick's feelings were hurt, he was sobbing. He tried to jump up and run away but the door was locked.

The screaming went on and he whirled around, trying to find something to cover himself, but Charlton was gone. The Countess was still screaming, her pendulous breasts flapping like gills. Her arm shot up pointing at the ceiling. "Save him! Save him!" A giant bat flew over his head, grazing his cheek. . . . Something was in the bat's mouth, something bleeding and barking! Tou Tou!! The puppy was yelping in fear. "Let Charlton save him, if you like him so much, you whore."

The screaming had turned to pounding. Derrick's heart? Was it him? The pounding grew louder. He sat up. *Holy Mary, what a dream. What now?* Someone was pounding on his door. He stumbled around in the darkened cabin. The clock said 6:30. *Two hours' sleep, he was done for.* His head felt like it was stuffed with ball bearings. He grabbed for the door, not even bothering to find a robe. *This better be good.*

Nurse Peggy dressed in her uniform and ready for war; her thin, lipless mouth, stretched wide in disaffect, pushed forward, without so much as a good morning, or sorry to wake you.

"What in hell's bells are you doing here? I just got to sleep."

"If I didn't sleep, why should your whining merit my sympathy? You weren't the only one dealing with that mess."

"Oh, my, touchy, touchy. At least you can rest if the clinic's quiet, I've got to organize the Talent Show and we've got everything from a paralyzed centenarian from Milwaukee who's going to sing the *Battle Hymn of the Republic* accompanied by her eighty year old son on the mouth organ, to a Drag Queen from San Francisco doing an original modern dance to *"I Am What I Am"* and Hensler's called an emergency staff meeting in his office and . . . oh never mind. I am whining. So what can I do for you this fine morning?"

"You've got to come back to the clinic and deal with the Countess. She won't leave and we've got to wrap the dog up and put him in the morgue and if she sees any of that she's going to lose it. You're the only one who can calm her down. I want you to help me get her back to her room and then I can give her a sedative."

"She seemed fine when I left her. The Worths were taking her back up."

"She went up and then twenty minutes later, there she was, hysterical and demanding to see her dog. She's down there now, holding the corpse in her arms and wailing away. Passengers are starting to come in and it's a very disturbing sight and you know how Hensler feels about anything that isn't upbeat on view for the guests."

Derrick sat down. "You don't happen to have your B-12 needle on you?"

Nurse Peggy reached into her pocket and pulled out a syringe. "Nothing for nothing."

He turned sideways while she jabbed the relief into his buttocks. "Thank you, my dear. Just let me jump in the shower. I'll be there in fifteen minutes. But I've only got an hour. Hensler wants me at 8 and I have to get my schedule together and have some caffeine first."

"I've got a pot on downstairs so hurry along. I can't have her running in and out of the morgue. But she won't listen to me. Just keeping the animal in there instead of burying him at sea is against the rules, but she's a guest of the Talbotts and Dr. Worth insisted. She wants to take the body home. I've never seen such carrying on. You'd think it was her husband."

Derrick laughed. "Oh, Nurse Peggy, you old spinster you. I guarantee that little poochie meant far more to her than any of her husbands, all of her friends and probably several of her children. Try to have some compassion. She came home feeling light as a goose feather, we were going to have a nightcap, but she wanted to check on little Tou Tou first. I settled down on the couch, and the next thing I know, bloodcurdling screams are coming from her room. It was like a horror movie version of *Night at the Opera*. Doors opening, people in nightclothes running everywhere, and the Countess racing back and forth with the pup in her arms."

"You don't have to tell me. I was sound asleep in the office lounge and then pandemonium. Never heard such a ruckus, not even when a human passenger croaks. A dead little mutt wearing a diaper! Such nonsense. Rich people. Just as bad as the Jews. Spoiled and demanding one and all. Except Mrs. Talbott, now there's a class act. Anyway, get yourself together and come deal with her. And you must make her understand that when I zip the dog up and put him in the freezer, that's it until we dock in Puerto Rico. Hensler or no Hensler. Got it?"

"Aye, Aye, Sir. I'll do my best."

Nurse Peggy replaced the syringe in her pocket, smoothed her uniform and went back to work.

✑

THE WAITING ROOM of Heinrich Hensler's office would probably rank equally to the engine room, the clinic surgery and the sewage container area as the crew's least favorite visitation sites. Not that anything in its décor was unpleasing, in fact there was usually a coffee carafe and a plate of pastries, though no crew member ever felt welcome to partake.

Pleasant music was piped in through the audio system and pictures of the grand old cruisers of the past, tastefully framed and captioned, gave the small space an intimate, nautical dignity.

But the anxiety attending a call to visit Mr. Hensler, was akin to a call from the IRS, Cold Case Files Squad or the Biopsy Result Lab. No one ever wanted to take it.

Flora Frampton had never been there before and this only increased her dread at what she was certain would be the axe dropping on her career. She had watched his face during her last night's show and while she was entertaining at the Talbotts' party and it had seemed to her, paranoia aside, that the word "stony" had been invented for the way he observed her performance.

If she wasn't so in love and in possession of an innately provocative nature, which found such obvious indifference a challenge, she would have been unnerved. Also, when Rory was on board she picked up a lot of her "Fuck You Fella," bravado, which helped.

The irony was, Rory said it but was a softie inside, and she was all Gothic Goo outside but she had that Scarlet thing in her guts. Tough all the way through, except for her fella. But still, she was scared. Passion and lust and love talk were one thing, but it didn't pay the bills and so far there was no mention of a future. She sighed and looked around for diversion.

The door opened and Monroe, the head of Spa services came out of Hensler's office looking as if he'd been sucker punched.

He sat down beside her and shrugged his pumped-up shoulders. "I should have slept the extra hour."

"Tell Momma, I might as well be prepared. Is he icy calm or cords standing out in the neck or cocky swagger?"

"Shhh, I'm convinced the office is bugged. Where's his secretary?"

"In the little girls' and I'm early, so what'd he do?'

"Me and my stupid ethics. Don't laugh, but I wanted to report sexual harassment by various passengers. The staff is really fed up and now that Collie's actually been attacked, I though it might be connected."

"Attacked? How? When?" Flora leaned toward him.

"Night before last she was pushed into her cabin, beaten to a pulp raped and sodomized."

"Oh, God, Oh my God! How did I not hear this?"

"This one really got buttoned up. But I wanted to see Hensler because she'd had a flasher and I've had a grinder already and both keep booking appointments and other masseuses are getting fed up, too."

"What do you mean? Flasher and grinder?"

"Occupational hazard. Well, the flashers, expose themselves to the female and sometimes the male therapists. You know, the lights are low and they're nicely covered with a sheet or supposed to be and you enter the room and start and then suddenly, the sheet is no longer covering and then depending on how big a prick the guy is, figuratively speaking, you deal with it."

"That's revolting."

"You have *no* idea. And most of the time they get a little persistent. It's very distressing and insulting to our profession, you can imagine."

"Graphically. What's a grinder?"

"I had one last night. Middle-aged woman, they're almost *always* middle-aged women, horny as hell and neglected by their husbands. Anyway, I was doing an aromatherapy massage on the wife and the husband was getting a facial in the *next* room and I'm getting my oils all blended and she starts grinding herself into the table and moaning; she's getting herself off and *loudly* and I'm thinking the husband's going to march in and deck me, so I'm trying to talk sense to her and she's pulling at my uniform and trying to grab my Johnson. "Oh, please ram me, baby, suck my vee vee. . . .""

"Her Vee Vee? No way. Vee Vee?'

"Vee Vee." It would be laughable except we could get sued or fired. You know the drill, The customer's always right. But no one on my staff is gonna put up with that crap or suck some withered old Vee Vee, not for anything, so after what happened to Collie, I thought I've gotta be strong and report it to Hensler and see if he can get the Head of Security to check it out and call a meeting of the Spa staff to address the issue and give us some support on how to handle this stuff."

"I had no clue. So what did Heir Hensler do?"

"Shhh, Flora, he could open that door. I should go, anyway, he'd freak if he saw me talking to you. He did zippo. He said the security chief is investigating what happened to Collie and he doesn't have time to get involved with the 'silly annoyances of the Spa staff'. It's my problem and I can hold a meeting, but no one is to offend a client no matter what."

"So I guess that rules out hot wax in the Vee Vees or Glycolic Acid peel on the Pee Pees."

"You're too much, but I may consider it, anyway."

"Where's Collie? I want to see her."

"They put her in a private cabin behind the kitchen. It says 'Out of Service' on the door. No one's supposed to know because they haven't caught the creep, yet."

"Poor Collie, she must be terrified, he'll come back. She needs protection. I'm going down there as soon as this is over."

"Please don't tell anyone I told you, especially not Hensler. You know he's been popping her and he's acting all distressed about this, so it's especially touchy. He's having a big security meeting again today."

"My southern lips are sealed. It's not the first time, ya know."

"I've heard rumors on every ship I've worked, but this is the first time it's someone I work with and it was really brutal. Gotta go. Good luck in there."

Flora looked at her watch and eyed the coffee pot. So what would he do to her if she had some? Especially if she was about to be fired anyway. Fuck it, as Rory would say. She helped herself and sat back down, more uneasy than ever.

What happened to people to make them turn into sons of bitches like Hensler? Why was it always the innocents, the givers like Collie that got the raw deals? Predators and prey, sometimes it seemed almost that simple. It wasn't though; it would be easier if it was.

She sipped the coffee, her heart beating faster, waiting now for the secretary to re-appear and her time to come.

Oh, Sweet Lord. She knew. She swallowed wrong and coughed, choking until tears sprung from her carefully made-up early morning eyes. *Hensler did it.*

Lorraine, the longsuffering assistant entered, followed by Derrick Doolittle and what seemed to be the entire entourage of the Talbotts' suite and the rabbi from the lecture series. Were they all together? Or was this just a typical 8 a.m. deal in the swine's pen?

"Ms. Frampton, Mr. Hensler will see you now. Sorry for the delay."

She stood up and realized her knees were shaking. Thirty years of work seemed about to end. "Wish me luck," she whispered to Derrick who looked the way she felt. She stood up, harnessing all her southern charm and vamp amour to face the beast.

Flora knocked on the door, regressing forty years—standing outside the principal's office at P.S. 146 in Savannah waiting to explain the circumstances that had led her to throw an entire cup full of grape juice into the face of Pepper Pruell, the class bully and her personal tormentor.

Actually, Flora thought, nothing much had changed. She still raged at injustice, at all imbalances of power, of needing to subserve in order to survive, which seemed to be the lot of most of the inhabitants of earth. Flora waited, the still closed door becoming a provocation, a symbol of everything she hated. *He's gonna let me sweat.*

If she hadn't had some talent and won the Miss Savannah contest and gone on to the finals of Miss Georgia, she would have been a union organizer or some sort of radical southern suffragette. Maybe she still could be.

The door swung open startling her. She had expected a terse, "Please enter," but not physical proximity. Flora moved back slightly, instinctively re-setting the boundary and the beast smiled, taking one step forward. An act Flora saw as arrogant and aggressive.

"Well, Miss Frampton, what a pleasure. Don't worry. I do not bite. Unless I'm asked to, that is. Please come in."

He stood still forcing Flora to squeeze by him into the room, as if entering an interrogation cell.

He stayed behind her, waiting, she imagined, for her to sit down, so he could tower over her. His presence was very disturbing, filled with a particular kind of male menace, a mocking sexuality usually reserved for the use of construction workers on female pedestrians. Flora sat and crossed her legs.

Hensler walked around her, reappearing behind his desk and lowering his tall, well-built form into his black leather chair, crossing his own legs. Everything he did seemed to her sly and taunting.

She smiled, softly dissembling while her solar plexus or whatever Collie called that part of her diaphragm, was coiling up into a tight hard lump of tension.

"So, Miss Frampton, a rare pleasure. I think this is the first time we have ever sat quietly across from one another. What a shame because you are a fascinating woman and our star attraction. Unfortunately, the demands of this job preclude such lovely diversions. Just now I have an enormous crisis with the beef supply. Thirty-six restaurants and bars and half the beef was not boarded! Such sloppiness! Most of the employees do not match your standard of excellence."

The compliments unnerved her. Whatever she had expected, it did not include flattery. Now she saw a bit of what Collie must see. He could be charming, well why the hell not, even Hitler was supposed to be Chuckie Charm himself when he needed something. Germany was still crawling with decomposing old dames who'd been totally enraptured with him. Was she really comparing Heinrich to Adolf! Why did she go so dark about this guy? Woman's intuition plus too many bad boys in her past, perhaps. *Hang on to yourself Flora; it's a trap.*

"Well, thank yew, Mr. Hensler, I do my best, but I must say I find my fellow crew to be professional across the board and considering how hard they work, such long hours with so many months away from home, I think for the most part they're heroic."

"Ah, yes. Well, it is a very different perspective that a co-worker has, so I must be the bad cop and look for the miscreants."

Flora's stomach was tying itself in a bow. "I guess that's why I sing and dance and leave management to managers, Mr. Hensler."

"Please, call me Henrich, and may I call you, Flora?"

The forced and synthetic intimacy request made her skin itch, as if consenting to such a seemingly small social act, the use of his first name, would be an enormous self-betrayal. He leaned back in his chair, smiling with perfect white teeth.

"Of course." Flora raised her long graceful fingers, flicking a stray hair from her forehead, the tingle of panic edging toward her, popping sweat on to her upper lip. *Yew are not going to have a hot flash here. Not a chance.* She remembered something she'd read. "The toe you step on today, may be connected to the ass you must kiss tomorrow." *Steady on, girl. Yew still need this job.*

"Good. Now we may talk as friends."

Uh oh, here it comes. Flora re-crossed her legs using stage presence to cover her fear.

"So, *Flora*, I appreciate your coming in at such an early hour. I know you are rehearsing a new show in addition to your evening performances, but we have had a distressing incident involving a member of the Spa staff, whom I believe is a personal acquaintance of yours and because of the delicate nature of the situation, I have decided to break official policy and take you into my confidence."

"Oh, my, it sounds serious."

Hensler sat forward, bringing his menace closer. "Well, I do not mean to alarm you, but it is rather serious. I am assuming that you are aware of my personal relationship with Miss O'Brian, we have become friends and so I am quite concerned about her attack."

"Attack? Good Lord! Is she alright?"

"Yes, I have been told by Dr. Padma that she is recovering nicely. I have not been down to see her myself, and I am rather pleased that you did not know, we are making an enormous effort to find the attacker, without upsetting the passengers. I'm sure you can understand. And, of course, with the owners on board, it is even more delicate."

"Oh, I see, that would explain the coffee klatch in your waiting room."

"I see you are no fool, Flora."

"Only for love, but everyone's a fool for something, if yew think about it."

"I do not spend time on such thoughts: men tend to focus on more immediate problems. He paused, and his smile grew wider, leaving his ice blue eyes stranded as if they were left over from someone else's face.

"Do you like Renoir, Flora?"

"Yes, all romantics like Renoir, especially southern ones."

"German nihilists also like Renoir. The women, mainly. I find his women violently erotic. Renoir said that he could only paint women who did not think."

Flora was trying to swallow, her throat felt as if all the moisture in her system had been sponged up. "Well, I guess I'd flunk the Renoir model competition."

"Yes. So, what do I do with a woman who thinks and who has a prominent position with many of the young women on the ship and is a friend of Miss O'Brian's?"

"Mr. Hensler, I'm from Georgia and I can go round and round like this with yew till the cows deliver the rest of your beef order themselves, but I know you're a busy boy and I'm a busy gal, so shall we fast forward this a tad? Are you saying yew want me to reassure the cast and my buddies in the Spa and go see Collie and reassure her and sort of play Mother Hen during this crisis?"

"Call me Henrich, please. And that is exactly what I would like. I apologize for the, how is it said here? 'Beating about the brush'?"

"Around the *bush*."

"Around the bush. It is quite an unpleasant subject to discuss with a female. I have written down the cabin number where we have taken Miss O'Brian, for her own safety and I would be most grateful if you would buzz me after you see her and let me know how she is recuperating. I have spoken to her several times, but with another woman, a friend, she may be more, relaxed."

"Well, I will go right away. No offense sir, but whatever is said between friends, I most certainly cannot repeat unless Collie wants me to."

The smile retreated, evenly and slowly. Flora stared, fascinated, watching his tide go out—everything under the water, now glistening and exposed. A flurry of un-Renoir thoughts flashed through her head. She imagined herself thrust into an old Nazi war movie, the terrified nightclub singer who caught the eye and then displeased the SS officer.

"Of course I admire your loyalty. It is a rare trait these days. I am just concerned for her well-being and it is a difficult subject to speak of with a gentleman."

"I don't even know what happened, but it would seem she should be talking to security and to the police."

"Mr. Rogers has, of course, interviewed her. But, we must be careful not to start a panic and as I'm sure you know, the laws of land are not easily enforceable at sea; it is a very cloudy area, and not your concern."

He seemed to have finished, clicking off like an expired parking meter, even the glint in his eyes dimmed. Flora sat forward not quite knowing what to do. She debated leaping up and running or seductively swaggering out, just like in the movies—shoulders squared, waiting for him to stop her or . . .

"So, if that's all, I'll be going now."

"Yes, yes, but there is one more small matter. He broke eye contact for the first time, rummaging around on his orderly desk, finding a folder. "I see that your contract is about to expire. My, my, you have been performing with Empire for quite a long time."

"Yes, I have." Flora was no longer swallowing or breathing.

"And you are happy with the new ship and the larger theater?"

"Extremely."

"Good. Very good. It is important that our cast feel comfortable and enthusiastic. When they are not, it shows in their performance."

"I think we are all more professional than that. The show comes first."

"Of course. But we are all victims of time and gravity."

Flora's stomach knot re-tied itself, making a bigger bow. *Careful, darlin, it's a "coon trap" not even covered by twigs.* "I don't know what yew mean, Mr. Hensler?"

"Nothing at all. I was simply making a philosophical observation. No need to continue. As I said, men are not good at such talk." Hensler suddenly stood up, starling her.

Do not jump up Flora, take your time and look him right in his beady blue eyes. She rose slowly, her knees shaking slightly, but always the pro, knowing this was just another kind of performance.

"Well, Flora, I've enjoyed our conversation and I look forward to hearing from you later."

"I'm sure Collie will want me to send her regards."

She turned, forcing herself to saunter and headed for the door, waiting for the bullet in the back or the dreaded exit line, "There's just one more thing." But the Beast was silent. The meter was empty.

She opened the door and moved quickly past the owners and their guests, out where she could breathe, sweat pouring over her, a fierce heat flash crackling across her skin like an explosion of rage. *He did it! That's why he called me in, to see if Collie'd told me. To let me know if I tell, I'm toast.* She pulled a tissue from her pocket and patted her face. Pleased, at least, that she never called him Heinrich.

"DERRICK, PLEASE sit down. I'm sorry to make you wait; as you can see, it's turning into a complicated morning."

"I would say so. I've seen everyone from Jo Jo and Flora Frampton to the Talbotts and it's only eight a.m. I was about ready to start an impromptu Jeopardy game just to keep them in good humor."

Derrick watched his boss's face to see if he was connecting, but the smile was so automatic it was hard to say.

He conducted a quick internal scan of his own behavior for the last twenty-four hours trolling for possible offenses that might have prompted this command appearance.

Jo Jo had looked desperate and so had Flora so his neck was likely in the same noose. *It must be about the Countess . . . hells bells what's my defense? Well, he did ask me to escort her so. . . .*

Heinrich tapped his silver pen on his desk as if sending morse code to himself before he spoke. Derrick could almost see the wheels turning inside his skull. He envied the way Hensler could just take his time, letting the other person wait until he knew exactly what he wanted to say—allowing the awkwardness of the space between with absolutely no discomfort or regard for the feelings of the waitee. He would never be able to pull something like that off. Mr. Fill-those-conversational-cracks. Mr. Keep-the-patter-pumping. Mr. "Yakety Yak, Yak, Mr. Blah, Blah, Blah. A wave of self-disgust crashed over him. *I'm becoming a buffoon.*

"Derrick, you have a fine record with us. Your evaluations are excellent, excellent. I think you are possibly the best Cruise Director we have in the fleet and so I am going to take you into my confidence a bit more than usual."

This he had not prepared for. This was a pop fly instead of a foul. What was he in for? Historically, Hensler could barely make polite small talk with him. He had always assumed it was his lowly status, so what was this about? If only he'd been able to ask Flora or even Jo Jo, but there had been no time and he was still unnerved from his visit with the Countess.

Something about that whole thing made no sense. When he'd raced down there to handle her for Nurse Peggy, she was sitting in the back of the treatment room behind a screen, quietly holding the poor dead creature in her arms. She wasn't in anyone's way or view and she most certainly wasn't making a scene, so what was Peggy's problem? The poor woman could not have been more dignified. She let Peggy take the dog and she'd left without a word. She held his arm and asked to go outside on deck and they'd stood very peacefully and looked at the sea.

"In the end Derrick, it all comes down to one thing. If you've loved anyone or anything with an open heart, that's what saves you and the irony of it is, you don't even know sometimes until you lose them. Ain't life a pisser?"

He was not used to such realness and he started to babble something about the show must go on, something dreadful and cheap and he felt ashamed because of his wicked dream that morning and confused by his feelings for her, by any feelings at all for anyone and threatened, but touched and when he was in that kind of danger, he talked; the way smokers reached compulsively for cigarettes, as an escape from feeling, he reached for words, and she put her long well-tended index finger over his mouth and said the most astonishing thing.

He still didn't quite believe it or certainly he doubted it was true but she was so serene when she said it.

"Shhhh, please don't talk. I have to tell you something. Sacred trust. Only you and I will ever know this. My grandson killed Tou Tou. God forgive him. He did."

How could he get away! He felt desperate to remove himself from her presence, the intimacy of the sharing, the smell of her perfumed finger, his eyes blinking wildly unable to meet her need or even understand what was being asked of him. Sacred trust! He did not *do* sacred trust with anyone!!! Let alone an almost total stranger! Confessions, personal revelations!

He felt as if he were back in Norman on his Aunt Gracie's screened porch. How he'd hated screened porches, closing him in, like monkey cages for human beings.

The Countess took her finger off his mouth and smiled at him, tears, streaming down her re-surfaced but well-worn face. "Scared ya, didn't I? It's okay, Derrick, just my gut, honey. Just my little old Texas twister. You don't have to say anything. Take me back up now, Derrick. I'll be fine."

He walked her up, but really she was taking him. Her strength shamed him. He was lost, lost in her truthfulness, unable to move forward or run away. The screen porch with mosquitoes swarming all over it. No place to escape and stinging danger everywhere.

Heinrich Hensler dropped his pen on the desk, snapping Derrick out of his reverie. Had he missed something? So unlike him to wander off like that especially in front of someone who intimidated him.

"Well, Mr. Hensler, I am flattered that you have chosen to . . ."

"Yes, yes. Well, you are the likely choice. So let me begin with the most immediate situation. The reason the Talbotts and their guests are outside. We have had a very unfortunate incident involving Miss O'Brian from the Spa. She was attacked the first night and of course the owners were told and having attractive young daughters on board, they are quite agitated and eager to resolve this.

"Also, we do not want to alarm the passengers, so we are conducting as private an investigation as possible. If you have heard anything, I want to know and if you hear any rumors or see any untoward behavior, I want you to report it to me personally, at once. We have undercover people as you know, but I need trustworthy staff to help keep this quiet."

"My heavens!" How terrible." Derrick paused not wanting to seem callous. "I don't mean to make light of this, Mr. Hensler, but I'm sure you know this happens. Usually more what they call 'date rape' incidents, but there have been complaints filed on every ship I've been on."

"I'd rather not dwell on this, Derrick. I am certainly aware of incidents, but not with such viciousness and not in the presence of the owners of the cruise line and their desirable offspring. So, I am assuming you have no information at this time."

"None. I'm shocked. I haven't even heard a rumor. Can she describe him?"

"No. It was very dark, his face was covered. She is still quite upset and very sedated. So, it is not all clear."

"Well, I will say, this is a very rowdy manifest. Lots of party boys, and I know several of the cocktail waitresses have complained to the bartenders about the behavior."

"If you can discreetly inquire, maybe one or two of them stand out."

"I will. May I inform my staff? They're all over the ship all the time and they have great antennae for the creeps."

"Please, but I would like Mr. Rogers to be present or one of his staff."

"Certainly. You do know that once I have that meeting the rumor mill starts on overtime."

"I do. But I have the Talbotts in my outer office and we have thus far been unable to find the attacker and I must show, shall we say, reasonable diligence."

"Would you like me to reassure them in some way?"

"That would be fine. So, let us move on to the next matter. I am aware that you have been entertaining the Countess and I appreciate your efforts to soothe her after the death of her animal. Please continue to do so.

"This is another ghastly situation; even though we are blameless, it casts a negative pall over their voyage and that, of course, human nature being what it is, will always be associated with *Palace of the Dolphins*. So anything you can do to make the experience of the Talbotts, the Worths and the Countess more enjoyable will be highly valued, even if it means, delegating some of your usual duties to others. You have my full support in this."

Derrick exhaled for the first time. "Thank you, Mr. Hensler. I'll do my best. I must say I find the Countess to be a delightful woman and I . . ."

"Now, the final matter, of which you may know. The steward, Jo Jo, whom you mentioned earlier, has told me that two passengers failed to return to the ship when we left St. Thomas. They were on your bus tour of the island. A most unpleasant couple, the husband had been complaining about everything. Their luggage was quite late and they did not like their cabin, their dinner table, the usual.

"A note was found by Jo Jo, who was their steward, saying they were getting off because of their dissatisfaction, but as you well know, the complainers never actually leave, they usually re-book before the cruise is over.

"So it is distressing that they would leave on the second day. They were not in an expensive cabin, so it is unlikely the cost of the trip was of no matter and it is even more confusing that they went on the tour. Their luggage and all their belongings are gone. Do you know anything about this?"

"You must mean the Karmajians. He's one of the 'do you know who I am' types, that's what we call those passengers. And you're right, they bitch and moan, but they *never* get off. I'm shocked again! First, because no one informed me and second because they had signed up for the talent show, seems he's an opera buff, and for a Catamaran cruise today and they acted like they were enjoying the tour. They certainly didn't tell me they were leaving or ask for any sort of rebate, which always happens when passengers leave that way. I'll check with my staff at once."

"Please. I was most disturbed that the names were not immediately reported. What do we have State of the Art boarding passes for? This is unacceptable and I will find the responsible crew member. How do such people choose a vacation? What ignorance! Do they not do research? If this ship isn't enough for them, they should stay home."

Hensler's eyes sparkled with fury as if the rejection was a personal affront to his worth and importance. To be dismissed by such inferiors was intolerable.

Derrick was starting to enjoy this. He had never seen any weak spot in his boss, but now one emerged. Hubris. Hensler saw the ship as a reflection of his own value. *Tread lightly now.*

"Well, I certainly agree, Mr. Hensler. Some people are just not worthy of this experience, but you know, just like the, the sexual incidents, it happens on every cruise on a ship this size. People change their minds or sometimes they go ashore and get loaded or fall asleep on the beach, even if they're having the time of their lives, these things happen."

"Yes, yes. I am not stupid. I know this. But I still find it sloppy and unsettling."

"We both should have been told at once. You're absolutely right. I'll look into it from my end, though I must say, good riddance. I spotted him right when they boarded. They ruin the experience for the other passengers; they need a lot of attention, any way they can get it." Derrick sat up straighter.

Hensler stood up suddenly, startling Derrick, as it had Flora. "I will see to everything and report back to you as soon as I can, Mr. Hensler."

"Yes, yes, good. Now I must assuage the Talbotts and may I tell them you will come to see them before lunch?"

"I'll be there. Maybe I'll have Chef Jean prepare his Sea Special Platter, it's fantastic. Some Dom Perignon and caviar, fresh Lobster, and I'll bring entertainment. I'll cheer them up. Fear not."

"I fear nothing, Derrick. Good day."

Derrick rose quickly and moved past him, without shaking hands. A headache was now forming from somewhere in his back and shooting mercilessly up the entire left side of his body and into his head. He checked his watch. 8:30 a.m. and he already felt as if he were at the end of the longest shift of his career.

⚮

FLORA AT THE DOOR marked "Out of Service", knocking softly, then knocking less softly. No response. What to do? A sense of urgency pushing at her. The southern thing in her blood, strong women to the rescue, velvet covering steel. Maybe it was just what childless women did with all that biology. Need to Nurture 101. She didn't want to wake her up but, still . . .

"Collie? Collie honey, it's Flora."

Silence. Maybe she should find Roy and get the master key card? Maybe she should run along and mind her own business and not get caught in what might well be Hensler's possum trap.

"Collie, Hensler sent me down. It's okay. Open up."

Flora listening—a rustle and someone moving. Say the secret word and the damn duck bobs up. Only Hensler was not Groucho Marx and she was not gonna win anything but maybe a six-month reprieve until her next contract review. *No, don't think like that; Collie's your pal.* A surge of longing rolled through her belly, untying the bow knot left by Hensler. She had a fella now, filling that place she had almost desperately used friends to fill. Mother Henning her way around the cast and the crew, gathering chicks, and comforting herself in the process. *If only I could just fold into him, let him carry me away, all the way away . . .*

Collie opening the door wide enough for one eye to look out. One swollen purple prune-puckered eye. Flora looking back, sucking in air in startled gulps. *Holy Mary.* Had she ever actually seen a battered woman? Up close? Flora giving silent thanks for the blessings at hand. No one had ever bashed her around. Not virtually. Not like that.

"Collie, honey, Hensler just told me. Can I come in?"

Flora bracing for more. Wordlessly, the door opened. Can you prepare, really ever, for anything awful? The other eye was worse. Her lips looked like, what? Strawberry jam, the kind with the big chunks in it. Almost yummy if they weren't part of a face. A pretty, sweet face, open and shy and innocent. Not anymore, gone forever, that innocent face. *God only knows what the rest of her looks like.*

Collie, shuffling like an old Georgia farm wife going for the morning mail, for the paper in the misty cold, like her Gram, like her mother, like herself someday far away. What could she possibly say?

The Irish girl easing herself onto the cabin bed as if it were made of nails. *Only good thing about it, she now had her own cabin.* Flora pondering, trying to remember living with someone else so close, like college girls, no privacy for months on end.

Had she really ever been that young and flexible and without secrets and the need to self-protect? The need for the comfort of the privately closed door. Of course she'd done it, hadn't minded a twit. College, summer stock, first years on the road. So long ago the memories felt as if she were watching an old home movie of a stranger's life.

The girl settled in, flesh flashing beneath her nighty, red and black bruises, cuts and scratches, like a collage of shame, seared into her silky white skin.

Flora sitting down beside her and taking her hand, putting it to her cheek and pressing it, passing compassion, avoiding any blunder with a piece of human porcelain.

The girl, reading her mind. "I can't talk about it, Flora. If I could, I would have rung you up. I can't and I won't."

"I don't care about that. I just want to help."

"You're a love. Really. I know you do. I, just . . . I'm still very hazy. Heinrich is helping. Giving me this cabin and protection, too. The security people are going to be watching over me, and Dr. Padma. I hate that people will talk about me. That's the Irish in me, land of gossips and rumormongers. Hate that!"

"It's been very hushed up. Don't even think about it. Yew have to get off the ship and to a proper hospital."

"No. No. I won't go! I look horrible, but it isn't so bad. I'm using my own herbal remedies. I am not leaving this cabin. Heinrich will see to everything."

Flora patting her hand. Flora letting go of her hand. Flora not knowing what to do. Was she wrong? What if it wasn't him? She'd been so certain. But what was life but one certainty turning to doubt and back again in every relationship and thought and feeling, well not every, but . . . *he's a pig and a sadist, maybe Collie didn't know it was him, but she seems so, so clear. . . .*

"Flora, it wasn't Heinrich. I know what you're thinking. You don't like him; every time I say his name your whole face squeezes up and your shoulders tense so hard I can see them lock. It's my work, you know, to observe the body. I sleep with him, I would know. I know his feel and his smell, even if I couldn't see and if I had seen him, I would scream bloody murder!

"I may look like a plum pudding, but I'm no wimp. That's why I didn't want to talk about it. I knew you'd be trotting down here, hoping it was him, wanting to save me. I know you mean well, luv, but it's too painful. Besides, there was, never mind. I can't talk about it."

"Okay, I believe yew. I'm sorry. I worry about you girls. I loathe the man, but really, I'm relieved if it isn't him. I am, it's just that, well he . . ."

"You said 'if'! You don't believe me! I already have a mum, Flora. I left home and went to sea to get away from meddling. My entire family is made up of female meddlers. My mum, and my grand-mum and my aunts and my great aunts and my six older sisters! I can't bear it!

"I mean no disrespect. You are an awesome person. I am in awe of you, truly. And I'm so flattered, that you find the time of day for me, but even if this awful thing has happened to me, I don't want to go back to meddling mums figuring everything out and telling me how to live my life, like they always know best and I never do. I attracted this, the universe gave this to me for a reason and I must now be very quiet in myself and try to find out the meaning of the message."

Hurt. It hurt, the words hurt. Sticks and stones but words can never . . . who'd written that lie? Words were the worst, not that Collie was being mean, but, so well, so ungrateful? She was always there for her bunnies, her pals—for advice, a loan, a shoulder. When they needed her she was a peach pie, but when they didn't want to face up to something she was a "meddling Mum". Well, the hell with it. Okay, so maybe it was her need, too, after all Collie hadn't called *her*, but what were friends for if not to come to your rescue when you were in trouble? Well you can't have a friend who's "in awe." Awe is a way of distancing, it can't be reciprocated. *Scratch a rescuer and you'll find a victim.* . . . who said that? . . .

"I've upset you, see? That's why I didn't call you, Flora! I just can't talk about it, yet."

"Yeah, yew did and now *you're* upset and that really stinks and I feel awful and I guess it's the old 'No good deed' deal, but I feel kind of used too, because I didn't know a thing and then Hensler called me in and gave me the old razzle dazzle and asked me to talk to yew and the cast and reassure 'the girls'. I wasn't trying to meddle. I've got enough problems of my own, frankly, Collie dear.

"Yew are very right. I'm not your mother and I do sort of cluck over y'all; he asked me and I did think yew might need some support.

"But my concern about him is based on the way he's behaved with other girls, long before yew came on board. He's not so nice once he tires of his plaything. He smacked around one of my backup singers pretty good and she left in the middle of her contract.

"So, my concern wasn't based on some Irish granny suspicion. I'm not so foolish as that, but I apologize for treating yew like a child or doubting your word or whatever. I'm deeply sorry, but pa-leaze don't start that massage school mumbo jumbo about how you attracted this to heal yourself! Then I *will* start acting like your mother!

"Sometimes things just happen and we deal and we learn and we cope and we get stronger or we don't, but it doesn't all fit into those neat little spiritual do-gooder packets. That doesn't help yew face up to life."

"I don't believe that. And it's my right not to and this isn't helpful to my healing, Flora."

Flora standing up, feeling like strangling someone. Anger and hurt feelings, anger at who? Not the girl, not even Hensler. Who was left? Maybe herself? Trotted on down, fell into his trap? The right thing for the wrong reason or the wrong thing for the wrong reason? Her own need? What *she* would want? Needing to be needed, trying to please the Beast.

All puffed up, thinking she'd stood up for herself by not calling him Heinrich, and then practically prancing down at his command? Was that too harsh? Her friend was attacked and her instinct was to help, so, what had she missed here?

This was really screwed up. Now she was mad and hurt and had made things worse and what she'd come for was to help and to make things better and maybe Collie was right, this *was* happening to show her something. The universe trying to get her attention (whatever that meant, she'd never been really sure, it was such a big concept but . . .).

All she cared about right now was getting out of there, away from the prunes and the strawberry jam that used to be Collie's face and trying to leave a message for her fella.

Rory was right.

He melted her all the way through, but it was wrong, and she was a fool.

"I'm gonna go, honey. I'm there if yew need me. I'll let you deal with Hensler. He thought yew might feel more comfortable talking to a woman about what happened, but it didn't work out that way, so . . ."

The girl was crying now, not so tough or without Meddling Mum need. Her own confusion emerging now that the moment of the withdrawal of compassion was at hand.

"What happened was, they grabbed me as I was opening my door, taped my mouth, bashed my face into the floor taped my eyes, tortured me with metal things, burned me, raped me, sodomized me, taunted me, called me horrible names, gave me drugs and left me on the floor, hog-tied like an animal! That's what happened!!!"

Flora on her knees by the bed, knowing what to do now, holding the woman who could have been her daughter, offering the pure part of rescue. But her head was elsewhere, stopped at a yellow light flashing one word. *They.*

⚮

"*Where am I going and what will I find? What's in this grab bag that I call my mind?*" *I could probably get through the rest of my life in musical fragments and never use one single non-lyrical word for communication purposes. . . .* "*Well, I think I'm going out of my mind, over you. . . .*" *What to do with all these feelings? All this unexpected emotion bubbling up and bursting forth, back to Hot Pot in Iceland fantasy . . .*

Amazing . . . no, no, can't use that word, too awards-show-acceptance-speechish, but well, it was . . . is . . .

How did I walk around all these years sitting on all these feelings and still function? Why didn't I just blow apart, like a hamster in a microwave . . . a poor trapped creature put under extreme pressure and splat. . . . Nice self-image Rory. . . . A hamster in a microwave?

What time is it? Oh shit, I'm going to be late for rehearsal. But I have to stop at the gift shop. . . . Have to buy him something. I just need to do something like that . . . so high school Ror, well yes but, God what this feels like! I never have felt anything like this, "*Bewitched, Bothered and Bewildered am I.*"

Oh God, I had sex. Amazing!! No, don't call it that . . . too Golden Globes, too, "I want to thank my amazing cast and my publicists and my dental hygienist and . . ." What was I doing with all that stuff all these years? Talk about like "riding a bicycle". Not that either of us was so great at it, but the power of the connection was . . . Oh fuck it, AMAZING! No one ever held me like that. Tenderly . . . "The evening breeze, caressed the trees, Tenderly . . ."

I told him about Billy! . . . Talk about an emotional avalanche! Talk about opening the intimacy closet! Talk about trusting someone! Did I do it because I had an orgasm? Was it like one huge and powerful release led to the big one? Or did I have the orgasm because I trusted him and so telling him was actually the secondary part? And why did this matter anyway? "Nothing's gonna harm you, not while I'm around. . . ."

I think I told him because I felt safe and I have never actually felt safe before. . . . "There's a wall in China that's 1,000 miles long to keep out the foreigners, they made it strong, and there's a wall around me that no one can see, it takes a little time to get near me. . . ." Oh shit, I'm going to cry again. No, Ror, no red-eyes at rehearsal, Flora will be all over it. . . .

How did it happen? They were dozing off and he was holding her and she had never fallen asleep with someone holding her like that and she started to tense up and he noticed.

"What is it?" he said and she said, "I have to tell you something." She didn't know she was going to say that! But she knew she did, have to, tell him.

"Anything," he said and he sat up and moved her away slightly so he could see her and she'd pulled up the sheet, protection of sorts.

"All my bullshit about being so honest and I didn't tell you the most important thing about me. I've never told anyone since it happened, anyone who didn't know at the time and I was on the road, so, no one in New York ever knew . . . and . . ."

"Tell me."

". . . I, have a son. Billy. His name is Billy. I hate the name but I loved that song in Carousel, 'My Boy Bill will be strong and as tall as a tree. . . .' So . . . God, I loved him. Love him. . . . Love him. I didn't think I could have a baby and then I did and my husband, Jesse, I told you about Jesse, well, he wasn't until Billy, but then we got married, we'd been on the road for a long time, and we were in Las Vegas and it was pretty bad, he was pretty bad and

I was pretty lost and then Billy was born and for five years I was happy.

"Mostly it was me and Billy, Jesse was gone a lot, gambled a lot, cheated a lot and then I had this sort of awakening about my work and myself and what I wanted for my son and I told him I was leaving him and moving back to New York and settling down into a real life and I took Billy to school and when I went to pick him up . . . Oh, fuck, I don't think I can do this, I . . ."

"Look at me, just keep looking at me. Tell me, Rory, please."

"He took him!! Jesse took him!! From his school . . . picked him up and vanished, evaporated. Gone!! Eighteen Years!! Eighteen Years!! He's a man, now! Oh My God! He's a man, even if I found him now. . . . He's a man. He was five years old and I can never have him back, have my little boy . . . back . . ."

He was so still. He never took his eyes off her; he left her alone but it felt like he was holding her up, allowing her to explore this long buried truth relic, dig it up and dust it off and gently but firmly examine it, see what it looked like in reality, after all those years of being buried alive, like some sort of Egyptologist with a newly uncovered tomb, some unearthed mummy that might simply crumble into dust when exposed to the light, leaving the scientist who had quested for so long with nothing to hold onto but disappointment.

"I searched, I looked everywhere! Seven Years! Seven years! I never stopped. He was even on a fucking milk carton! I went through every cent I had in the world. Everything I'd earned and what I'd been left when my family died, I'd put that in a trust for Billy, but I had to use it and then I turned forty and I had nothing left and I needed . . . I had to stop or I , I . . . wouldn't have survived much longer and I had to survive in case he needed me, in case he was looking for me and that's why I kept Jesse's name, so Billy could find me and I went back to New York and tried to re-start my life.

"I'd been sort of a bright little up and coming talent, but it was too late, and I had to earn money, so I could keep trying and I just did whatever I could and now . . . this is so, so embarrassing, I mean you're a fucking shrink!!! But I've only understood this minute that to keep from accepting it, I froze him in place! He's been five years old all this time! I'd find him and he'd still be five even if I was in my fifties and I'd get to raise him and I would never, ever, never have to face the loss.

"I did the same thing you did with your daughter and your wife, I held on and refused to move on. I was going to stay right where I was when I lost him! But you, looking at you. . . . Oh God, he's a man! He's a grownup! Even if he found me, he wouldn't remember, he's probably had another mother, knowing Jesse and I don't think I could . . . she just better have loved him, taken care of him . . . or I'll, I'll . . . the worst of it, is, is I couldn't find them so I couldn't murder his father . . . no way to unload all the rage, so helpless, so . . . unbearable . . . right now, it feels so unbearable . . . no wonder I never faced this! Maybe this wasn't such a good idea. . . .

"Oh, shit, Poe. . . . Billy's a grown man!!! He's never coming back, my baby's gone, forever ! Jesse didn't even like him, never seemed to care, it was just to punish me and have another ego prop.

"I never even got to decide to stay! If he had threatened me, I could of at least decided to stay. Oh, God, Oh my God! I saw Leah's daughter and she asked me . . . she asked me if I had kids and I ran, I ran right into you and I can't go back now I . . . I . . ."

He stayed still while she thrashed around, hyperventilating and venting and sobbing and choking and panicking. Wow! How fortuitous to fall in love with a trained professional just in time to crack like a fucking teutonic plate, just crack open like a long dormant fault line and spill thousands of pounds of unfelt feelings out of the core of your being.

"I'm right here Rory, don't be afraid. You won't die, I promise you".

She believed him and she kept going. She had never trusted anyone before, like a little child, she kept her eyes on him and she kept going until there was no more wrath, no more anguish. Peace. She actually felt something like peace.

All those cornball things she made fun of but she'd let go of something huge.

The orgasm had just been a little snack, this was fucking Thanksgiving dinner! Two days, not even three yet, and she'd been completely re-upholstered, like some lumpy old sofa, ripped open, re-stuffed and wrapped up in a shiny new casing. An emotional Extreme Make-over . . . amazing!

"I'd like to thank my uncaring and long dead parents, my uncaring and long dead grandparents, my sociopathic kidnapping bum of an ex-husband, my first heartbreak, Walter Worth, my long lost friend Leah Worth and, of course, Poe Evanoff, without whom I would not be standing before you tonight, fucking AMAZING!

Where the hell am I? Promenade Deck, somewhere. Where's the damn gift shop? I've never shopped on board before. There must be a hundred different stores here! I can't even begin to deal with this.

Rory stopped and leaned against the glass wall in front of a toy store. The window was completely filled with Barbies. Baywatch Barbie and Nightclub Barbie and every conceivable manifestation, slutty, strutty, punky, funky, the same frozen face and fabricated femininity as when she was a little girl. All those new generations of innocence to be exploited.

She was exhausted, the lack of sleep and all the emotion and the enormity of the physical space all smacking into her.

Maybe they've got a funny little bald Curious George Monkey thing, something silly. She looked into the store, which was filled with people. Nothing looked appealing. She checked her watch. Fifteen minutes. *Shit.*

Just do it, Rory, walk into the store like a normal person. She scanned the shelves, overwhelmed by the sheer magnitude of choices. *There are people actively sitting in rooms in factories somewhere inventing all this junk?* Shelf-lined walls crammed with stuffed things: pigs, and cows and bunnies and ducks and teddys and puppies—lifelike and whimsical, squishy and snuggly and furry and enormous and minute.

Do-It-Yourself kits, art supplies and coloring books and story books and jewelry and games for every age and interest and learning toys and interactive toys and mechanical battery-operated toys and old fashioned retro toys and gimmicky toys and thoughtful toys and books-by-celebrity-moms and CD's and DVD's of every-movie-ever-made-for-children and Make Up kits and Dress-up kits and balls of every size and shape and color and bounce—soft bounce and high bounce, and funny cartoon character clothes and doll clothes and dolls, dolls, dolls: human looking and Asian and Black and blonde and life size and baby size and dolls that burp, and poop and drink water and talk and cry and . . . No Curious George. No Snoopy.

She turned and started back out. An older woman was standing in front of the stuffed animal wall and something about her posture caught Rory's eye. *I've seen that woman somewhere. . . .* She moved closer. It was the Old Swami dame from the first night at the Talbotts.

The woman's hand was shaking and as Rory moved past her, she thought she saw tears running down her cheeks. The woman reached forward and pulled out a life-like little stuffed puppy and snatched it to her, holding it against her stomach and marching off to the check-out line.

Re-think the gift choice, Rory. The way the woman attached the stuffed thing to her was not exactly the message she wanted to send. *I told him about Billy and I'm still alive.*

⌣∕ℓ⌣

THE COUNTESS VON ESSEN slid onto a stool in the Krazy Kat's Koffee Kup and looked at the Krazy Kat clock over the counter. She was early for her lunch date with Derrick Doolittle. Good, give her some time to settle down. She opened her Hermes Tote bag for one last look at her new, padded version of Tou Tou, and patted it. What should she call it? Tou *Two*? She chuckled and put the bag on the floor. This would have to be her little secret, or Ian would use it as an excuse to have her committed.

Was it so unusual for a lonely old woman to want something snuggly to help her through a period of grief? Is it any harder for a toddler to deal with insecurity, night fears, the need for something comforting to cling to than for a senior?

A perky young girl with a name tag that said, "Hi! I'm your Kool Kat Kitty" stopped to take her order. Was that really her name? Doubtful. "Coffee please, with real cream, dear," Her voice sounded strange to her, shaky and tense, not her normal voice at all.

Well, her whole being felt shaky and tense, so why shouldn't the sounds emanating from her. She put on her glasses and looked around. It was cute, if theme dining was your cup of catnip. Must be why Derrick had suggested meeting there.

Comfort food. At least it wouldn't be pretentious. What was that horrible stuff Sissy had ordered for them at dinner last night? Monkfish stacked on top of turnips mashed with cinnamon and turmeric and leeks with lobster sauce on top of that. Absolutely revolting. Not that she'd ever understood the concept of "stacked" food, anyway.

The older she got the more she wanted to eat like her grandchildren, nothing touching the thing next to it. Each food group doing what it was supposed to do with no strange substances snuck into anything just to show off and charge more. A discerning three year old can spot one fleck of basil in the tomato sauce from across the table.

As far as she could tell the only reason for all the pretentious food nonsense, was to give the hooty-tooties she knew something to chat about while dining. No one had real conversations anymore. Too many politically correct no-no's. No one dared go out on a limb or risk separating from the "group think" of whatever group it was.

"Never discuss Israel or the economy at dinner," a socialite Washington friend once told her. Well, the list was a lot longer than that these days. Social conversation was now a hockey game of potential wild pucks, not worth the risk, or maybe no one she knew really cared enough about anything anymore to fight for an unpopular opinion.

Well, that was one good thing about getting to be her age and being alone. She wasn't on anyone's "A" list and she wasn't much interested in going along, not that she ever had been, but she'd gotten away with murder by playing the kooky Countess and of course, having all that money. But she wasn't kooky, and she was damned tired of the role, even if she'd cast herself in the part. "Umm, the lobster sauce blending into the turnips, how intriguing." Pa-leeze.

"Here ya go." The Kitty Kat put a nice big mug of hot coffee and a little pitcher of what at least appeared to be real cream before her and she was filled with a moment of pure joy. She poured the cream and added two nice big teaspoons of sugar and took a sip. *Delicious.* She was actually enjoying herself. Maybe they had tapioca pudding or a nice big slice of banana cream pie.

A well-dressed country clubbish couple came in and sat to the left of her. The wife was carrying a shopping bag from one of those horrific boutiques.

Looks like Texas to me. She could spot her fellow Longhorns in any crowd. Always a little too well-turned out. Everything a bit too contrived, one piece of everything too many. If it was Chanel then every single thing they had on would be Chanel. The whole look of well-tended Texas was as if they were compensating for not being New York. Philadelphia new money did the same thing. *My, oh My Mimsie, what a wealth of meaningless social trivia you've amassed over the decades.*

The wife reached into the shopping bag and pulled out several cashmere sweaters in various ice cream colors. "These are gonna be ga-reat for Scotland, hon."

"We're goin to Vienna."

"Whatever."

Mimsie took another sip, trying to conceal her eavesdropping. The wife reminded her of a younger version of so many of her friends and luncheon pals. Slitting and cutting and injecting globules of butt fat and syringes full of plague, sandpapering off layers of their faces, sucking out pounds of their insides, lazering and stapling away at themselves in between shopping excursions to buy overpriced ridiculous outfits for trips to "whatever" locations.

The trips were an excuse for the shopping; the socializing was an excuse for slicing themselves up. But in the end it was just a way to fill all that spare time. If they stopped socializing and taking vacations and jetting about to attend one another's momentous occasions and recovering from elective cosmetic surgery, well, what on earth would they do all day? *Don't go there Mims, you haven't even had a grilled cheese sandwich yet.*

She looked toward the door, though Derrick was still not due for several minutes and she was in no hurry. In fact she regretted having made the date. He was being kind and they were all worried that she might fling herself overboard from her loss, not that she hadn't thought about it for a minute or two, but somehow, buying the weird little stuffed creature had calmed her down immensely and she felt rather alright and in no need of any conversation but her own.

A group of elderly passengers was being led into the restaurant by what must be their caregivers. *Goodness mercy!* Walkers and wheelchairs, a line-up of decrepit oldsters: enfeebled, frail specters of who they must have been. Crippled, paper white, stunned by time and patronized by their attendants like pre-schoolers. *How did God work this one out? We begin with soft, silky innocence and end up like this heap of compost? Gumming jello and creeping around the cruise of a lifetime? Not far away from that yourself, Mimsie, so be gentle.*

She turned back to her cup, shaking off the nearness of what lay ahead.

Two of the more agile of the group sat down at the counter on her right. She was encircled now, Texas and the past on one side and the near future on the other.

She glanced over, trying not to be obvious. The women were most probably no older than she was but had clearly not had the advantages of good dental care or moisturizer let alone the cosmetic overhauling of the Texas tootsie on her other side, or of her very own self, though it was just one face-lift twenty years ago which cured her forever. It had felt as if someone had wrapped a boa constrictor around her throat and it had been months before her head felt remotely like her own. Horrible, bloody, bruisy mess of agony and no one even thought she looked any different!

The woman closest to her had a pack of cigarettes sticking out of her pocket, but Mimsie would have known she was a smoker even without the clue. *You can always spot a fellow puffer.* She sighed. Not a drag in ten years but the very sight of a pack could double her over with craving.

"Four orders of white toast, hon, and two cups a java. We're sharing."

The other woman was very small and resembled, Mimsie thought, a white raisin. She had an oxygen tube in her nose and strapped around her head and connected to a small portable unit on her walker.

The feistier woman next to her spread a newspaper out on the counter.

"Remember Gert, I told youse about the old lady with the Alzheimers—froze to death on the roof of that nursing home? Well, it's happenin' all over. Cut backs. All the homes are cuttin' back. Look, says right here, 'Easy Livin' Lodge' where your son stuck youse? Inspectors undercover caught them puttin' the oldies to bed nekked! Let 'em eat breakfast covered in—says right here—Their own feces! A nurse got fired for tryin' to clean 'em up before they ate."

"He didn't know about that, Janet. He put me somewhere nice."

"Nice! Didn't youse just tell me about your roommate with the Parkinson's havin a dirty tube rammed down her throat when she was fillin' up?"

"We complained about that and it's better now. When my son comes, he asks me. He looks out for me."

"Gertie, he hasn't been to see youse since last summer! You're livin' in La La land. Get outa that hole and come live with me."

"I'm fine. I need my treatments, ya know. Look at where we are. They arranged this trip. Got all the consents. Got a special price. Took us ones up to it, even let youse come with."

"Yeah, well, only cause I volunteer, but I'm not goin in. They'll have to come with a warrant and drag me out! I'll go down smokin' and fightin'. Look here . . . some poor old fool with the paralysis, they dropped him on the floor and broke his nose!"

"Things happen. That's life."

Mimsie shuddered, she'd forgotten about the down side of sitting at a counter, that's how long it had been since she's actually done it. Now she had images in her head, even more disturbing than poor Tou Tou. Old people like her very self being dropped on their heads, withered naked bodies slopping down waffles in their own filth.

Well, the one thing money could buy was not having to end up like that. She felt a sudden urge to ask the feisty lady for a smoke, ask her to join her for dinner, a new friend, someone who would go down, "smokin' and fightin'". The O.K. Corral version of old age. She rather liked that.

She glanced back at the door. Derrick was waving to her and pointing toward a small booth in the corner. She placed a five dollar tip on the counter and picked up her fake puppy, holding herself as countess-like as possible, determined to not be mistaken for one of the "group" and went to meet him. She was grateful now for the company, knowing that if she sat there any longer, she would have had no place to go with her thoughts but to Ian and she was not ready yet for that part of the voyage.

⌁

"LEAH? IT'S RORY."

"Oh, Rory, you were reading my mind! I was going to call you right after my yoga class to see if we could all get together tonight."

"Well, that's why I'm calling; it may not be what you want to do but I guess I'm having a little Fairfax High nostalgia, and I read in the ship's newsletter that they're having a 'Seder at Sea' no shellfish I'm sure, but anyway, it reminded me of all those Passovers at your Mother's house and I thought, maybe you and Walter and Clarissa, might want to go and if so I thought I'd ask, um, Dr. Evanoff and we could go dance or something afterward, work off the matzah balls."

"Oh, Rory, what a lovely idea! I'm so touched that you would think of that. I'm ashamed of myself, I completely forgot it was tonight. Clarissa's ashore with her friends, but she's got such a crush on you I know she'll want to come. Can I ask Walter and call you back?"

"That's fine. They say the seating is limited, of course they always say things like that and it's competing with the ice show and some special theme dinner deal, so it may not be a problem, but I think I should reserve the seats pretty soon, Jews cruise you know and a standing room only Seder would be pretty uncomfortable."

"Poe, uh, Dr. Evanoff said the rabbi's not exactly Moses material, but he should be interesting."

"Oh, yes! Uri Dayan. I sat next to him at dinner the first night, at the Captain's table. He's very charming and awfully smart."

"You think everyone is very charming and smart, but I'm willing to keep an open mind."

"Oh, Rory, you make me laugh. I do do that, don't I? But most people I meet really are."

"Really? Well I either want to smoke what you smoke or move to whatever new planet you've inhabited."

"Well maybe it's planet Lost in Space. I must say, as I get older, I have a tougher time holding onto my optimism."

"Leah, optimism is great, as long as reality is the starting point. But, it's part of your charm and probably why you haven't aged a day. So maybe we'll meet in the middle."

"Sounds like a good idea. Shall we get together before?"

"Well, they say it starts at sundown which means around 5:30 somewhere called the 'Pirate's Cove' dining room, doesn't sound ko-sher to me. I've got rehearsal until 4:30, so let's just meet there."

"Fine. The ship leaves at 4:30 so Clarissa will be back in plenty of time."

"Great, so unless Walter revolts, we're on."

"He won't, but even if he does, Clarissa and I will be there with bells on."

"As long as they're temple bells. See you later."

Leah Worth put down the phone and smiled. What a wonderful surprise! Rory wasn't indifferent to her, whatever had happened that drove her away, she clearly cared enough and had thought enough about them to plan this special evening.

What a lovely symbolic gesture! To remember her family and the Passovers they'd spent together. She finished the last bite of her lunch, feeling better than she had since they'd left Puerto Rico.

That's why she was so optimistic! Things usually turned out to be far better than we think they will and all that needless worry was such a waste of precious time. She picked up her yoga matt and went into the living room.

Sissy was having a manicure on the private deck. No one else was around.

"Sissy, have you seen Walter? He's been gone since breakfast and I need to ask him about going to a Passover dinner tonight if it's alright with you and Teddy of course."

Sissy put down her magazine. "Haven't seen Walter or Teddy all morning. They were dressed for golf, so they may be on the putting green or practicing their swings or maybe they went ashore to play. I was having a massage and they were gone when I came back."

"Well, I guess I'll leave a note, I'm going to the yoga meditation workshop."

"Sounds soothing. Maybe I'll join you, if my nails dry. I'm waiting for that nurse to give me a shot and then I can exercise a bit more."

"It starts in twenty minutes. It's not strenuous. It may help your back. Do come."

"I'll see how I feel."

"Is it alright about the dinner tonight? I hope it won't interfere with any plans?"

"No, no. We're having a few people for drinks, ship executives that Teddy has to be nice to and then we'll take the Countess and whomever to that little Italian supper club; it's supposed to be marvelous for a ship like this, anyway—trying to cheer her up, poor dear. Is Clarissa going with you?"

"Yes, I'll leave a note for her, too."

"Well, I envy you, a daughter who would willingly go to a religious occasion! Twinkle hasn't set foot in our church since her communion and she only did that because we promised her a pony! We'll be lucky if they have dinner with us once this week."

"I know it's hard to face the fact they have lives of their own and they don't need us the same way anymore."

"Yes, yes, it is." Sissy picked up her magazine, signaling the intimacy was over.

"Well, maybe I'll see you at yoga."

"Ummm, if my nails dry and the nurse comes in the next five minutes. Have fun."

Leah went back inside to write her notes, trying not to let the awkwardness of her Sissy interlude affect the excitement she felt about the dinner date.

Rory put down the phone and frowned. *No taking it back, now.* Why had she wanted to do this? This was almost like *entertaining*! Well, maybe it was like sex and the bicycle deal, it would come back to her, this world of social living, inviting and being invited, renewing old friendships, telling a friend something personal about her past. *Trusting people.* Maybe it was the "Lovelight in her eyes," or maybe it was more like . . . "So we talked about the old times and we had ourselves some beers, still crazy after all these years."

"It was an impulse and she had acted on it. Highly unusual for her, being more compulsive than impulsive by nature. How about some of wanting to appear with her fella, let Leah and Walter see her as an elbow-wobbler? A tad, not much.

It seemed like the right thing to do and she'd meant what she said, those dinners at Leah's house were the closest thing to a warm loving family she had ever seen. She owed Leah some explanation for her desertion; jealousy she could cop to, but without the Walter trigger it seemed too lame and she couldn't tell Leah about that if she didn't know. No way. Oy, now it was feeling messy. Now a nice quiet pizza for two in her cabin was seeming like a much better choice. Well, too late, even she couldn't cancel out now.

One thing about the absence of a social life she already missed, was not having to make all these choices and plan events. Rory sighed and picked up the phone. Passover in the Pirate's Cove. It didn't even have rhyming possibilities.

～～

URI DAYAN PAUSED at the railing and looked out into the sea. The sun was setting and the sky was streaked with gold and purple. A perfect night for a Seder. He took a long deep breath and let it out. *Ahhhh.* The breeze was warm and the feeling of the enormous ship moving so effortlessly through the ocean gave him a rush of excitement, an actual thrill in his being.

He was looking forward to this, which surprised him. He had only agreed as a courtesy, but now it felt far more serious, a moral imperative almost. He actually felt stirred in a deeper, rabbinical sense — pride at being a Jew, which he rarely felt, though he'd never admitted that before, even to himself.

What an extraordinary two days! He really had Poe Evanoff to thank for everything. If he hadn't had that disturbing conversation with him, which led to the panic attack, which led to his terrible encounter with that anti-Semite nurse, which led to all of his soul searching and re-evaluating his life's purpose he would not have undergone such profound change and growth.

He felt so, alive. More alive and strong in himself than he had in years, maybe than he ever had. It had stirred passion in him and changed his sense of purpose about his mission as a spiritual communicator and he was looking forward to speaking to an audience of his fellow Jews and expressing his feelings. He'd done his homework, too. And he also had Evanoff to thank for that!

Incredible what he'd uncovered on the computer in the ship's library about the resurgence of anti-Semitism since 9/11, the horrible things going on in so-called civilized Europe and the rest of the world, to the point where Israeli's survival was at risk, making the unthinkable possible. New pogroms without any safe haven, without the right of return.

French Jews were immigrating to *Israel*! *Now* in the Twenty-First Century! Sixty-odd years after the Holocaust, Jews were emigrating to escape persecution in *Paris*! He would speak of this and weave it into the story of Passover and record it for his book.

He smiled into the wind. Life was wondrous. Everything was a gift. He *could* feel the way he'd felt after that woman gave him the shot, without drugs.

He reached into his pocket and checked to see if he had the tranquilizers, just in case. At least when he complained to Mr. Hensler he had been accommodating enough to send the doctor to his cabin with some medication in case it happened again. But Hensler had been aloof and defensive about the nurse and he'd left feeling horrified at how smug and callous these people were, not even trying to conceal their prejudice.

This was the most alarming thing of all. It was as if the world now saw the Jews as close to another annihilation and without power, between the Palestinian time-bomb and the resurgence of anti-Semitism everywhere in the world: in the U.N., Italy, Germany and of course, the bastions of bigotry, Russia and Eastern Europe and even among the liberal democrats who were turning on Israel and bonding with its enemies and this was without the Saudis, the Syrians, and Iran and he would address this and take this zeal back to his work. And he would even thank Poe Evanoff in the forward of his book for opening his eyes. Yes, he'd be a mensch and a real Rabbi.

The Pirate's Cove dining room was filled. Long tables decorated in blue and white with baskets of matzos and carafes of red wine and roses, not lilies. Someone had done their homework, no Easter flowers in sight. Little bouquets of roses and azaleas? Or maybe they were carnations.

His heart beat a bit faster. There must be 200 people there! All nicely dressed and looking eager and serious. They were expecting something special from him. *He could fail*; this thought had not occurred to him before. He smiled, making his way around the room to the place of honor at the center of the head table. A podium was set up with all the Seder equipment. The herbs and the eggs and the chalice and the nuts and the apples. No pillows to lean on, but that would have been too much and since this was most likely a reformed group, no one would actually expect a table arrangement set with cushions. . . .

"Why do we lean on a pillow tonight? To be comfortable as a reminder that we were once slaves, but now we are free . . ." He needed to choose a young person to ask the questions. He had forgotten about that. What if no children were there?

His heart pounded harder, he was beginning to feel a bit queasy as he reached his place and looked out into the faces, still chatting with one another but some already turning toward him, waiting for him to transport them into reverence, to affect them in some way.

He felt the confidence of just moments ago begin to slip into stage fright. *Relax yourself. You are a professional. You have taken audiences ten times this size and moved them to tears, to awareness and pride.*

He reached down and picked up a glass of water on the table and sipped, playing for time as the attendees began quieting down and settling in for the ceremony. *Make eye contact, Uri, bring them into you.*

He looked from guest to guest, nodding slightly and asserting his role. He saw the beautiful red-haired woman from the Captain's dinner with her husband and a young woman who must be her daughter and the Doris Day look-alike he had seen with . . . Evanoff, sitting beside her! He hadn't foreseen this. Evanoff was *here*, looking at him with that steady, mocking look. Was it mocking or was he imagining it? Why would he come?

His knees were shaking and his heart was now racing much too fast. Reflexively, he reached into his pocket and pushed one of the tranquilizers out of its foil packet and turned away from the room, away from Evanoff's eyes which were reading his face and judging, judging his integrity, his authenticity. He swallowed the pill dry and wiped the sweat on his forehead. *God sends us what we need, so my lesson is not over.*

The thought surprised him because he realized he believed it, even if it had sprung from panic. He turned back to face this new test of himself.

"Good Evening ladies and gentlemen and children who are merely small ladies and gentlemen! It is a great honor to be here at the first Seder, marking the first night of Passover the most important event in the eight day holiday. In a moment I am going to ask one of the children in the room to help in the ceremony, to ask the four questions which define the meaning of Passover and that is the job of the youngest child at the table and it is a very big table!

"As many of you know, children are very much a part of this holiday which celebrates the story of the Exodus and that is because of the commandment in the Old Testament, 'And thou shall tell thy son.' . . ."

Rory was trying to concentrate. Poe on one side, Walter on the other. Leah Frankel and her daughter—one big happy family at a Seder at Sea! But she was distracted by the last sentence coming from the twerpy guy Poe had told her about. *Tell thy son . . .* she'd told Poe and now she would probably open her big trap in the heat of the occasion or its aftermath and tell Leah and they would all join hands and comfort her and she would re-join the normal world and why did none of that seem so appealing?

Maybe because the pain still pulsing through her entire being had shifted into a new gear, something approaching acceptance even while still idling somewhere between neutral and the demon's desire for reverse. Her son Billy was no longer a child and that reality spoken out loud slammed her out of the past and back into life.

Also, she was really aware of Walter's presence. He was so, unnerving. She could feel the heat coming off him, the smell of something delectable, he was all wavy and tawny and manicured and perfectly put together—*molto elegante* the Italians called it. He could *be* an Italian mogul or something. The posture, the presence, the way he sat so straight but at ease and cool—well Poe was cool and sat straight and seemed at ease but he certainly wasn't like Walter, no wavy for starters, no perfectly tailored, presence though he had and . . . What was she *talking* about? Here she was at a floating Passover comparing her first love and most likely her last love? Was this a joke or what.

Leah was beaming, like having them all together was her aim in life. Leah was filled with sweetness and delight toward her as if she'd cooked the entire fucking Seder and set the table for two hundred herself! All she did was call and say "Five for the Pirate's Cove," nothing had changed! Leah's oblivious niceness still made her shrivel up inside with self-hate. *She's so good and I'm so . . . not good.*

"So, Leah, here's the truth. The reason I dropped out of your life and became the former Best Friend and forever letter-downer and meanie and abandoner of a wonderful and caring person is that I gave my virginity to your husband and would have probably given my life . . . jumped up and down on his pee pee in the back seat of his Buick convertible (top up of course) in front of my grandparent's Four-Plex and he took my virginity and my hope and dumped me for you without a word, which given the fact that I was so envious of everything you had and so jealous of you and Walter that I could barely look at you, well, it seemed like the best choice and so . . ." Did it still matter after all this time? You never know about that kind of stuff until you open your big fat mouth and then it's too late. *I don't want to hurt them. . . .*

Poe reached over and squeezed her hand. Could he read minds, too?

"So God unleashed a series of ten terrible plagues on the people of Egypt and still the Pharaoh refused to listen to Moses' plea, 'Let my people go,' and God told the Israelites to mark their dwellings with lamb's blood so the Angel of Death could 'pass over' their houses and not kill their first born sons, but would kill only the first born sons of the Egyptians. . . ."

Clarissa was trying to listen, but she was too uneasy. The whole day on shore had been so weird, she felt like the Israelites waiting to see if they would be saved. Totally stressed out day.

Ian and Twinkle were wasted by noon and really obnoxious and then, Ian, Oh my God! He made jokes about smothering his grandmother's dog to punish her for asking him to take Tou Tou out!! Bragging and laughing on the beach! She'd almost vomited. He was not just a spoiled snob, he was a monster! And Twinkle, laughing and imitating the Countess mourning her puppy and those creepy island guys coming on to all of them. Drug dealers for sure, and off they'd gone with them!

"Come on Clarissa, we're going to mingle and tingle, get a touch of Island Fever."

Horrible! She'd tried to stop them. The ship was leaving in just a few hours and when they started, they could party for days!! And those guys were completely scary. What could she do? She'd warned them and left them on the beach. That was it. She had to tell her Dad after the Seder.

And her parents didn't even know about the cell phone message to Mrs. Talbott!

"Clarissa dear, may I have a word."

"Of course Mrs. Talbott."

"When did you last see Twinkle and Ian?"

"On the beach around noon."

"Did they say anything to you about going to a party with some friends from New York?"

"Well, they . . ."

"No nonsense, Clarissa. I know you're trying to protect them, but this is serious. I must have an honest answer."

"They met some people who invited them to a party and they went off with them. I told them there wasn't much time, but they went anyway and I came back to the boat."

"I want you to listen to this message on my cell phone."

"Mother dearest, we've met some pals and we're going to party awhile and we've decided to cut out on the rest of the trip. It's just too played out for us.

"We've got our passports and credit cards and we hardly need any clothes, so we're all set. Sorry for ducking out, but we really like the vibe here, so we'll hang for a few days and then wend our way back to the City. Oh, Ian says to tell his grandmother thanks and he's very sad about Tou Tou and he'll buy her a new pup when he gets back. Love to Daddy. Ciao, all!"

"Did they tell you they weren't coming back?"

"No, ma'am. They said they'd only stay an hour or two. I'm so sorry, but I'm sure they'll be fine. They're like that, you know, living in the moment. They were getting bored and they hate that more than anything."

"Yes, they do. Her father is going to be furious and how do I tell the Countess that her own grandson took off in the middle of her tragedy?"

"I can talk to her if you'd like."

"That would be very kind of you Clarissa, I'm not good at that sort of thing."

"And the First Born son of the Pharaoh was dead and he relented and agreed to let the Israelites go . . ."

Clarissa shuddered. The only good thing about it was she wouldn't have to see Twinkle and Ian for the rest of the trip! Not very noble of her but at least she was telling herself the truth.

Uri was soaring. The pill had worked wonders! He had risen up from doubt once again to perform his best Seder. All the Poe Evanoffs in the world could not shake him when he was on stage. He was at home before an audience or a room of powerful people in a way he was not at home anywhere else; that was his gift. How could he have been so weak? What power did Evanoff have but his contempt?

The room was his, from the smallest child up. He focused on the lovely red-headed woman, and played to her. She was enrapt, transported. He saw tears in her eyes when he segued to compare the Exodus to the Holocaust; the room had gasped out loud at the figures: 15 million Jews left on the face of the earth but without the Holocaust there would have been more than 150 million, equal to the entire population of the United States in 1945!

The power of the numbers, gave magnitude to the historical loss and the fragility of those who remain. He was so quiet, so without theatrics when he described the Nazis using the pelvises of gassed Jews for ashtrays — or the ovens specially built by the top bakery supply company in Berlin to handle the incinerating of Jewish corpses. He had found a new voice in the cruise ship's library, all thanks to Evanoff. The hell with him and his judgment! He had taken something negative and turned it into a golden gift, and he had conquered his fear once again.

No one had ever given a Seder like this, combining the Exodus and the Holocaust. The room was so alive with feeling he could barely contain his own emotion.

"There is a word that linguists consider to be the most untranslatable word in the world. The word is *Ilunga*, a Bantu word. It means 'a person ready to forgive any abuse the first time, to tolerate it a second time, but never a third time.' We, as Jews, must never allow a third time. Bless you all and Good Yontif."

They were standing, lifting him up to that magic place only a triumph before a large group of people can ever lift anyone. Women and grown men had tears running down their faces. This was his gift, his calling!

Evanoff was nothing. A jealous old cynic who hadn't the potential to move masses of people with his words, his charisma. He had won. Now he could look at him, now they were eye to eye, through the glass darkly but face to face: biblical!

Where was he? It must have been too much competition for him. How could he have left without me seeing? Evanoff had gone.

"Solly, I need air. Let's take a walk on the deck. My God, Solly, look at my arm! I have goose bumps. I have never had goose bumps in my life except when we walked inside the portals of St. Peter's and tonight. I am moved beyond words. That rabbi was, like a prophet! I feel so, so connected to my fellow man, to everyone. I am so glad we went to that. Where have we been all our lives? In a coma? I am so proud of us, to do that. To be so open to new ideas!

"If I hadn't run into that darling lady from the face-reading thing, we would never have done this. Solly, we have to tell our children how important this is: to be more aware of Israel and the plight of our Jewish friends. Look at my arm! I am swelling with emotion from this experience."

"Well, I'm swelling with gas from that food. My Neapolitan stomach would never have made it to the Red Sea. Gotta go to the cabin for some Tums. Then we're gonna trip the light fantastic, enough death for one night. That thing about drawing obscene pictures on human skin while I was trying to swallow the Filthy fish or whatever the hell that stuff was, will haunt my dreams. A little Tony Bennett or something is what I need."

"Yes. Yes, enough. I agree. I'll go with you. I could actually use a little something. Maybe a slice."

"Good, let's go. And if you're still swollen with passion later on, let's try substituting a little ensuite Porno for Adolf Hitler and see what happens."

"Oh Solly, you're my prophet."

"Yeah, but no more funny hats. I've got a dent in my head from that yamkala."

"I'll gel it when we get to the room."

⌒⁄⌒

My darling Maria,

I have only a moment, but I had to add to my last letter. More bad news I'm afraid. I may decide not to send these letters at all, but writing them to you is so very helpful. We have had a terrible thing happen. The little dog of the Countess was found dead and everyone has been upset, but most especially the Countess.

I feel myself responsible, because I left the dog with her grandson and I did not check on him and I do not think he was caring of the animal or of his grandmother.

And more things. The two young people, Miss Twinkle and Mr. Ian, they did not come back before the ship departed. This is quite unsettling. I do not know what I can do, but the good spirit is gone and I know this is selfish, but I fear it will reflect badly on me with Mr. Hensler.

And the last thing is about my friend Jo Jo. I went to him to try and talk with him to see if he was still upset and he was very nervous. He would not look into my eyes and he told me he could not tell me what it was, "for my own good." This was so strange and when he left he said something even more strange. He said, "Elonzito, if Mr. Hensler asks you to do any special favors for him, no matter what you have to say, don't agree, don't let him go any further. Tell him you're too busy, tell him anything. Trust me. It's too late for me, save yourself."

And he raced off! His face was so troubled. And now I fear what Momma would call the Evil Eye is on us. I do not want to think like this and I do not want you to worry. I am fine. But this is beyond my experience. I am thinking that I would prefer to go back to being a steward on a lower deck. I am

*not worldly enough to deal with these important people. It is
quite a different way they live their lives. Now I must go . . .
the third day is ending. I cannot say I will be sorry for this
cruise to finish.*

Your adoring husband, E

Chapter Four: Day Four

LATITUDE

Your Daily At Sea Newspaper

Are we having fun or what? We've had great cruise buzz about our whirlwind day in St. John's, so, of course, we've got to top it in Bridgetown, the gem of Barbados!

Though Barbados became independent in 1966, the influence of its former ruler, Great Britain is evident in everything from its cricket playing to the fantastic chocolate and china products.

For those of you history and culture buffs who didn't make it to our Cruise Director, Derrick Doolittle's lecture last evening, you can re-play the event en-suite before you go ashore.

And for the truly intrigued, a cricket demonstration will be held on the Sports Deck at 9:30 a.m. If you plan to play some yourself or have a round of golf at the Sandy Lane Golf Club, be sure to do it before you attempt the Mount Gay Rum Distillery tour, just in case the tasting room lures you!!

For those staying aboard, we have a few special treats. Our very own Taffy Daniels will bring her dancing expertise to a rip-roaring Texas Two step class and barbeque lunch, no experience required. We'll even provide the Long Necks and the cowboy hats! Or if crooning is more your style, join our Flamingo lounge headliner, Freddy Fratelli and try your hand at sing-a-long with Como, Sinatra, Damone and all your favorite oldies. Bring your grandkids and give them a musical history lesson!

For our more religious passengers, the Reverend Otis Ohrmond from the First Baptist Church of Mobile, Alabama will give a talk on the Resurrection and the true meaning of Easter in the Yoga Pavilion right after the Not for Sissies, Hot Room advanced Ashtanga class (and yes, if you have to ask what that means, you won't like it!) Also, the Reverend Father, William O'Malley will provide counseling and confession in the chapel between two and four today, for those of you who may have been overdoing the fun part of our journey! Just kidding cruisers!!

The dress tonight is informal. And if you've mastered your two-step, there's a Country Western Shindig after the second Dinner seating with our own good old band, the Horny Hornets.

Have a great day in Bridgetown. Remember we set sail promptly at 6 p.m.!

RINGING, RINGING, forcing her up, don't want to go, sleeping was so sweet, sleep like this, no demon dreams, no grinding jaw, lolling, lazing, peaceful sleep, baby sleep, down deep, make it stop ringing. . . . I want more. . . .

"Rory?"

No more ringing. A voice now. A man's voice, saying her name. A husky, Cary Granty sort of voice calling her up from such lovely peace. . . .

Pressure on the bed. The voice closer. "Rory, there's a call."

She opened her eyes. It was dark in the cabin and the dimness played tricks with his face, his bald head casting shadows, hollowing out his cheeks. His eyes were smiling. She'd never really seen his eyes like that, glassless, vulnerable.

A man in a white Hotel-At-Sea provided bathrobe, murmuring her name in the morning light. She smiled up at him. Even weirder, morning was not her smiley time. It took hours for her to commit to actually being up and dealing with the day.

"Unless it's good news, tell them to call later. I was having the most peaceful sleep and I don't have rehearsal until 12."

"Well, I don't think it's good news but whatever it is, it's Leah Worth and she sounds a bit urgent. Shall I inquire further?"

Rory sat up. So much for peaceful sleep-ins. "You're sure it's not just a social protocol-call?"

"Instinct says no."

"Okay, I'm up. I'll get it here."

He stood up and she felt the movement, the loss of his warmth and heaviness as a new emptiness.

"Leah?"

"Oh, Rory, I'm sorry to call so early. Please forgive me. I just had to ask you something about last night."

"Of course, anything. Not much happened."

"After we left, was Clarissa with you the entire evening?"

Rory was wide-awake now. Something wasn't good about this.

"Well, most of it. We took Clarissa to the Grotto disco and she wasn't feeling well. I think she was getting her period, she said she had terrible cramps and I offered her some Advil, but she said it wouldn't help, so Poe suggested she go down to the clinic and get something stronger and maybe a heating pad and off she went."

"Do you remember what time that was?"

"I think it must have been around 11, not too late. We wanted to go with her, but she said that would be 'totally embarrassing', her words, actually she just told me, she didn't want Poe to know. I told her we were going back to my cabin if she needed anything. Why Leah, what happened?"

"Did she say anything else about what she might do after?"

"Let me think. Oh, she said if the pills worked, she might hook up with a guy she'd met that afternoon and go back to the disco. They'd had some tentative sort of, maybe we'll hang-out deal, you know the way kids date now."

"Did she mention a name?"

"If she did, it's left my grey matter, but after I have a large coffee it may come back. What's going on?"

"Oh, God, I'm probably just being a Jewish mother, but, Rory, she didn't come back to her room last night. When Walter woke up he went to check and her bed hasn't been slept in and after what happened to that young woman the first night . . . I'm trying to stay calm but I'm really frantic. It's not like her. She's so reliable and she knows it would frighten us. I didn't want to make a fuss or have Walter call security until I'd spoken with you."

"Oh, sure, I understand. Of course you're frantic. But the way this ship works, things are on a twenty-four hour clock. The casino is open very late and there's the all-night After Hours club and these kids, they party away until six and then go have breakfast. She may just be waiting so she doesn't call and wake you up.

"Let me get myself together and I'll ask Poe if he knows anything else and I'll meet you by the main pool in an hour, okay? We'll find her."

"Oh, Rory, you're an angel. Thank you."

"Don't worry."

Rory sat up. What a throw away line. She *should* be worried. Clarissa wasn't in a party mood last night and she sure as hell didn't seem like that kind of kid . . . twenty-three, smenty-three . . . kids they still were. Also she was almost doubled over with cramps. She said she was going to get some meds and go to bed. The "I shall return" line had sounded to her like bravado for Poe's benefit if anything, so he wouldn't insist on going with her.

They still hadn't caught whoever attacked Collie, which she'd only just heard about through the rehearsal rumor-mill, but it sounded truly unnerving.

So now she and Leah were bonding over a *missing* child! Talk about irony. Talk about how she would not have chosen to start this precious day.

She sighed and slid off the bed and padded over to the little junior sitting area opening onto the small outside balcony where Poe had gone. The sun was shining on him and he was concentrating on some files. He looked so solid and sturdy and alive, and dependable. *And* trustworthy.

She wanted to throw herself onto him, clasp him around, bury herself against him and cover him with slobbery, weepy kisses of gratitude and slurping, puppy-panting need. But instead she planted a small peck on the top of his sunburning head and sat down next to him. There was, after all, only so much emotion a three and a half day old love affair could handle.

"What are you reading?" Rory poured herself a cup of coffee from the room service pot. There was a warm, gentle breeze, a blue, cloudless sky, and the water so far below them was glistening silvery green as they whizzed along, like some enormous sea monster, disturbing the deepest privacy of the natural world.

We have no business here, she thought and turned to tell him. Whoa. A coffee companion, a fellow tooth-brusher in a matching white robe—a couple of sorts, asking things like, "what are you reading" and passing the sugar and all these domestic actions repeated a million times a minute all over the planet by couples of all conceivable sorts and now she was, one of them, a sharer-wither.

"I'm reading a hodgepodge of material about the Nature of Evil for an article I've been working on. Not exactly sunshine and sea air fare, but fascinating."

He paused and smiled at her. "What did Leah Worth want?"

"It's very unsettling. Clarissa never came back to their suite last night. She wanted to know how long she'd been with us. I'm going to meet her in an hour. I didn't know what else to do. I'm sure she's fine, but after the attack on Collie O'Brian, I told you about that, well I don't blame her for being freaked out."

"Can I help?"

"I'll let you know after I see Leah. Hopefully, Clarissa's on her way back from some all-night party-hardy deal in someone's cabin."

He didn't smile. "Awfully ironic for you to be offering help to her concerning a missing child."

A moment of utter suspension of belief. A second of time-stopping, her coffee half-swallowed, her hand frozen on the cup. She gasped, tears washing her face, a gush of them, how many more could there possibly be?

He laughed, head thrown back, hearty and full of vibrato. "Good God, Rory, if that made you sob, you most certainly don't want to hear about the nature of evil."

"No, it's so pathetic. I was thinking the same thing when I was talking to Leah and then you said it back to me, like you'd been inside my head. I've never had anyone do anything like that before. This is truly maudlin."

He reached over and took her free hand and gently squeezed it.

"You must stop doing this, you know, justifying your feelings, degrading them. Every single one of them is a gift.

"I've spent thirty years watching injured people struggle to reclaim them, to feel anything; so much damage was done to their ability to express what was in their hearts and souls, and that's partly what this article is about. Can't quite believe that natural selection wouldn't have disposed of all those messy emotions only we humans are capable of, envy and lust and rage and frustration and fear and jealousy and grief and the rest if they served no purpose, if they were not, in fact, essential to our survival and growth.

"They would have shriveled by now, don't you think, gone the way of the semi-erect posture and the grunt?

"And also, what you've just described is one of the rarest and most extraordinary of human interactions. Connection. A moment of being received. Oh well, look at that. I made a speech. That's what three cups of coffee before breakfast will do to me."

"This is good. This can be a morning routine. I sob and you give impassioned, brilliant responses and then we order omelettes. I like this."

She wiped her face and resumed sipping her coffee and they were quiet for a moment, nothing but the sound of the ship barreling forward toward their dockage in Bridgetown.

"Speaking of natural selection, what I was going to say before the waterworks was, we don't belong out here. These ships don't belong here; it's like putting the Chrysler building on rudders and launching one every day. It's horrible.

"I hate being a part of it, I gotta tell you. Well, we're both a part of it. But, if I can make this new show work I don't want to write this crap, anymore. Every time I have to come on board to work, I'm a neurotic wreck for at least a week before. I keep wanting to apologize to the ocean for doing this to it."

He laughed again, more like a chuckle this time, his eyes crinkling, making her heart flutter. "Well, if I ever need to find someone to accept blame for anything, I know exactly where to look. You are absolutely adorable, you know. If there is an opposite of evil, it isn't good, it's you."

"Wow. What a thing to say! Thanks, Doc. I wish I had a tape recorder out here. I'd replay it when I get home if I'm feeling low." More tears glistening without quite falling now.

He stopped smiling. In fact she had never seen a face get more serious, more suddenly than his was now. . . .

"You won't need a tape recorder because I will be there to tell you myself every day for the rest of my life if you'll let me."

Up. She was up. Not knowing where to go, but needing to go somewhere. The magnitude alone, the thought alone, the no-way-back-of-it all, slammed into her like a sea gull into plate glass.

"Oh, shit, Poe. I gotta get ready to meet Leah. Shit, shit, shit! How can I . . . this is way too Lifetime-for-Women for me. You can't *know* that. You can't ask me to *trust* that! Please. *Please.* It's way too scary. I'll call you after I find out something. Don't take it back, but don't say it again, okay?"

He looked so sad, she felt so bad, but it was all she could do not to jump off the balcony.

"I'm sorry I scared you. I won't take it back and I won't say it again until you're ready. It was arrogant of me and you're right to push away. I know you're scared and I'm not scared because I'm so sure of who you are, but you have no way of being sure of who I am and you're right not to trust me.

"There's an ancient Chinese proverb, excuse the lameness of that line, but one of the endless ancient Chinese proverbs says, 'Go straight to the heart of danger for there you will find safety.' Maybe that will help a bit."

"And there's an ancient Irish proverb that says, Oy. Oh and one from George Bernard Shaw, another ancient Irishman who said, 'the two greatest tragedies of life are not getting your heart's desire and getting your heart's desire.' So maybe if we smoosh the Jews, the Irish and the Chinese together, we'll figure this stuff out."

His eyes crinkled again, but his mouth was still sad and she wanted to lean over and kiss him and she did and neither of them said one more word. That, she thought afterward, was the very best part.

"So SUE ME, I'm vain. I don't give a crap what my wife thinks, so I work out a lot. Nothing is gonna come between me having a 33 inch waist and a constant weight of 170! I'm gonna maintain my 'plant', okay?

"She's all on my case because I wanna take Brutus our Great Dane in for a dye job and maybe a little work on his chin. When I see him looking old, it bums me out—not the image I project, man.

"I had my eyes done, why shouldn't Brutus look good? It's depressing to see him looking old and I'm in my prime. Forty is the new 25.

"I get almond scrubs and sea algae facials, and weekly massages and mannies and peddies. Any opportunity for the nasty, I know I'm tip top I'm good to go at any time, if you catch my drift. My wife can't stand it, thinks it's fruity and she gets all competitive, 'You look better than I do,' and I do.

"So it's really her fault if women want me, ya know? If she jiggles and has chipped toenails, why wouldn't I stray? So it may all go down over Brutus. She says she'll leave me if try to de-age him, so let it be. Old dog, old wife, get past it and on with life.

"I made that up, sort of my morning mantra for the trip, though she's still clueless and I gotta tell ya pal, with the Botox and Viagra, I'm gonna be like, ageless!

"Check out that suckable little babe in the red thong over by the bar. No more than what? 19? Did her in her cabin first night out. Banged her boobies off. She thought I was 28! Ah, life is sweet. And I even have a pre-nup. So, it's all cool. Good genes, good jeans, 4 hours per in the gym, no pain, no gain and the rest is medical science, what a great time to be living."

Rory turned her head as far to the side as possible to see the reciter of this revolting but captivating little biography. His back was to her but he looked pretty much as advertised. He was wearing a too tight tank top, of course, gotta maximize all that gym time, four hours a day! She was still working on four hours a week as a goal, talk about jiggle.

The back of his tank top said, "If you can read this, the bitch fell off." Very cute. Wonder if his wife picked it out. Maybe they were Hell's Angels from the Yuppie division. Did Hell's Angels have divisions? Probably not.

A tiny, slickly bronzed, top heavy brunette stumbled along into his lear range on huge, clunky, cork-soled gold platform sandals, that looked almost like stilts with laces that wrapped half way up her well-muscled calves.

How long would that take, Rory wondered. All that winding things around and tying them up? Did the girl actually think no one could tell she was really short? It was like the fake boob thing . . . *we know*. So then what's the point, hobbling around like that with your calves cramping and rope burns probably on your skin and all the time it must take to get them on and off and *we know you're short*. Nothing made any sense to her anymore. Face lifts for dogs? Maybe they offer twofers, poochie and parent, under the knife together, an anthropomorphic family rate.

She looked at her watch. She was early. Fifteen minutes until Leah arrived. Good. She needed to focus and figure something out.

Poe said every day for the rest of his life. Terror dripped down the back of her neck in ripples, like sweat.

I've only been a fool for love twice. Walter and Jesse, otherwise I've had a pretty good grip on reality. . . . People lied. People said things they didn't mean. People said things they did mean at the time, but changed their minds. People used other people for their own gains. People made promises they did not keep. People disappeared forever. People died.

This she knew. This she had found out all by herself during her 52 years on the planet by experiencing all the above. Not many illusions left, for which she was actually very grateful. Flora gushing on about her "fella" made her squirm.

I do not want to be a gusher-oner, I do not want to be a fool and trust another narcissist or sociopathic son of a bitch, who says things like, "For the rest of my life" and doesn't mean it or says it before

*I've decided if I mean it. So, Poe, reap and sow . . . ice and snow . . .
on with the show . . . how do you know . . . love can go . . . say it isn't
so. You're rhyming again, Rory. Haven't done that for three days. Is
this good or bad?*

"I know $2,000 is a lot for a crib, but it's for two babies and
I've already spent $20,000 on the nursery. It's their environment,
why shouldn't it be the best? I waited so long to have them; I want
excellence everywhere.

"Like this cruise, start them seeing the world, and being open-
minded and flexible. I have French language tapes playing every
night and, I have CD's of Einstein's theories, sort of Einstein for
Dummies, and I play them at nap times. I really do believe they are
capable of so much more than we even understand."

Rory opened her eyes, this she had to see. Two women who
looked like older versions of that bride-to-be and her friend the
un-Stacy from the first day in the Jacuzzi were pushing twin stroll-
ers, one holding triplets and the one who had the nursery that cost
more than her rent for the year had one containing twins.

The twins were still in the drooling-pacifier stage; Einstein and
French conjugations seemed a stretch but hey, why not! Skip right
the fuck over the Alphabet song, Barney and Big Bird to Proust,
and quantum physics.

And what was with all of these multiple births everywhere?
Central Park on a Saturday afternoon looked like Yorkshire in April,
bursting with litters or flocks or whatever the human equivalent
might be. Middle-aged mothers and their fertility drugs, the new
way of breeding. *Too bad, they were still mammals . . . if we figure
out a way for them to lay eggs . . . out come the double-wide stroll-
ers, . . . have to widen all the sidewalks and jogging paths and the
roadways and build bigger SUV's and drive the environmental
activists further insane. . . .*

*Your brain is overheating, again. This was supposed to be quiet,
thought time. Uh, Oh . . . they're passing right by the "bitch fell off"
guy . . . eye contact? Nope . . . at least he isn't the father of the mul-
tiples. Something to be glad about, human potential wise. . . .*

*Oh, Boy, Leah's right behind them . . . what am I doing here . . .
acting like this is no big deal . . . a little normal-just-another-daily-
old- friend encounter . . . I'm getting into something I don't want to
get into . . . look at her . . . serenely gliding, waving, smiling, Jackie
Kennedy at the funeral—is that good? Why does everyone think it's*

so great when women rise above, no tears, no falling down in a faint at the casket, or no hysterical sobbing at the thought that your kid might be the victim of a brutal rapist.

Why is this good? The elegant Jackie, perfectly coiffed, holding the hands of her perfectly outfitted, perfectly gorgeous, every-hair-in-place . . . (one gift, one great little Irish gift, the kids had great hair, all that great-in-a-crisis-hair) . . . and Mom standing tall and regal and brave . . . all those other emotions Poe was talking about, so what about that?

Leah the Jewish Jackie . . . grace under pressure . . . never see her sweat, never see her frown, never hear a spontaneously-unpleasant-or-negative-or-angry-or-gross-or-imperfect word or snort or burp or fart or inappropriate comment or gesture or . . . if someone seems too good to be true they are.

Shit, I'm in it now, right back in it. Might as well be thirty years ago. . . . All I need is my Drill Team outfit and a Pez machine. How did I get myself into this? How could I not know I can't handle this? Me and my big mouth. Me and my Seder at Sea. What about the ol'unconscious, Ror? What about all that therapy?

Get a grip, she's almost here. . . . Well, she does look a little strained, tired maybe. Something sort of human to relate to . . . not so completely Jackie With The Kids, maybe a little Liz Taylor after Mike Todd died . . . even worse! Damsel in Distress, and I get to be, who? Fucking Eddie Fisher. . . .

"Rory, you came! Oh, thank you. Bless you for coming."

"Of course I came. Do you think I have the sort of life where I get lots of calls from distraught friends asking me to help them find their missing daughters? Like I'm up to my ears in such requests, can't even process them all even on cruises, so it's easy for me to just forget and not show up?"

"Oh, no. I'm so sorry, that must have sounded awful! I meant it was so lovely of you, I invaded your privacy and everything and it's so good to see you, just the two of us. Forgive me, it's been a very distressing morning so far."

"Forgive me too, I'm feeling a tad edgy myself. So let's have it. What's happened?"

Tears falling from the damsel's eyes, far more Liz than Jackie. What was the word for it . . . limpid . . . yes, "eyes like limpid pools" . . . irresistible, she really was. . . . I am fucking Eddie . . . gonna blow my entire life as a person of common sense to go to her aid. . . .

"Oh, Rory, I'm so afraid. Walter's with the security people. We've looked everywhere we can think of. No one's seen her."

"Well, *someone's* seen her, just not the someones you've talked to."

Here it comes, here you go Rory, you knew it would come out of your trap, so just get it over with . . . help her out here . . . what was that song Eddie sang, 'Oh my Poppa'? God I hated that song. . . .

"Leah, I want to tell you something that may be of help. I have a son somewhere. He's older than Clarissa. His father kidnapped him when he was five and I've never found him . . ."

"Oh, my God. Oh Rory, I . . ."

"No, no. Please. I'm not telling you to bond over missing children or for sympathy or anything. I just, the thing is, I spent so many years searching and I worked with a lot of private detectives and I know how to look for someone. So, if you want, I'll try and find out what I can. I'm pretty good at it and I know the ship's security guys and they like me so if you want help, I'll do my best."

"Oh, Rory, I would be so grateful for anything you could do! I didn't know you had a child. And to lose him like that, I can't even imagine what you've been through, and if this brings it all back and it's too painful, I really understand. It is so unbelievable, isn't it? To find one another again like this? It really does make you believe in a higher power.

"I'm trying to stay calm and in the present, God only knows I've spent enough time in Yoga classes learning how to do it, but I just, I feel so guilty. I let her down, Rory. She's been having a great struggle with her friends. I don't want to break her confidence, but I don't think she'd mind; she really adored you, but I didn't support her, I was terrible.

"I guess I have such a hard time looking at anyone critically, it scared me. I'm just not like that, I always see good and want to like everyone and look for the silver-lining. My mother always said if there were Jewish nuns, I'd be one, but Clarissa needed me to be more supportive and I'm afraid I upset something in her and maybe because of that she used bad judgment and I'm so worried about Walter, she's his pride and joy, I've never seen him so distressed. I really didn't know where to turn.

"I don't want to burden him any more and I want to do something, not just sit around and worry and be selfish. . . ."

So how did it go down? Eddie rushed to Liz's side when her flamboyant-bigger than life-movie mogul-older husband who she leaned on and needed . . . her sparring partner and giver of furs and jewels and probably serious orgasms was killed in a plane crash and Eddie offered nice, menschy, Boy Singer comfort and held her elbow (OY not a good sign) and then she let him hold other things and before ya knew it, he'd abandoned Debbie Reynolds, the spunky tap-dancing heroine and their two small kids . . . and Eddie took the plunge and ended up singing, "Oh My Papa," in retirement homes or something and Liz rallied all the way up to Richard Burton and the biggest diamond in the world and got even more beautiful and famous and so what is going on here Rory?

A smallish victim script? A succubus fear? A good old fashioned trust your gut instinct about Leah and the possibility you were right to run and your long ago resentment and anger was a pretty decent attempt at self-protection and marshmallows may be great over a nice hot hibachi, but in human form they are pretty tricky . . . can't see in and wherever you press they change shape and then bounce right back to that same marshmallowy form . . . so unless you plan to set her aflame maybe you . . .

"Worry is selfish, don't you think? I try to do my part, I don't want Walter to shoulder this alone, I . . ."

"You know what I think, Leah? I think *everything* is selfish. *Everything*. We start with the self, and sure we have moments of 'lessness' here and there, but the selfish concept is just too hard for most women to face.

"You don't see guys all tortured and hand-wringing about their selfishness, they even think it's macho and a sign that they're tough and driven, a success totem or something. Mainly, I don't even think men think about that kind of stuff.

"For women, for *mothers*, Hello and Howdy Do, to guilt about selfishness, forever and ever! But the truth is, how can Motherhood not be selfish? We can't say we did it for our child, because when the decision to have one is made, there *is* no child. *We* want to be mothers. And why? Because we're selfish!

"We want someone to love, to love us, need us, take care of us when we're old and donked out, give us status, a reason to live, to fit in with our peers, to compete with our peers, to please our spouses and parents — to have someone who adores us and looks up to us and brings us pools of soppy joy and gives meaning to our otherwise ordinary lives — to be the most important person in the world to *someone*, to be irreplaceable.

"Even the instinct to fuck in the first place, is pure animal need and selfishness. What is the sex drive but the meeting of an immediate selfish need, to bring us pleasure? Nothing noble or motherly about the old sex drive, which is good or there would be no more mothers to worry about whether they let their kids down.

"Leah, try to look at it that way for a minute, look at it as an endless set-up for self-abuse. Mothers are supposed to be entirely un-selfish, taking the food from their mouths, tits, wherever to sustain their young; flinging themselves in front of trains, planes and automobiles; fighting off attackers and lifting car wheels with super human strength; foregoing any thought of self for the rest of their lives to protect, guide, nurture and support their off-spring. Unlike, I might add, any other maternal creature in creation. Every other one of them from Caribous to cockroaches, drop the kid, get it fed until it can survive by itself and then it's 'Later, Larry' time. Mom moves on.

"The fact that human mothers are almost incapable of 'moving on', even when their kids are *old*, says something! I'm not quite sure what, but it is about *our* need for them, our *selfish* interest in them to brighten our lives and it's really only the little *toe* of why mothers are so angst-ridden, self-tortured piles of stress at least from my observations and the little . . . the time I had with my son, from what I saw and felt myself. And this is what the *good* mothers go through! The bad mothers just check out or blame everything on *their* mothers or their kids or their husbands or the school system.

"Please, don't look so horrified, please Leah! I'm trying to stoke you up a little with that reality thing you were talking about. The point is, give yourself a little break here or you won't be able to help Clarissa. You're just a decent human being who has a daughter who's missing for the moment.

"This is not anymore your fault than if she'd been kidnapped by aliens. And believe me I know, it took me years of therapy to take the axe out of my own back, okay? So, I'm going to start where I last saw her and you're going to find Walter and let's meet back here in two hours. I don't have rehearsal until 12 and it's only 8. We'll be docking soon, which is good. We'll find her. I have a few ideas."

Jesus Herbie, look at her face. I went too far, I did, she has clearly never conceived of her self as anything but noble and nice. I hit something, some nerve . . . shit, Rory, why couldn't you just put on your "nice" mask... when talking to marshmallows, "nice" masks are a very good protective mechanism... oh, I get it, I know.... I got rid of Eddie... no "Oh My Poppa" refrains, no way.

"Well, Rory, I must say, that was really, I think, overpowering. Such a, a new way of seeing things. So much to absorb! Fascinating, and I'm so grateful you shared it with me, after what you've been through, you see things so much more clearly. I have so much to tell Clarissa, so much to still learn. I just hope she won't blame me too much. I'd better try and find Walter and see what the security people know. Thank you, Rory, really."

"I haven't done anything, yet. It's going to be alright, Leah. You'll all be back to normal by wine and dine time."

Look at this! She's morphing back into perfect, poreless composure... always her necessary posture... seamless, never revealing anything less than serenity.... Here she is... right here.... Seamless and beauteous and I wouldn't want to be her for anything....

Where to start? All those episodes of Without a Trace... all those years looking for Billy... and here I am... need a new visual... not Jackie and the kids... not Eddie and Liz... how about Angelina Jolie in Lara Croft? Craft?... someone gorgeous with tattoos... wild and free... who never fails and never takes any shit from anyone... yes, also supernatural powers... much better.... I've been dating myself with my visuals.... Clarissa could have been my daughter... I never used any birth control with Walter... did he? He must have, but still... think of that, she could be my... stop this... concentrate... you were in the disco... she was dancing with someone with very curly hair... tall... maybe Hispanic or Italian and she came back to the table and said she had cramps and she left... go back there, maybe someone saw something....

What was she wearing... oh right, someone would remember that.... Flora's gold sequined skirt with all the rhinestones... and a black sleeveless turtleneck... quite the fashion observer you are there... how did she get Flora's skirt? She told you... after the Seder, she went backstage with who? Walter. Yes, her father took her backstage because the Talbotts invited them, and he wanted to make an appearance because they hadn't gone to dinner and Flora was holding court and Clarissa admired one of her outfits and Flora said, "It's yours for the evening, Princess that's my lucky boogie skirt, I met the man of my dreams wearin' that. You will, too." And she put it on, which means she left her skirt there.... Find Flora.

Maybe Clarissa went back to change . . . didn't want to get her period and bleed on Flora's special skirt. She would do something like that . . . start there. Then the clinic . . . if she made it there . . . someone would remember . . . don't say things like "if"—Lara Croft or Craft would not say "if"—Goddesses with snake tattoos never doubted a positive, triumphant outcome . . . this was way better than Eddie or Jackie even. . . .

I should call Poe . . . tell him I'm not coming back now . . . maybe that's too . . . what? Too much like we're a couple . . . too close to 'for the rest of my life-ish' . . . how about just polite, Rory. Can't one little spontaneous gesture ever occur with you?

Wait, he has a lecture today. Yes . . . yes . . . maybe I'll just swing by after instead . . . rather than interrupt his Evil research . . . oh boy . . . is he so interested in that stuff because he might actually himself be evil? Stop it . . . keep moving forward, now, you're almost out of passenger range . . . there's Derrick with the Talbotts, god damn, he really does do the cruise and schmooze deal better than anyone . . . he's practically gargoyle level . . . wonder if he saw Clarissa?

Later, I'll save him for after . . . oh, the Dog dame is with him. . . . Clarissa said she was in the dressing room too, she might know something . . . not yet . . . keep moving . . . the skirt, follow the skirt. . . .

What the hell deck am I on? Never been on this one . . . kiddie pool, rock climbing wall . . . too many people . . . look at that, miniature golf, jungle gyms, do they still call them that? Parents galore . . . how many swing pushes can anyone do . . . how many, "oh good girl Tiffany, do that little belly flop again so Mommy can take a picture." . . . yak . . . yak . . . yak, passenger chit chat . . . what do they talk about all day . . . standing around watching their traveling buddies partake of all these goofy activities? Love to listen . . . wish I was not only invisible but had X-ray ears . . . gotta find the crew door down to the back stairs of the theater.

What's the picture on that woman's tee shirt? A little fish called "Darwin" being eaten by a big fish called . . . he's wrinkling up . . . what's the word? "Truth." . . . Oh brother.

In the twenty-first century, roll right back past evolution . . . imagine being raised like that . . . better to be neglected, at least I didn't end up like one of those glazed-over ladies, warbling for the Lord on Sunday cable channels. . . . Go Genesis . . . if it were only that simple . . . people need to make it so simple . . . life's too hard to handle—all those uncertainties. . . . Good Things Happening to Bad

People, Bad Things Happening to Bad People, Bad things happening to Completely Ordinary People.... Day Six the Dinosaurs... fuck carbon dating....

Gotta get past this crowd and out of here.... Okay, there's the door....

Down and down I go, round and round I go... stage door... love backstage... love that feeling of the process... the change from empty to magic... precious private world of creating it... empty theaters are so, hopeful... loss and hope... round and round... no one here yet.... Flora's probably still in her cabin sleeping....

Knock first.... "Flora? Flor, it's Rory." No one in there... don't even know where her cabin is.... Please door... be open.... Let the creationist chick with the anti-evolution Tee shirt get the Lord to open it. Yes....

Okay. Here we go.... Feels really weird.... Flora won't like this, she's so private... underneath all the southern hospitality stuff... we share that... only I don't do the hospitality part... smells like her... powder and gardenias... Flora... Floral... so girlie... everything is so fem... family pictures... lots of plucky old ladies... all that history stuff.... Flora pictures... why would anyone have pictures of themselves to look at?... Get real....

She'll hate this... maybe I should try and call her first and tell her I'm in here... just look around Rory, you're not doing anything wrong, Flora is the one freaking out about the rapist, rallying the cast, she'll understand... over in the corner on the chair... looks like street clothes, look there first... what was Clarissa wearing before? Something simple, because of the Seder... a black skirt. Yes, silky and short.... Shit. It's still here! She never came back for it. This is not good. Clarissa would have come back to change....

What now? The clinic? Or.... Photo gallery! They took pictures at the Seder.... Maybe a photo would help. I'll go there first, then I'll call Flora, then I'll hit the clinic.... Good... forward momentum, that's what Irving the Vegas P.I. always said, "keep moving forward, don't look back."... good life advice generally speaking... unless you're in Freudian Analysis... not even Woody Allen is still in Freudian Analysis....

What time is it? I've already taken twenty minutes... photo gallery's too far... take too long. A beautiful young woman with bright red hair and a gold skirt is enough.... I'll just go down to the clinic... I'm only two decks away. Do that first... then Flora...

Down and Down . . . when was I in the clinic? Oh God, two cruises ago . . . stepped on that hornet on the beach . . . so painful . . . never thought anything could hurt so much . . . screaming out loud . . . all alone . . . so scared . . . that terrible old bitch . . . Nurse Pammy? Something like that . . . so mean. . . . Dr. Padma . . . Derrick's chess buddy . . . sweet to me . . . good Daddy man . . . put that morphine drip in my arm and I cried in his arms . . . regressed all the way back to the Four-Plex . . . sobbing my heart out . . . "My family's dead, my Dad never held me. . . . I don't want to die. . . ." kind . . . stroked my hair. . . . "You're not going to die, dear . . . you had the misfortune to step on one of the two most painful sites in the human body for such a wound . . . you will be fine as soon as the medicine begins to work . . . do not worry . . . I will stay with you.". . . Maybe he's there, maybe he'll remember me. . . .

Oh shit, it's Nurse Nightmare . . . look at her face . . . talk about a pickle puss . . . she could have popped right out of one of the old Canter's Deli barrels. . . . Be nice, Rory, put your nice mask on. . . .

"May I help you?"

"I hope so. My name is Rory Saltz, I'm a writer for the show and I'm trying to find my friend's daughter. A redheaded young woman named Clarissa Worth? She was wearing a black sleeveless turtleneck and a gold sequined skirt and she left us last night about 11; she had cramps and we told her to come down here for some medication and no one's seen her since and her family is quite concerned, so I was wondering if you or whoever was on duty saw her or treated her."

"Nope. I was here. If she'd been in, I would have seen her."

"Is it possible you might have gone on a break or something?"

"No."

"Okay, well, what if she came in much later? Maybe she went and took a nap and then got up and came down after you went off duty?"

"I didn't go off duty."

"Oh, so you're like, what? Nurse Vampire? Work all night and all day."

Easy, Rory, your mouth is going to mess this up.

"Very funny. None of your business, is it now. I'm a former marine. We know how to pace and we know how to work, unlike some others I could name."

"Was Dr. Padma around at all? He treated me for a bee sting a couple of months ago."

"Oh, now I remember you. Screamed like you'd lost a leg. No, he was not."

"Look, it's really serious, she's not the kind of girl to stay out all night and not tell her parents. They're very worried, especially after the attack on Collie O'Brian."

"So, why should I tell you, anyway? You're a writer or so you say, not the F.B.I. It's security's business and they haven't been in. These sleazy kids are the bane of the clinic. All of their parents think they're living saints and you wouldn't believe the garbage that goes on or what staggers in here—dead drunk, overdosing, bingeing, group sex—makes me sick. She's probably passed out in some guy's cabin. She'll turn up."

"Okay, Nurse, Scrooge was it?"

"Look, lady, your friend's kid is not my problem."

"No, your problem is more clinical."

Good, Rory, very nice. Look at that face . . . her eyes are actually sparking with fury . . . like the top of her head's going to blow . . . like a sort of human pickle version of Mt. Ranier, but she's not saying anything . . . why isn't she retorting? This is a very retortable type person. . . . Something's not right. . . . I don't believe her. . . .

Why would she lie? But she is, she's hiding something . . . the old overheating in your head could really run you ragged now . . . keep it simple . . . don't tell her what you think . . . just go before she leaps up and injects you in the back of the neck with some horrible deadly substance . . . back out, Rory . . . just to be safe.

"Well, okay. You have a nice day, Nurse."

Look at her, we're in some eye lock power thing. . . . I'm not looking away . . . this is what they mean by "if looks could kill" . . . stare the witch down. . . . Oh God, she's lying. . . . This is not good at all. . . .

Close the door, go call Flora. . . . That is one scary person. . . . Could it be some plot? Holding Clarissa for ransom? Keep it simple. . . . Picklette could even be right . . . the curly headed guy, maybe she went with him and . . . naw . . . don't believe that . . . Clarissa would have returned the skirt if she thought she was getting her period and she would have gone to get some meds if she was worse . . . I'm trusting what Irving taught me. . . . "If you trust yourself, you don't have to trust anyone else and you don't have to be right."

⤮

WALTER WORTH SLID onto one of the fake wicker stools of the Polynesian Pool bar with the easy elegance of the aging athlete and ordered a beer. Probably not a great idea. Coffee would better fit the situation at hand, but he'd already had too much and his nerves were so tight, anything that calmed him down seemed preferable.

He lowered his polarized sunglasses and looked out across the pool, wanting to dive in. Everyone was ashore, or so it seemed. An empty pool, mindless laps, cutting through cool, silent water. God how he missed California and swimming all year round. How could he even think of such a thing when Clarissa was missing!

He sipped the beer, the cold, fizzy bitterness offering a moment of pleasure. This trip was now officially a nightmare. How much longer could he keep this up? Everything was already closing in on him even before Clarissa.

What the hell could have happened to her? She had to be alright. She was alright. The only good to come out of his entire wasted life. And if she wasn't alright he couldn't possibly go through with the rest. No way.

He needed a "Nes"; he'd never heard the word before the Rabbi at the Seder. Hebrew word for miracle. If he'd known it when Clarissa was born, he'd have named her that. Listen to him, he sounded as if *he'd* given birth to her, as if Leah had no say, but he'd always assumed she'd do whatever he wanted or so it looked from the surface. And it had only taken him 30 years to find a snorkel. Leah had always been the hardest part of his war with himself. The trouble with being at war with yourself was you were fighting an enemy you didn't really want to defeat.

Damn it. Damn all of it. What a mess! What a fucking mess he'd made. Imagine saying that out loud in front of Leah! He smiled and took another sip. Maybe he'd just sit here in the sun by the fake Polynesian-theme pool and get smashed and let Leah find Clarissa all by herself.

Walter buddy, you are not thinking clearly and it is very important that you think clearly for the remainder of this cruise from Hell: too much at stake: too much to lose. Teddy is already twitchy enough. All this planning, all this time, think of the pot of gold at the end of this ridiculous rainbow. Keep your eye on the prize, on the Prizes, don't forget why you've done all this.

Despair washed through him, chasing the beer. *I've lived my entire life without doing one thing that brings me joy. No. Not true! Clarissa brings me joy. Sports bring me joy. Thank God, it isn't that bleak!* Imagine saying something like *that* to Leah? She was completely freaked out because Rory Riley said she was selfish! Some damn babble about motherhood and reality.

Great. Now I have to deal with Rory Riley. Why the hell did she have to bring her into this? We've already had thirty years of Rory, like Elijah in our house. Obsessive, crazy damn thing. Talk about not being able to stand rejection! Well, Rory was the only person who ever left Leah. *Look who's talking. No one ever left you, period.*

Mr. Winner at everything. What a joke. But no one ever had left, not yet, anyway. Not Rory. The way Leah held onto her, it was almost like she knew about what had happened between them, but there was no way. God knows Rory didn't tell her. Rory was like one of the guys, she had a guy kind of class about her, good character. What was that quote he'd read, "Brains are like muscles, you can hire both by the hour; the only thing that's not for sale is character."

Rory had character. He had brains and muscles, fucking hired help. All he'd ever been. An agile, cocky, good-looking suit full of brains and muscle, held together by the love of two good women, one wife and one daughter and a lot of hubris.

For sure. And the expectations of others, ever since he was a kid. His mother looked at him the same damn way Leah did; his Father looked at him like that, too. All those expectations, Great White Jewish Hope, he had been. Star athlete, scholarship to Med school, rise above their modest circumstances, the few L.A. Jews who had failed to make it across Doheny Drive. Walter would do it for them.

He drained the dregs and slammed the bottle down, anger bubbling up, fizzing up like the beer inside him. *All I've ever done since I was five years old is work the room, work my stuff to keep that look in all those idolizing eyes. Clarissa has got to be okay or everything I'm doing is irredeemable.*

He smiled. Talk about selfish. He checked his watch. Where the hell were they, anyway? Leah was checking the cabin, again. Damn it! He did not want to have to deal with Rory without Leah there! The Seder had been hard enough with the polite good old days small talk but her eyes were looking all the way through his skull and screaming, "Bullshit, Walter!"

She had not been one of his finer moments. He'd treated her like garbage. Used her and run away and the worst of it was, she was the only one in his callow young life, who didn't just see his package, the only one he felt safe with and that was the problem; there it was. The last thing he'd wanted was someone who would let him be *Walter* and make him see himself like that—brains and muscle for hire. No way, not then. *Damn it. Here she comes.* Leah was nowhere in sight.

God, I want to swim. Plunge right in and butterfly stroke my way into oblivion. He sighed and watched her approach from behind his glasses. *If I'd married Rory my entire life would be different. I would not have failed.*

What a joke life was, the opposite of what he'd believed then, was the truth. He'd dumped Rory for the crown jewel in the high school collection and sold his soul, not a moment's peace since, not a day without the background hum of low-grade depression, "Mood Dysphoria," Evanoff called it. He was so used to it, he'd almost missed it when everything started to change, when hope had appeared out of nowhere and lifted him back up into himself. He was so close to being free now. If only his daughter was okay.

While Rory made her way around the pool thirty-four years disappeared. He was no longer watching from the synthetic wicker bar stool, he was watching from the front seat of his Buick, waiting for her to turn the corner onto Curson St. in front of her grandfather's apartment building. He'd get hard just anticipating the contact.

So innocent, so milky white and scared and Irish, the sin of it all, nice Jewish boy that he was supposed to be—damn it. *Don't even think about that now.* She saw him and he saluted and she slowed down, still walking the same way, like an Our Gang comedy kid, like Mickey Rooney, spunky little Mick with that side to side toes turned out kind of stride. She didn't want to be alone with him, either.

"Hi, Walter."

"Hi, Mickey."

"Oh boy. Don't you dare. Really, bad, Walter."

"You still walk just like him."

"And you're still a patronizing prick."

"Well, at least we don't have to waste time on small talk."

"Or large talk. Or any talk. Where's Leah?"

"I don't know. She went to check the cabin again. In case Clarissa came back. She should be here by now."

"Okay, so now what?"

"Rory, would you accept an apology, could we start there?"

"I don't know. I need to hear it, first."

"Man oh man, I'd forgotten what talking to you was like. Okay, I behaved abominably. I was a coward and a schmuck and I am deeply and truly sorry for hurting you and betraying your trust."

"That's it?"

"It's the truth, I was and I am."

"Wow. All the years I've fantasized this moment, bringing you to your knees, making you pay while you pleaded and cried and begged for forgiveness and told me I was the only woman you ever loved and now you're right here in the flesh and you apologized and told the truth and it sucks."

"Would you prefer a lie?"

"Yes. Something along the lines of you found out I was your half-sister and wanted to spare me the pain and fell on your sword or . . . Okay, no. The truth it is."

"Can I say that like everything else, the truth isn't always that simple, but it's the only version I can give you without compromising other people."

"Much better. That I like. Gallant with a little cliff-hanger. So, now that we've dispensed with the past, I don't have very good news."

"Christ. I was hoping you'd had better luck than we've had. The security people are frantic because of the Talbotts and no one knows anything. We did find the guy she was dancing with; he speaks about ten words of English, but he said she never came back. And numerous witnesses saw him there for hours afterward. This is all my fault."

"Woah. Enough. Your wife thinks it's all *her* fault, now you think it's all *your* fault; do not do this—I will not get into this breast-beating bullshit. And we're wasting time. So let's find someone neutral to blame. How about the *Bosa Nova*? Okay? We'll Blame it on the *Bosa Nova*, lousy song, good idea. So before Leah comes back, let me tell you and you can ease her into this.

"Clarissa's skirt was in Flora's dressing room. You took her there, she borrowed Flora's gold skirt and she was wearing it when she came to meet us, remember? She had cramps, probably getting her period, she set off to get meds from the clinic, but she did not go change back into her own skirt. She would have done that, I think. And I went to the clinic, have you had the pleasure of meeting Nurse Peggy?

"Yes, many times. I consult to the clinics on technology and equipment."

"I rest my case. Left over from the Snake Pit or something—anyway, she was pretty horrible and I think she's lying about not seeing Clarissa."

"Why? Why would she lie?"

"I have not one clue. I know I have a vivid and sometimes paranoid imagination from growing up glued to television screens and triple matinees at the Fairfax Theater, but my good old gut says, she's hiding something."

"Remember the Saturday matinee horror festivals, we'd sit there until our eyes froze."

"*The Thing, The Werewolf, It Came From Outer Space, War of the Worlds. . . .* heaven."

Silence. They'd come at one another full speed, the wounder and the wounded, not really so much different after all, but the injury had detached them from all the other things, good things they had shared and felt for one another; that's the problem with human pain: it distorts everything good around it, tilts the memories in favor of the pain and away from the healing gift of fairness to the self. In fairness to themselves, they were silent.

Walter took off his glasses and smiled at her and she punched his arm, one of her old Mickey moves, when things were getting too close or too corny and they both laughed.

"So, okay, that's done. I'm going to try and catch Flora now, she wasn't in her cabin or her dressing room, but we've got rehearsal in an hour. Maybe she saw her later. Maybe you'd like to take another crack at 'Peg O' My Heart' but don't take Leah. I think she does better with guys. Something smells from herring about this, Walter. I don't want to scare you, I think Clarissa's okay, but maybe we should even go ashore and talk to the police."

"They have no jurisdiction and they're even worse than ship security. Rory, thank you. I don't know what Flora, what's her name? Frameson?"

"Frampton."

"Right, she invited us for a glass of champagne and Clarissa borrowed a skirt, but what would she know?"

"Maybe Clarissa called her or something. I'm just following my instinct, here. Check the nasty nurse. Who knows, maybe Clarissa's back in the cabin and that's why Leah didn't show up."

"Maybe. I'll go there first. No damn cell service on board."

"Yeah, but great exercise. Bye, Walter."

He watched her go, duck-walking like Micky or a ballerina, hardly changed from high school . . . if he could turn it all back and start over. Or at least the last week of it.

⁓

HEINRICH HENSLER ROLLED the flat-chested little acrobat from the Ice Spectacle onto her stomach and entered her. Backwards with the bosomless, frontwards with the buxom. With Collie, always from the front and he could even screw her with his eyes open. He liked to look at her, so pink and plump and delicious. With this one he would need to use his imagination.

Ah . . . he was at least in, and she was, at least wet and excited or faking, but something, not as bad as most of them—doormouses or dead meat, lying there as if that was enough, allowing him entry was all that was required of them. How stupid most women were.

The young ones were the worst. Lazy and ignorant, taking male lust for granted. Perfect was about forty, unsure of their appeal, not so self-confident anymore, but still firm and experienced enough to know what to do and trying harder to please . . . not getting so much anymore and eager to make the most of it. Yes, forty was about perfect.

Collie was the exception, young but with the other attributes. Ah well, that was probably over. At least for now, possibly for good. She was tainted now. He would never be able to touch her and not remember her debasement.

"Heinrich, that hurts!" The ice skater stiffened.

What was her name? Emily? No that was yesterday, the dancer with the nice ass this was, can't remember, free associate . . . she has a parrot and six cats and eight dogs and a pet monkey and her name is? . . . She looks like a monkey . . . maybe . . . the Bonobos . . . dirty monkeys . . . fuck everyone . . . yes. . . . Human nature in primate form. . . . The Bonobos fuck their mothers, their fathers, their children, their sons and daughters and grandmothers . . . everyone . . . solve all their social problems sexually. . . . Monkeys are keeping me hard! This is interesting . . . frightened monkeys, was that Skinner? Experiments with fear . . . maybe the Nazis? Tests on monkeys . . . scaring them and putting a nurturing presence and food before them and they would starve to death trying to get to the nurturer . . . love more important than life? Impossible. . . . Maybe it was Watson . . . ah Watson, so Nietzchian . . . so cynical and clear. . . . "The two biggest lies ever told are, 'Love thy enemy' and 'the meek shall inherit the earth.' " . . . Exactly! . . . That makes me hard . . . power, control. . . . Think of something else . . . great ships. . . . Lusitania, Mauritania, Ille de France. . . . Paris . . . someday an apartment in the Maurais, near Victor Hugo's museum. . . . Victor Hugo could fuck nine times a day. . . . Prodigious giant of a human . . . fucked his son's mistress, prostitutes . . . nine times a day and wrote and wrote, giant energy. . . .

"Oh, Heinrich, Oh, that's so good, I'm so hot . . . you're totally sexy . . . oh, yes . . . yes . . ."

France. . . . Hugo, Renoir. . . . Renoir . . . could only paint women who couldn't think. I can only fuck women who can't think . . . dumb is the turn-on. . . . Collie is dumb and bovine . . . so sexy. . . . Oh, such bad thoughts, such hurting thoughts . . . what if I said it out loud? What if we said things out loud . . . deadly wounding, quick as whiplash, leaving no mark . . . when I fuck them it's like that . . . like I'm puncturing, wounding with my thoughts . . . transferring the contempt . . . such frustration. . . . I feel such frustration . . . cannot stand not being in charge of it all . . . cannot stand having to wait to be the boss . . . cannot stand kowtowing to the Talbotts . . . prigs and idiots. . . . But I have them. . . . I have them . . . now. . . . Oh, Yes, that makes me very hard . . . fuck them all. . . . I will. . . . I will . . . have everything. . . . Shumann's Bar in Munich: I will live near Shumann's Bar and go there every night with a different big-breasted beauty . . . plump in the right places and all pink and white . . . no more compromises, no more frustration. . . . French wine and German women . . . dumb and juicy. . . .

"Oh, Heinrich, I'm going to . . . I'm going to . . . oh, oh . . . oh."

Stab it through her and get on with things. Jo Jo is waiting for me. . . . Come like a monkey, do it, do it. . . . Ahhh. . . . Done, frustration is a little better . . . that's why Hugo did it so much . . . his frustration with the lesser men . . . not enough control over his life. Sex is the answer. . . . I need something more, this was barely . . . satisfying . . . got to find someone more appealing. . . . Older, more anxious and with breasts or a bigger ass at least. What is her damn name . . . I'll call her, dear girl . . . and get in the shower.

~

Jo Jo MARQUES sat on his hands in Heinrich Hensler's waiting room, trying to stop them from shaking. He must settle down or Mr. Hensler would see it and know he was hiding something.

What could he do? He should have gone to Elonzito and told him everything. Elonzito was his friend, and older and wiser. But then his friend would be in danger too, and that was not how he was raised. He had to do this himself.

But, he was lost. What could he have been thinking? To believe he could handle a world like this, people like Mr. Hensler. He had walked right into his trap. All he'd wanted was to make a good impression on his boss. Advance himself, make some extra money to send home.

What a child! Had he learned nothing from his grandparents! All the Sunday dinners after mass when his Abuelito would talk about honor and freedom, and only behaving in a way that Jesus would approve, no matter how "shiny the apple": that is what his Abuelito would say. He'd grabbed the first apple offered him and become a spy and now he knew terrible things and Mr. Hensler owned him. He had seen too much, and he knew too much and now he knew things even Mr. Hensler did not know and that was the only thing that might save him.

Why did he say "save"? Did he believe that his life might be in danger? Would Mr. Hensler go that far to keep his mouth shut?

Oh, Father in Heaven, please help me, I do not know what to do. I must get control of my fear, think of my family, think of the fishing boat. If I can put him off, tell him just enough to appease him until we get back to San Juan, I'll take what he owes me and I'll disappear during the clean-up. I just need a few more days, and I must use my wits. I must grow up very quickly. Father in Heaven, forgive me for I have sinned, forgive your sinner and help me, and I swear on the head of my son, I swear, I will sin no more.

Jo Jo stood up and walked over to the table where Mr. Hensler kept the sweets for his visitors. He had never taken one before, but something in him said, "take one" and he reached out and popped a small chocolate into his mouth. His hands had stopped shaking.

The Savior would see him through this. The Lord had suffered so he could have another chance.

The door opened and he could feel his heart pounding into his throat. He swallowed the chocolate and turned to face his corrupter.

Jo Jo had never seen anyone as immaculate and menacing as his boss. He was so tall, so handsome and polished, he almost sparkled. Mr. Hensler's eyes snapped over him like blue camera lens, clicking and evaluating, making him flush with fear. *Father please . . .*

"Come, come, Jo Jo, I'm very busy, let's have our little chat and we can both go on with our work. I am very eager to hear your report. Very eager!"

Jo Jo followed him in. *Like a fly, I am like a stupid, dirty little fly and he is the tarantula, a huge white tarantula. Father, please, forgive me. . . . I was greedy, a greedy, stupid sinner. . . . Help me please. . . .*

Jo Jo licked the last of the chocolate off the inside of his mouth and sat down across from his boss. He could smell soap, something that reminded him of home . . . lime oil and pine. He forced himself to look up, feeling the Father was with him, whispering inside his head; he could hear the voice, not his own frightened whine—another voice, giving him courage. This is what he would listen to, not the other voice that made his hands shake, left him filled with doubt and fear; this voice, the one that told him to eat the chocolate, this was the Lord, answering his prayer.

Look into his eyes, do not be afraid. This man is a bully and only has the power you allow. You have the information. He needs you. You have the power because you do not crave power. He is the weak one, because he wants so much, needs so much. You can go home in the Shoes of the Fisherman and be happy.

Something astonishing was happening to him. As if he had been asleep all of his life, and just now, this minute in this lonely and dangerous room with this terrible man, he had found himself, found the voice of his manhood, the voice of his God. A wonderful quiet seemed to pass through him. He could feel the beating of his heart slowing down, and he surrendered to this new voice, coming from a place within him, he had never known was there. The voice said, "wait for him to speak first" and he did.

"So, let us begin with Mr. Talbott and then Mrs. Talbott and then we'll move on to the new events."

ᘓᕈᕈᕉ

"FLORA? It's Rory, open up, it's important!"

Flora at the door, looking slightly woozy . . . that southern, sensual thing . . . sultry women were like that . . . was it possible to be that relaxed . . . like children, no tension or so it seemed. Wonder if I lifted her arm if it would flop right back down, with no resistance.

"What's the problem, honey lamb? We've got to be on stage in ten minutes. We're running your blues song and I'm still not off book."

"I tried you in your room. I've been up and down between here and all your haunts enough to gain muscle mass. There's a situation."

"Oh, sweet savior, not another rape!"

"Well, we don't know. Do you remember last night, Walter Worth, the handsome doctor who's staying with the Talbotts?

"Sure. He came down with his adorable daughter after your Seder dinner, with that hoot of a Texas Countess dame and we drank some champagne and I lent her my gold skirt. What a little darling thing she is."

"Well, she is a darling thing and she's missing; never came back to their suite and I was down here earlier looking for you and I saw her skirt was here, so she never came back to return it and so that is really weird and I thought maybe you'd talked to her or she said something to you about where she would be or something.

"Her parents are completely frantic, especially because of what happened to Collie, so I'm helping them check out possible leads and you're my last hope."

"Oh, no. No. No. No!"

"What the hell does that mean? What's with the, 'Oh no, no, no.' No what?"

"I can't talk about it, Rory. I don't know anything and I can't tell yew anything. I'm just stunned and upset. Okay?"

"Now it's my turn. . . . Oh no, no, no, you don't! I'm looking at your face. Your perfect camellia-like complexion has turned into a rosacea ad. A young woman's life may be in danger, so this is not the time for Fainting Chaise behavior! Look at you, you're trembling all over. Sit down, I'm calling the stage manager and telling him to work around us."

Flora did as she was told, sliding down into her make-up chair with her performer's grace intact, while Rory made the call. "I'd kill for a brandy."

"First you talk, then you drink."

"Oh, Rory, yew don't know what you're asking of me. This is sacred trust, other people's feelings and lives are at stake here. I'm not a secretive person, I'd tell you anything, but this, I can't."

"Bullshit. You *are* a secretive person and you must tell me or Security or her parents. I just left her father and I can call him right now . . ."

"No, no! Please! I'll tell yew, please don't do that. Let me get a drink. The bottle's on my dressing table. Oh, God, what a mess."

"Just a sip and I'm pouring. And stop crying. You can't cry, yet. What? What did you see?"

Flora knocked back the brandy and wiped her face. Her hand was still trembling and a shudder ran down her entire body.

"*So?*"

Such was life, so gothic after all, no one ever got away with anything. Not one little ol' teeny, tiny anything.

"I did see her. She came to return the skirt and I was here with my fella and she saw us and I guess she got embarrassed, the door was closed and she just opened it, what a silly thing for me not to lock it, and we were, sort of, into foreplay and she saw me and I saw her, but he never did, his back was to her and I tried to wave to her, make less of it, but she ran off and she never came back."

"That's it?"

"Uh huh. That's it."

"Flora Frampton your cute little ol' southern schnozola is growing before my eyes. Clarissa is not a six year old and even a child wouldn't react in such horror they'd run off and disappear into the night over such a sight. I can understand her not barging in and changing her skirt, but your reaction, makes no sense and you know it. So what are you leaving out? You said the guy didn't see her?"

"No. No. And I didn't tell him anything."

"Well, was it someone she knew or a secret shipboard romance and she was two-timed by him with you? What?"

Flora looked up at her, tears streaming down her face again, leaving cracks in her perfect makeup, scarring her cheeks. "This is sacred trust, Rory?" Cross you little lapsed Catholic heart."

"I'm the fucking sphinx. Who?"

"It was her father. Walter Worth is my lover. He's the one I'm in love with. She saw me with her father and she ran, so there's a reason."

Rory reached over and poured herself a brandy. "The plot just thickened to taffy batter."

Amazing what discipline does, Rory thought, watching Flora on stage ten minutes later. No one would guess a thing; maybe that's what we're all like anyway, a horde of masked men, what you see is never what the deal is. If I just came in and was watching her, so poised . . . a perfect song bird . . . such a funny idea . . . song bird, never call a guy a song bird, but only male birds sing; Jesse told me that . . . one of the two interesting things he ever told me . . . the other was about canaries re-learning the same song every year. . . . Song bird, learning my song, . . . no one would think anything looking at you, either. Sitting here with your note pad and your specs, looking professional and immersed. . . .

My days are pretty simple, nothing much at all
I'm really only waiting for night to finally fall
Standing in the darkness at the center of the stage
The focus of all attention, the object of every gaze.

Shimmering in the shadows, totally in control
Waiting for the conductor, to tell me when to go.

I'm a Lady of the Cabaret, the bandstand is my home
Always living for the magic hour, when I'm never all alone.
When Life is clear as glass, and everything's all right.
The world is just a cheering crowd, applauding through the night.

I'm a Lady of the Torch, I'll sing until I drop.
Waiting for the cue to come, to tell me when to stop.

When life is sparkling wine, and everyone's my friend
The world is just a sing-a-long, the clapping never ends.

My days are pretty simple, nothing much at all.
I'm really only waiting for night to finally fall.
When life is sparkling wine and everyone's my friend
The world is just a sing-a-long, the clapping never ends. . . .

Well, she's singing from her gut, that's what love's given her. . . .

"Flora, that was wonderful. You nailed it. Are they going to block the Dog song or are we done?"

"Marvin said he'd do it with me later."

"Okay. We're gone."

Poor Flora, Walter would never leave Leah. Poor Leah, she was no way in this world equipped for this shit. Poor Clairssa, if ever there was a Daddy's girl, imagine walking in on that! Even my Aunt Maddie locked the door.

Too bad Flora never had any therapy, maybe the old unconscious was behind the "Oops! Forgot to lock it." . . . no accidents and no . . . oops's. . . . Tired of being the mistress and looking for a way to leap onto center stage without any Other Woman dirty tricks? How about forgetting to lock the el dooro and turning up the Passion? Oh, so what's that on your face, Rory? Is that a little smirk. Is that a little enjoyment over all of this? Very, very low.

No enjoyment over Clarissa or Flora, but the other two. . . . Fess up. Your face is smirking.

Oh, brother, what a performance Walter put on! "Flora Framson?" God I hate being played for such a dope. Now I'm going to have to hear the entire sordid story. Now that I know, she'll want to tell me everything. I would, too. And of course I'm almost dying to hear, but I also don't want to hear or know and how am I going to deal with Leah now?

Never mind that. What's important is getting Flora to take me down to wherever they've stashed Collie O'Brian.

What did Flora say before she went on? "Collie knows something but she's protecting Hensler!" If she saw someone, maybe she can give us a description. If she thinks there's another victim, she'll tell us. . . .

Shit! what time is it? Where's Poe? What a thought . . . where's Poe . . . like he's mine. I can feel him around me. I can smell him. . . . Want to just tell all of them to leave me out of this; I've got a "fella" myself, so there . . . want to run and find him. Hold him, be grateful. I have a lover, too! I have someone of my own and he said "forever" . . . he could help us . . .

No, no, don't go there, Ror . . . can't do that. I've got to do this alone. She could have been my kid. . . . Oh, for sure, don't go there. Should I tell Flora about me and Walter? What time is it? Where is she? She was right behind me.

There she is. Uh, oh, looks like she's been crying again. Maybe she called Walter's room? Don't ask. Don't ask, don't tell . . . like so much of life . . . pretend what is, isn't, turn away from the truth, so threatening to everything, how can something so major, be such a pisser. Lie, lie, lie about almost everything to almost everyone including ourselves until we die, die, die. I am not going to do that. . . . I am not ever going to do that about anything again. . . . I will not die not knowing what's true about myself and my life, no matter how scary or horrifying or lonely it may be. I refuse. . . .

"Rory, sorry, honey lamb, had to make a loo stop. My stomach is my major stress indicator. I know what yew want to do, see Collie, right?"

"Right. We've got to."

"We're going in way over our cute little heads, but I think she wanted to tell me and that was almost two days ago. She may be scared and mad, but she'll give up the ghost, so to speak, if another girl's been hurt."

"Well, we don't know anything, Flora. She could have been so freaked out at seeing you with her father, she just bolted, hung out somewhere until we docked and went ashore, like her pals."

"Oh good God, it's my fault! If that happened! How could I be so stupid, not to lock that door! I lock it if I'm just sittin' in there doing my nails. I'm so territorial. It is that Southern 'get off my land' gene or something."

"Let's walk and talk, okay? Do not start this conversation; trust me, you won't like it. I've had far too much therapy for such a chat with you and you've got to stand in line for awhile to even get to the front of the 'It's all my fault' group on this one, but how about letting Walter have that one for now, anyway."

"Oh, Rory, don't be so harsh. He's a good man; we never meant to fall in love. We're both pretty desperate and we saw something in one another and it just happened. He's been on a lot of these cruises, consulting on the clinics and things and yew know how it goes. He's heartsick about it and having his family with him makes it almost unbearable . . . the guilt and all . . ."

"Walter Worth desperate? Walter-the-Man-who-has-everything-and The Prom-Queen-desperate? Spare me. And I am harsh about him. But I'll save that for later. I am also a tad cynical about the degree of 'guilt' that leads to Dressing Room sex with wife and daughter close at hand, but hell, if I'd had to live all these years with

Leah Frankel, I'd be groping you in the Green Room, myself. None of this is coming out right. Where the hell are we going, anyway?"

"One more flight down, she's in an unoccupied cabin behind the kitchen near the dining room. Paying guests hate the noise and the smells, so they never can sell it."

"Oh, of course. Perfect for the rape and torture victim."

Flora laughed, "Now yew sound like me. I forgot yew knew Walter and his wife when y'all were kids. How bizarre is that, for yew and me and them to all be entwined! Gives me goosebumps!"

"Gives me hives. Don't say *entwined*. I can't take the visual."

"Here, Rory, it's this one."

"Great, knock."

"Okay. Should I tell her you're with me?"

"No. Not until she opens it."

Flora took a deep breath. "Here goes. Wish you'd let me have another toot of brandy."

"Knock."

"Collie. Collie honey, it's Flora."

The door flew open startling them both. Whatever they had expected, this was not it.

"Come in, quickly, before anyone sees you."

Rory followed Flora in. The cabin was small and dark and she felt a moment of panic, they were filling the space with too much raw female energy, sucking up all the available oxygen. She had only met Collie once, in another small dark room and she had cried her way through, hardly seeing or relating to the warm, strong hands and the soothing, good Mommy voice attached to this young woman.

Who could have imagined that three days later, the healer would be hurt and she would be standing over her, not to comfort even, but to extract and in the days between her entire life would have been turned on end.

"Collie honey, do yew remember Rory Saltz? You gave her a massage the day yew were attacked?"

Collie had climbed back into her bed and laid her head against the pillows. She nodded as if the walk to the door and back and the stimulus of their entry had used up all her energy.

"Collie, we would never come here like this, but something terrible has happened. A girl is missing. A lovely young woman, the daughter of old friends of Rory's and we're trying to help because you know how overloaded the Security guys are and if it's the same person who attacked yew and yew saw *anything*, please, please tell us.

"I know you're being loyal to Hensler and all, but you're a good girl, and another good girl may be in even worse shape. You said something when I was here before that confounded me, yew said 'they' as if more than one person attacked yew and I didn't ask yew anything, but now, now it's even more urgent so . . ."

"It's okay, Flora. I'm not protecting Heinrich anymore. He hasn't even come to see me and he's already screwing everything in sight, don't ask me how I know. I think he's using little Jo Jo the steward to spy on people, so he can use personal information against them. He told me it was a ship's politics issue when I asked why I couldn't tell anyone who attacked me. But I don't care now. I'm going to break my contract and go home and sue the company."

"Can yew do that?" Flora sat down beside her.

"I can try. Passengers can't attack personnel."

Rory took a deep breath. "Passengers. Then you saw who did it?"

"I did at that. But it wasn't them who had anything to do with your friend's daughter's disappearing, rest assured."

Flora reached over and took her hand. "How can yew be certain?"

"Because they left the ship. I know for a fact they got off in St. John's."

Rory and Flora looked at one another without saying a word. This was Collie's moment.

"It was the Talbott girl and her friend the Count or whatever he is. They did this to me. Monsters they are and powerful and Heinrich promised to protect me from them and from her father and all if I kept silent. But he didn't! He thinks I'm such a stupid cow, I'd believe anything and not doubt the 'great man' himself. But I'm not stupid and I'm not a coward and I want you two to know, just in case anything should happen to me. Someone needs to know the truth and not let any of them get away with it!"

Flora kissed her hand. "Nothing's gonna happen to yew, sweet pea. I'm getting Roy Rogers to put a guard on your door right now and Hensler won't dare do a damn thing. Don't yew worry about anything. The bastard."

"He promised he'd send a guard, but he didn't."

Tears popped from the girl's eyes, and she sunk deeper down

under the covers. "You were right, Flora. I was so silly, so in awe. If I hadn't gone to that fancy party, they would never have picked me out. It's my punishment for putting on airs and fornicating with a foreigner. I wish my Mum were here. I'm so scared, Flora. I want to go home. I just want to go home."

Rory kneeled down beside Flora and they offered what comfort they could. Two natural Mother Hens, neither with a chick of their own filling the void between what the girl needed and what they could provide.

When they left her, they were silent, exhausted by the force of all the emotion; the rush of adrenalin that had propelled them down there, replaced now by reality. They were nowhere closer to finding what had happened to Clarissa but they had added a layer of information neither of them could now turn away from.

You open your eyes in the morning and all bets are off. Rory looked at her watch. *Poe should be back from his lecture.* She had someone to tell all this to. *What a thing, to not go through everything alone. What a fucking thing.*

Maybe he could help her find the best way to tell Walter and Leah the disheartening new facts. She had lost Clairssa's scent, like a police dog at the end of the pier. So much for sleeping till noon and lolling around in the arms of her new love. The day was ending and the ship would be pulling out any minute and Leah's child was missing, like Billy.

ONE THING the stuffed creature that had replaced Tou Tou could not do was breathe. And one thing she could not do without that sound, that night comfort emanating from her formerly living, breathing, canine companion, was sleep.

At 3 a.m. the Countess gave up, got up, put on her French silk traveling robe, picked up Tou *Two* and left her room.

She had no destination or plan. She was not hungry, thirsty or even restless. An extraordinary form of numbness, unfamiliar to her, had crawled into every pore and crevice, vein and arterial flow connection of her being from the moment she had heard the cell message from her grandson and Twinkle.

It was as if some major electrical switch inside her very being had been thrown, the elevator moving up and down her heart and mind had stopped in mid-descent or ascent or whatever such things controlled. Everything in her had ceased moving. All power gone. Only this peculiar lack of movement, of inner emotional gurgle. Not like her at all.

The cool marble against her bare feet was the only reminder that she was still feeling anything. She pushed her toes down harder into the small available pleasure and walked slowly across the foyer of the enormous suite into the Great Room as such spaces were currently called in travel brochures and real estate ads.

The room itself had a life of its own; all rooms did and she felt like a voyeur, creeping around, invading its privacy, all the under sounds that rooms make when the people are gone. It was very dark with only the moonlight trickling in and the emergency lights and it relaxed her, loosened some of the paralysis: the hum of the ship and the ice maker and the refrigerator and the slight rattle of something not quite secured in a drawer.

The life of things, rather than people, offered some relief. She sighed and sat down in the far corner behind the grand piano, hidden away in a sort of little lair, adorned with stacks of silk and velvet pillows, a cozy cave-like place to hide away. From what she wasn't sure. Whatever was under the numbness?

She wrapped her arms around the stuffed creature who couldn't breathe and closed her eyes. It didn't take long. One word gently floating across her mind. *Grand.* Inner hell, breaking loose the numbness as if some comic book super hero had smashed through it and flipped the master switch back into full power.

Interior lights on everywhere. Rage blasted across her, so intensely and so suddenly she thought for a moment it would kill her off right there in the pretentious, over-decorated suite on the damn, goddamn *Chicken of the Sea* or whatever the hell this ship on which she was now hostage to her grief was called. No way. She was not going to join Tou Tou in a zip lock bag in that morgue. She took a deep breath and held her stuffed Comforter tighter.

Grand it was. *Grandmother. Grandchild.* What she had been led to believe that meant. Better than a parent, better than a child. The last hope of connection, of a bond that would outlast her—even one person, a grand-person who would hold her memory, remember her—a link between existence and dust. A living nod to the fact that she had been here at all. Her *grandson.* He had murdered her dog, an act of such violence against her as to be unspeakable. And he had abandoned her to that truth. Her last hope for some sort of redemption maybe. And why? Why now?

Oh, Mimsie, you have always known this. This is payback from God for the money. For wanting it. For having it. For using it to buy love. The link between love and money, the only two real power centers in so many family relationships. Relatives do not abandon other relatives when they truly love them or when they love their money.

And that was always the underlying threat. The line she never crossed, the bluff she never called unless the truth was more important than the need of the illusion. She had crossed the line to help her grandson. She had threatened the withdrawal of money for bad behavior. She had risked facing the truth.

He did not love her. He did not need her. He loved and needed only what she provided. *He loved her money.* She had said *no*, facing her own fear of his turning on her, or away from her forever, to save him.

"No," was her job. "No" is every parent's job. The right to say it. The need to say it when necessary, when the bullying or the self-ishness are destroying the child. When the spoiling is spoiling the child. A boundary, a forcing of responsibility for their own actions, for their own lives; a pushing back the blame; a standing up past her own guilt which left her so vulnerable, so easily manipulated. She had said NO. *You will walk the dog. We will make some changes or the money will stop.* And he had called her bluff.

She had been here before, but she had not taken the hit. She had moved faster, partied harder, traveled farther. So many children with so many different fathers. The ones who hadn't squandered their money didn't use their children as pawns, as bait to manipulate her because she loved them. The unspoken threat with the others was always there. *Give me what I want or I won't let you see your grandchildren.* The Grand-children, safer than the children, the innocence of their trust in her, the love freed of guilt, of the agony of doubt that walked hand in hand with motherhood. Once they spoke the threat, and her more desperate children had, *you owe us, you must make it up to us or . . . or . . . money for love.*

Grand-children as barter—push them at her, seduce her with her own heart, entice her in and then snatch them away as punishment. But once the line was crossed, once they voiced the threat. Once she said *No. No more money now. Now you must take charge of your choices. Now you must stop blaming others for your mistakes. Now you must grow up. No.*

Her job, not done soon enough, but with good intentions: the rubble of life. But, when they used their children as pawns, the trust was broken forever. Once she knew they were capable of that, of causing that agony, it could never be the same again.

The price of truth was sky high, and she had survived it before, but the losses compound, the pain of the restrictions, of the paltry options, changed the ease with which she was able to *Grandmother*; the fear was now always in place.

They would do it again, they would break her heart, again. Grandmothers do not want to self-protect with their grandchildren. Mothers do not want to self-protect with their children. This was monstrous, but this was true and necessary more often than not. She was not the only one. God knows.

Ian had been her hope. The one Grand-son who would not be used that way. His mother didn't care enough to pull him back *and* she had money of her own. Ian was her last chance to give all that love in a safe and wise way.

And he was a soulless creature. And she had always known it. Even at ten, he had the dead eyes, the frozen callous affect of the sociopath.

She had lied to herself and now she had to face it.

Curled in this pasha pigeonhole, with a stuffed creature replacing all the potential grief of the living losses, she had to tell the truth. All of those children, and friends and men and grandchildren had led her to the place she had feared most, the living nightmare of her entire life. She really was this alone.

A sound startled her, the reality of the present intruding. Someone had entered the room. She hesitated, not having any sense of what to do: announce herself or sink further back into the darkness? Something about the movement, the excessive stealth-like quiet decided for her. She curled deeper into the cushions and waited for a chance to escape.

Slipper sounds, almost on tip-toe, but a man's sound. Walter or Teddy were the only choices now that Ian was gone.

Maybe he'd come back! Maybe she was wrong, just too suspicious and looking for trouble! Maybe he was sorry and he would beg her forgiveness and they would be able to heal and she would help him become a better man or . . .

The sliver of hope gave her courage and she leaned slightly forward, trying to see who it was. It was too dark to tell, but she could follow the sounds across the room and into the kitchen. Something was being poured. From where she was, it was possible for her to stand now and peek around the side of the curved wall and creep slightly forward without being seen.

She pulled herself up and moved closer. Ice cubes rattled and a hand stilled them. She was afraid now. She did not want to be caught here like this. Someone was knocking ever so quietly at the back door to the suite, the door that led from the kitchen to the service stairway. The man inside moved over to open the door and in the light from the hall she saw Teddy Talbott's face. Someone entered, someone smaller, much smaller and in a uniform. They were whispering. Oh God, if she could just disappear!

Teddy picked up his glass and drank something, scotch probably and handed it to the other man. How peculiar! What on earth could he be doing?

She moved a few steps closer, braver now that the path from where she was to her room seemed reachable without calling attention to herself. The smaller man was gone! But the door hadn't opened again or she would have seen the light. A rustle. Then another sound coming from Teddy.

Goddamn! The man wasn't gone. He was on his *knees,* on his damn knees in front of Teddy Talbott on the floor of the kitchen, "suckin his longneck" as they used to say back home! The last thing she saw before she made her dash to safety was Teddy's bald birdlike head thrown back, mouth as wide as if waiting for a nice juicy worm to land inside. Moaning in the moonlight, and this sight, as repulsive as it was, strengthened her. Providing the comfort of knowing that nothing is ever what it seems and no one is ever anything but alone in the moonlight with themselves. . . .

Chapter Five: Day Five

LATITUDE
Your Daily At Sea Newspaper

Bonjour cruisers! For those of you up with the Pelicans, you have already watched our entry into the Beautiful port of St. Lucia, an exciting combination of British and French Colonial history, with battles back and forth for 150 years; so even though this stunning island with the world's only drive-through volcano has been part of the British commonwealth since 1803, the presence of its French occupiers is all around, from the patois patter of the St. Lucians to the food.

So, welcome to Day 5 and we sincerely hope you haven't used up all your energy preparing for the Talent Show, or the Two-Step shindig or in the gym or on Barbados yesterday, because St. Lucia is spectacular from our incredible tours of the rain forests, the banana plantations, the beaches, the amazing Batik factory, fishing villages, Pigeon Island Park or just wandering the town and eating at one of the fabulous Creole restaurants. We have tours for every taste. So that's the good news! The bad news is we will only be in port from 8 a. m. until 5 p.m. Sooooo much to see and do and soooo little time!!!!

For those of you (and there are many) who see the Ship itself as the vacation, we have fun, fun, fun planned! A highlight for the wacky among us is our always-jammed Silly Animal Seminar. This week, ferrets are featured and the Editor in Chief of *Ferret Living* is on board to fill your sun-drenched minds with fascinating ferret trivia such as: the ferret/hamster No No!, elderly ferrets and what to expect, potty training, dental hygiene, ferrets as great pets for urban dwellers and free funny ferret costume posters will be given to all attendees!

Tonight is semi-formal cruisers, so get those shoes shined! We have a pull-out-the-stops Grand Buffet in the main Dining room and the always packed, Comedy Club featuring our own hilarious Corky Conchlin and his improv troupe as well as fellow cruisers, who will compete for best amateur. This is way better than Karaoke dudes, so be there!!!

The drink special is the Va Va Voomer; if you have to ask what's in it, you don't deserve it!!! The spa is open all day and through the evening. Jazz is featured in the Sea Spray lounge; Irish Step-Dancing lessons will be given in the Aerobics Room off the fitness Center by our own brilliant Katie Malone (now this is a work-out to end all!) There will also be a Kitchen tour fascinating to see, and lots of yummy samples and insider info. For example: the *Dolphin* stocks 1,200 gallons of milk and 5,800 pounds of cheese, 64,000 lbs. of fresh vegetables on each cruise. Ask Rubiroso Montenegro, the executive chef, how many desserts are prepared each week. Want a hint? 70,000!

Have a great Day!

ELONZITO CARRIED the coffee carafes into the dining room and set them down beside the lavish selection of choices he had meticulously arranged for breakfast. The morning ritual always gave him pleasure. The beginning of a new day with the freshness of everything, the hope that it would be happy and bring new experiences and pleasures to those in his charge.

The morning had a cheerfulness to it he did not find quite the same at the other end of the day when he prepared the drinks and hors d'oeurves for the socializing before the evening started. There was always something less relaxed about that part of the day; they seemed restless, eager for the first cocktail to soften their disappointment or whatever it was. He could not know for sure.

In the morning, even if they were ill or had not slept well, they were kinder and less on guard with one another.

He put the coffee down and went to bring the pots of different milks, each carefully marked as to fat content, something he could not understand. In his country leite was leite and coffee came with it hot and frothy and no one he knew had ever asked for a different kind or a special butter that was not butter and all the other confusing selections that Americans wanted.

A longing for his family, homesickness, soul sickness flooded his entire being, bringing tears to his eyes. He put down the pitchers of different milks and shuddered.

He had never felt so lonely and so unhappy about his job. He had always enjoyed what he did, even if it took him from his loved ones. It made him feel special to know he was providing so much for them and for their future, and proud because he had gone further than anyone in his family.

He knew people from all over the world, he'd seen places they had only dreamed of and learned so much about so many different things, things he could teach his children and show them in all the pictures he took. Stories he would tell his grandchildren so they would remember him, long after he was gone. He felt such pride in what he had accomplished and in doing his work well: love of the sea and the romance of the ship's life and seeing people having a magical experience.

He wiped his eyes and picked the milk up. Now it was all changed for him. The three young people were gone. Two by their choice, but leaving such discord and now Miss Clarissa. He could not walk around the suite without hearing crying or raised voices from some room. The poor Countess, who had lost her precious little companion and then was abandoned by her grandson when she most needed comfort and the Worths, such nice people, such a lovely family, having their only child vanish with all the terrible possibilities.

He prayed on his way up to the Suite at dawn that she had returned and the day would begin with bright spirit. But he did not believe this was true. The rooms were cold and silent, a door opened and he heard the Talbotts' voices. This was unusual; Mr. Talbott was always first and he brought Mrs. Talbott's first cup of coffee to her room. But he could see them both, dressed in exercise clothing instead of bathrobes. Mr. Talbott was smiling, this was a good sign. A very good sign. Maybe he was wrong and the day was not lost after all.

"Elonzito, good morning to you! I woke up with a craving for buttermilk pancakes and well-done sausage. If you could order that for me, I'd be most obliged. My wife will just pick at the buffet as usual. Girlish figure, you know."

"Teddy please, it's too early for nonsense. Elonzito, Mr. Doolittle and Mr. Hensler and Mr. Rogers are joining us for coffee, so make sure there's enough. We won't want to be interrupted once they've arrived."

"Yes, very well, Mrs. Talbott."

Elonzito went back into the kitchen to place Mr. Talbott's order, his heart speeding up. Clearly this breakfast was going to be about

Miss Clarissa and the attacker who was still uncaught. He should not be listening or wanting to listen to what the conversation would be, but his nature was curious and it was exciting to be an invisible witness to a fascinating drama as terrible as it was; it was almost like being in a movie audience, so different was this world and these events from anything before in his life. He felt guilty but he was eager to overhear what he could.

And there was still Jo Jo, as much as he didn't want to believe his friend could be part of anything bad or dishonest, he knew something was very wrong and Jo Jo would not tell him.

He could hear the Worths crossing the foyer. This was also different. Dr. Worth was always the first one up and out for his morning run on the track and he had not gone this morning. Elonzito walked back out to greet them and ask if they wanted anything special from the kitchen. He could see how they had changed in just one day. Mrs. Worth's eyes were swollen and puffy making her beautiful face look distorted, as if the slightest physical alteration was too much for her delicate looks to adjust to.

Dr. Worth did not look as if he had been crying or was in any outward way affected, but he seemed smaller and less immaculate, something in his posture and the combing of his hair was not as careful.

He had seemed to Elonzito from the first moment, as a man totally in control and immaculate in his behavior and looks and manner, not with the stiffness of Mr. Hensler, but with a confidence that was also not quite natural, almost a protection from closeness.

"Good morning Elonzito. How are you this morning?" Dr. Worth smiled at him, but there was hurt in his eyes.

"I am well, Sir. May I order you and Mrs. Worth something?"

"No, no, there's a bounty already here. Not that hungry this morning. Are you, Leah?"

"No, thank you. I'd love a cup of tea. Chamomile if you have some."

"I will check and if not, I'll have it sent right up."

Elonzito went back into the kitchen, knowing that soon the conversation would begin, and the people he served would talk about personal, private things or fight or behave strangely in his presence, as if, to them, he was not quite real, was not a man or even a human being, but some combination of robot and pet, who would never react, repeat or even absorb any action or conversation.

Sometimes it hurt his pride, but mostly it gave him an enjoyable opportunity to observe and learn more about his fellow man than people with other jobs could ever know.

"Walter my man, I've got the *New York Times* printout if you'd like a look."

"Thanks, Teddy. Maybe later."

"Well, the liberal rag is quite a good read this morning. Nice piece about the Bayeaux tapestry. Ever been to see it?"

"No, we did make it to Normandy, walked the beach and the cemetery, but we didn't have time to stop in Bayeaux."

"Damn shame, to be so close. I was there for the 50th D Day Anniversary. One proud moment in our history. My Uncle's buried there, saw the marker, cried like a babe. The towns were filled with old heroes and their families walking around wearing their 'I Like Ike' buttons, felt like I'd lost 50 years.

"The French even had old jeeps and ambulances driving the vets and dignitaries around. We still had values then, war was clear, good versus evil, harked back to ancient battles. Spartans versus Athenians. Simple moral warriors against hedonists. Archimedes for instance, in my humble opinion, was the first Bill Clinton. History only repeats, nothing new in war when one studies history. When I came home wearing my 'I Like Ike' button, Sissy said it was a clear sign of middle age when Ike starts to look like a hero and that was over a decade ago!

"Where was I? Oh, Bayeaux, another example of war and history repeating itself. The tapestry is fantastic. Unbelievable! It's rather like an enormous, medieval comic book, telling this incredible story of the Battle of Hastings, fills room after room. Absolutely riveting to follow it through.

"Harold promised William that when Edward died, he would support William for the throne. But he lied of course and when Edward died, he crowned himself. So William invades, Harold is shot through the eye and William the Conqueror is crowned. Perfect tale of loyalty betrayed by ambition. History repeats, however WWII was the last war about anything comprehensible."

"I do agree, Teddy. The Hindu Kush is a long way from Omaha Beach. You may know it's where Alexander the Great lost an entire division. The Russians didn't even bother to go up there. There won't be any more wars of honor; the rogue states have entirely different agendas."

"Exactly! Even when the British burned Washington we weren't in this much danger."

"Oh, for God's sake, Teddy, please! We haven't even finished our first cup of coffee and things are grim enough without the end of the world conversation. I think we should talk about what we want to ask Mr. Hensler and the Head of Security, whatever his name is. Have you been able to reach Twinkle on her phone yet?"

"No, my dear. I have not. There seems to be no service. But I will go ashore directly after our breakfast meeting and try again. I don't suppose you've heard anything from Ian, Countess?"

"No, no. But I didn't expect to. He's very frivolous about his phone. I haven't looked, but he may not even have it. When he doesn't want to hear from me or anyone else, he simply turns it off or he leaves it behind. But I don't think Ian and Twinkle are the main problem. They've behaved badly, but they're most likely drinking champagne in some Jacuzzi somewhere. It's really Clarissa that we should be focusing on."

"Oh God, I don't think I can bear this! I just cannot believe this is happening to us! I was so sure she'd just appear!!! Something terrible has happened. I can feel it!!!"

"Now, now, Leah dear. Get a hold of yourself. Elonzito! Please bring that tea for Mrs. Worth. Walter, you must have some tranquilizers in your bag. Give her a valium or a xanax or something to calm her down. We have to keep clear heads."

"I'm so sorry to make a fuss, Sissy. I'm too emotional, I know. I have taken something. I'll be fine. It's just hearing it out loud like that, suddenly makes it so real. Forgive me my outburst."

"Don't be silly, Leah, nothing to apologize for. Here comes your tea. Let's all take a nice deep breath and get our wits together, shall we. Elonzito, will you please listen for the door?"

"Yes, Mrs. Talbott. I'll be back in a moment. I have Mr. Talbott's breakfast, just coming now."

"Good show. I'm unusually hungry this morning. Hearty appetite, every time I'm on board."

"Maybe you've gotten in a bit of *vigorous* exercise, Teddy."

"Right about that Countess! Worked with a trainer yesterday. Didn't do too badly, rather be golfing or fishing any day, but it did get the blood pumping."

"I bet it did, Teddy. Leah, I'm so sorry if I upset you, I meant to do exactly the opposite."

"No, no Countess. I'm very grateful. As I said, it was hearing it out loud like that."

Elonzito re-appeared carrying a silver lidded dish containing Teddy Talbott's comfort food and placed it before him. Everyone else was picking at a bit of fruit or muffin and he found it strange to see the glee which Mr. Talbott displayed over his breakfast.

Maybe deep inside Mr. Talbott was upset, but he did not appear to be in any way distressed by the situation affecting the others.

Perhaps this was the only way to have a happy and carefree life: to be able to cut oneself off from all unpleasantness, to put it away somewhere it would not interfere with a good meal or a night's sleep.

Elonzito pondered this possibility, wondering whether this was something to be envied or pitied. Mr. Talbott poured a small pitcher of honey all over his pancakes, spilling over onto the sausages, and took a bite.

"Delicious! Reminds me of the breakfasts my mother's cook Edwina used to make for us children during those wonderful Newport summers when I was a child."

"Teddy, please. Let's get on with things. Elonzito, would you call the clinic and make sure Nurse Peggy is coming this morning with the shot for my back?"

"Yes, Mrs Talbott. I'll see to it at once."

"Thank you. Alright, Walter would you like to take charge of this? I'm afraid I have nothing to report. I haven't seen Clarissa since before you all went to dinner with Rabbi Dayan."

"Well, I'm afraid Leah and I don't have much additional information. We've met several times with Roy Rogers the Head of Security and . . ."

"Is that his first name? Sissy, did you hear that? *Roy* Rogers, my childhood hero! Best damn cowboy movie star Hollywood ever produced. Wonder if he's a relative. Never knew that was his first name. Well, well . . ."

"Teddy, for heaven's sake. . . . Walter, go on. . . ."

"Well, we've met with Rogers and Leah's childhood friend Rory Saltz, who writes for the shows; she's been a great help and we have traced Clarissa back to around midnight of the night she disappeared, but the trail goes cold then."

"I haven't spoken with Mrs. Saltz yet this morning, so she might have some more information. Frankly, we're at our wits' end. I'm going ashore to talk to the authorities, and the authorities on Barbados have been notified but we . . .

"Oh, God, please, forgive me, I can't sit here . . . I really can't! I have to go lie down a bit. I'm so sorry. Really, I just can't bear this . . ."

"Leah, yes, let me walk you back. Please excuse us for a moment."

"Of course Walter, Leah must rest, no point in putting her through this now. Elonzito, I heard the bell! Oh dear, are we ready for them? Well, I guess it doesn't matter. Unless someone else has been attacked or disappeared!

"This is just absolute madness, this entire cruise business! No control over anything! I do not understand this sort of vacationing and I never will. I understand private yachts and sailing, but this is so horrific! Too many people from God knows where! We're probably brushing past the rapist every day! And I can't even imagine how many other unsavory characters are mingling among us, squeezed into those little dark cabins, piled up like prisoners!

"Revolting, Teddy! This isn't us and I want you to get out of this business. There is going to be a scandal over all this. You must know that! And lawsuits. I will never set foot on one of these ships again. That's a promise! Even your own daughter couldn't bear it."

Elonzito rushed to answer the door for Mr. Hensler and Mr. Doolittle and Mr. Rogers. He felt like a small boy leading these tall, somber men into the suite—so elegant and serious and official in their duties. He felt overwhelmed and unprofessional. Between Mrs. Talbott's snapping orders at him and the tension, his pride in his work and his confidence had slipped away from him. He could see himself in their eyes, trotting before these men, looking childish and silly.

"May I bring you coffee?" he said, and his voice sounded faint and high.

"Yes, you may," Mr. Hensler answered for all of them without inquiring. Even Mr. Doolittle did not acknowledge him or make a joke. Mr. Hensler had that affect on everyone who worked for him. It was not possible to feel any ease in his presence.

"I'll bring a fresh pot at once,"

Elonzito turned and started for the kitchen, forgetting in his nervousness to check the plates of his employers.

"Elonzito, please take my plate before I eat anymore of this wonderful breakfast. Everything in moderation. Never saw such a huge portion."

Elonzito flushed, afraid to look up, in case Mr. Hensler was glaring at him.

"Certainly, sir. I'll fetch a tray and be right back."

Elonzito raced to the kitchen for the tray and placed the fresh pot of coffee on it. They were already discussing Miss Clarissa without even the normal amount of polite greeting conversation.

He carried in the tray and placed the coffee on the buffet before picking up Mr. Talbott's half-finished breakfast and the other half-picked meals around him.

Doctor Worth had returned to the table and was talking about his daughter.

"I was with her in Miss Frampton's dressing room with the Countess and some other passengers and Miss Frampton took a shine to her and offered her a sparkling gold skirt to wear for the evening. Clarissa was delighted. She put it on and she was wearing it later in the disco. She never returned it to Miss Frampton and no one saw her at the clinic where she said she was going and no one has seen her since."

Shattering sounds. Bomblike, an explosion of sound, startling the table full of intent grown-ups, who jumped up, instinct overtaking any real possible threat. Elonzito was kneeling on the floor, in the middle of debris from the tray's contents.

Hunks of teeth-marked pancakes and half-eaten sausage and pools of orange juice and honey and melted butter and shards of china and glass. He had lost control, the tray slamming down on the marble floor in a dissonant cacophony, like cymbals clanging or buses backfiring. He had dropped the first tray of his entire career in front of his boss and his boss's boss.

Mr. Doolittle and Dr. Worth rushed to his aid, only codifying his despair and humiliation. "No, please, please! I am fine. I will have it cleaned in a moment. Please! I am so regretful. So, very sorry. Please . . ."

He piled pieces of China and food back onto the tray using the soiled napkins and his hands, utterly desperate, humiliation flooding his entire being. He could feel Mr. Hensler's eyes on his back as he scurried back and forth, scampering like a baboon, like something less human than the others, clearing the wreckage, the reminder of his failure.

His legs could hardly hold him, but he stood up running to the kitchen with the worst of it and returning with cleaning aids, blotting up his disgrace.

He wanted to yell out his defense. It was not his fault! It was not clumsiness or inadequacy! It was the description given by Dr. Worth.

The skirt of shiny gold. Mother of God! Had he seen her? He had seen a shiny falling gold object hurling over the side of the ship when he'd gone out on deck to look at the moon before going to bed.

A flashing bit of gold, falling over the side. He had thought it was one of the costumes from the talent show, moving very fast and disappearing. This could mean Miss Clarissa had disappeared into the water with it! It had been so black, he'd never even considered it might be attached to a person! It was so far away from where he was standing, just a golden flash, falling from the top deck.

Mercifully, Mr. Hensler and the others sat back down and resumed their conversation, allowing him to return to invisibility. The floor was now spotless, no reminder of the embarrassment and shock, no tangible speck of evidence connecting him to the debacle.

He stood up as quietly as he could, not even putting his heels on the ground until he was safely back in the kitchen.

What could he do! He must tell someone! But who? It was certainly not possible to blurt it out to the Worths and the Talbotts nor to Mr. Hensler. He must use his head and start with someone more accessible, but who was in some position to give him guidance or take the information forward?

After all, he could be mistaken. There were many gold objects and items of clothing on the ship. It could have belonged to anyone and there was certainly no way to know if a young woman was wearing it. It could even have been Miss Clarissa, who for some unknown reason had taken the skirt off and thrown it overboard. But he must tell someone.

He dropped all the debris into the trash bin and washed his still-shaking hands. *If only Maria was here,* he thought. His wife, his beautiful, strong wife, so clear in her thinking, so much better at seeing around the corners of any situation. He was not good at that; most men were not, as far as he had seen. Women were much better at the "Big Picture" as Mr. Doolittle called it. He saw this difference even in the way his daughter and his son played.

His son, rushing forth, all eagerness and without thought of anything but the moment and his daughter always holding back just a bit until she had gotten her bearings. Who would Maria choose?

Dios mio, he had said it himself. Mr. Doolittle! He would tell Mr. Doolittle after the breakfast and then he would try to find Jo Jo. Jo Jo was acting so strangely, maybe he knew something about all of this.

He simply must proceed as if he had not suffered a disgrace, as if Mr. Hensler would not mark him up or even demote him—as if the gold shiny thing he saw fall was not possibly covering the body of the lovely young daughter of his passengers. He must do what was right before him: finish serving the guests and find a way to communicate to Mr. Doolittle his need for a conversation.

His Ava had told him so many times when he was a boy that the most wonderful and terrible thing about life was having no idea what would happen and never being able to plan or control anything. Now his grandmother was all around him and those long ago words, wisdom, not valued then, came back to him now as a man, when he was ready to understand. A gift without measure.

WHEN SISSY TALBOTT slipped into her cabin, leaving the breakfast group to wind down without her, Nurse Peggy had been waiting for almost 15 minutes. Sissy had quickly learned that Nurse Peggy did not like to be kept waiting—all that military discipline, she assumed.

The syringe was filled and resting on a piece of plastic next to a sterile swab. Nurse Peggy had seated herself in the large reading chair rather than the small desk chair next to her medical bag. Sissy noted this small act of insolence, the assumption of equality, but quickly discarded the thought. She had made the Nurse an offer she probably couldn't refuse and had put the offer on the table.

"I do so apologize Nurse Peggy, we're in the middle of a nightmare here. I'm sure you've heard some of it, people being who they are. I had to find a proper moment to excuse myself. I'm in considerable pain today and I'm sure the stress hasn't helped."

"Right about that, Mrs. Talbott. I have everything ready for you. Let's get you feeling better and then we can discuss your most flattering suggestion."

"By all means." Sissy lay down on her side and waited for the magic to take hold. She was no dope. She understood that Nurse Peggy was quite aware her employment offer had everything to do with her desire to have a personal medical assistant to supply her with her medications without unnecessary frustration or the need to deal with probing eyes or reluctant physicians. This most likely explained Nurse Peggy's taking a bit of status liberty with her furniture.

The shot jolted her and she could feel the tension drain away, the euphoria and energy filled her being with warm, fragrant bliss.

Nurse Peggy put the evidence into the proper receptacles and sat down in the smaller chair facing Sissy and picked up a folder she had left under her bag.

"You just rest a bit, Mrs. Talbott and I'll speak about your offer and what I've been thinking myself for awhile, if you don't mind."

"No, no, that's quite alright. This is a serious decision for both of us. I don't hire people frivolously and I really know very little about you. I have been terribly impressed with your work ethic and professionalism, but beyond that I know nothing. I'm feeling so much better, so do go on."

"Well, let me say first, I am very honored by your offer. I have found you and Mr. Talbott to be a cut above, if you will. I see so many people and my opinion of my fellow man between the ship and the Army hasn't improved over the years. You and your husband have renewed my faith.

"So, that said, I have been pondering my future and wanting to make a change for quite some time and your kind offer may be just the ticket. You will get a days work for a dollar's pay, that I promise you.

"I know you wanted to see references, but unfortunately, being in the military all my adult life, I have only one personal reference, plus what the ship's people can tell you. I did have a one year job between the army and the *Dolphin* and I have a letter from those people, I can read to you."

"That would be fine, please read it."

"Dear Mrs. Crumm, (Mrs. Crumm was my adopted aunt: only living relative, now deceased) Since neither my husband nor I have writing ability, your Peggy does our writing for us.

"We wanted to write you this note to tell you what a wonderful help your Peggy has been for us this winter. Don't know how we'd have managed without her. Since I am a quadriplegic, Peggy does everything for me and also helps Henry outside.

"It has been a wonderful winter, beautiful weather and with Peggy's help one could say it was just about perfect. Sadly for us we will be leaving Peggy with you in Maine on our way South. We wish you all the best, The Butlers."

An urge to laugh pushed up and out of Sissy Talbott's throat forcing her to cover her mouth with both hands. The meds made her mirthful and the letter was just too tempting, absolutely irresistible.

"Oh, my, well, Nurse Peggy, ha, ha, ah, ha, so sorry, don't know what's come over me. It's a very, ha, ha, good letter, but my, oh my, if the woman is, sadly, very sadly, but a ha, ha, quadriplegic, well, she could, might have actually been screaming for help! Ha, ha, and you might be writing 'I'm the Bee's knees' you know, it's ha, ha. Please forgive me, I don't mean to imply that, oh dear. . . ."

Sissy opened her eyes and looked quickly over at Nurse Peggy, fearing the worst, but surprisingly, she was smiling. *Careful Sissy, you need this one.*

"Mrs. Talbott, I do understand the humor of it, I can only say I am a person of honor."

"I can see that. Well then, I will discuss this with my husband and get back to you before the end of the day with a formal offer. If we come to terms, when would you be able to start?"

"I have two more cruises before my current contract expires and I had already decided not to renew, so I'm free at the end of this month."

"That would be fine. May I ask why you'd decided not to continue on the *Dolphin*?"

"Let's just say, the ilk of the persons I'm required to care for is not to my standard. I have a nest egg and I am tired of putting up with such nonsense."

Sissy sat up, feelings of endless possibilities and fondness for this woman, who would devote herself to her care and accompany her on her travels and see to her needs. A companion, but one without the frustrations of a husband or the guilt of a failed motherhood as were her most available alternative choices. This was just the ticket. This woman and she would see eye to eye. The future looked brighter already.

"Nurse Peggy, I'm feeling so much better and I look forward to our making an arrangement."

The soon-to-be companion of Sissy Talbott stood up and briskly cleaned up the debris from her medical procedure, snapping her bag shut and turning toward her patroness, standing so straight, Sissy half expected her to click her heels and salute.

"One thought, Mrs. Talbott, if I may be so bold: since Mr. Talbott is the owner of the cruise line and the boss of my employer, Mr. Hensler, a word from him might make it possible for me to finish my duties sooner and even, perhaps, I might leave the ship when this cruise is over. If that would be more convenient for you, I would be happy to make the accommodation."

Sissy lifted her head. Now that the possibility of her own personal quasi-physician was at hand, well, the sooner, the better. "Why that's a wonderful idea, Nurse Peggy. I'll speak to Teddy at once. You could come back to New York with us and get settled in right away."

"Yes, Ma'am. Right away would be fine."

When Sissy returned to the dining room Teddy was alone at the huge granite table, sitting with a cup of tea in front of him, swirling it with a spoon. This startled her, slightly cooling her euphoric high. She had never seen him doing anything like that before. Teddy was not the kind of man who sat alone and pondered. He was certainly not an introspector or a solitary spoon swirler.

She searched her memory for another such moment. Blank. What a strange thing to realize! He was always engaged even when alone, he was puttering around doing this or that. Re-arranging his desk or his wine bottles or his cigar boxes or preparing to leave for some sporting activity requiring special attire and equipment, or surrounded by his minions or groundsmen or chauffer or interfering with the cook's menu or pontificating to his endless array of good fellows from one club or board or the other or scanning the papers or watching the Discovery channel or reading his history tomes. Sitting alone and stirring, this was entirely new and most likely attached to some dreadful news that she was in no mood to hear.

She sighed and let the medicine lift her back up, forming an invisible internal shield against anything appalling or upsetting that her husband might be waiting to divulge.

"Well, that was quick. I thought you'd be at it for hours."

Teddy Talbott put down his spoon, handling it with such care, it might have been made of glass and looked up at his wife, with his watery blue avian-eyes.

"There was not a great deal to report. They've all gone to investigate further and Leah is asleep."

"Rather abrupt departure."

"Not at all. You obviously dozed off. It's been more than an hour. Your nurse left quite some time ago. I've had two meetings since you excused yourself."

Sissy gasped and checked her watch. "Good grief! That medicine is much stronger than I thought. Sorry for that, but I feel so much better and I want to discuss Nurse Peggy with you, anyway. She's accepted my offer and I'd like to hire her and take her home with us if you can be a dear and get Heinrich to let her out of the rest of her contract. I'm very pleased about this. She's going to be just the ticket for our waning years."

Teddy sighed and crossed his long, liver spotted fingers in front of him, resting them on the table. This was beginning to be very unpleasant. He had never *sighed* before! Sighing was just not something they did. She had always considered sighing an ethnic behavior, something for emotional peoples like the Jews and the Italians. A sign of bad breeding or some sort of moral weakness.

"Teddy, for heaven's sakes! You're behaving so strangely. What on earth is the matter with you?"

"Sit down, Sissy. We have to talk," he said and she did.

RORY TOOK A BIG sip of coffee and looked at her watch. Flora was late. Roy Rogers was late. Maybe Trigger was acting out. Maybe he'd gotten his balls caught in his lasso. Maybe she should think about something else and avoid the possibility of making bad jokes about his unfortunate name.

She yawned. Romance was not turning her into an early riser or an under eater, two of the potential perks she had read about. Oh well. What an incredible evening they'd had. What an incredible thing to wake up and want to spend your day re-living your previous evening.

She should have brought something to read or at least a pad and pen so she could do some work. She reached into her bag and pulled out a catalogue someone had left on the counter. *Good thinking Ror, better than staring into space.*

Lifecycles: The Better Living Catalogue. Maybe not better than staring into space. She took another sip of coffee. *You know better, Rory. This is not in your best interests.* She had sworn off all catalogues and women's magazines and was now in on-going recovery. *I'll just look at the pictures. Oh, sure . . . you will . . .*

Look Younger Instantly! . . . Microdermabrasion System Produces Collagen for a Natural Face Lift!!!! . . . Total Odor Eliminating Body Mints, Leaves Your Entire Body Odor-Free Around the Clock!!!!!! . . . Eliminate Unsightly Nose and Ear Hair!!!!! Expel Fat, and Inhibit toxins!!!!! . . . Shrink Your Belly Fat and Eliminate Cellulite!!!! More energy, Less Fat, Fewer Wrinkles!!!!! Penetrating Gel Emulsifies Fat on Contact!!!!! Grow Thicker, Longer Lashes!!!!! Dramatically Reduce Wrinkles While you Sleep!!!!! Melt Away Wrinkles in Three Easy Steps!!!!! . . . Anti-Aging Breakthrough—Better Than Botox!!!! . . . Anti-Aging Cell Protection!!! Anti-Sag Facelift Serum!!!! Anti-Wrinkle Infusion!!!! . . . Fuller, Plumper Lips!!! Clinically Proven!!! Wake Up With the Skin you were Meant To HAVE!!!! Erase Lip Lines!!! Six Shades Whiter Teeth in Minutes!!!! End Ingrown Toenails!!! Conceal Varicose Veins!!!! Soften Dry Scaly Feet!!! Clear Infected Nails!!! Fade Age Spots!!! Look Ten Years Younger in Minutes!!! Painless Hair Removal for Your Entire Body!!!! Look Twenty Years Younger Instantly!!!! Reduce Under-Eye circles!!! Dry up Pimples Overnight!!! Stop Acne, Eczema, Warts, Herpes!!!! Shrink Pores Fast!!!! Extract Whiteheads and Blackheads with Ease!!!

Rory, this is turning into a serious relapse. You are circling items. This is not good. This is the catalogue junkie's version of Falling Off the Wagon. This is serious. Put your pen away. Take the catalogue and toss it onto the next booth. Ah, just a couple more pages. Some of this stuff sounds pretty amazing . . . . No . . . do not listen to that voice . . . that is not you . . . that is The Demon . . . close it up . . . think of something more connected to reality—like, what? Well, like how revolting it is to be an aging woman? No, think about how great it is to be an aging woman who refuses to buy into all of this bullshit. Yes, okay, but . . . that one about instant fat emulsifying for your belly, now that. . . . No. . . . Stop this. Think of this the way an alcoholic thinks about a bottle of gin . . . not one sip. . . . You've already re-lapsed. Toss it. Now. . . .

Rory tossed the catalogue over onto the table behind her, using all her will power. *Whew. That was a close one. I was ready to buy the entire inventory.* Perfect distraction, though. Deadly and perfect.

Well, not deadly, let's not get overdramatic. She finished her coffee and tried to find a waitress.

Think about something else.

Herman. I'll think about Herman. When I get home, I'm going to pick Herman up at the kennel and take him out for a nice, special walk.

She smiled, thinking about Herman. Before Poe, her dog had been her favorite living creature, and New York City had suddenly become the most dog-friendly place on earth—go figure. Everywhere she tried to take him outside of the city had great big signs with pictures of dogs on leashes with thick red diagonal lines across them and also a written warning NO PETS in case English was not your first language or you were just a really defiant kind of person.

You could no longer walk your dog on the beach or at any of the nearby nature preserves, but half the restaurants in her neighborhood said "Dogs Welcome" and some even put out little water bowls and doggy treats. All kinds of pups were trotting around the cosmetics departments of Saks and Bergdorf's, where those zombie saleswomen even squirted them with Evian water in the summer. So Herman was How-de-Dood and red-carpeted in chic little bistros and major department stores, but not allowed on the *beach*?

What would it do to Herman's world view? This was interesting to ponder. What if dogs began to think that Saks was their natural habitat and chasing sticks in the park was a BAD THING?

Some hotels even had special spa packages for pets, with special outfits and massages and food choices. Gone were the days of Fido and the doghouse. Maybe it was time to think about relocating before Herman turned into a spoiled brat.

Whoa, there, Rory . . . could this idea have anything to do with Poe's future plans? That little house on that island somewhere she'd never even heard of? Let's hope not. No self-improvement catalogues and no day-dreaming about you know what. *Think about something else.*

Before she had time to think about anything else, Flora Frampton and the head of Security, Roy Rogers arrived, looking very much like a couple. Rory waved and they waved back, Flora leading the way to her table. Incredible Flora's fella would turn out to be Walter! Rory had always thought she and Roy were perfect for one another. At least he was single—but then again, who the hell knew? Maybe he was a multiple bigamist with wives and children in every port like that guy in New Jersey she'd read about or maybe he was gay or into teenagers or . . . too bad though, if he was just a decent guy who probably wouldn't break her heart like dear old Walter was most certain to do.

Flora slid into the booth facing her, without even a second of awkwardness. No matter what she was doing, she moved as if she were on stage, without effort or anything but poise.

Stomach muscles, Ror, gotta . . . what had that trainer at the spa told her? Gotta "engage" her stomach muscles. *Well, I don't believe in long engagements, I just want a single ring and a marriage certificate and I don't find my stomach muscles the least bit sexy or a good potential companion.*

"Sorry we're late, Rory lamb. Roy was meeting with Hensler and the Talbotts and then it took us forever to get across the sports deck. They're havin' some volleyball extravaganza and every jocko on the ship is up there."

"No problem, I was perfectly content nodding off and thinking about my dog. Hi Roy."

"Hiya Rory. What kind of dog do ya have?"

"A Bassett Hound, Lab and some kind of maybe Beagle mix. When I got him the shelter lady said, the only thing they were sure of was he isn't a Great Dane. He's the ultimate mutt."

"I gotta Wheaten Terrier, which makes people snigger. They seem to think it's a weird dog for a man, but I saw her in a window, Doggy in the Window, just like the song and my heart went pitter-pat and I just marched right in and took her out of that place. Had her 5 years now and I can't imagine life without her."

"What's her name?"

"Lola, like that Barry Manilow song, Copacabana?" She's my showgirl. When she sees me packing for a cruise, she jumps right up into my suitcase and looks up at me with her big black eyes and it's all I can do to leave her."

"How about 'Whatever Lola wants, Lola gets, and little man, little Lola wants you'? Great song from *Damn Yankees*."

"That's the ticket. I'd do anything for her. My gal friends all give up. They say I love her more than them. One of 'em even bought me a book called *Men Who Love Their Dogs Obsessively* and I read it and decided it was true. If I had to choose between Lola and the ladies, Lola wins hands down."

"Funny idea though, Roy, having the girlfriend and the terrier lined up waiting for you to make your selection: 'She goes or I go'.

"You're brave to buy her from a pet store. There's a very upscale popular one in Manhattan and they always have the cutest pups in the window, sort of like shoe stores putting their hottest brands on display to lure you in; so one day, in I went, this was before Herman and before the economy tanked, and they had these glass doored cubbies with very unusual looking dogs in each one and a lot of Mink-Coatie type customers asking to see this one or that one and the pet store employees would open the doors and plop the little pooch down and they'd look it over, turn it upside down like they were handbags at one of those fancy boutiques — really, really creepy. 'How much for the Japanese Chin?' It was sort of like the canine slave trade."

"Well, this old store was in my hometown in Florida, and I guarantee there was none of that."

"Heloo, everyone? You've got a cat person here and one who is in desperate need of some coffee and eggs. Let's get a waitress and get on with this. I'm starting to get very feline in my attention span."

Roy Rogers stood up, using his long lanky cowboyesque frame to catch the eye of the waitress. "Excuse me Ladies, let me try and facilitate your breakfast."

The waitress responded instantly, picking up the coffee pot and racing to the table.

Rory rolled her eyes at Flora. "Unfucking believable. I've been trying for twenty minutes. I was about to jump up on the table and scream fire."

Flora laughed. "Rory, lamb, yew are so new to the planet for such a snappy girl. He's a guy and a cute straight one at that. You can't possibly think she's gonna hot foot it over for yew."

"I refuse to accept that reality however many times I'm confronted by it."

"Better let Roy order everything otherwise she'll probably 'forget' what we tell her."

Rory wasn't sure, but it looked to her as if the slightly shopworn, but still, as they said in the singles bars, "fuckable" blonde with the "Hi, I'm Daisy" name tag placed at the top of her probably artificially inflated bosoms, had sucked in her stomach right before she made her perky dash to their booth.

Roy did the ordering and the waitress wrote it all down with several hair tosses and boob thrusts and a couple of well-placed giggles and cute one-liners and she and Flora watched, not saying anything, but communicating in the way women who are both beaming into the same frequency can "hear" one another and Rory knew if they were alone they would be pondering how "Daisy" would look with all her little white petals plucked right out of her stem and how being middle-aged women they could think such things now without even pausing to consider whether this was politically correct or anti-feminist or anything else.

Roy sat back down and grinned at them. "I can read you two like the Tallahassee Yellow Pages. You hate me right now, but you're glad I'm here."

"Rory and I don't hate yew, a fine 'sort-of' southern gentleman like yourself. You saved me from hypoglycemia and catty behavior. We hate ol' Daisy Mae and her bouncing boobies. It's a chick thing, Roy, don't even ask."

He grinned broader and Rory thought again, it was a shame Flora didn't like him. He had a nice gangly look and he loved his dog *and* this was really none of her business. She was having trouble remembering why they were here in the first place.

He stopped grinning as if reading her mind and his eyes narrowed in that sort of slightly Roy Rogers way, kind of oriental at the sides if she remembered correctly, though she had always hated westerns, even that one with Marlon Brando in it and Yul. Oh boy, Yul had gotten her motor going all those years ago, so no wonder Poe had appealed to her right away . . .

Roy leaned forward "I know we have some serious business, I don't mean to make light of it. Rory, I shouldn't be here at all, ya know. If Hensler knew I was talking to you two, he'd fire my ass, but Flora said you knew something important and we're completely out of leads; I can feel the heat from the Talbotts and Hensler, three decks down; I'm trusting you gals and taking one helluva risk. So shoot. What have you got?"

"Okay, but the reason Flora and I thought we should tell you together is we're very concerned about compromising Collie O'Brian, so before we say a word, we need your promise that you'll send one of your guys to stand guard outside her cabin until we get back to San Juan."

"You want me to promise before I know why for?"

"Yep. Hensler was supposed to handle it and he didn't which is most of why she talked to us in the first place."

"Hey ladies, you know this is a cruise ship in the Caribbean, not Special Victims Unit. It's not like I have a staff really equipped for this as it is. We're covering 4,500 passengers, 1,600 crew members and it seems an increasingly, raunchy, rock and rolling crowd and I'm not just talking about the younguns.

"You wouldn't believe the stuff that goes down on one of these trips. I could use five more guys just to handle the drunken spousal punch fests and the sex in public places attempts; we got more shoplifting, bar altercations, petty theft, you name it.

"Now what happened to Miss O'Brian is way over the usual, and the disappearance of Clarissa Worth, that is all consuming, I gotta tell you.

"It's the hierarchy, the way the deal works. A staff member being brutally raped and beaten half to death is not anywhere near as important to these folks as a fancy guest gone missing and Hensler and the Talbotts are freaking out because of the bad press possibilities, so a full-time guard down there is going to get me in serious hot water and I don't have anyone to spare."

Flora leaned over and touched his arm. "Find someone, Roy dear, 'cause it's a condition, just like a plea bargain on T.V. No security, no talkee and believe me, you're gonna want to know what we know and Hensler will not dare do a tiny little ol' anything."

Before Roy Rogers could answer, Waitress Daisy returned with a full tray and they waited while she plopped all the appropriate food orders down and refilled their coffee cups, leaving with a glistening smile for their ambushed security head.

Flora dug right into her breakfast, leaving Rory to close the deal. Rory watched Flora daintily devour her omelet. Flora and she did have great chemistry. They instinctively knew how to work as a team, Flora the charmer and she the Closer.

Roy grinned again and shook his head. "Whoa, now ladies. You got me cornered. This was one fine set-up and I admire your grit. Remind me never to play poker with you two."

They waited while he made a messy little sandwich with his over-easy eggs and white toast, watching him soak everything in ketchup and too much salt and smash his home fries into the middle of it.

They were engrossed the way women can be engrossed watching a skinny guy eat. He took a big bite and chewed slowly, taking his time as a bluff and a way of saving his manhood before the fury of motivated female energy.

"So?" Rory leaned forward, looking down at her oatmeal as if it were some Twistian gruel. "You'd better do it, Roy, because if I have to sit here much longer and watch you eat with all that greasy gusto, I'm going to put a fork through your hand."

Roy laughed, bits of egg appearing at the sides of his well-formed mouth. "Now, now, no need for violence. You can't have all the good cards. I'm a cop after all." He washed his food down with a deep gulp of o.j. and looked across at Rory. "Okay, we've got a deal."

"Good I won't stab you. You eat, we'll talk. We know who attacked Collie and it wasn't some mad rapist crew member and it isn't connected to whatever happened to Clarissa Worth."

"Collie O'Brian *saw* who attacked her?"

"Yes, sir."

"Well, why the hell wouldn't she tell us, especially if she's still terrified?"

"She told Hensler and he said he'd take care of it and he buried it."

"What!! You've got to be kidding me! I just sat up there with him ragging on my ass for thirty minutes about why we didn't have any leads and how it was most certainly the same person who abducted Clarissa Worth!"

"Well, Roy, he's a liar. He knows. He must have some really sinister reason for doing this, but he knows. Collie has *no* reason to lie."

"Leaping Lizards. I'm freaking here. He's my boss."

"We know. But we have no one else to go to with this."

"Well, hell, I'm glad about that. So okay, who did it?"

"The Talbotts' daughter Twinkle and her pal the Countess's kid. They left the ship in St. John's, probably worried Collie might have seen them. They don't know she did, but I can understand them not wanting to hang around with Momsey and Popsey just in case. So if Hensler's your boss, well the Talbotts are *his* boss and his career is on the line, so maybe he thought it best not to tell the social-leaders-and-prominent-community-members that their kids are rapist thugs."

Roy Rogers scratched his head, and rubbed his eyes and pushed his plate away. "What a freaking thing. I gotta mull this over. You got the guard, though if the *perps* are gone, it must be Hensler she's afraid of and this means that whatever happened to the Worth girl is even more disturbing and unknown. It makes my nose twitch though. Too much coincidence always does. There's gotta be a connection, we can't see it, but I can feel it. I don't like this a bit."

"No shit. Clarissa is a great kid. Collie is, too. So we're doing what we can."

Roy Rogers looked at his watch and winked at them. "You're good people, you gals. This is now a blood trust, okay? No gabbing, not to anyone."

Flora gave Roy her stage smile. "On a stack of Florida flapjacks or holy books, whichever yew take more seriously, Roy dear."

"Oh, now that's a relief." He stood up and shook his head at them, his eyes crinkling into the other Roy's famous look. "We never had this breakfast, okay?"

Rory looked up at him thinking again how good he would be for Flora after Walter broke her heart. "Okay, then if we never had it, I can finish your food."

"Be my guest. Us dog lovers have to watch one another's backs."

"Flora, too. Even cat people can be trustworthy, sometimes."

Flora slid out beside him with cat-like slink. "Gotta go. I'll see yew at rehearsal."

Rory nodded and watched them leave, waiting until they disappeared out the door: two long lean southerners as unlike herself as possible, but part of her life, a life that until this cruise was made up entirely of people with whom she had no history or any real links, which was the way she'd liked it. She sighed and pulled the half-finished plate of the lanky law man's hearty meal in front of her, pushing the oatmeal off to the side.

She had promised and Flora had promised, but they both knew they would tell their fellas. Some things required more willpower and aloneness than was bearable, once you had the temptation before you, and options, something she'd never thought she'd have. Screw the oatmeal, and screw the vow of silence. She had to tell Poe.

DERRICK DOOLITTLE STOOD in the back of the theater, watching Sylvia and Fernando the ballroom dance instructors, lead the candidates for the "So You Think You Can Dance," the *Dolphin's* rip-off of the television show, prepare for their competition.

God Bless reality T.V. It had given him an endless new selection of on-board activities and as teeth-gritting as some of the performances were, it was at least more entertaining than bad magic tricks and baton twirlers, though they'd never completely eliminate those, since the Talent Show was still one of their most popular events. Some people took the cruise just for the chance to sing "Climb Every Mountain" in the wrong key, clad in a rented powder blue tuxedo with the sleeves too short, before hundreds of snickering strangers. The joke was always on them, which didn't faze them a tad. Anything for a moment of glory, a sip from the cup of celebrity — a taste of being special.

Cruisers arrived on board with tubas and hula skirts, top hats and tap shoes. They rehearsed as if talent scouts from Hollywood were attending. Who could possibly know how much delusion anyone had about their lives? Thank God he was only the Cruise Director and not their father, not that some of them didn't try and turn him into that, but if he'd learned nothing else, he'd become a master at the internal unplugging.

Nothing on the outside changed, not even the width of his smile, but the lights went out. He just switched off and let them prattle on about high school pom pom victories and opera company auditions.

It was probably the same thing he did with everyone, not even a choice. An invisible, silent internal shield that automatically slid into place when any intimacy or sharing of vulnerability threatened his "Life is a Beach" façade. Which was most likely why this new relationship with the Countess had so unsettled him. She had broken through his shield and he hadn't been able to shut her back out.

He leaned back against the faux marble wall watching the Russolinis, the gregarious Italian couple from Long Island who he'd at first dismissed as "fantasticers" but had come to see as just a couple of innocents abroad, but down-to-earth and with a jolly energy, a by-product of good heartedness — a kind of honesty that makes them essential for entertainment events because they bring good spirit and enthusiasm, but they don't just love everything, so they keep the steppers stepping.

People like that rarely join in; they participate from the sidelines, but these two clearly loved to dance and danced with that kind of unfakable ease only well-married people had. They knew how to move together and a tango, no less. Some dance studio in Great

Neck had made a pile on those two and they could win it, because people would like them and see themselves in their earnest effort. *Give me more passengers like Vera and Solly and I may make it through the rest of my career.*

He looked at the clock. Ten more minutes here and then he had to check on the Volleyball tournament and see how his staff was doing with the island tours. He pulled his activities schedule out of his pocket and re-checked his notes. Damn, he'd forgotten about the Encore Comedy night! God he hated that one. Bad dancing or Karaoke had *nothing* on bad comedy.

Once when he was drunk, he and his staff had tried to come up with the most ridiculous possible activities they could conceive of, all of which sounded hilarious to them at the time. Ear wiggling lessons, corn cob sculpting, Amish sock darning techniques and after they sobered up they'd decided to sneak each one of the bad joke activities onto the program one very quiet cruise when Hensler was in Germany and no one was paying much attention.

Passengers came to *all* of them. Even the Hair Ball Decorating Session. What was it about human nature that made this sort of mindless seeking of instruction, of any kind of expert telling you any kind of drivel or the need to fill every second with things outside of yourself, the fear of being, of self-guidance, of space between, of what? And this of course, was his problem, too.

In twenty years, he'd never put anything on the program or had any guest lecturer stand before an empty room. They came for anything. *Anything.* They dressed up in silly clothes, allowed intrusions and humiliations, invasions of privacy, and he was very glad they did, but he had become contemptuous. During the Ferret Seminar, he'd fought the urge to shout out, "What's the matter with you people!! Get a grip. Get a life!! Go home!!"

And who was he really talking to? Them or himself? And where did Countess Mimsie fit in to all of this?

He was now her cruise companion and confidant and what was more, he was confessing back! Sharing these very personal thoughts, telling her about himself and he was looking forward to her company. His shield was shrinking, leaving him in quite a state, lost in uncharted inner territory, triggering panic as well as pleasure, but he didn't seem able to re-seal himself and with all the horrific things going on around them, he didn't have much time or desire to try.

"Mr. Derrick, may I talk with you for a moment?"

Derrick stiffened as if caught doing something unseemly, even if the activity was only taking place inside his head. It was dark and it took him a moment to recognize Elonzito. His heart speeded up, the fight or flight neurons kicking in. He already knew whatever he was about to hear, was not going to make his day better.

"Yes, of course. Let's go backstage, the Green Room should be quiet. I only have a few minutes though."

"I am very sorry to disturb you. I will be brief."

Derrick led the nervous young man across the back of the theater and through the emergency exit leading to the dressing rooms and opened the door to the Green Room. Elonzito followed him docilely, and, Derrick thought, with a certain desperation. Could this be about the dropped tray and some fear that Hensler would fire him?

At least that was fairly simple to address and give the man some reassurance. Elonzito was probably the best butler on the ship or on any of their ships and no one on the staff would stand by and let Hensler axe him for something like that, however humiliating it must have been for someone with Elonzito's pride in his work.

When Derrick turned on the lights and saw Elonzito's face, his shoulders tensed. This was not about a dropped tray. He braced himself, trying to keep his own mounting urge to run, to bolt, to push his hands over his ears and keep out whatever information this worried and decent man held. If he didn't receive it, he wasn't responsible for doing anything about it.

"What is it, Elonzito? You look like the captain of *Titanic* after the iceberg."

"I'm very sorry, if I'm looking so, but I overheard something this morning, when you were all meeting with Mr. and Mrs. Talbott and I have been very, very concerned and Mr. Derrick, I do not know who to trust but you or how to tell Mr. Hensler. So I came to find you. I did not know what else to do."

Derrick could feel the tension crawling all over his body. *Oh, how I do not want to hear this.*

"Let's sit down," he said, hardly recognizing his own voice, which was usually deeper and controlled by all that public speaking and breathing work he'd done. He sounded like he'd just inhaled helium.

They sat facing one another and he realized he had never sat facing this man, had only seen him in subservient roles, rushing to bring something or waiting on him or passing by in the halls. He had such a soulful face. Beautiful big dark eyes and strong features. It was impossible to tell his age, probably 30 or so. What could he possibly be so upset about that he needed his help?

"So, Elonzito, what's the problem? I'm flattered you feel you can trust me, but are you sure I'm the right choice?"

"'I'm not sure of anything, Mr. Derrick. But you're very smart and a nice person and I have to tell someone right away, because Miss Clarissa's life is at stake and . . .'"

Derrick felt his stomach turn over in his body as if someone had reached inside and twisted it around. "What! What are you saying?"

"Mr. Derrick, this is the trouble, I am not sure what I am saying. This morning, when I dropped the tray, it was not clumsiness, it was because I heard, I was not trying to listen, but I heard Dr. Worth saying how Miss Clarissa was wearing a shiny gold skirt borrowed from Miss Frampton on the night she became missing.

"I was on the crew deck having a moment before I went to sleep and I saw, it was far away, and it was very dark, no moonlight, but I saw something like that, gold and shiny fall over the side of the ship, the starboard aft side, from one of the top decks. But I thought nothing about it until this morning when I heard about the skirt. I became so afraid it was possible it could have been Miss Clarissa falling over the side, but you can see how I could not say such a thought out loud and I may be wrong.

"I did not see a person, just something gold falling, and it was so far from me and the noise from the engines, you know how hard it is to hear from our deck, but I cannot just pretend I never saw it and I thought you might be better to tell them or to tell Mr. Rogers. I do not want to put you in the midst of this, but I did not know what else to do."

Derrick's body felt as if he had suddenly been stuffed into a space shuttle or submerged in a diving bell. His stomach flopping back and forth, his neck and back tightened into an almost rigor state of fear.

"Elonzito, well, I, I see why you didn't want to share this with Hensler or the Talbotts and the Worths this morning. Let me think here a moment; this is serious enough, we don't want to get this wrong."

"No, no sir. I do not want that!"

The young man's eyes were full and Derrick was afraid he might start crying, but he blinked them back. After all his years in the diplomatic corps, it was second nature to him to never show doubt or anger or weakness in any negotiation no matter what was churning away inside.

Derrick leaned forward and touched Elonzito's shoulder. "I want you to listen very carefully because we are not going to meet like this again. Okay?"

"Yes, yes, Mr. Derrick. I will. I understand."

"This is what I want you to do. Nothing. You go back to work and put this out of your mind as much as possible. I'm going to tell Roy Rogers. If he wants to tell any of the others that's his business, but knowing him and a bit about how security people think, I would be very surprised if he didn't keep this information to himself until he had checked it thoroughly; there are surveillance cameras almost everywhere. It may well be on file.

"I don't think he'd tell Hensler, and I promise you I won't use your name, but no one will ask because it doesn't matter at all who saw the gold thing. . . . I hope it's a thing, let's not even think about any other possibility. I will protect you but it only works if you tell no one and I mean *no* one. Don't even put it in a letter to your wife. This is for your safety. You haven't told anyone else have you?"

"No, no. I swear on the Virgin. No one."

"Good. You've done the right thing and I'll do my best to see that Rogers takes it the next step, but we have little to go on and frankly, if the girl was in the gold skirt, there is nothing to be done and there wasn't anything to be done even when it happened. I've been at sea a long time Elonzito, when you go over the side of one of these babies, it's most likely over."

"But, but, Mr. Derrick, why? She was a happy girl. A well-raised young lady. She would not have done something like this and she would not have fallen off! If she went over, Mr. Derrick, someone pushed her! Someone killed her! Oh, Mother of God, then there is a murderer still on board and someone else could be hurt!"

"Elonzito, remember what I said. You go back to work and put such thoughts out of your mind. We are going to keep this simple and you are not to worry about it. Now it's for the professionals to handle."

Derrick stood up, reinforcing his words with action. The conversation and the gruesome speculation had to end or the young man would not be able to keep his promise.

"Let it go now. We'll not speak of this together again until this cruise and this mess is behind us."

Elonzito stood and looked up at the older, bigger than life man, who looked to him now so heroic and strong. "I will do as you said. Bless you Mr. Derrick you have taken a great burden from me."

Derrick waited until his penitent had left, not wanting to be seen anywhere near him. He moved toward the stage exit, catching sight of his reflection in the mirrors lining the wall. Was that him? He looked so, worn. Bloated and worn. More than a quick shot of B-12 and some oxygen was going to be needed to get him through this. Elonzito had transferred his burden, and he was already buckling under the unwanted weight.

"GOOD MORNING, *Mr.* Rogers."

"Derrick, my friend, if you've come to try and enlist me in any morale lifting crew activity, the answer is, I'm busy that month. What brings you down to the bowels in the height of hive buzzing?"

"I'm here as a damn messenger, so please holster your weapon before I drop this one on you."

"Sounds serious. No weapons, I promise and I've already had my major morning piece of bad news, so I'm resigned in advance."

"I hope so. I just finished a conversation with one of our most trustworthy crew members, who's name I will withhold permanently. He's scared enough already and it's unimportant, just believe me this is a solid person. He told me he saw a shiny gold something fall, or drop or whatever off the left starboard side of one of the top decks of the ship, the night Clarissa Worth went missing. He was too far away to see if the object was being worn by a human being, but he felt compelled to pass along the information to someone he trusts and telling Hensler was way too terrifying."

"Holy Hosiah! You gotta be kidding me! You believe him?"

"Completely, but it doesn't mean it was her, lots of gold stuff on this ship, or she could have tossed the skirt or someone else could, like the rapist who's still at large . . ."

"Nope. No rapist still at large and don't ask me any questions. I don't like this, Derrick. Something is happening on this ship that reaches way beyond the Collie O'Brian deal. I don't have a Caribbean clue what it is, but it's bad news and it ain't over. Thanks, for coming down. I appreciate your coming to me first."

"Well, I may be a bit burnt out and waterlogged but I'm not crazy enough to drop this little mega bite on The Man and knowing him, he'd probably bury it just to keep an even keel with the owners."

"Yeah, well now the gator's on my gangplank. Though I may have to just throw myself on top of it and take the hit."

"If I can help, just page me."

"Count on it."

⌒⑭⌒

SHE WAS LATE. Poe was already at the lectern. She thought she'd caught his eye but maybe it was just the light; though a crouching white haired woman creeping across the back of the lecture hall was sort of hard to miss.

Not many people. But then, he hadn't expected many. A talk about the nature of Evil, or a day at Limbo Beach, hmmm, lemme see. She sat down near the exit and checked her watch. Well, not too bad, she should be able to hear his talk and grab some lunch with him before she went back to rehearsal.

Now that she had made the decision to tell him about her meeting with Roy Rogers and what Collie had told her and Flora and to generally blurt out everything she'd been up to, she could barely wait.

He was smiling at his audience, that sweetly irresistible, to her anyway, smile that made his eyes twinkle. She could picture him shooting up out of a toilet bowl, chipper and immaculate and laughing at his own little inner bowl joke, up to any of life's realities, even the inside of some foul-excreter's latrine.

"Well, I must say, I am most flattered to find anyone here on this beautiful day. I hesitated to put the subject of this talk on the program; I thought it would put everyone off, but I decided it would be worse bringing you in from some far more entertaining activity under false pretenses. May I make an assumption that most of you are either students of psychology or professionals or involved in law enforcement or possibly just evil yourselves?"

Rory laughed too loud. *Ror, you're not his mother.* Sitting in the back was good, because she could watch reactions. People were nodding and laughing back. *Good, very good start.*

"I have a confession to make. You are my guinea pigs; this is the first time I've given this talk and it's part of a rather ambitious research project and I do find hearing myself talk in a socially acceptable way, not locked in my bathroom or to strangers on the subway, is extremely helpful and I welcome any questions.

"So, evil. What the hell does it mean in the ways less obvious than the usual suspects?

"If some of you were at the talk I gave at the beginning of the cruise about my main work which is the reading of faces, a technique which has mapped the emotions of the human face, you may remember that it is now being used in increasing frequency by therapists and police to help recognize emotions such as fear and rage and to identify lying and it is proving to be remarkably effective as a tool.

"But what about evil? Can we see evil? Or is evil the ultimate dissembler? Obviously if someone is hurtling toward you down a dark alley, with his teeth bared and a knife in his hand even animals, birds, infants can 'see' that. But if evil were 'readable' then would any young woman get into a stranger's car, or an otherwise intelligent and savvy businessman trust his savings to a charlatan?

"In my work, I have learned that the most evil face is the one that is unreadable. Without emotion. The far extreme of sociopathia, of what is often referred to as 'detachment.' The muscle contractions that have been mapped to help face readers decipher emotion, do not react accordingly. Unreadable is the true nature of evil.

"In a fascinating article in the *New Yorker* on the 'Nature of Evil' by John Updike, he quoted from the work of the psychoanalyst Carl Goldberg. Dr. Goldberg prefers the word 'malevolence' which he defines (borrowed loosely from Nathaniel Hawthorne) as 'The deliberate infliction of cruel, painful suffering on another human being.'

"I rather like that definition, because it encompasses a much denied, but omnipresent component of human nature and one does not have to commit murder or rape or steal the life savings of widows and orphans to commit such acts, which often unfold without any conscious awareness.

"Those of you who watch nature programs and are followers of the Discovery channel, can probably rattle off endless examples of animals such as the spotted Hyena, who when barely out of the womb, attack their siblings in a vicious deadly response to eliminate any competition.

"Updike sites numerous examples of animals and birds, learning to cheat, and deceive to gain maternal favor and more food and then moving toward mammals he sites the trial of a sociopathic ten year old boy, Robert Thomson described in a work by Lyall Watson, who kidnapped a two year old child from a mall outside Liverpool, brutally murdered him and then went round to buy videos.

"At his trial Watson described the killer as having, 'A blank face. . . . Just blank, a mask without identity, dead skin over dead eyes.' Which is what I mentioned earlier about unreadable faces. What is key is the absence of human reaction or emotion.

"Are we all capable of evil? Most certainly. Does that mean that it is in our nature to be evil? Most certainly not. Patients who have sustained severe damage to the small gland in the brain called the amygdala, which processes emotional content and aids us in the appraisal of danger, lose the ability to discern fear or anger in others. They simply cannot interpret it, leaving them unable to recognize danger and enlist the fight or flight response.

"These emotions, the most primal ones, the first ones we as humans are capable of feeling, are necessary for self-protection, every bit as essential to survival, whether physical or emotional, as in the animal kingdom. And protection from what? A speeding car, a flashing light at a train crossing, a bomb going off, or most importantly, one another.

"We all have our own definitions of what I call 'meat and potatoes evil', the obvious war criminals and serial killers, Ted Bundy for example. Mr. Bundy, who was the penultimate study, the epicenter of verisimilitude. The unreadable fine young fellow to whom innocent women reacted as if they were one of the victims of a shrunken amygdala. As we can all be in true evil's presence. So, evil, again. Wolves in sheep's clothing. False friends. Traitors. Pension fund fraud.

"Where are the lines to be drawn in a free society? The used car salesman who sizes up his mark and lies through his shiny capped teeth, pawning off a lemon on a poor and vulnerable young single mother? Politicians who take bribes and betray the faith and trust of working people or union members and sell them out for a speedboat and a spa vacation?

"Reality television programs such as *The Apprentice* or *Survivor*, where vicious conniving and deceit and manipulation of their fellow aspirers' weaknesses or humanness? Is this evil or the way to make your dreams come true?

"It may be the very definition of evil has been changed forever by a society that celebrates success and winning over everything else.

"These are questions I am in the process of exploring and I would be most appreciative if all of you would fill out the questionnaires I left on the table. They are pretty straightforward and you can remain anonymous if that's more comfortable.

"What I would very much like to know, is what your definition of evil is and what either you have done or someone has done to you that you would consider evil, or at least of which you have had shame or regret.

"Whatever the true nature of a human being is, a range of normal from Rwanda and Adolf Hitler and *The Killing Fields* of the world, to spreading malicious gossip about a colleague who's job you want, what is a normal range?

"Are we civilized and behaving ourselves pretty well, most of the time, because of laws and state troopers and our desire for a beach house and a nice car, but when Bosnia appears, we will rape and slaughter our neighbor's children and burn the houses of innocent old women?

"How far have we evolved in our Darwinian diaspora and how do we as civilized human beings, living in a world still filled with predators of all levels, from scam artists and trust betrayers to pedophiles and psychopaths, learn to use the animal instincts to preserve, not diminish our humanity?

"Thank you very much, and I'll be happy to take a few questions."

He's looking at me. He's winking at me. He's happy I'm here. Wonder why he's so into this stuff? No Ror, that's not where you want to focus, that will lead back to "maybe he's evil." Look at that punim. Does he look evil? He looks like the Pillsbury Dough Boy with more testosterone.

Oh, shit, I just want to hold him so tight, hold him against me and sink right into him. . . . Someone to love me too much, someone to know me too well. . . . I'll just sing my requests into one of his shiny little ears. The audience is scooping up the questionnaires, and now he's going to be with me and I'm going to trust him and tell him and blab, blab, blab and break a promise. Does that make me evil? Well, then it's a really huge club, but I didn't promise Roy, I just sort of nodded, no blood oath or secret handshake or anything. He's smiling at me and his eyes are so kind.

He was beside her, taking her hand, pulling her gently forward. "Come, come with me, I have a surprise."

"But, I thought we'd have a bite, I have rehearsal in an hour and I want to talk to you about . . ."

"I know, trust me, let's go quickly before someone stops us for a question or we'll never get free. Keep moving forward, we're going to my cabin."

He let go of her hand and grabbed onto her elbow maneuvering her out of the room, down the hall, through the main atrium past all the little shops bulging with Ka Ka: clocks shaped like cruise ships, silver anchor earrings, angora sweaters covered with sequined naval insignias, trinkets and mementoes of every conceivable sort: souvenirs of experience, the ultimate impulse buys.

Shoe stores, and crystal stores and personalized coffee mug kiosks and bathing suits and sunglasses and evening gowns and mink coats and watches, and more watches and watches again; time was of the essence . . . time marches on . . . time goes by . . . time after time . . . the time is now . . . time heals all wounds . . . I don't have time for this . . . you're wasting my precious time . . . a stitch in time . . . that's another one of those . . . things we say. We don't have a clue what they mean. . . . She let him lead her, keeping her mouth shut, feeling his urgency. . . .

Down that ugly fake glass staircase, so Fred and Ginger, but they were dead and she and Poe were not gonna break into a foxtrot. Here was that elbow-wobbler deal again. His fingers were pressing harder. Almost ouchish, but she didn't want to say anything, better a bruise than him letting go. She did not want him to let go, that she knew. "Everytime we say good-by, I die a little. . . ."

Down the food hall deck, past the pizza place and the gourmet coffee stand and the exotic martini bar and the pastry shop . . . hmm, I could go for a little something sweet, but he kept moving . . . and he looked so serious, so unlike he'd looked on the stage . . . what the fuck was up here? His fingers were warm and dry, and strong against her skin, it felt good, a little tight but, secure . . . and she was tripping along, trying to move gracefully like Flora, didn't want to trip and fall flat, that she didn't want big time. Ginger never fell flat.... Deborah Kerr, An Affair to Remember, not a chance... he didn't turn his head at all, not looking at her....

"Everytime we say good-by, I wonder why a little"... Oh God she was in love, she was, absolutely in love really for the first, the only time in her life, nothing had ever felt like this—not even Walter.

"Why the Gods above me, who must be in the know, think so little of me, they'd allow you to go...." No, I don't want him to go....

Down the escalator, using them like stairs, still holding her arm and down the hall to his cabin, nicer than hers, at the door now, he let go and faced her and smiled. What a relief, to see that smile. She smiled back, still not talking, very unlike herself.

He pulled out his key card and opened the door and she saw a room service set-up with a little half bottle of champagne and two silver domes over what must be lunch and flowers. He had planned this. What a thing; what a nice thing.

"I know you don't have much time, I wanted to surprise you, but then I realized you might not show up at my talk and then I'd have to go all day without you and I.... Oh my God, Rory, Rory, Rory! I didn't count on this, could not have imagined this, seeing you at the back there today, it was all I could do to finish. I love you Rory. God help us both, I truly love you."

He was crying and he pulled her to him, engulfed her with his warmth and his passion and his need, kissing her cheeks and her neck and her face and she felt his tears and his erection, but this wasn't about that, not really, it was coming from something deeper, and she kissed him back, trying to find her own way through this and she was holding his head in her hands and she was saying it, back ... she was saying it out loud. "I love you, too. Poe, I do, love you."

She could feel him beginning to relax against her, now that they had claimed this thing and taken responsibility for it. He took a long breath and she could feel his ribs expanding against her and she moved slightly and he did too and they looked at one another, two middle-aged lovers with tear-streaked faces and some diffidence and she did the only thing she knew how to do in such a predicament.

"Well, so okay, what's for lunch?"

He laughed and walked over to the room service table and picked up the silver domes revealing two giant hamburgers with

Suzie Q fries, which she had told him she loved and could never find anywhere since they tore down the old Delores's Drive-in in L.A. and how she longed for them sometimes at night, with tartar sauce and a great big chocolate malt and there they were.

"Get real," she said and started to cry all over again, which didn't stop her from digging in and totally forgetting all that she had wanted to tell him and then the hour was up and they hadn't done anything even about his erection, let alone her Nancy Drew adventures, but that was the thing, the best thing. She would see him for dinner and she would have all the time in the world to tell him everything she had ever wanted to tell anyone.

⟶

THE COUNTESS WAS lying on her bed, Tou Two snuggled against her side, leafing through one of Ian's notebooks filled with quotes from his readings. She was looking for something, anything, to give her a clue about what he was up to, or, if she was being truly honest, to who he was. This was not the time in her life for any illusions. She was not going to turn into one of those fuzzy-headed fade-outs who sink into Blanche DuBois–land before the final curtain. Rip those damn drapes down and face up to life it would be for her. Head on, no more wishful thinking.

Ian had lots of Tennesse Williams quotes speaking of Blanche, but not that play. Ian hated that play. *Can't read his writing, looks like, "Sissy Gorforth." Funny it would be "Sissy", not a common name, a character I assume.* "Everything we do is a way of—not thinking about it. Meaning of life, and meaning of death . . . just going from one goddam frantic distraction to another, 'til finally one too many goddam frantic distractions leads to disaster."

I don't like this at all.

She tossed the notebook aside and pulled Tou Two up to her chest, tears filling her eyes. *I miss my dog.* She rocked back and forth, remembering the comfort of the living animal, the enormous joy he had given her.

A knock. She tossed the stuffed creature aside, as if she'd been caught with a vibrator or doing some other private and unbecoming act. "Come in."

The other Sissy stood in the doorway, looking slightly bombed and strained at the same time.

"I hope you weren't sleeping."

"Not a chance. I was contemplating."

"We have to talk, Countess."

"So, I assumed. Come on in and take a load off. Actually you look a bit, well, loaded."

Sissy stiffened as if the Countess had jumped up on the bed and somersaulted into her arms. *Uh, oh, too much reality for Mrs. Talbott.*

"Sissy, that was a joke, I apologize."

Sissy Talbott's body did not seem to return to its former, only slightly less tense posture, but she advanced into the cabin and lowered herself carefully into the arm chair next to the Countess's bed as if entering into a slightly too hot tub.

"Well, I'm not too quick with jokes, but you're right, I am. A nice big vodka on top of my pain medication and you may need one yourself in a minute."

The Countess felt her heart skipping beats in her chest. She was too old for this kind of conversation. Maybe everyone was too old for this. "Spit it out Sissy, I don't have the stamina for bad news foreplay."

"I apologize, I'm still trying to get a grip on it myself. Believe me, if I felt there was any way I could avoid discussing this or mentioning it at all, I would, but I can't because it involves both our children."

"What!" The Countess put Tou Two back onto her lap without even realizing what she was doing.

"Oh dear, I hate this. I'm so truly terrible at this sort of thing."

"Sissy, speak!"

"Alright, alright. After we all met this morning, I went to get my back medication from Nurse Peggy and I apparently fell asleep and when I came out Teddy was alone and acting very oddly and he told me that Heinrich Hensler had stayed after the others had left because he had, as he said, 'deeply sensitive and disturbing information about Ian and Twinkle that he wanted to deliver personally.'"

"Dear God, are they hurt?"

"I assume they are fit as fiddles, but what Heinrich told him was horrifying. He said that they were the ones who attacked that young woman. Ian and Twinkle beat her up and you know, did those things and he was not only told by the victim, but he has a witness, the cabin boy Jo Jo, who saw them go into her cabin."

The Countess Von Essen, stroked the head of her stuffed companion and closed her eyes. *No more illusions it will be, Mimsie.*

"Well, this is a living nightmare, but I already knew it."

"How! Did he tell you? How could you possibly have known such a thing and let us run around in fear and not lock them in their rooms and hustle them off the ship or whatever we had to do to stop this scandal from leaving this cabin!!"

"Calm on down, Sissy. No one *told* me. Ian doesn't even tell me good news, let alone true confessions of revolting criminal activity. When I first heard about the poor girl, I had a terrible flash and I remember praying, please don't let it be Ian. Twinkle never entered my mind. So, I'm distressed, but unfortunately, not surprised."

"This is shocking! For you to think such a thing about your grandson! If I had known, I would never have let him near Twinkle."

"He murdered my Tou Tou, and I know that the same way and believe you me, if I had had this information I would have never set foot on this ship and I would have taken what action I could. But to be blunt, Sissy, Twinkle and Ian are two of a kind, which has now been proved. No one made anyone do anything, and Lord only knows what else they've been up to.

"The fact is they are both adults and have their own incomes and there really isn't a goddamn thing we can do about their behavior. Well, I do have control of Ian's trust and threatening him with a possible cut-off is why he killed my dog. So, it's time we faced up to the truth. We've both got a Bad Seed in our feed bags and that's just the way it is. Welcome to Motherhood without the good parts."

"Frankly, Countess, at this point I might as well confess, I've never really thought motherhood *had* any good parts. We never planned it and we are both disastrous at it, though we do love Twinkle in our way, but we ruined her. We never held her accountable, spoiled her *and* neglected her, but this, this is so beyond the norm for children of our circle!

"Teddy said that Hensler will make sure it never leaves the ship, there are no jurisdictions, all the laws are very murky and the girl will never pursue it. He thinks we should make a very generous cash settlement to her immediately and have her given a royal escort off the ship and send her home on our private jet before she has time to re-consider. There is no proof, only her word and it was dark and it can be said she was drinking and, good grief! I can't believe we're talking about this, but at least it does seem we won't have to face some unimaginable public disgrace and they won't be sent to prison."

"Well they should be, but I agree this is best and how we each handle it afterward is more important. As far as Ian is concerned, money is the only thing he really cares about, meaning not having to earn any, so I know what to do about that, but that does not absolve us from our responsibility to society. No one just behaves like this once Sissy and what we do about that, I haven't a clue."

"Well there are treatment centers and private clinics and medications . . ."

"And chastity belts and the stocks. Face up my dear, it is not going to go away."

"Hensler said he would have our security people track them down and bring them back to New York and keep them sequestered until we get off this damn cruise."

"Now we're talking. And what does Mr. Hensler expect in return for all of this covering up and facilitating the obstruction of justice?"

"Why, I, well, I don't really know. I expect, it is part of his job, and in his best interests. I do think, I had the feeling, he may have insinuated to Teddy that he expected to be rewarded in some way. It is a kind of blackmail after all, if he wanted to use it, I suppose."

"Hmmm. Now that rings the dinner bell. Wouldn't be the least bit surprised from what I've heard about the fellow and observed with my own little peepers, if he doesn't have some powerful leverage even beyond our children. He's a cunning and voraciously ambitious sort. Bet there's a big promotion in his very near future."

"Well, that may be, Teddy is so weak and utterly distraught over this, but what do you mean by 'even beyond our children'? Do you think he has spies or knows, well what could he . . ."

Careful Mimsie, Teddy's midnight delight in the kitchen is not something she needs to know. "Nothing Sissy, I watch too much television. But ambition does lead to certain ruthless acts of self-interest and it is not uncommon for men in positions of oversight with small fiefdom kinds of power like Hensler, to have his toadies reporting on all kinds of things. After all, he can't be everywhere and on a ship like this, anything going on can come back to haunt him. So even if it's basically benign, they need other sets of eyes."

"Yes, yes, I see. Well, frankly, I don't care if Teddy makes him Chairman of the Board as long as we can keep this quiet and get those kids home and end this horror as quickly as possible. Will you please talk to Teddy about the financial settlement with that young woman? Hensler was going to speak to her the moment that's settled, so the sooner the better."

The Countess gave Tou Two one last pat and shook her head feeling the beginnings of a migraine coming on. "Yes, Sissy, I will, but it's a bitter pill and I guarantee whatever it is, Ian will be debited the entire amount and I would strongly suggest you apply similar punishments to Twinkle. And they must agree to go into therapy or I'll go to the authorities myself."

✿

ROY ROGERS LEANED in, taking advantage of his boss's slightly open door.

"Mr. Hensler."

"Mr. Rogers."

"I know I have no appointment, but it's most important that we speak as soon as possible."

"I'm just preparing to leave for a cocktail party in the Captain's suite, but I do have a few minutes."

"May I sit down?"

"Certainly. How may I assist you?"

"Well, now right there, we have the central issue. This is the problem. I'm not here with a clear and clean request or report and in my job, I never talk to management unless I have both, but these are unique circumstances and I don't like to waste anyone's time so I ask your patience while I find a way through this gulf grass."

"Yes, yes. I will indulge you."

"Mr. Hensler, you are a gentleman from Munich and I am a gentleman from Tallahassee and we don't speak the same language on most things I would reckon a guess, but when it comes to this ship and keeping an eagle eye or a hawk's eye at least out for trouble, I think we're pretty much alike. And I smell big trouble but I have no facts which makes this a bit risky to come to you about."

"I have the feeling, Mr. Rogers, that in spite of some rather charming dirt kicking, you have more than you are saying, so proceed."

"Okee doke. Well, after our meeting with the Talbotts and the Worths this a.m. I got pretty, shall we say, aggressive with my people and followed up on several tips given to me by unbiased observers and I've found out several disturbing pieces of coincidence."

"Such as?"

"Well for starters, two passengers, a couple from Philadelphia I believe, abruptly left the ship after the second day without any real triggering event and they have not been seen since. So Twinkle Talbott and Von Essen were not the first to jump ship. We did a search of all the hotels on near-by islands, flights back to the states, even to Europe over the last few days but no luck. Nothing but one cell phone message."

"This does not seem odd. They could be staying at a private house on numerous islands or a yacht having one big week long orgy and not exactly in shape for long chats with mommy and daddy."

"Yes, true and so it may be, but we have pretty good relations with the local police and coast guard. Some of the local private cops also think something's fishy, and then there's the Worth girl."

"Has she been found?"

"Nope. But, and I have hesitated to tell you this, because it's very, very sketchy, but one of the crew saw something gold and shiny fall over the side of the starboard bow around 2 a.m. the night she disappeared and it's possible it was her. So far, nothing's showing on the video tapes.

"I was on this like mosquitoes on the bayou and I managed to find a very nervous member of the cleaning staff who saw a young woman meeting her description being chased down one of the crew halls near the clinic by two big guys in maintenance outfits.

"She couldn't see the faces and she just thought the girl was caught in some crew cabin committing illicit acts or doing drugs and they were trying to get her out of there, but the timing fits.

"She could have been pushed overboard, for some mysterious reason, but we have pulled up anchor and we'll soon be on our way to St. Marteen, and then we're at sea until we dock in San Juan. So if there has indeed been more foul play and they boogy off tomorrow, we're out of luck and if they don't, someone else could be killed."

"Please, do not say 'someone else'. At this moment we have absolutely no proof anyone has been injured except for the unfortunate Miss O'Brian. The departing of disgruntled passengers before the end of the voyage is a fact of life you well know and it is still entirely possible Miss Worth is sleeping off some debauchery somewhere on the ship and whatever went over the side could either have been her shedding her clothes in a moment of abandon, or a completely unrelated incident. This is all circumstantial and we are both men who like order and fact, so I understand your hesitance to report and I'm not so convinced you should not have waited."

"Well, I pretty much figured you'd feel like that. I do have a couple more aces to play. I do know it was the Talbott girl and her pal who attacked Collie O'Brian, so the mad rapist theory is over, and with all due respect, it was unethical of you, Mr. Hensler, to withhold that from your Head of Security—caused a lot of wheel spinning and unnecessary anxiety.

"I also know you have spies on board who find whatever dirt they can for you to use to your advantage, but hey, man, I watch reality T.V. Winning is not about swimming with the sharks, it's about swallowing them whole and becoming them, so, what the hay.

"But, my good ol' panhandle paranoia sees some connection going on here, one I don't think you have any involvement in, so relax, but something very dicey is going on right under your sniffer and that is why I'm here.

"No matter what kinda J. Edgar Hoover game you're running on the Talbotts, if something really sinister goes down on your watch, well, Talbott may be the owner, but he also has a very powerful and conservative Board and they can toss both our asses right out of here, so I suggest you work with me on this and share whatever gossip or spy reports you have before it's too late."

"Well, well, Mr. Rogers, what a pleasant surprise. I have grossly underestimated you. Too bad, we might have spent some pleasant evenings together. I won't bother trying to find out how you have gotten your information. But I have a few thoughts. I will check some of this out and contact you within an hour."

"We'll be at sea by then."

"Yes, very true. But I am not the police and as far as my concerns and the welfare of the *Dolphin* and the Empire Cruise Line, that is very much in our best interests. And it is your problem to follow up those loose ends with the local authorities."

"I will do so and we are being extra careful about checking the manifest for anyone not returning to the ship. But you know the local authorities, they make those dodos in Aruba on the Natalie Holloway case look like the CIA. On second thought that probably isn't the best example."

"What you need is German secret police. Americans still prefer to be liked rather than feared and so you will always be weak in the face of criminals and terrorists."

"Well now, that's a sitting and rocking conversation best left for another time. I'll be in touch."

"Where are you going now?"

"I got a little sea bird on my shoulder, tells me a nice friendly chat with our own Nurse Peggy and some of her co-workers might reveal some missing pieces."

"Oh, well. For her, the Gestapo would probably be a good back-up."

"I must say, Mr. Hensler. I agree with you on that one. I'll letcha know."

WALTER WORTH WAS a strider, all that old football training, all that new gym pumping, and pilates crap and running and swimming and keeping himself together. And he was moving even faster, straighter, and cockier, because he was fueled by so much rage, self-rage and repressed rage and "up to here" rage and somehow, as out of line as it was, some very powerful righteous indignation rage and the need, the sudden, overwhelming, almost uncontrollable need to tell his wife the truth.

Possibly it was the fallout from his very traumatic just-ended encounter with Teddy Talbott and also possibly because even with Clarissa still missing he'd made a decision and having made a decision it was now unbearable to keep the secret inside him anymore, even if, or maybe especially if, something unthinkable had happened to his daughter. He was going to have to let her go, anyway.

He was crossing the spa now in search of his wife who was supposedly taking some cockamamie meditation class. Well, she would need it a lot more later.

There she was, looking dewy and wistful, walking toward the water fountain with a sweatband around her hair. He slowed a moment, catching his breath. Would he really be able to do this? Yes, he would. He put his hand up, towering over the other heads and caught her eye and she waved and blew him a little kiss.

He moved across the gym and she moved toward him and smiled. She looked so sad, but he was still so mad, he didn't even care.

"What are you doing here? I thought you were meeting with Teddy?"

"I was. I did and now I have to meet with you in the cabin, right away."

"Oh, God, Walter, it isn't something bad about Clarissa?"

"No, nothing new on that. This is about us and it can't wait."

"Us? Oh dear, did I do something to displease you? I haven't done really anything since this morning but sleep and cry."

"Come on, it's not something specific."

They walked side by side, Leah working to keep his pace and stealing glances at him. This was so unusual, he was never abrupt with her and he never confronted her or lost his temper. What on earth could it be? Maybe because she'd fallen apart and wasn't helping enough to find Clarissa. But she had been handing out snap shots from the ship's photographer and looking everywhere she could think. It couldn't be that, not to make him this upset.

He opened the door to the suite and she followed him into their room and sat down on the bed while he closed the door and put the privacy sign outside.

This was starting to alarm her. He was always so gentle and protective with her. She'd never seen him like this.

"Have you taken any more medication, Leah?"

"No, I still feel rather woozy from what you gave me this morning. Why, did I take too much?"

"No, I was hoping you were in a relaxed state, because I have some very, very tough things to say to you and I'm doing it brutally and without warning."

"Walter! What in the world! You're frightening me!"

"Good. Why should you be the only one who never has to be frightened?"

"You're angry at me. I've been feeling it for weeks. I thought it was just the stress of waiting for Teddy to sign the agreement. What is it? What did I do?"

He paced back and forth, thrusting his hands into his thick curly hair as if trying to pull the conflict out of his head. "Well, if it was something you *did*, that would be easy. We'd argue, you'd apologize and we'd go forward. But this is not about something you did, it's about who you are and that my beautiful, genteel bride cannot be altered."

"Who I am? You love who I am. All you ever tell me is how

perfect I am. When I criticize myself or doubt myself, that's what you say, 'Leah, you're perfect, knock it off.' "

"Yes. YES!!!! Exactly! You are. Perfect and delusive. I've had a lifetime of serving your image of perfection and you know what? I hate your fucking perfection. It's phony like the rest of our life. I hate you for wanting the lie and settling for perfect. Perfect is a big fucking lie.

"I see your face, you're horrified. But it is, yes it is. You never allowed any reality. Well, this cruise is a great big fat reality check! And I've just had an incredibly sleazy and disconcerting encounter with our host and I don't care much more since my daughter went missing about lying or protecting your narcissism. So I'm going to tell you something, I've been waiting for over a year to find a way to soften this, but there is no way, I let it go on too long."

Leah crawled onto her hands and knees and tried to get off the bed and away from him. "No, you're not yourself. You don't want to do this and I refuse to hear anymore!"

He grabbed her leg and flipped her over, forcing her to look at him. "No more refusing to face reality! I'm snapping under the strain of living like this! If I have to fucking deal with it, so do you! I'm in love with someone else and I'm leaving you. I won't be going back to New York with you and Clarissa when she's found.

"I've made arrangements. The apartment is paid off and in your name and when you sell it, you'll make a good profit. Also in the back of my closet in a duffel bag is enough cash to take care of you for the rest of your life even if you don't work, not at the level you're used to but sufficient. I have a separate account set up for Clarissa which she'll receive when she's thirty. I owe you that and I've done terrible things to get it."

"Oh my God, Oh my God! This is not happening, Walter! You're, you're just exhausted from the stress. You're not well, you love me and I, I've given you everything, you've been my whole life! We've been so happy! Why? Why? What could anyone give you that I haven't given you?"

"Why? I just told you why. Because you're so professionally perfect and she isn't. She is flawed and chipped and pervious. Yes. Pervious. And you are impervious and I have been trying to live up to your expectations and delusions and fantasies about me since high school and I can't do it a day longer. I'm not perfect, Leah. I'm not who you think I am or expect me to be and God knows I've tried to tell you.

"Sometimes I've really pushed the envelope, but even if I left a dossier of misdeeds in an open drawer in our fucking bedroom, and set it on fire to get you to see, to look, you'd just close it and spray some fancy perfume all over it!

"I can't live like this anymore. I'm a failure, Leah. I'm a fraud."

"No, no, don't say that! You're a brilliant scientist and you're so close to having the patents and if something went wrong with Teddy, you're just upset and even if you've had, a, a little fling, well, I can accept that. I'm willing to overlook it . . . we're a team and you're so close to seeing your dream come true. . . ."

"No dream. Lies to protect you and live up to your image of me! Do you want the truth? No of course not! Take your hand away from your eyes. Look at me, dammit! *See* me! Big strong, brilliant Dr. Worth. Do you know how I've supported you all these years? I run a pill mill. I do unsavory private operations on society women. I do internet medicine for drug traffickers. Didn't it ever occur to you to come see my 'office' where I'm creating all these astonishing new medical tools? You never wanted to look any further than the tip of your perfect little nose.

"Do you know what my business arrangement with Teddy Talbott is really about? Why we became socially acceptable and cruise companions and all? Why I got that contract to consult on the clinics?"

"No, no more . . . stop this!!!"

"No. I won't. This is yours too! Teddy is in love with me, that's why we're here! There he was down on his bandy knees, throwing his arms around my ass and begging me to let him fuck me.

"Surprised? Horrified? Well I've led him on for the last three years. I saw his deal that first party we went to. And one day when we were alone in his penthouse, I let him suck my cock. And everything that's happened since has come from his romantic fantasy that I will do it again, or do more. So I hustled him for the contract and there is no patent, just a fat retainer that's kept you in designer clothes and illusions of better things to come."

"Oh my God, you're trying to kill me!! To do this now with our daughter gone! I, I, I, don't believe you! You've lost your mind, temporarily. I will not believe this!"

"Believe it or not, it's true. Desperate men do desperate things and I did worse. Far worse, so don't ask where the money in the closet came from or how I have enough to get off this ship and take my woman and disappear."

Leah was screaming now, very unlike herself, and he didn't care. He'd punched Teddy Talbott in the jaw and the cat was definitely out of the bag and now all he cared about was being with Flora and getting away from everything that reminded him of the duplicitous filth of his so-called charmed life and even though the price might be losing Clarissa forever, he would pay it. He had given her the best he could and he knew she knew he loved her and he had written it all to her and he hoped she would forgive him and if not, he was going anyway.

Leah was curled on her side sobbing uncontrollably and he found he had no impulse to comfort her, no guilt at least yet and no second thoughts.

"I love you so Walter, you're the only man I've ever loved, you're my life. I'll die without you. I don't care what you've done. Please don't leave me!"

"You don't *love* me! You can't love a fantasy. You've learned nothing! Nothing! You haven't changed a hair since Fairfax. Love looks *out*. You only look at yourself. I can't live up to it anymore.

"We are both responsible, though you will never get that. You never had any fucking subtext, Leah.

"I'll let you know if I have news about Clarissa, but I won't be staying in our cabin again.

"Our daughter was the glue, but she's a grown up now, whatever else we have to accept about her disappearance, so there's really no more reason to pretend. You'll be fine, Leah, that much I know for certain. Peachy keen, always the Prom Queen."

And with that, Walter Worth, threw some clothes, sloppily, very unlike himself, into a suitcase and left the cabin without saying another word, ending thirty-four years of perfection.

URI DAYAN STEPPED out of the shower and pulled the oversize *Palace of the Dolphins* robe from its hook and wrapped himself into it, nice and tight. Ah, comfort. Who said that comfort was what America had given to the world? Mark Twain had said Europeans created it, but he was talking about a more balanced lifestyle not material objects. Interesting concept, he should make a note of that.

All in all it had been an excellent day. He reached for one of the little monogrammed hand towels, chuckling to himself. Everything was branding these days. Every single thing of use in the cabin and on the ship was branded with the name, as if in management's marketing department, they had anticipated the pilfering of Kleenex boxes and hand towels and soap dishes and were actively encouraging the taking of anything that kept their name with the passenger.

He wiped his face and then used the towel to clean the moisture off the mirror over the sink. The bathroom was so small, it was like a steam cabinet. He opened the door into the cabin and the air conditioning began evaporating the moisture, clearing the mirror and revealing his face for his approval. He looked at himself closely. He had changed in a week, less than a week.

He looked, younger. Yes, he did. Maybe he should shave his beard? A symbol, an external symbol of his inner transformation. Quite fascinating to see such a thing actually happen to him. He had spoken of such things for years, read aloud from the Talmud, but he'd never really witnessed such a thing or believed it, but now he was living proof. He looked, stronger and more virile. More manly.

He took out the state-of-the-art electric toothbrush his wife had given him for Christmas and pushed the button that brought the paste up the shaft automatically. Such a strange present. He had thought it to be impersonal or a hint about his hygiene. He grinned at himself, checking his teeth for the return of the yellowing he had undergone light treatments to lessen. They looked fine. Maybe his wife had been sending some unconscious sexual message. The paste moving up the shaft of the brush and oozing out of the tip?

The thought caught him off guard. Her fantasy or his? He could feel his penis begin to tighten and swell against the robe. All kinds of reawakenings were occurring, it would seem. Transformations. From ignorance to self-awareness leading him closer to God's purpose for his life?

He pushed the whirring bristles up and down and back and forth, enjoying the sexual tension and looking forward to releasing it and falling into sleep. A man of God, but still a man, after all. He clicked off the brush and rinsed, looking at himself again. He looked, Christ-like. Was that hubris? No, he did. The Sermon on the Mount. Jesus said, "Behold I send you out as sheep in the midst of wolves; therefore be shrewd as serpents and innocent as doves."

Yes! Yes! That was what he was learning to do! That is what

had come from his encounter with Poe Evanoff, in his panic and uncertainty; he had grown-up. He had moved beyond his ego and insecurity and faced himself at a deeper level and he now had so much more to bring to his work, to his book and his new center. What had seemed to be the darkness, was in fact, the dawn!

He wiped his mouth and picked up the *Palace of the Dolphins* moisturizer, smiling again at the marketing moxie, and patted some over his Christ-like face. No, the beard should stay.

His cock was harder now, a delicious sense of self-love flooded his entire being, a sort of euphoria, a peace and excitement, overwhelmed him with conflicting waves of emotion. Onanism really was a product of this form of grace.

He turned out the light and picked up the discarded hand towel, taking it with him to his bed and pulled down the sheets, undoing the steward Jo Jo's careful shaping of the top into some fish-like form.

A knock, a tapping at the door. He turned, startled by the intrusion into his exquisite reverie, feeling his erection soften. Who on earth?

He moved back to the door and put his eye to the peephole, the memory of the attack on the young woman, making him hesitant and the lines from Jesus seeming now, like a warning from his intuition, "shrewd as serpents" it would be.

A mane of red hair was all he could see, the face, a female face, lowered, but it could only be Leah Worth or her daughter. He reached for the latch, unlocking the door, almost dizzy with the oddity of this, but excited also, by this startling imposition. He was in the hands of a bigger force, working through his consciousness, bringing the lessons he needed and he was stimulated beyond his experience by this week of new adventures within himself. His erection had vanished but not his excitement.

FLORA FRAMPTON SITTING in the dark waiting for something. Waiting for a whisper, what she called God. Some inner tiny little voice to tell her what to do with all this fear and longing and guilt and information she was too scared to look at.

Flora Frampton alone in the dark, listening to the sounds of the ship and the tinkling piano music from the Martini Bar above her.

Stripped of all her armor: no make-up, no hot rollered curls, no push-up bra or pull-in body shaper. No southern charm, no energy or attitude or elegant posture.

Flora Frampton was slouching, her stomach just so slightly loosened under her comfort gown. No silk or flounces or décolletage, just her favorite white flannel nightie with long sleeves and little fake pearl buttons. An old lady's sleeper, what a woman could wear when the game was over, when men were no longer part of your yearning or your quest. And she was fine with it, preparing for it.

Walter hadn't shown up after the show. Walter would most likely never show up again. Their daughter was missing and she knew something more about that than he did. He had gone back to his wife. They would have to face a horrible thing very soon and there was no way, no way she could compete with that nor would she try. Nor would she want to.

Cold cream and dead dreams and saggy abs and flannel nighties and no new contract and no place to go and maybe Georgia on her mind.

Flora Frampton just sitting, trying to tell the truth, trying to know what she even felt about all of this. Morose, but relieved. Yes, there was a kind of letting her breath out, no more anticipation of heartbreak and loss. At least now she knew what she was dealing with.

Banging on the door. She barely changed position, not caring who or what it was. She glanced over at her clock. After midnight. Who? Him?

She got up slowly, and didn't even glance in the mirror. As Rory would say, Fuck it. This is me. Deal with it.

Flora Frampton moving across her small cabin and opening her door without looking, not much caring if it was a frothing maniac.

Walter Worth was the frothing maniac. Flora backed up and let him in, not even happy he had come back. He was agitated, really almost frothing and she stood there and let him. She did not offer comfort, a wet cloth, a shot of whiskey, a hot shower, she watched him froth, tears streaming from his eyes, his hair bunched into knots as if he had been trying to tear it out of his head: his eyes red and swollen, his clothes disheveled, his face puffy and unshaven.

Not anything like the man she loved nor was she anything like the coquette in costume, the vixen in bed; the two very put-together passion puddles looked like a couple of swamp rats. *Well he's at least man enough to come and tell me it's over in person. No Ship's post card slipped under my door with some kiss off promise of filthy lucre or a new car waiting for me at my Momma's nursing home.*

Flora Frampton moving away from her lover and re-settling herself in the chair, like an old woman interviewing her new caregiver.

"I know why you're here, Walter, it's okay. I guess I've been expecting it all along, so when yew stood me up tonight I just knew."

"Oh no, no, Flora, Flora, no! I've been crazy, crazy because I have so much, so much to tell you. I had an encounter with Teddy Talbott. I thought it would just be a brief, business drink thing, but it turned into something terrible and it well, I think it's good, because it just accelerated everything, and I guess I just flipped out from holding so much in for so long and with Clarissa still missing and I decided . . . I was on the way to see Leah, because I . . . I had to tell her, but I ran into Roy Rogers and he told me something . . . he felt he had to tell me, it wasn't right not to and he was going down to the clinic and that's well . . . I can't tell you so many things yet, but he told me that someone, a crew member had seen a gold shiny thing go over the side, and . . . and it might have been . . ."

Flora Frampton, pulling herself forward, stomach now held in, dancer's posture returning, "Like my skirt? Yew don't think that I . . ."

"No, God, no! But it might have been Clarissa!! Oh Christ, it might have been! Someone saw her being chased down a hall from outside the clinic, and I . . . oh don't, I can't tell you about that now . . . but she may . . . oh God . . . she may be dead, and then I think my control snapped and I just let it all go. I told Leah about us, not your name, not who, but that I was leaving and look, look I have my suitcase and I can't go back, won't and . . ."

"Yew told her Clarissa might have gone over the side of the ship!"

"No, no, of course not. But when it became a possibility it was too much to keep holding in, and I didn't care anymore then, couldn't pretend anymore . . . couldn't keep it up and I hit Teddy Talbott so . . ."

"Oh, Lordy be! This is, well, a hooter tooter, talk about your yin and yang! I don't know whether to laugh, cry or faint dead away which is how my aunties raised me to handle such gothic startlements!"

He was on his knees holding onto her flannelly covered legs, her hero, her knight, her unreachable, impossible dream of a man, was crouched before her, sobbing into her lap.

"Oh Flora, Flora, forgive me for hurting you, making you think I'd left you. I love you. I need you so much. I told my wife I'm not coming back. I've given her enough to take care of her and I have enough for us and I want you to come away with me. I want you to come with me and trust me and never look back."

Flora Frampton sitting still, something she rarely did, wishing she had a rocking chair. Much easier to think about things in a rocking chair—so long ago on her grandmother's porch, rocking and thinking little girl thoughts, until she was dizzy and her brain was tired.

She was silent and he let her go and stood up looking like her man again. A less attractive version, but a more loveable one, a real one, a man who needed her, who had given up everything for her and wanted to take her away from all of this and who had chosen her above his own family. Someone loved her for herself. Cold creamed and plain and without stage presence or cleavage.

Flora Frampton from Savannah, Georgia a 45 year old woman whose knees ached and she loved him, too. Whoever he was and whatever he'd done or wherever they ended up. She was ready.

⁓

LEAH WORTH STAGGERED and Uri Dayan reached out to steady her, pulling her forward into his cabin, performing an awkward sort of fox trot, he in his big fluffy robe and she in hers.

Had she wandered all the way from the Owner's Suite to his cabin in her bathrobe? Was she drunk? What if someone saw him pulling her into his room? She was a guest of the owner! He was just beginning a relationship with this company! What should he do with her? He couldn't leave her out there, sobbing and half-dressed and he certainly couldn't call her husband or . . . *shrewd as a serpent, innocent as a dove.* He must remain steady and find out what this was about. Another message was being sent to him.

"Please, please, Mrs. Worth, sit down. Let me get you something. Would you like a brandy? I have some left from the Seder. Are you ill?" Leah Worth sat, looking up at him, her large green eyes spilling tears, the ultimate damsel in distress.

"Leah, please, call me Leah."

"Yes, of course, *Leah*. What can I do? Are you in some kind of trouble?

"Oh, yes. Rabbi, I am in terrible trouble. I, I had to talk to someone, someone who would understand and there was no one, no one because my daughter is gone and my husband is gone and I, I didn't know where to turn and then I remembered your wonderful sermon at the Seder and our lovely talk at dinner and I just, I'm so sorry, to intrude, I hope I didn't wake you, this is, so, so such a, an imposition, so inappropriate, but I, I just, Oh God, I need help. . . ."

Uri Dayan opened the bottle of brandy and poured them each a drink. He felt a thrill like a chill down his spine. He felt so powerful, so masculine and strong. This rich beautiful woman, feminine and vulnerable, nothing like his wife, who was the only woman he had been with, the only woman, he realized, he had ever seen in a bathrobe!

All of his energy went into building his career, and raising their children; not that women didn't make themselves available to him, all men who seemed to have answers, who stood on stages and offered wisdom or hope had women who wanted to be close to them, but he had been too smart for that; he had seen colleagues ruin their lives that way.

And it hadn't appealed to him, sex had been more about having his family and relieving tension than passion. His wife had never triggered great lust in him and as good a partner as she was, she was hardly a woman like this, at least ten years older than he was, probably fifteen but so desirable. So out of his reach, he had not even allowed a thought of her, well maybe a thought, because she had looked at him with such admiration and trust, but here, she was here, in his cabin. In tears and a bathrobe in the middle of the night!

He handed her the brandy and took a big sip himself, watching as she swallowed, and wiped her eyes and took a long deep breath, that he thought as he watched her, was the most sensual thing he had ever seen a woman do.

He sat across from her in the little desk chair, aware of how small the cabin was with such an intoxicating presence added. "How may I help you, Leah?"

Tears again. She took another sip and set down her glass, shaking her tousled red hair back and forth almost puppet-like.

"No one can help me. No one, I just needed, someone to be with me for awhile. Please, if I can just sit here for a little while."

"Of course, but I have found in my work, that when you can talk about whatever the problem is, no matter how overwhelming it may seem, it does help."

She looked up at him again, her eyes begging him for something intangible, something vast and bottomless and slightly frightening. Too much need, too spoiled and used to attention and for someone like this, there could never be enough attention.

"Do you know that my daughter Clarissa has been missing for the last two days and we don't know what has happened to her?"

"My God! No, no. I have no knowledge of this! No wonder you are distraught."

"Yes, yes, well it's been very, very difficult, but as long as Walter and I, as long as we were together, I could find the strength, somehow, as weak as I am, to go on and have hope, but then, then tonight, he, my husband, he seems to have had some form of a breakdown and he, he confronted me and told me that he . . . oh God, I don't know if I can, say this . . ."

"Please, you can trust me. Please go on."

"Oh Rabbi, he's all I ever wanted, my only love and he told me he's in love with someone else and he's leaving and never coming back, even if Clarissa is gone and it . . . he, hates me! It was horrible, unbearable and then he packed some things and he left. My whole life is broken, broken in bits. And I, I, Oh please, please help me!!"

Leah Worth threw herself onto his pillow, sobbing in spasms, her robe pulling up around her thighs. "I have nothing left to live for . . ."

He stood up and moved to the bed, sitting down beside her, knowing this was a mistake, knowing without thinking it, the serpent was eating the dove, a tiny bite at a time before he could notice.

"Leah, Leah, please, please believe me as terrible as this is, it will pass and it will lead you to places within yourself, open windows into your soul and your humanity you cannot yet imagine. Feel your pain, let it flow through you and it will open you up and it will make you stronger."

The half-naked white-thighed woman rolled onto her back and reached out for him, throwing him off balance and off-guard. "Oh Rabbi, please, hold me, hold me! Your words are so wonderful, you are so wonderful. Please take me, take me, make love to me, want me, please, please help me! Fuck me. I need you. I need you to make love to me. Please, please!"

He could feel her body pressing against him and his erection returned, stronger than anything he could remember: a lust that was unfamiliar in his experience, a boy's lust. Serpent in the Garden, serpent in his groin. He pulled away, knowing it was for show, for her benefit really, not that he would have admitted it, but needing to justify himself at least that much.

"Leah, you don't know what you're asking, this is just the emotion talking. We mustn't. I can counsel you, but this is not the answer."

"Oh, God, Rabbi, please, you can't reject me, too! I'm a woman who's lost everything, give me this, want me. Please want me!" She untied her robe and pulled it down revealing herself naked underneath. A beautiful milky white temptress, a Circe, a wanton voluptuous creature, kissing him, moaning against him with a passion he had never brought forward in his wife or in himself.

By then, it was no longer a choice of will, it was no longer about carefully crafted words delivered from a podium with the smugness of the untempted. Then it was about lust. It was ego and the baseness of man, overcome by Jesus, but well known to God. And fuck her he did.

Chapter Six: Day Six

LATITUDE
Your Daily At Sea Newspaper

Good Morning Cruisers and welcome to the incredible split personality island of St. Martin/ St. Maarten and its quaint Dutch capital of Philipsburg! If you've watched our indefatigable Cruise Director Derrick Doolittle's ensuite lecture or attended in person, you already know that this amazing little paradise, is half French and half Dutch. So Welkom/Bienvenue and get ready for the grand finale of your Voyager week. . . . So much to do, so little time as we seem to keep saying and hearing our passengers say!

Hard to believe this is our last land day, tomorrow we head out to sea for your final 24 hours of continuous cruising (veteran cruisers swear that's the best part) until we dock back where we began in San Juan on Sunday.

So, no time to lose reading this!!!! Let's get going! It's not often you can experience the language, architecture and food of two European countries and also sail, snorkel, swim, loll on some of the most pristine beaches in the Caribbean or flap your wings with the inhabitants of the island's amazing "Butterfly Sphere," but this doesn't even half cover the possibilities, so please check the activities list for other exhilarating adventures. And once again, for those of you who choose the ship as your activity of choice, well we won't disappoint. Today on board we are focusing on fitness, with a Wally ball tournament in the gym, a Spinning marathon, matt Pilates for beginners and advanced Pilates for jocks (for those cruisers over 50—yes, it really is the old calisthenics we hated in high school re-packaged for the Twenty-First century, no pain, no gain for these jocksters!)

Our water nymph, Natalie will be leading aqua-Cardio and Power Plunge classes in the main pool and Irina Sobovitch one of our lovely Ice Extravaganza stars will teach you to twirl and swirl and work on your triple axels (just kid-

ding) on the ice rink at 2 p.m. a
one time only opportunity.

Whew! Tired already? We
haven't scratched the surface!
There are several fascinating lectures: Bingo for Bimbos (Don't
get huffy, it's for laughs, dudes),
Bridge for Brides and oh, of
course, for all our Talent Show

Contestants, final rehearsal as
the tension mounts!!!

So, have a blast, your last day
ashore with options galore, and
tonight so much more, Formal
dress encore! And just a reminder from our official Party
Poopers, we sail promptly at 6,
so take your watches!!!!

My darling wife,

I am writing this hastily, because I must get ready for the day and the breakfast and I have overslept. I know when you will finally receive all of these letters, much time will have passed and the things that are happening may by then make you laugh and shake your pretty head and even make you glad we have the life we have rather than your fantasy of the exciting adventures of myself and my passengers. But for now, I am so very miserable and so many things have been happen-ing to add to my distress, I am now praying I can maintain myself for the last two days of this trip. So very quickly I will update you.

The children of the Talbotts and the Countess have not returned nor has the daughter of the Worths been found. This as you can imagine, has caused great distress and the mood in the suite is quite depressed. Then last evening when I was preparing for the cocktail hour, which is not so much work now, because no guests are coming and no one is sitting together, but just taking their drink at different times and not conversing or enjoying the hors d'oeurves, but I am still trying to prepare nicely and do my work.

Mr. Talbott has been acting very oddly, he is usually rather pleasant in his behavior and his treatment of me, but he now seems distracted and Mrs. Talbott has become more rude, very difficult to please and quite curt in her attitude. I am afraid of making a mistake and upsetting her and having a bad report and you know how I am, I do not work well under disapproval; it is a weakness in my character, to not perform well under stress.

I must be rather immature, for it is childish to expect people to always be polite, but when Mrs. Talbott picks on me, maybe because she needs someone to put her unhappiness on, I begin to doubt my work. I am trying to think of how I can do better under the circumstances.

I wish my dearest wife that this was the end of it, but it is not. Last evening I did the turn-down and set up the things for today's breakfast and checked everyone's cabin for water and fresh towels. I had decided to not disturb Mrs. Worth, who did not leave her cabin or have dinner, but on my way down to my cabin to sleep, Jo Jo appeared in the hall and told me he must speak to me and pulled me into a service closet.

He was shaking and very frightened and he said he was going to leave the boat this morning and not return and of course, I told him this was madness, but he said, he had seen something so terrible he had no choice and he would not tell me, because he wanted to protect me, but I should be very careful.

I asked if he had his travel documents and enough money and he laughed, but not a happy laugh and said, yes, he did. Mr. Hensler had given them to him because "he owes me" and I asked him what on earth he meant and he told me that he had been a spy for Mr. Hensler, who wanted information on senior staff, but mainly on the Talbotts and he had done terrible things for which he was ashamed.

He said he had brought cabin boys to Mr. Talbott for acts against our faith and he said it was Miss Twinkle and Mr. Ian who had attacked our fellow staff member and Mr. Hensler was using this information to blackmail Mr. Talbott. He had been given money for his spying and he was afraid if he refused, Mr. Hensler might seek revenge, so he had told Mr. Hensler he had new information for him, but he wanted the rest of the money he was owed and his travel documents so he could take some time off and Mr. Hensler agreed.

He was scheduled to meet with him after we docked today in Phillipsberg, but he was too frightened by what he had seen and afraid Mr. Hensler might even be involved, so he was going AWOL! He asked if I could contact his family and tell them he was okay and on his way home.

He said he had "Sold his soul, but only half of it," and he had enough money to buy his boat so it was worth it, but he was crying when he said it.

I felt such concern for him and so helpless and worried. He said he was going to hide for the night "just in case" and that sounded almost like something from the television, but he may be right and I am just too ignorant to understand what is happening around me.

So I did not sleep most of the night and now I am starting this day, very tired and confused and worried about my friend Jo Jo, but I must put on my most pleasant and blank face and greet Mr. Talbott and Mrs. Worth and the others. I am praying for wisdom to help me through this day.

I long for you to be in my arms, to be safe in our little house. I will try to write again tonight.

Your devoted husband

～

"Mr. Hensler."

"Mr. Rogers."

"May I have a moment of your time?"

"Certainly. Come in. Would you like coffee and a sweet? Help yourself. They are just baked. Very delicious."

"Don't mind if I do. Been on the internet most of the night, and I haven't had my breakfast yet. Most important meal of the day, my Grandma told me and I can feel the hollow in my belly, but I wanted to get you first thing, before anyone goes ashore."

"That sounds ominous. Not so nice a way to begin the day."

"No, sir, it most certainly isn't, I'm sorry to say, but it's my job and what you asked me to do and I've found out some disturbing information but fascinating for an old cop like myself. Just let me gobble one of these yummies and have a sip of Joe and then I'll be up to it."

"Yes, yes, of course. I assume what you have found is something about the Talbott daughter or the Worth girl?"

"Hmm, well yes and no. Maybe, I guess. Let me wash this down, my Grandma always frowned on conversations with a mouth full. Mmmmm, that was as advertised. Delicious."

"Yes, I brought a brilliant pastry chef from Newschwanstein

my hometown in Bavaria, the site of the famous castle of the King called Mad Ludwig. It makes me less homesick when I taste these tastes. You must try his apple strudel, it is world class."

"Don't think I've ever had apple strudel, more of a pie man, myself. You know, I never thought there was a real Mad Ludwig, always assumed it was something from the fairy tales."

"Ah, what a shame, Mr. Rogers, so little real history and certainly German history is taught in your schools. You should go and see. The castle is fascinating, a lesson in gaudy excess and erotic indulgence, but he was not really mad, just eccentric and artistic, a patron of Wagner; he loved the operas, Lohengrin especially, but he became King too young; he was only eighteen and he was extravagant and reclusive.

"He antagonized the court so he was victimized and plotted against, deceived and betrayed. He could have been an interesting ruler but he was overthrown and his body and that of his psychiatrist were found floating in Lake Starnberg, the lake of my childhood. He was actually called the Swan King. It is a region of swans."

"Well, thank you for the history lesson. I will start with the strudel and then cruise the net for some info on Mad Ludwig, maybe even name my next dog after him. Ludwig is a very interesting name, don't cha think?"

"Yes, I do. So, what is this distressing dossier under your arm?"

"Well, here's the thing. I didn't find anything more about the Talbott girl or Von Essen or Clarissa Worth. No sightings on any of the nearby islands and they haven't headed home to New York. But what I did find, it took hours, but what I'm seeing is a pattern going back for years and crossing over to all the Empire ships."

"Pattern? What kind of pattern?"

"Look here. I've printed everything out. In the last six years, 27 passengers who have cruised with us have gotten off the ship, made calls, or left letters or cell or text messages explaining why they've disembarked and have never re-appeared. Just gone missing."

"What? What are you saying? How could you possibly know it had anything to do with our ships? People leave all the time, there must be hundreds of passengers who have not completed their cruises if you count all the ships in the line for over half a decade! How did you track those twenty-seven?"

"Well, that's what detectives do, sir. Look for links, clues, patterns. And lo and behold, there they were. Now mind you, the randomness of the events and the number of ships and cruises, no one ever filed suit, though missing persons reports were made by families, but nothing ever linked back to any of the ships.

"They were all seen safely on shore, so law enforcement just looked on land. No bodies, zilch. But you gotta admit, it is too much coincidence, and I hate coincidence from the get go. Twenty-seven disappeared passengers and now on this ship we have Worth and Talbott and Von Essen but we also have the Karmajians from the second day.

"Karmajians?" Yes, Armenians, I think. Yes, we spoke of this. They left a note. I remember their steward Jo Jo bringing it to me, he said they were quite unpleasant and Derrick had an incident also, typical complainers. Has anyone reported them missing?"

"Nope. But then, even their family, if they have a family, with the exception of the owners and their guest, none of the others really had families to speak of, but even if they did, they wouldn't be expecting them home for at least another few days, so, they wouldn't be concerned yet. So, that makes a total of 30 cruisers gone missing. Something smells like bad bait here, Mr.Hensler, sir."

"But there is nothing, from what you've said, that could connect these, these lost people to the cruise company! It is entirely possible they were victims of some ring of kidnappers or whatever, operating in the Islands. You know how unsavory the underbelly of many of these places is! This could cause a scandal and lawsuits and investigations and the media frenzy of speculation for nothing!"

"I am well aware of all those possibilities and believe you, me, I wasn't looking for trouble, but out it popped. Too much damn coincidence, man oh man, I hate that, gets me twitchy and obsessive."

"I do not want you to discuss this with anyone. Do you understand?"

"Absolute a dooty. That's why I was at your door with my belly growling. However, I did think you might want to tell Mr. Talbott, sort of a bait and switch if you will, gives him something else to focus on and gets the pressure off, so we can look deeper without my men standing guard all over and working double shifts."

"I am not sure of the wisdom of this. I am in, shall we say, rather delicate negotiations with Mr. Talbott and I am not at all . . . never mind. What is this 'Bait and Switch'. I do not know this term. Is it a police tactic?"

"Well, I can tell you're not a fishing man. It's more of a con man tactic, but it means throwing the customer off, re-directing his attention. Manipulating him away from what he came in for and selling him what you want him to buy."

"Hmm. I like this term, 'Bait and Switch'. Well, this is very unsettling, but I must warn you again, basically you have smoke and we do not want to blow smoke, another one of your American sayings, so continue looking for more, but this must not leave this office. Am I very clear?"

"As a mountain spring. I'm going to keep poking around, because if there is any connection and something's going on, something really bad, believe me, you don't want to be caught off guard. You want to nail it first and do damage control on your terms."

"Yes, Mr. Rogers. Neither of us wants to end up like the poor King Ludwig, not seeing out from the isolation of the schloss. As you said, we must 'nail it' first! So please proceed."

COME ON, COME ON, *let's get it moving, come on Rory, we're do-ing this . . . ten laps around the track . . . nice brisk pace . . . help you think, burn off some nerves . . . show opens tomorrow . . . what did Derrick say? Two producers from New York and some agents and show bizzers asking about it. . . . Oy . . . What you hoped, but not so fast . . . okay, okay . . . what the hell. . . . Go for it . . . just the beginning anyway . . . gotta take it out of the cabaret deal . . . flesh it out . . . open it up . . . don't wander off . . . keep the pace . . . take your mind off it . . . still haven't talked to Poe about every-thing going on . . . why didn't I tell him last night? Hmmmm, well* Romance for Dummies, *couple of saps we were, mooning and spooning . . . dancing and prancing . . . best sex we've had, starting to get the hang of it, not so scared, not so rusty . . . greasing those hinges. . . .*

Leah, shit! I didn't return her call . . . more than one, I bet. Guilty, I feel the Catholic part AND the Jewish part, all bogged down with it. . . .

Grandpa had the Bog deal down . . . look like giant broccoli, always think of that when I eat them . . . stunted forests . . . soggy and mysterious . . . glaciers melted, so sad in a way . . . every-thing malformed, struggling to grow . . . like us, like humans sort of . . . pushing forward against all odds, trying not to get "bogged down". . . .

Wish I'd never started this re-kindling with Leah. So hard to re-enter old friendships, friendships need continual closet-cleaning . . . must keep tossing and sorting out . . . what really fits now and what is causing clutter and confusion and doesn't fit right anymore . . . need to look at people in our lives like that . . . a lot of old out-moded junk, a few great finds, some trendy impulse buys that you're mad about for a season and then can't imagine what you were thinking or who you were to have bought it and the hardest stuff . . . when you pull out your favorite back-up outfit and it looks like shit; so then . . . no more back-up, just a huge empty space in the closet . . .

So the trick of relationships is . . . to not just fill in the empty space, not rush out and buy some second-rate, not-really-good-enough-fear-binder schmota, but to learn to live with the empty spaces . . .

Oy, closet metaphors . . . not that my closet all these many years has been overflowing . . . more bog-like than Saks-like.

Rats, it's nine o'clock! Gotta get ready for rehearsal . . . no time to have breakfast with Poe. Gotta try and call Leah though, guilt it is . . . and what can I even tell her?

Dead ends everywhere. I don't even know who else to ask . . . could try Rogers again before I go to rehearsal, but I don't know what else to do. Why should he tell me anything, anyway . . . we're totally out of the loop . . . maybe Flora's heard more. . . . Maybe Walter's told her some news . . . does not look good. What in the hell could have happened to her?

✑

"GOOD MORNING, the Talbotts' suite."

"Elonzito?"

"Yes, speaking."

"Hi kiddo, it's Rory Saltz. How's it going?"

"Oh fine, Miss Saltz. I hope for you, too."

"Great, but that's what we'd both say even if everything sucked."

"Oh, Mrs. Saltz, you are a very wise and honest person."

"Yeah, well, that and a quarter. . . . never mind. I'm trying to reach Mrs. Worth and this is the only number I have. Is she there?"

"I believe so, but she has not come out of her room yet and I think she may be still sleeping."

"Oh, okay, I don't want to bother her. When she gets up will you please tell her I'm returning her call."

"Yes, of course I will. Is there a place she can reach you? Oh, if you can hold for a moment, I believe I heard her door open."

"Oh, it's not important, she can call me back."

"Just one moment, she's coming now."

If I'd kept my mouth shut that last 5 seconds, I could have boogeyed off before she came out . . . don't want to do this, donot wanta toa doa thisa . . . God she makes me so, so, what? Guilty. Yes! . . . just hearing her voice turns me into some confession booth case. Why the hell is that? I . . . there it is again, she's so "nice". . . . What a stupid, meaningless word . . . the human being equivalent of a salt-free diet . . . what can I tell her anyway . . . can't tell her about Clarissa's buddies the rapist sickos; can't tell her I think nurse Peggums is lying . . . can't tell her Walter is fucking the Star of the Show. . . .

"Rory? Thank God!"

"Hi, Leah, that 'thank God' after my name makes me really, really nervous."

"It's just, I'm so glad you called, so much has happened, can I see you? I know your show is opening tomorrow, but oh, Rory, I'm just losing my mind and if I could just talk to you for a few minutes. I'll meet you anywhere, I'd be so grateful."

"Well, sure. I'm sorry I didn't call back sooner. I was hoping to have something to report, but . . ."

"No, no don't tell me on the phone! Where are you?"

"I'm in my cabin changing. I've got to be at rehearsal in an hour and I wanted to try and see Roy Rogers first, so it's tight, but sure, come on down. I'll be cleaned up by then, I went for a walk. I've got coffee."

"Oh, bless you! I'm on my way."

Okay, Rory my dear, what a predicament . . . something's going on, she's going to tell me something I don't want to know and I can't stop her because . . . there's that guilt-trippy thing again! Why the fuck not? Well, the old deserting-best-friend thing and the missing daughter thing and the . . . button pushing thing.

Now that part, I can stop. Glue that fucker down. No button pushing allowed! I'm a healed woman . . . in love for the very first time and I'm too old for that stuff, takes two for that tango. She does it to everyone, has that effect . . . what's that saying? God gave us two eyes, two ears and ONE *mouth. Shut up and let her do the talking. Write that on your hand if necessary, but do it.*

Shit, she's knocking, must have done the Road Runner pace down here. . . . Open the door and get this over with. . . .

"Leah, come on in. I've just got to put my shoes on and grab my briefcase. There's coffee on the table, help yourself."

"Oh, bless you, Rory. I didn't sleep much and I need to be alert. Take your time. This is so cozy. I actually like these cabins better than the suite. Up there you don't even have a sense of being on a ship."

Something is definitely going on. She looks so, hmm, altered. Not together. Never seen her not totally together. She looks a little askew. Where are my shoes? Under the bed. Okay, shoes, now briefcase. Show notes, in. Make-up bag, in, just in case we run way over. Okay. Funny, to have her here and not feel, not really care much, not using a sledgehammer to kill an ant. Now that's interesting, quite the metaphorer we are. . . .

"Rory, I love your style. You always look so casually chic, I have to spend so much time putting myself together."

"Casually chic, eh. Never thought of myself that way. Lazy and scared of change is more my fashion style. But thanks, I like that idea, especially coming from someone who always has the latest and most stylish everything."

"Well, that's kind of you, but I don't and even if I did, it doesn't make anyone love you or want you or . . . oh God, Rory, I'm so unhappy! I don't know where to turn and I did something very, very stupid last night and I . . . Rory, Walter left me! He's in love with someone else!!

"In the middle of this nightmare with Clarissa still missing, he, he turned on me, he was almost violent and he attacked me and I don't know who this person is, but I think she's on the ship and he left to be with her and I can't face the Talbotts or anyone! He had an altercation of some sort with Teddy and I think he's lost his mind, but he said the most horrible things to me and he packed a bag and he said he wasn't coming back, even if Clarissa is found!

"I think I went out of my mind, and I found myself at the Rabbi's door, looking for help and I, I had sex with him Rory and now I'm so ashamed. I just feel so lost, I don't know what to do. I know you have Poe, you have someone now. Ironic isn't it our roles have switched! I know he knows Walter and maybe he knows who this, this woman is and . . ."

"Whoa, time out. I need a time out, here Leah. Take a deep breath. I haven't even poured a cup of coffee yet. So slow it down. Give me a minute."

"Of course, of course, you're right. It's just, I've been up for most of the night, after I left the Rabbi and it's all just pouring out of me and . . ."

"Leah, breathe. I'm drinking. I'm thinking. Whew! First of all, I'm really sorry about Walter, I can only imagine what you're going through, but I am not going to get involved in that. I'm no quisling and I'm not going to go to Poe and even if he knew or I knew who, it isn't going to help you and it doesn't change anything.

"I know it's painful, probably unbearable right now, though, boy, you found a sub pretty fast, amazing antennae you have, so, but, the point is, when someone doesn't love you anymore there's nothing you can do and why or who or none of it makes any difference and will not make you feel better.

"Finding your daughter will make you feel better so I would suggest you try to focus on that and pull yourself together for the next couple of days and then when you get home you can collapse in a safe place and with support and shrinks or whatever you need to get through this. I guess this is one of those, 'Snap out of it' conversations I tend to favor and you tend to hate, but I can only tell you what feels right for the situation and for how I understand you."

"Yes, yes. I know you're right, but you sound so, so harsh, Rory. You are my best friend and I guess I expected more, more compassion."

"Leah, I am *not* your best friend! I haven't seen you in *thirty-five years* for chrissakes, get a grip! Do not lay that on me. I'm sure you have drawers full of extra friends, I'm the loner, remember? I just happen to be here now and yes we have history and yes, we *were* best friends, but it wasn't even real, I was too envious for it to be real and that's the truth. We're too different, we see the world too differently to ever be close and we always did, so let's leave that alone. I'm sorry I sound harsh, I don't mean to, it just comes out like that sometimes when something feels inauthentic. . . ."

"Inauthentic? The other day you called me selfish and now I'm inauthentic? My daughter's missing and my husband has left me for another woman and I'm inauthentic? I can't believe you could talk to me like this . . ."

"Well, I'm sorry but, you found your way to the Rabbi's cabin, 'in an altered state'? Give me a tiny break here. This ship is like a fucking jigsaw puzzle. How did you manage to get his cabin number? And after all that trauma, you took off in the wee hours or whatever and happened to choose exactly the right person to turn to, to get exactly what you needed? A good fuck and another adorer? Yes, it does feel inauthentic; that was more important to you, someone to reassure you of your desirability, than finding Clarissa? And you chose Havah Nagila dude?

"I mean, pa-leeze. This is the meaning of 'over-sharing' and believe me, I don't want to know any of this, but here you are and you came to me because you wanted information—wanted to manipulate me into asking Poe about the third party, not because I matter to you. And I am not going to take it back or let you make me feel guilty for telling the truth. You are *so* good and I am *so* bad. I'm sure that's what drove Walter nuts too, now that's really harsh, but the truth is like that sometimes."

"I can't believe this! This is like a bad dream, no matter where I turn, there's more pain, more duplicity and rejection! The two most important people in my life hate me! I never, ever stopped believing in our friendship and thinking some day you would call. This is like a knife in my heart for you to judge me and turn on me now."

"Do not do this! I want you to go. You are impossible. Go. I'm deeply sorry about Clarissa and I'll keep trying to find her, for her, not for *you*. But I want you to leave now. I'm doing you a big favor, because, if you don't leave I know my mouth and I'll say stuff you really, really don't want to hear, so please go now. Just go."

"You know, don't you? You know who he's with! That's why you've turned against me. You always liked Walter and he chose me! You're jealous and you're trying to hurt me. I understand Rory, I do, but please, for all that my family did for you, for my mother, please tell me. You owe me that much."

"Oh boy, you are amazing. Truly. Even if I knew, I wouldn't tell you and I don't want to discuss this and I want you to leave and take the fucking past with you. I'll write your mother an apology letter, with real blood on the page. Now out! Out! I refuse to allow you to take over the most precious week of my life and use me for what *you* need! So save it for the Rabbi or the hordes who will line up to comfort you. Go away Leah and leave me alone."

"I'm going. I am trying very hard not to judge you, to understand and forgive you. I will always love you Rory, no matter how you treat me. I'm sorry to have bothered you. Good-bye."

Maybe if I put my fist in my mouth it will muffle my primal scream. I need air, move, go see Rogers, too close, that came too fucking close . . . could have really messed that up. . . . Could have compromised Flora big time, cost her her gig and certainly . . . not that I'm not stunned . . . who woulda thunk it. . . . Go Walter! He really did it . . . good for them . . . wrong on that one . . . never would have believed it . . . so glad I resisted telling her about Walter and me . . . now THAT would have made me feel guilty . . . if you feel guilty or start obsessing, you're being manipulated . . . where did I read that?

Hot damn, Walter left her! Wonder what he said, wonder what he's doing?

Hope Flora's alright . . . Hope Leah doesn't find out who it is before the show opens . . . now, now, selfish, selfish . . . Flora could eat her for an afternoon snack and not even burp . . . they'll be fine. . . . Poor Clarissa to come back to this if . . .

Oh shit, maybe I was too harsh . . . her kid and her husband . . . why couldn't I just shut up? See! Guilt, she got ya. . . . Husband of thirty-odd years drops her on her perfect red head and she's banging Seder Schmuck by lights out . . . stay with that train of thought, fight that guilt and do not obsess about it. . . . Okay. . . . One more punishable Good deed and I'm done . . .

"Come in."

"Hey, Roy, got a minute?"

"Yep, funny, I was just going to call you and ask you to meet me at the Koffee Kup. Heard they've got buttermilk biscuit hot cakes featured this morning."

"With whipped butter I bet."

"Count on it."

."This is best. I'm still digesting your discarded breakfast from yesterday or was it the day before? I'm starting to lose track, that Cruiseheimer's thing sets in about now."

"Yesterday. So, you first. What brings you by?"

"Oh, well, guilt, mainly. I promised to help find Clarissa and I've sort of lost the scent, so I was just checking in to see if anything was new that you could reveal to an outsider."

"Yes and no."

"Yes there is and no you can't tell me?"

"Yep, but I can tell you we have no new leads and she has not been found, which doesn't look good."

"Did you talk to Nurse Snake Pit again?"

"Yep. Immovable object, swears she never saw her."

"Did you believe her?"

"Nope, so I had a meeting with Dr. Padma. He was asleep at the time and I did believe him. She seems to rule the roost down there; everyone's scared of her, even the Docs. It went nowhere. She told me this was her last cruise anyway, bragging to beat the band about Mrs. Talbott making her a fantastic offer to be their private nurse/companion and she was leaving with them in Puerto Rico."

"No shit. Imagine making her your choice of personal care-giver?"

"Takes all kinds. Anyway, she's leaving and she certainly ain't kissing and telling."

"Hey, I just had a very dim light switching on. My friend, Poe Evanoff, he reads faces for a living. He's a shrink and he's trained to tell when someone's lying by how the muscles in their faces contract; it's complicated, but maybe if he went down to talk to her and confronted her, she might open up."

"Unlikely. I know the type and why should she? If she did see something or did something to the girl, she'd hardly be eager to tell us and then she knows the Eyes of the Law are on her. I think it's better for now to watch and not let her know we're watching."

"You're right. What an awful mess. So, I'm out of suggestions and I've got a final rehearsal with the band. Why were you going to call me?"

"I wanted to ask you a few questions, but you can't ask me anything back."

"Gee, remind me never to play Charades with you. Okay, I'll try, but I can't promise. I'm really nosy."

"Trying is fine. I'll hold the defensive line. First question. How old is your dog?"

"This is controversial? He's five and I miss him so much that bringing him up makes my stomach hurt. So why did you ask me that?"

"I was curious. When we talked about our dogs, I didn't get to inquire. It's very hard to have a dog discussion when a cat person's with you."

"Very true."

"Also, I wanted to see if you could get through one question without questioning the question and you flunked."

"Also true."

"The next question is really several small questions."

"Shoot. I'm concentrating on the short, to-the-point answer technique I've learned from ten years of Law and Order re-runs."

"You're a hoot, you know that? Wonder why we never got together. I like your style."

"Hmm, well first I'm not much of a mingler and I tend to hole up when I'm on board and second, you never asked."

"Story of my life. Okay, back to business. How long have you been working for Empire?"

"Eight years plus change."

"Have you been on board a cross-section of the ships and traveled most of their routes?"

"Yes. I think I've probably worked on material for all the ships shows and I've certainly followed the Flora acts. We've worked together a lot."

"Got it. So, on any of these cruises, were you ever aware of passengers who went missing like on this one?"

"Oy. I hate that term. Gives me the heebie jeebies. Sore spot with me, Roy, really personal."

"Not trying to pry, Rory. It's important."

"Okay. Let me think. No, not that I recall, though as I said, I come on board, do my thing, retreat to my cabin. I don't do the booze and schmooze deal and I don't try to make new friends from each excursion, no ships that pass stuff. So I'm out of the rumor mill. I mean, I hear stuff in rehearsal and when I have a drink with the cast or Flora gives me some dish, like about Collie, but I don't remember anything about missing passengers.

"Whoa, one thing, I do remember! About three years ago, after I came home from the first cruising of the *Dolphin*, I was reading the *New York Post* and there was an item about a couple who were on the ship for their honeymoon. They went off in St. Thomas I think and never returned.

"Their parents flew down there when they didn't come home and searched for weeks. I was really into missing persons stories then and so I clipped it. But you know, St. Thomas? Talk about sketchy! So the authorities assumed they'd gotten loaded and mugged by some dope fiends and tossed in the water somewhere. No leads and I never read any follow-up."

"That is most helpful. Thank you kindly."

"So, that's it? Do you think there's some conspiracy going on or a serial killer or someone, stalking cruise ships?"

"Unuh, no questions remember?"

"It's my nature. I should get credit for lasting until the end."

"Credit given. Sorry I can't give you more info. Believe me, this is nothing compared to what I'm facing with Hensler and the families."

"I can only imagine. Gotta go. Sorry about the pancakes, but if you hurry over, you've still got time."

"Tell Flora I'm coming to see the show."

"I will. Good luck today. I guess if we don't find anything before they pull out tonight, it's very bad news."

"I won't lie to ya, Rory. I'd say the chances of Clarissa Worth still being alive are pretty small. We're thinking of doing a cabin by cabin search. We've been doing an unofficial one, just having the stewards report, I mean they sure as hell would know if someone was drugged out in a cabin or being held prisoner and we've checked every crew cabin and all the other possible hiding places, even the life boats and they come up empty, so unless she somehow snuck off with someone when we docked . . . but there are no missing clothes and she didn't have her passport or wallet and she was wearing Flora Frampton's dancing skirt. Unlikely she'd go like that from everything we've heard about this girl."

"Oh migod! What you're saying is, you think she's in the water!"

"Can't comment, but it's pointing that way."

"Let me offer a word of warning. I would not tell her parents that, especially her mother. You really do not want to go there, ever. But certainly not today."

"I have no such intention, but thanks anyway."

"This is really, really awful. What a scary place the world is."

"Well now, that's why things like dogs and pancakes become so important as time goes by."

"Amen to that. I'm late."

⚜

PAIN FALLING LIKE RAIN all over her heart. Clarissa and Billy . . . missing people . . . sides of milk cartons, backs of buses, ads in newspapers . . . please call home, all is forgiven . . . if you have seen . . . any information leading to the whereabouts . . . tears falling like pain, falling like rain, like drops off awnings after a deluge.

Rory walking — from the back looking so jaunty, from the front, looking so sad, sadder than anyone ever lets themselves look in public.

How was this all clicking into place? Her lost son and Leah's lost daughter, all these years between—the image of Clarissa—a shining bright creature, a rare fresh fine young lady, capable of having a happy life, not many people really were. Capable of becoming self-actualized, whole. A short list that. Abraham Lincoln, Albert Einstein: she had read that they were and it had become her goal, to be like that. The definition she had seen somewhere. Capable of self-acceptance and of acceptance of others, to act spontaneously, perceive reality efficiently, never fake anything, resilient when faced with difficulties, creative in finding solutions and focusing on the problem not the people involved in the problem including themselves; do not rely on others for their happiness or to fulfill their needs; values and ethics of high standard and respect for personal privacy, though values may be individual, not social norm. Constant striving to reach highest human potential. Humanism; human beingism.

She had tried to be like that, for Billy, for coping with his loss, for accepting her aloneness, her past, her wrath. She tried, Leah aside, she did. Jessie aside and Walter Worth aside and any of the other injurers to her sense of justice.

She had tried for so long to get back all those feelings she'd shut down, disassociated from herself, way, way back at the Four-Plex—just turned them off, like Sybil or Three Faces of Eve only not so radical, but not admitting how much it hurt and how mad she was and it had taken her so long to be able to reclaim enough and so here it was, yippee kiyay.

All she could see was that beautiful, innocent-of-heart young woman who had the potential for happiness being thrown off the side of the Sea Monster intruder. The terror and the horror and the waste and the evil, sheer evil of it and the senselessness, like Billy—mean and senseless and untenable but not without some hope: not hopelessly final, not the deep-black-endless-sea-final! Even if her son was lost to her forever, he was alive somewhere, capable of having a good life, a better life than she had had or his father or most people.

Grief drizzled down her being, making everything else seem meaningless: shows and careers and almost everything else, but dogs and pancakes and someone to love.

She stopped in the ladies' room outside the theater lobby and wiped her face and blew her nose, not even bothering to check for smudges and puffy lids, the outside of everything seemed completely irrelevant to her, almost a betrayal of the emotion stirred by the fight with Leah and the conversation with Roy. *Keep moving forward, Rory, whatever is going to happen next you are not going to be able to anticipate.*

She felt the bad vibes the minute she opened the swinging doors and walked into the theater. A weird quiet, not the normal restless, anxious, getting ready to put it together quiet, not that show in the making mixture of anticipation and preoccupation but a dull, empty kind of quiet. *Whoa, something is going on here. Self actualize exercise number 4 million: accurate perception of reality. . . .*

The band was there, looking glum. The composer was there looking pissed off. Derrick was there looking like he always looked to her, how she described him to Poe, "I guess you'd call him a deeply shallow man."

Derrick saluted her, one of his cute little trademark greetings, some kind of Naval Kitschy gesture he probably saw in that old movie with Gene Kelly and Frank Sinatra—*On the Town*? High energy charmers in tap shoes and navy whites hit Manhattan on leave . . . salutey tooty.

He was smiling, but only his zygomatic major muscles were moving. She had learned that from Poe. She could *tell* his smile was fake. Very, very cool. Derrick was obviously the bearer, striding up the aisle to greet her. What was missing here. Missing, missing, missing . . . the word de jour. Where was Flora?

"Rory, we were waiting for you, we need to talk for a moment, let's go out to the lounge."

"Oh boy, it's one of those step outside conversations?"

"I'm afraid so. Come on, I've got some coffee out there for us."

She followed, trying to swallow her fear, feeling her throat swelling over it, making it necessary to think about the act of moving saliva down where it was supposed to go.

They sat and Derrick poured coffee, cutting the smile. She watched him, realizing she had never seen him without his smile. It was like seeing a woman without her make-up on for the first time; sometimes a totally different person emerged. He looked entirely different. Better. How about that, he looked so much better. Handsomer and kind of smart.

"Okay, let me have it. The tension is lethal."

"Well, this is one of those 'don't shoot the messenger' reports and I'm it. I've been put in that position big time on this cruise, must be my Karmic necessity or so the Countess seems to feel such things mean, but I am, so here goes.

"Rory, Flora is gone and the show can't open tomorrow without her. I know how hard you've worked and how excited you were that there were theater people on board who were interested in seeing it. We were all excited about premiering something special and a cut above the usual, setting a new standard and the press was interested, because it made it possible to see the entertainment part of these ships as having broader potential and attracting better acts and material, the whole nine yards, but she's gone."

"Holy shit, Derrick. You don't mean 'gone' like Clarissa, not like foul play or something?"

"No. Oh, sorry, I should have been clearer. No, like, 'I'm in love and I'm out of here, sorry guys. I'm head over heels and my man needs me' gone."

"Oh, that kind of gone."

"You don't seem shocked or furious or any of the emotions the cast would have predicted or are experiencing themselves."

"Nope. The truth is Derrick, I'm not surprised. I know about the guy and the situation was very dicy and I think she knew the end was near as far as where her ship career was heading, and so she just took her shot. If you knew who the man was, you'd understand."

"Oh, pa-leeze do not tell me. I can feel the heat already and I'm sure I'll have to know sooner than I want to, anyway."

"No problem with that one. Frankly, I really don't think it's ready. I've seen so many things I want to change and expand and I'd rather wait then have it out there too soon. It was great they let us do it but I think I'm sort of relieved. More relief than regret, which is one of my signals, so relax. I'm not going to throw hot coffee in your face or have to be carted off to the sedation section. I'm just sorry for the cast. I'll go talk to them. Good for Flora. Better on her terms than Hensler's. Know what I mean?"

"Oh, Lordy be. I do indeed."

"So, gee. I guess I'm off duty."

"Not a chance. In fact we're all on overload. We're going to have to pull your old Broadway Baby revue—Serena Coffey understudied Flora on that and she's the only one who can carry it. But a lot of the patter and dialogue needs updating. So I'm afraid you'll be working most of the day and night. We're going to have to do an emergency rehearsal after the 10 p.m. show tonight. That's what they're waiting to set up with you."

"Sorry, Derrick. Guess I blanked out there for a minute. Let's get to it."

"I almost forgot, Flora left you a letter."

Derrick Doolitle handed the note to Rory without even once re-attaching his smile, which for some reason cheered her up. She took it, smelling Flora on the paper and went in to talk to her colleagues, astounded to find that something that only a week ago had seemed to be the center of her life and her hope and her motivation for getting up was now almost completely irrelevant to her reason for living.

~/c~

POE EVANOFF SAT on a lounge chair by the Aphrodite pool, the sun pleasantly searing his bald head, which he knew he should cover, but the warmth and the breeze gently ruffling his papers, was simply too pleasant to interrupt. He put on his sunglasses and looked around. The last day ashore, was always his favorite on board. At some moments he almost had the feeling of being on his own private mega yacht, having entire sections of ship deck all to himself.

He took a sip of his iced tea and turned on his phone to see if Rory had called. He could still smell her on his hands and hear her in his head and see her in his heart and every hour away from her seemed endless and there were many, but it was good, good because it gave him time to think about what he wanted to tell her and what he hoped might happen after they got back to New York.

Nothing even in his wildest fantasies could have prepared him for her. His plans for the future had been set up so scrupulously, down to the last detail of banking arrangements and even the kind of patio chairs he wanted for his little Azorean compound and his new life.

He had been completely ready; contracts fulfilled, office sub-letted, apartment sold. Everything was in order, until that shaggy white head had bounced up at him like some enchanting jack in the box and thrown his entire, carefully controlled and arid life into a tempest of tornado force emotional storm activity.

If he'd only had pre-cognition, witchcraft, the twilight zone, visitations from the dead, anything at all to foreshadow such an unlikely event, he would have done so many things differently.

How he would change the last ten years! But that isn't the way it works, not ever and so all he could do was play this set of aces and jokers as well as possible under the circumstances.

She'd left a message and he felt his heart quicken as he punched in the proper code and waited for her voice.

"Oh Poe, ho ho ho! They cancelled my show! Really a blow, the cast is so low. This is the scoop: Flora blew the coop, took her fella who's totally yella, quit and they split and I've kept my mouth shut, but I wanted to blab, hope to tell you at lunch, got a very big hunch. How 'bout Paddy's pub, get some Irish grub, need some bangers and mash and I'll give you the trash, gotta work all today and most of tonight, on with the show, and you don't want to know why this is in rhyme, as a symptom of mental decline—the songwriter's curse, I stoop to verse, but it sure could be worse, I could sing it in reverse!

"Sorry for this. But I hope we can at least have a lunch bite, since I won't see you tonight. There I go again. Gotta get back. So Paddy's at one unless I get a call back. I miss you. I do. Bye."

He sat back in his chair and laughed, playing the message over again. Someone like this, bringing him back to life with all the messy humanness that entailed—someone to live for, to change for, to dream again—but without any assurance this precious creature would agree to go with him.

If it took her some time, even if it took her a long time, he would go to the Azores and he would wait for her to finish what she needed, and to trust him enough.

He would wait for her and his life would be full in the way solitude made happiness possible, what Proust said, 'True happiness can only be found in solitude,' but Proust punted himself, his solitude being ameliorated by his loving grandmother and his parents and some feeling of support underneath.

He had learned to love solitude but he would probably be better at the aloneness, knowing she might join him and whatever time they had left to live, they would have it together.

What was that terrible, true line in Ulysses about long married couples? "Someone has to go first, someone must always go first." He had lived through it before, and it held no fear for him, only a humbling sense of life as it was meant to be lived, without the terror of loss corroding our ability to give freely and completely of ourselves.

He closed his eyes, letting the sun soothe him and played her message again.

⚛

SO THE LAST DAY of shore adventure ended and by 6 p.m. all the stragglers were accounted for, the passengers returning with bags of memories, and sun-scorched patches of skin, slightly dizzy with the overdoing of stimuli or slightly depressed at the finale, the approaching end of, for many, a long anticipated experience—something to look forward to, to make the mundane, the tedious, the daily grind of life lighter, "just three more weeks honey and we'll be sipping Mai Tais and jet skiing."

Whatever was hoped for, whatever the personal fantasy, all of those tangible and intangible reasons for leaving home, day dreaming about exotic places, and saving for the Cruise of a Lifetime. Whatever the needs filled, or partly filled by pleasure cruising, they were back on board now for the last time; they were on their way home.

The ship sat waiting for them, always receiving them without a hint of irritation or boredom or exhaustion—always right where they had left her, at their disposal, offering comfort and luxury and endless forms of sustenance to soothe their disappointment or heighten their excitement. Filling their bellies and their gullets and their senses, then transporting them safely back to their real lives; not a cure for anything, only a respite, a segue from the form of their rituals, their obligations and frustrations.

The ship never judged, never noted them at all, it did what it was told by men and computers; it carried them from place to place and returned them to themselves. The rest was not its responsibility.

So the boarding was completed and the horn was blown and the massive *Dolphin* put out to sea, taking thousands of interchangeable inhabitants with her. Week by week, horde by horde, all the same to her—taking them now farther away from land, heading back.

The ship picked up speed, the lights went on.

She was oblivious to the results of her journey, indifferent to all that had happened and all that was still to happen. Quite removed from the endless combinations of event and emotion, the result of confining large numbers of human beings in space and time and on the ocean. The power of the mixture would never lessen as long as there were people and there was water.

✑

"OHMIGAWD, SOLLY, I think I am inebriated. I am swaying around here, Solly, I can't carry the trophy another foot. You're going to have to take over. I'm tilting slightly here and I have to pee so bad, I may not make it.

"Wait, Solly, slow down! I need you to carry this and I need to lean on you and I've got to take my Manolos off or I'll end up like my Aunt Margarita with those hammer-toes. Ohmigawd, Solly, my head is spinning, my feet are bleeding, my bladder's bursting and I've never been happier in my entire life!"

"Vera, what am I going to do with you? Okay, first give me the friggin trophy. Jesus, it must weigh twenty pounds, it's like a friggin bar bell. How the hell did you carry it all this way?"

"I was highly motivated, I'm not proud of it, but I was showing off. My sister is going to drop totally dead! Solly, here, I'm putting my shoes in your pockets. Oh Mother of God! I am giving up high fashion, look at my toes! The blisters have turned into bloody, ooz-ing skin pods or something like on CSI."

"Jesus, you are not kidding. Those are the friggin shoes that on sale cost more than my Tuxedo? Enough, Vera. You aren't going to turn into one of those fashion victim broads like your cousin Mario married. We have children in college; this is a month's al-lowance. How the hell did you dance in those? You danced like friggin Cyd Charrise! I felt like I was tangoing with a movie star, and this is what was happening inside those things? I woulda had to be carried off the stage."

"Didn't feel a thing till after, just the thrill. OhmiGawd, Solly, we won! We won First Prize Most Talented on the ship! In front of all those people, clapping for us, calling our names! You and me, like we had wings on our shoes!

"The only thing I ever won before this in my entire life was that little red dinosaur bean bag by swatting those rubber rats that kept popping up out of those holes at the arcade in Disneyworld. My sister will be green, beyond green, purple. What happens if you mix green and purple? She'll be that. We won!"

"We won our *category*, let's not get crazy here. They had a lot of categories, they're not dumbnuts, they can't let all the people who've been practicing and taking it so serious go home with nuthin. We did great, but don't tell your sister we won the whole talent show. She'll be all over that."

"I know, just let me have my moment, my fifteen minutes, okay Solly? What's the harm? See, that's what the counselor said, you bring me down, see, that's an example. Gotta deflate my little triumph."

"Here Vera, lean against me, we're almost at the cabin. I'm tryin, I know how you feel when I say something like that, but it's not because I'm not happy for you or I want to take the wind out of your sails, it's nuthin like that, I just, I'm trying to protect you. I just don't want you to get hurt."

"Oh Solly, that was very sweet. I do know that. I really do. But, it's just you and me here? We tangoed and we won a prize! Solly! All those classes I dragged you to, we were like Susan Sarandon and Richard Gere in that movie. I still cannot believe it! First thing in the morning, Solly, we gotta get up there and buy those pictures the photographer took! The kids are going to fall down. Their parents, the nobodys, won first prize in the ballroom dance competition!"

"In the over 40 category."

"I know, there you go again. Oh, Uh oh, Solly, I don't think I'm going to make it. I think I'm having one of those urgent bladder episodes. Remember those 'gotta go, gotta go' commercials. I can't hold it another minute."

"Do the thing you tell me, take deep breaths, think about the dancing. We're right here. I just gotta get the card key and we're in. Oh, man, where's the friggin key?"

"Solly, enough, you've used that word about ten times in the last ten minutes."

"Well, you're gonna use it too, cause, I can't find the key. Did you bring yours?"

"I gave them both to you."

"Smart, we've both pazzo. Vera, I gotta go all the way back and have them make up a new one."

"Ohmigawd, Solly, I can't pee in the hallway! What do I do?"

"I dunno. You could use one of those friggin shoes."

"Hello? They have open sides."

"I can cup my hands, you can pee into my hands and I'll go around the corner and dump it down the service stairs and we can towel it up when I come back."

"Oh, Solly, you'd do that! No, it's no use. I've got a flood thing, it'd be all over the place and you can't go back to the lobby with pee pee all over your hands. OHmigawd, I really can't hold it. I'll have a hernia or something."

"Vera, honey, maybe if you just sit down and take the pressure off. I'll run. I'll go as fast as I can. Maybe I'll find a steward and he can open us up."

"You go, just go. I'll slide down and wait. If I pee, at least it'll go right into the carpet. This is not how I thought we'd end the most fantastic night of our lives except for our wedding and the kids' births. Go, I'll be okay."

"I'm gonna go as fast as I can. Take those deep breaths, honey. And, hey, not Susan Friggin Sarandon, it was Jennifer Lopez; you look like her and you dance better than her. I'll be right back."

Okay Vera, think about the dancing, ohmigawd, wait, wait a minute. There's a service closet right across from our cabin. Maybe it isn't locked. If I can crawl. . . . Vera you must be drunk, you're talking outloud to yourself! Maybe I'm hallucinating from the excitement and the foot pain and the pressure on my bladder or is it my kidneys? Crawl, I'll crawl across and try the door. Okay, I'm doing it. Ohmigawd! It's open. I can pee in there. I bet there's a bucket or something.

Vera Russollini of Great Neck, Long Island, winner of the first prize trophy for the Tango in the over 40 competition of the most popular entertainment event of the week on the *Palace of the Dolphins*, pulled herself up and opened the service closet door and stumbled inside. It was very dark and she reached for the switch, squeezing her vaginal muscles so tight her eyes teared, but before she could flip it up, she heard a moan.

"Please don't turn on the light," a voice from somewhere in the blackness whispered and Vera obeyed. She grabbed for a towel and stuffed it between her legs and peed into it as if she were a diapered baby, which at that moment, was about how she felt.

LATITUDE

Your Daily At Sea Newspaper

GOOD MORNING CRUISERS! As we bid farewell to the sumptuous island charms of St. Marteen, we can say, "Hello Stranger" to the equally sumptuous Palace Charm, the incredible $1 billion dollar Baby, your home for this week and hopefully for many weeks in your future: The one and only, the top of the top! *PALACE OF THE DOLPHINS.*

We *are* prejudiced, but we do think we've saved the best for last. It is a *cruise* and for the next 24 hours that is what you'll be doing and we've pulled out all the proverbial stops to ensure you'll have choices galore and land will not be missed, however many adventures you've had on shore this week.

There are so many activities planned for today, we're not even going to start listing. Yes, you do know the drill! Check the attached activities schedule and take your pick. We know you've got packing to do and we have all that luggage to collect for arrival in Puerto Rico mañana, so tonight is casual.

Wear anything but your bathrobe for our Barbeque Buffet farewell dinner. This is the real deal folks, so make sure you spend some time in the pool, on the Rock wall, the putting green, the In-Line skate rink, the basketball court, the boxing ring, or in our state-of-the-art fitness center, take a karate class, Tai-Chi, Spinning—sweat it out in the sauna, but be prepared to chow down and dance the night away to the Texas Twisters and don't forget to pick up your photo memories from the guest services desk before midnight.

So, here we go, on with the show. Have a fabulous day on board the greatest cruise ship in the world!!!! And don't forget to LOOK OVER THE SIDE. The ocean is the main attraction today, dudes!!!!

"Hɪ."

"Hi. I didn't expect to find you up and dressed so early."

"I'm not up and dressed so early, I haven't really been to bed, yet. We rehearsed until almost 4, and I came back and sort of collapsed. When you called I was face down, like a floater. I'm way too old for all-nighters, but we finished, or I finished. They've got another run-through, but they probably won't need me."

"I'm sorry I woke you. I wanted to see how it went and I was being selfish. I missed you madly."

"I'm blushing, aren't I?"

"Yes. Big red splotches on your beautiful cheek bones."

"That's even more embarrassing, since I probably look like an army cot after basic training. How about you order breakfast and I'll jump in the shower."

"Sounds like a plan. What do you fancy?"

"Everything. I want one of everything except any of the granola-y stuff. I'm starving and it's the last day of free food and I am Irish after all. Order up. I have so much to tell you."

"In addition to all your other charms, you have a lusty appetite and I cannot tell you how refreshing it is to find a woman who eats."

"Well, save it for the day I can't fit into my fat clothes. I may need to remind you."

Okay, Rory, you wanted to talk to him, couldn't wait to talk to him, oh, oh, oh, God damn this is the best shower I've ever had, everything feels so intense . . . that's because I'm overtired . . . always feel like that when I'm too tired . . . but also . . . he's here and this is the first day since we met . . . he has nothing more to do . . . I have nothing more to do . . . oy . . . all day and all night and tomorrow we dock and then what?

Ship Board romance. . . . An Affair To Remember, Deborah and Cary. . . . plan to meet again in six months . . . no way . . . I am not getting hit by a taxi . . . he could get hit by a taxi . . . why are you thinking like that? Everything about this week is too surreal . . . so how do I get off and what do we do with one another? Will he offer to take me home? Can't visualize him in the East Village. I have to pick up Herman . . . what if he doesn't like Herman? What if Herman doesn't like him? How do I incorporate him into Herman and my routine? What makes you think that will be an issue? Talk about anticipating . . . talk about not living in the present. Don't go there, Ror, you've made such progress. . . .

What do I do with him all day? Oh, boy, I'm really scared now. All night? What if all of a sudden it's just over, run out of fuel, steam . . . momentum . . . summer love . . . that Ship Board thing again . . . why do they call it that . . . because it's a, a thing . . . my neighbor Merry went on that freighter, fell madly in love (he said he missed me madly) where was I . . . oh . . . Merry and the freighter Captain . . . torrid affair for the entire trip and then they docked and he met her on shore in regular clothes and without the uniform, he was just a guy . . . all done, she was . . . all done. The whole thing was just an illusion. It was the uniform, not the person.

Well . . . hello there! Who are we talking about? Crazy Merry, who sleeps with a snake, who lives on Ativan and Mojitos? You are not Merry. This is not an illusion. He is not wearing a uniform. No place to hide anymore. . . . You are going to towel off and go back out there and the fear will go . . . now. . . . Rory . . . move it now.

Once she started eating she was fine. In her element, eating and gabbing simultaneously and he was quiet. A gentleman, a neat eater, well-brought up, clearly from a well-mannered family who sat at a real table and used proper utensils and did not talk with their mouths full, not a family of isolated loners who ate off T.V. trays all facing forward toward the human contact substitute, the screen of denial and separation that filled millions of family rooms and living rooms and provided the illusion of connection, verbal and visual musak, the light offering a kind of cozy feel, a flickering of warmth like a fake fire, softening the sorrow.

Only on St. Patrick's Day, Christmas and Thanksgiving did they ever seem to eat as a family and that was where she learned to be sloppy and talkative, the sheer joy of the connection, however forced or whatever the under-emotions, the mood enhanced by Irish whiskey and beer and corned beef and cabbage or turkey and stuffing or ham and beans and the lulling upper of aromas and booze and tastes were so exciting to her—so out of the ordinary and spoke to her longing for what she saw at Leah's house, what she saw on television, what she dreamed of having. She could never control herself; it was her rare moment of center stage, since none of the adults really had anything to say to one another, too many secrets and resentments and jealousies.

Maddie would seeth and drink too much, her mother would

smile that vacuous dead-eyed smile and focus on her father who would sulk and smoke and ignore her and her grandparents would set their mouths in two straight red lines and shovel the food in and listen to her, watching all the participants as if they were a television program that didn't much interest them, but it was the family or a test pattern.

So she talked. Entertained with jokes and stories, recitations of poems and songs, mimicry, reenactments of daily events—afraid to stop and risk being ignored again, or worse, much worse, a fight starting or, worst of all, silence. Chewing sounds and knives and forks scraping and tense, empty space. Not worth the risk, even now with Poe, she was afraid to stop and lose her audience.

And, also, she had so much to tell, so much had built up and like all good story tellers (there was that Irish thing again) she loved to spin a yarn and she had quite a yarn to work with. So she ate and she talked to him.

She threaded her loom beginning with Eggs Benedict and Nurse Peggy, moving on to Flora and Collie O'Brian with the Buttermilk pancakes and then Flora and Walter with some smoked salmon and onions, then back to Collie and Flora and the attack by Ian and Twinkle with some of Poe's corned beef hash and on to Flora and Roy Rogers and Clarissa Worth, then her fight with Leah washed down by fresh squeezed orange juice and one nice slice of Canadian bacon swallowed with more coffee and ending with Flora and Walter leaving the ship.

She stopped and wiped her mouth and put on her glasses, which she had avoided doing, but now she wanted to see his face better because something was going wrong and she needed the information.

He was cutting his food very slowly and carefully as if every bite was of extreme importance. He was too serious about what was on his plate and not responding with his usual lively intent love look, his happiness look, which she had learned from him how to read—all the muscle combinations showing spontaneous happiness; he was looking down and she couldn't see his eyes. The abruptness with which she had finished talking created a space she was not willing to fill, and he looked up.

"What makes you think the Nurse was lying? Why would she do that?" he said, so somberly her heart began to pound.

"Well, exactly, why would she? Roy thinks something's very fishy, but he couldn't share any of his thoughts with us. I have no idea, I just knew she was."

Her throat was getting tight and her chest was squeezing up and she was having a little trouble breathing, familiar signs of something not kosher, some untruth, her body barometer never lied, even when she desperately wanted to run from whatever it was that was too hard, too threatening and painful to face; it forced her to face it, a blessing in the end but never in the process.

"Rory, are you alright? You look very upset."

"Oh, boy. Poe. I am, not feeling so great right about now."

"Well, it could have something to do with the gargantuan amount of foodstuffs you've inhaled along with all the air from eating and talking simultaneously."

"I thought you liked that about me."

"I do. I love it, but it does have a price at your end."

"It's not the eating and talking. I've got a cast iron stomach and I've mastered the art. It's you."

"Me. I've barely said a word."

"Yeah, well, that too. It's your face. Your face isn't right."

"Not right. You mean like something on it? Ketchup? Bits of food stuck to it?"

"No, like fear or lying. You're U one, two and four and maybe twenty-five and twenty-six: Your inner brow raiser plus the outer brow raiser, plus the, I forget the names, the depressor, supercilli? I think, and the upper lid raiser, whatever it's called; your face is scaring the shit out of me and I . . ."

The phone was ringing and she jumped up and ran for it, terrified to continue and yet knowing there was no way back, never really is any way back once the truth has been laid out on the table with the half-eaten bagels and the soggy French Toast.

"Hello? This is Rory. Who? Oh Yes, of course I remember. From the seminar and the Seder, sort of your own S S, just kidding. *Now?* Well, I'm with someone and we're having breakfast and I've been up almost all night working so it's really not a . . . Oh . . . Oh my. . . . Okay. Okay. What's your cabin number? I'll be there as soon as I can. I promise. I'm on my way."

He was watching her and the scary look was gone, now all she saw was such enormous sadness, she didn't need to be an expert to read it.

"What the hell was that about?"

"I'm not sure, but my Nancy Drew career is not over. I have to go see this woman, Vera Russolini, the lady you picked out in your first seminar for having an open, honest face? She said it's urgent but she couldn't tell me why over the phone, but I believe her. She said I must come down there, someone needs me."

"Good God Rory, she's a stranger and you're exhausted. Can I go instead?"

"No, no, I promised. I'll call you here or in your cabin when I get there. I gotta go, now."

"Rory, wait one minute."

She didn't want to, did not want to wait even one minute, did not want to risk him telling her anything, but he came to her and turned her around and all the hurt, which she could barely stand to see, was still there.

"Rory, you are right and when you come back I will explain, but don't think it has anything to do with you or my love for you, don't be afraid. It's going to be alright."

She looked at him and her eyes filled and she closed them, blinking back the fear. "Why is it when someone says that it's always the opposite."

And he smiled, and kissed her so softly on the cheek. She smelled coffee and butter and marmalade and eggs and his agreement.

"I'll call you when I can." She said and moved toward the door.

✑

Two MIDDLE-AGED people in jogging suits sipping coffee from disposable cups, standing outside their cabin waiting for her with visible anxiety, looking exhausted but stimulated, much like herself.

"Solly, she's here!"

Uh oh. Savior Saltz to the rescue. What could they possibly want?

"Thank God you're here, Miss Saltz. . . . Solly, where can we talk? We can't just stand here in the hall."

"We have no choice Vera, she's asleep, we can't go in and we shouldn't go too far away just in case."

"I have no idea what the hell you're talking about, but the 'Thank God' before my name makes me very uneasy and please call me Rory."

"You're right, *Rory*, and it's Vera and Solly, I think you met my husband at the Sedar."

"Yes, I did . . . So, who's in there and why am I here?"

"Ms. S . . . Rory, this whole thing is unbelievable. Ohmigawd, it's like from a movie script! I'll try and tell you as quickly as possible; we're just innocent bystanders, and so are you, so don't be nervous. Let me try and explain, I just, it was all so dramatic and we were a little tipsy when she, when it."

"Vera, just tell her what happened."

"Alright. Alright. I'm taking a cleansing breath. Last night it was close to 2 a.m. and we were coming back to the cabin, we won the Talent Show . . ."

"In our category, Vera . . ."

"Yes, in the over-40 ballroom category and I had to pee, OhMigawd, it was like Mt. Vesuvius was in my bladder and Solly couldn't find the key, so he went back and I didn't want to . . . you're a woman, you know. . . . I didn't want to pee in the hall and the storage closet was unlocked and I went in and a voice said 'don't turn on the light' and I found her in there and she was all bloody and traumatized, like you wouldn't believe to go through something so terrible and she was terrified, out of her mind almost with fear and pain!

"I think she's got at least a couple of broken ribs and her wrist for sure and abrasions and cuts and maybe a concussion, bruised and battered and I just sat with her until Solly came and he carried her into our cabin and I said I was going to call the clinic and get a doctor and she became hysterical, pleaded with us not to! She said 'it wasn't safe' and that they had tried to kill her! Two men had chased her and thrown her over the side of the ship!"

"Is it Clarissa Worth?"

"Exactly right! She said she fell onto a lifeboat that hadn't been pulled in and crashed through the top and was unconscious until the next day and then she waited for it to be dark and managed to pull herself onto the deck and she'd been hiding in the storage room behind the towels ever since. It's unbelievable! Tell her Solly, what she was like."

"We got kids a little younger, so we know from theatrics and drama queen deals, and this kid is not scamming. She's in fear of her life and she needs a doctor and medication. She needs her parents, but she went ballistic when we said we should call them and they seem like such lovely people, but she made us promise.

"Vera had to calm her down, and she cleaned her up my wife is a walking medical emergency kit, so she had antiseptics and bandages and she gave her . . . what the hell did you give her? Advil or something and a valium, because she had to calm her down; the kid hadn't slept, but you know, we're not equipped, we could be liable and we didn't know what to do, but we did believe her.

"So finally this morning, we told her we had to have some help, she needed some help and she said the only person she trusted was you, to call you."

"I thought . . . we were all beginning to think she was dead, so excuse me if I sob away here, but this is one of those bad news, good news things. She's alive! That's, so wonderful! You were really great, to trust her, to take her word like that. I've got to think this through."

"She wants to talk to you. Don't worry about waking her up. You go in and we'll go eat a little something and give you some time, but then, we've got to get some rest and pack and we don't know what to do with her, but if she's in danger, well, we'll just have to sleep in shifts, right Solly?"

"Right."

"You two go eat. We'll figure it out somehow."

"Here, I'm giving you one of our keys, just in case, but leave the Do Not Disturb out, she'll freak out if the steward comes in."

"I'll put on the inside lock so when you come back knock three times."

"Solly, do you believe this? It is like a movie. Can we bring you a little something? Maybe a bagel?"

"I've just eaten the most massive breakfast of my entire life. I'm good for decades. But thanks."

"We'll bring food for Clarissa, not to worry."

The two decent married people in almost matching exercise attire walked quickly and in almost lock step down the hall away from her. The husband reached out and put his arm around his wife and Rory felt a knot of longing in the bottom of her belly; to have a comrade, a life companion, she had almost allowed herself to hope, but his face up there . . . first things first. She inserted the key and moved quietly into the darkened cabin, knowing that whatever Clarissa was about to tell her would change her life again, forever.

Red hair fanned out on white pillow, pale young woman softly sleeping. Rory stood beside her unable to break into her release from reality, envying her deep, silent slumber, a time-out; the idea of a medically induced coma had always fascinated her; it sounded almost pleasant, like a long winter nap. A release from the tension of the endless shiftings of consciousness, the doubts and fears, the mendacity and complexity and alternating daily perceptions of awareness. Facts, differing points of view, conflicting emotions, truth or duplicity, self deception or self-awareness and the past and the future and calorie counting and tooth brushing and libido needs and fashion issues, money problems, loneliness, menopause and guilt and shadows of Billy. Old plumbing and street crime and everything else all the time getting in the way of her joy and peace of mind. A little floatie here and there—a nice quiet but harmless coma for a day or two now and then.

Clarissa was *alive* and not lying at the bottom of that enormous watery endlessness, not decomposing and picked over by passing predators instead of bouncing down Broadway or somewhere, full of exuberance, a golden girl if ever there was one.

She knew the moment she touched her, called her name, brought her back from the safe place that sleep is, both of them would have to deal with something deeper and darker than either of them had anticipated. The very act of sharing it back and forth, whatever it turned out to be, would turn it from the ether and deniable, to the concrete in your face.

Rory wiped her eyes and sat down beside her, smelling the Russollinis' lime aftershave and Gardenia perfume, hair spray and Lavoris and drying underwear, so personal to be in someone else's intimate space. A cabin or a hotel room, like the private parts of someone's home where guests never ventured, almost illicit to be in there without them.

She waited, hoping Clarissa would wake up on her own, but she was too deep in her time-out, her escape from the power of the present.

Rory reached out and rested her hand on the cool silky white arm, the Leah-like arm of Leah's daughter and her eyes fluttered and then opened. Walter's eyes, such a miracle these genetic soups, stirred by invisible, unknowable, unfathomable alchemy—creating each single being one at a time, each mold shattering immediately afterward. Walter's eyes in Leah's face looked up at her.

"Rory, you came."

"Of course I came, best offer I've had in years."

"Don't make me laugh, I think my ribs are broken."

"Now you must know that all you have to do is say something like that and it will automatically trigger compulsive hilarity. I will be funnier than I've ever been and you will yuck your heart out."

"You're right I take it back. Anyway, this is so not funny, it probably wouldn't happen for long." Tears now, pouring down her unlined, untouched face, dropping onto her neck and trickling onto the Russollini's body-scented sheets.

"They're dead, Rory. I saw them both. They've been murdered and they were . . . parts of them were off, cut off."

"Who? Parts of who? It's okay, I'm right here. Who?"

"Ian and Twinkle! They were on tables, like operating tables in the clinic. After I left you, I went to lie down in my room, but the pain got worse and I got up and went down to the clinic; there was this big guy in some kind of maintenance uniform and he was standing, like on guard outside the door and the lights in the hallway were off, so he didn't see me.

He kept looking at his watch and he was shifting around, like maybe he had to use the bathroom and he must have because all of a sudden he left. There was a "closed" sign on the door, but I guess he'd forgotten to lock it. I pushed and it opened and I went in, but no one was there so I walked back through and there were some weird lights on in the treatment room and people in surgery scrubs and I peeked in through those porthole windows they have and I saw — I saw Twinkle's . . . her face was . . . her eyes were gone! And she was all cut up! And Ian too, his arm still had his Rolex watch on it, but it was almost hanging off! I must have gasped, I don't know it was very dark, but someone in a mask looked up and saw me and yelled to someone, 'take care of her!' they said and I started to run and then two men were chasing me!

"I never looked back, I just ran and it was like in one of those dreams, my legs were heavy and I couldn't scream and I think one of them was the guy from the hall, they were big and they caught me and knocked me down and I must have passed out and then I was being shoved over and I heard them say something horrible and I was falling! I thought I was dying and that's all I remember until I woke up in the lifeboat! If they find out I'm alive, they'll kill me, because I saw, I saw it and I can't trust anyone now! Please, promise me you won't tell my parents, not yet, please!"

'I promise. Shhhhh, shhhhhh, don't worry about any of that, no one is going to hurt you. You're covered okay?"

"So what do we, what can I do?"

"Now that is a very good question. Give me a minute. We have to make some very serious choices and we have very little time, so I'm processing as quickly as my fevered little brain can sort this out."

"I've never heard a grown-up say anything like that before."

"Who said I was a grown-up?"

"Don't make me laugh, Rory. It really hurts."

"Who said I was being funny. Okay. Now, first, you need a doctor. Your wrist is a mess and it's important to know whether you can safely be moved, so . . ."

"No, no Rory, you promised! Only you! I can't take the chance. Please."

"Whoa, Clarissa, look at me. Here's some wisdom about life given to me a long time ago by a very smart man. The only person you ever need to trust completely is yourself, which is a lot harder than it sounds. And you, yourself, chose *me* to trust. So no bullshit, if you trusted me, then you have to *trust* me to make some decisions on your behalf. Sometimes we just have to and you need, *we* need help. We have to stabilize your injuries enough to get you off the boat tomorrow and to a hospital in Puerto Rico without anyone seeing you and we can't do that alone. Got it?"

"Yes. I wasn't thinking about any of that."

"You don't have to. Now, do you remember spending that last evening with me and my friend Doctor Evanoff?"

"Yes, but he's a shrink."

"Did you like him?"

"Yes, a lot. He has kind eyes."

"Yes and he's a psychiatrist, which means he's also a medical doctor and both his parents were medical doctors and since we can't trust anyone in the clinic, he's our basement in this hurricane and we're going to have to trust him. So, let's do that first. One trust at a time, okay?"

"Okay."

"I'm going to call him in front of you so you know exactly what I say."

"Thanks, Rory."

"I'm dialing. I think he's in my cabin. Poe? Listen closely, do you have a medical bag? Great! I need you to bring it and act nonchalant.

Come to G-Deck, cabin 6-302 and knock three times. I'll explain when you get here.

"Do not tell anyone where you're going. Maybe put your bag in a beach bag or something so no one thinks you're going to treat someone and if anyone's in the hall, wait until they pass. I don't mean to be too Forensic Files about this, but it's serious, like life and death level. Come quick. Bye.

"He's on his way."

She could see the relief on the young woman's face: the handing over of the responsibility to an older grown-up, someone who seemed sure of themselves, someone who could make decisions and take charge.

Three knocks. Clarissa's eyes were closed, she'd nodded off again. Rory tiptoed to the door and opened it onto the face of the man she almost trusted, the man she now loved and didn't know what to do with. He had come, without asking a question or hesitating. Maybe she'd misread his face.

She put her finger over her lips and he nodded and looked over her shoulder at the sleeping beauty.

"Is that Clarissa Worth?"

"Yes. Poe she's pretty badly hurt and terrified. The Russolini's gave her some Advil and a valium last night, but they were afraid to prescribe for her. She's had a horrible experience. I can only tell you that she was in the wrong place at the wrong time and two men threw her over the side of the ship, but she landed in a lifeboat. They don't know she's still alive.

"This is for real. Her wrist is broken and some ribs I think and I don't know if she has a concussion. But she won't go near the clinic and we have to find a way to get her off the ship in the morning and into an ambulance and to a hospital in Puerto Rico and I, she trusts me, so she let me call you. Can you help?"

"I'll do my best. You sit over there and have some water. You look awfully pale to me. Too little sleep and a lot of excitement."

She sat and did as she was told. She felt light-headed and exhausted and her pulse was very slow. How could he see that? She was very quiet, for her. No rustling or fidgeting. She watched him, sitting beside Clarissa, murmuring to her so gently, almost like a horse whisperer or a vet with a frightened pooch.

He asked questions and she nodded or answered and he patted and probed and she winced a couple of times and he took things out of his bag, he had all sorts of interesting things in there and he pulled them out and taped her ribs and splinted her wrist and looked into her eyes and asked her to say some words and move her head around and move her eyes around and then he asked her to sit up and he moved her legs and gave her some pills and checked his watch and settled her back and she closed her eyes again and Rory wanted to close hers too and lie down beside Clarissa and have him murmur to her and pat her and put his hand on her forehead and give her something to stop the confusion for just a little while.

He turned to her and motioned to the bathroom and she followed him in and closed the door behind them. The bathroom was very small and they were very close together and she could smell him.

"Is she alright?"

"Basically. I've done what I can, but she needs to get into a real hospital and have that wrist set, the sooner the better. She has a mild concussion, nothing serious, so I gave her something for the pain and to keep her calm. She's a brave young lady. You're going to need the Security Chief to get her off before anyone else and into an ambulance. Does she know her father's gone?"

"No. I'm taking her one step at a time. I need her to agree to let me call her mother. Leah's a lot of things, but she's certainly innocent of any involvement and she's absolutely frantic and I can't take over for her.

"Her mother is going to have to go with her to the hospital and it's only right she knows her daughter is alive. But she freaked out about telling them. I don't understand. I mean, I can see how she'd be very upset with her father, finding him with Flora, but still . . ."

"Rory, keep it simple. Her mother and Roy Rogers should be told, but all he needs to know is that she was injured and she's scared and wants to get off and to a hospital without anyone knowing.

"Tell him anything. She was drunk, she was with a guy and had an accident. Do not tell him what she told you. Do not get any further involved in this than you are. You must believe me. That will not only endanger her and her family, but you."

"But what if they come after her when they know she's alive? She saw something . . . I can't tell you what, but she's really in danger."

"No one will come after her if you leave it where it is."

"How do you *know* that?"

"It's a ship. Rogers has expensive former military muscle to deal with crimes at sea, such as piracy. They will handle it on board. It will end when she gets off."

"But, it won't because . . . look, I can't tell you, here. I'll tell you when I get back to the cabin. Will you be there?"

"All day if necessary. If you need anything else, call me. I'm leaving some medication with instructions. Talk to her and call her mother."

"She's not going to be happy."

"Not at first, but she will be when she sees her. Mom is Mom, even the bad ones."

"I guess, couldn't prove it by me. But Leah isn't such a bad one, and she loves her kid. So, thanks, Poe. I owe you."

"Not a chance. I'll be waiting."

She let him out and re-locked the door and went back to Clarissa to give her the second "trust me" option. Clarissa opened her eyes on her own this time and smiled at her, which was a good sign.

"Okay, kid, now, first choice was not bad? So, second one. We have to call your mother. She has to help you off the ship and in addition to thinking you may be dead, your father has walked out and off the ship with Flora Frampton and left her for, probably, ever, which is something you know and your mother doesn't know.

"And we also have to tell the head of security, because he's the only safe person who can get you off the ship and into an ambulance in the morning before anyone else, even Collie O'Brian."

"Rory, no. No! You can't tell anyone from the police! You can't! Those men, what they said, when they were throwing me off . . . it's so . . . you can't tell him!!!!!"

"Hey, hey. Trust is trust, remember. And he's not the police! I won't tell him anything you don't want me to. Poe agrees. How about I tell him you were partying with someone and you fell down some stairs and were too ashamed to face anyone and the guy let you stay in his cabin, but you're in bad shape and need to be in the hospital or I can try to think of something a bit more dramatic?"

"Okay, that's fine, but nothing about what really happened. Promise me!!!"

"I promise, but what the hell did they say? This is a lot to cover up. The Talbotts and the Countess have dead children here, Clarissa. This is something totally horrifying!"

"I know. I do know that! But they can't know about it! They can't because . . . I'll tell you, only you, but you can *never* tell the police. Promise me!"

"I'm probably out of my mind to promise this, but I promise."

⌒

HE WAS SITTING outside on her little balcony, just sitting very quietly, except she could read tension around his eyes and mouth, looking out at the water as the *Dolphin* thrust forward, pushing the sea aside.

All she'd had to do was worry for just a minute about how she would spend an entire day and night alone with him, just the thought was enough to unleash the Gods-of-Let's-Fuck-up-that-Waste-of-Good-Energy, and now half the day was over and in addition to everything else, all she wanted to do was throw herself face down and sleep forever.

She opened the sliding door and sat beside him.

"Hi."

"Hi."

"How is she?"

"Whatever you gave her really helped. She's mainly sleeping and the pain doesn't seem as bad."

"How did the rest of it turn out?"

"Well, it's a shame I never saved my Camp Fire Girl beads. I could've been an award winner. I am so tired, I'm having trouble forming my words, so the crib notes version is, she let me call her mother, and that was a huge relief. I left them alone with an enormous quantity of food that the Russolinis brought back. Boy, was she lucky to land in their lair. What a trip those two are. They have renewed my waning faith in my fellow man.

"So then, I went up to see Roy and gave him a plausible scenario and he was drilling me pretty hard, lots of intense, unwavering eye contact, but he took care of everything. She's going to be taken off, like the minute the ship pulls in; she and her mother and he's worked it out for their suitcases to be put ouside — on top of everything else there's all this luggage to deal with!

"Leah left a note for the Talbotts saying she was in her room and did not want to be disturbed; Elonzito will put her suitcases out and the Russolinis packed up and Leah will put *their* suitcases out and Leah and Clarissa will stay in *their* room and Roy gave me a pass key to Flora's cabin, so the Russolinis can sleep there and Leah has her passport and Clarissa's and all that stuff with her and we did a little arms around one another, forgiveness dance.

"You were right about the Mom is Mom. They need one another now. No more 'Daddy's little angel!' Actually, the role he played with both of them was pretty heavy on the Father Know's Best bullshit, so, oy, I don't feel so great. I thought I'd never eat again, but I think I'm hungry or something. I feel kind of shaky."

"I have sandwiches inside. I'll get them, but it may be more anxiety."

"I'm too tired to be anxious."

"Really? Your face says otherwise."

"Oh, I get it, we're going to do a micro-expression face-off. You'll read mine and I'll read yours and you'll tell me what I'm really feeling and I'll tell you what I think you're really feeling, but being a novice and not highly motivated to see what I saw in your face this morning again, I'll lose. I hate this."

"I know, but we must. I'll get the sandwiches and then we need to talk."

"Good, since I talk with my mouth full and I'm exhausted, I'll probably choke to death and solve all our problems. Or maybe not all, as a Woody Allen character once said, 'I'd commit suicide but it wouldn't solve all my problems.' "

"God, Rory, don't."

"What's the matter? Poe . . . you look . . . that was just funny. You look like I just flushed your donor organ down the toilet or something."

"What did you say?"

"I said you look like . . . you heard me . . . I was doing a little mood lightening, what's wrong? You look so, your face is . . . it's A.U. one? Anguish? Am I right? You're really scaring me. Oh, God, Poe! Are you crying? You're crying. What did I say? Are you waiting for an organ? Oh my God! You're sick and this is like your last love affair and I . . . ? What? Tell me!"

"Rory, come, come inside and sit with me. I want you to have some water and something to eat. I'm sorry to upset you. I'm not sick. Come."

Follow him, follow, follow . . . sit and swallow . . . he's cutting my sandwich. He's pouring my water . . . This is not good, I just don't know if I . . . I'm always expecting the worst on the surface, but not

*really . . . inside I always believe things will be okay but if I pretend
I think they won't be then I'll cheat fate . . . talk about self-deception. . . . So? You didn't really think this would happen even while
you were 'expecting the worst from him' and now he's going to break
your little Harp heart in a million pieces . . . he is, I know he is and
I think I can't stand it. . . .*

*Sing Rory, sing inside your head and then you won't really have
to hear him do it. Swallow . . . and sing . . . what would be appropriate? Lost love. . . . Man that Got Away? . . . Naw, too bitter. . . .
Something more romantic . . . how about My Romance? At least I
know the words. . . . My Romance, doesn't have to have a Moon in
the Sky. . . .*

"I love you, Rory. Please remember that because I have to tell
you some very tough stuff and I know you'll not want anything
to do with me after, but please, never, ever doubt, that I love you
beyond words and I never wanted you to know this but I owe this
to you. . . ."

My Romance doesn't need a Blue Lagoon sailing by

"Rory, I told you my daughter died, but I never told you why. She
was born with severe kidney malfunction and she was very low on
the donor list because she was already so ill by the time she was
correctly diagnosed and because she had my wife's blood type which
was quite rare and none of us were American citizens then.

"She died waiting for a transplant and my wife could not handle
the guilt, she blamed herself for everything. I told you this our first
night, except, possibly the extent of *my* guilt.

"I wasn't watching her closely enough. She was acting more positive and cheerful and we all thought the medication was working.
The morning of the day she killed herself she'd looked right into
my eyes and smiled, and told me she was fine and then she slit her
wrists and her throat. I started following Elkman and Tomkins,
because I'd read about the micro-expression work being used by
psychiatrists to tell when suicidal patients were lying. Even though
she was gone it made me feel less helpless, maybe I could save
someone else's wife or . . ."

No month of May, No Twinkling Stars . . .

"Then about three years later my mother died and I went to Israel for the funeral and of course all the loss caught up with me, the numbness cracked like a wine glass at a Jewish wedding, that's how I felt, like some overenthusiastic groom had just stomped his foot down on my heart and shattered it into shards and splinters and rage; unstoppable rage.

"I don't know if you've ever read Carl Jung or you know about his theory of synchronicity, but this was what happened to me in Israel. I was just wandering around in all this raw emotion, staying in my mother's house, reading her diaries about the Holocaust and exploding inside with so much anger; the word in Latin actually is *angere*, which means to strangle or confine, which is what it felt like.

"I hadn't talked to anyone in weeks when the phone rang one afternoon while I was strangling on my anger and a strange man told me he had a proposition for me I might find interesting but it must be conducted in utmost secrecy and I could not ask any questions. He said saving children's lives was involved and if I was interested, he would send a car for me in an hour. I was to wait inside and a blindfold would be slid under the door, then they would lead me to the car."

No hideaway, no soft guitars . . .

"Well, I didn't think I had a bloody thing to lose, even if they killed me, and being in Israel one never knew, and so off I went, just like in a spy film with the man who had called and a driver; none of us said a word for what seemed like hours until we reached our destination. They led me out and into a basement of some sort, and the amazing thing was, I was completely without apprehension.

"It was as if my entire life up until that moment had been leading exactly to this place. My purpose on earth was about to be revealed. I understand how ridiculous or sententious this sounds, but I believed it then and I believe it now. This stranger who stood over me was Abraham to my Isaac or God to my Abraham; it was the Holy Land after all.

"He told me he worked for an Israeli billionaire, a brilliant and driven man whose loved ones had been beset with genetic tragedy. Various rare forms of cancer of the kidneys and livers and lungs had devasted his family and his sibling's families.

"He had lost two of his own children and his sister and several nieces and nephews because Israel's laws on organ donation were impossible; the ultra orthodox Jews believed the Talmud forbade it as desecration of the body.

"In his despair and helplessness, he had decided to devote his life to finding healthy organs for the young. He set up private clinics in amenable countries like South Africa, Turkey, Russia and he put together an international network of middlemen and a few select doctors to find organs.

"Well, up to that point of course, it sounded like a dream come true for me, to be involved in something like that, but then the fine print got bigger.

My Romance, doesn't have to have a castle rising in Spain . . .

"I was not allowed to ask questions, but he knew my question would be, where do you find all the donors? In the U.S. alone there are more than 85,000 people on the list and thousands of them die every year waiting for a donor.

"Ah, ethics, what a luxury they are, Rory. What they were doing was harvesting bodies. Murdering people and then taking everything useable: eyes and ears and lungs, and livers and kidneys and hearts and skin grafts and cartilage.

"It was rather like Robin Hood. They targeted people that their scouts deemed to be physically healthy enough, but otherwise worthless or evil, made them disappear and put their beautiful living parts into dying children. Thousands and thousands of young lives were being saved.

"You cannot imagine what desperation is out there. Poor people are selling their kidneys and eyes, to feed their families! Unscrupulous organ brokers cheat many of these people out of the money owed them. Desperate families are commiting themselves to endless poverty to pay for botched illegal operations or they're having diseased organs transplanted by venal physicians. The world of the organ seekers is beyond anything imaginable to outsiders.

"This man told me, they had become increasingly concerned by how they were choosing donors, and they had read about me when I came for my mother's funeral and done some research and lo and behold, not only was I one of the few available practioneers of micro-expression science, but I had lost a daughter because of the donor waiting list!

"*And* I was right there in Haifa and a Landsman to boot! Ah, sychronicity. He told me I could take my time, that they knew it meant crossing an enormous line in terms of my oath as a doctor, etc. and I said, I didn't need any time, but I would never take one cent for my help and when I was ready to stop, I was out without any further connection or contact.

"He agreed and he asked me how I would choose and I said I would choose pathological narcissists and sociopaths because they only brought misery to the people who loved or trusted them and never, ever brought joy; they sucked life and energy out of the world and I was very good at spotting them now, by reading their faces.

"Maybe in the end we were upsetting the entire balance of the universe, the far bigger picture of how negative and positive energies work and if bats eat mosquitos, scary as they may be, they're valuable, but are mosquitos? Who can say.

"If Hitler played God, so could we. Medical vigilantes, the ends justifying the means; whatever it was, I didn't care. It was my mea culpa, or maybe it was just the strangling rage and the human need to release it outward.

"I made the decision and I never looked back or regretted it until today—or rather until the night I saw you and the idea of something to live for, to hope for, flushed all the dregs of the malice and guilt and plucked the shards and fragments of glass out of my broken being.

"But even then, Rory, my darling, Rory, even now, looking at you, seeing how frightened you are, I wouldn't take it back. I don't regret any of it! Countless lives have been saved, families spared. Good coming from however unlikely a source.

Nor a Dance with an endlessly surprising refrain . . .

"I love life, Rory, but I hate the world. I'm sick of the world and I don't see things from a socially acceptable point of view anymore. I see a world in which the very worst of us are often the most sought after, the most successful, famous, popular. I see a world where everyone lies to fit in and fitting in is more and more essential. No one wants to risk being outside the circle.

"The people who conquer whether in politics or the arts or

business, are generally the most ruthless, uncaring of others, self-centered, unreachable—but they *are* adorable, charming, charismatic, irresistible. No one sees through them and gets to stay close to the power and the light, so the choice we are confronted with more and more is our integrity and our truth or a place at the table.

"Everyone keeps circulating the same lies and when someone stands up to be counted and speaks an unpopular truth, they are set upon, left to crawl off in mortification and isolation and very few of us will risk that.

"Very few of us will even risk not going to boring parties or eliminating all the phony relationships that clutter our lives, so we get exactly the celebrities and leaders that such cowardice and self-deception provides. In other words, we get what we pay for.

"I think the price is too high, but it's easier for me, because I've already left the game. This cruise was my last job for the Israelis. I was finishing up and as soon as I got back to New York, I was going to leave forever. I have a house on this remote island called Flora in the Azores.

"Then we met and I let myself imagine you coming with me and feeling more joy than I thought was possible for me now. But the downside of synchronicity, I suppose, is the circle has to complete and with you came all of the connections between you and the Worths and . . .

Wide Awake, I can make my most fantastic dream come true . . .

"I can see in your eyes, you've just figured the rest of it out."

My Romance Doesn't need a thing, just you. . . .

"Oh, shit, I finished my song and I . . ."
"What song? What are you saying?"
"I was singing inside my head, so I could stay still and listen to you but I chose one that was too short and it didn't block enough out and then it was over and now . . . Now I guess I have to really face this and I . . . Did I ever tell you what my grandfather did in the old country?

"I know I didn't. I've never told anyone. . . . I mean it's not like he illuminated the Book of Kells or anything, but . . . he was a

Cooper, that's what the Irish call caskmakers. It's quite an amazing craft very speciliazed, takes years of apprenticing and training and its incredibly intricate . . . how they carve the casks, using mostly their eyes and the feel of the tools in their hands and their connection to the wood; it's very intense and it was a skill passed on from father to son, you sort of had to be born into it. It was one of those prideful professions.

"You know, casks have been around for thousands of years, they found them in the Egyptian tombs 4,500 years ago and my grandfather he worked for Guiness in Dublin, but they started to phase the Coopers out, stainless steel was new and cheaper by far and he was getting older and they let him go. It killed his spirit I think. He came to America and settled into a kind of sour emptiness.

"He became bitter and cold and when I was trying to blot out what you were saying, I kept seeing my grandfather whittling away at his casks, steaming the wood slats and shaping and pounding the copper bands around the top and bottom and sanding and shaving and doing it with such love, such concentration and pride and I envied that I guess.

"I, understand. I can understand how the chance to turn something so horrible into something meaningful, something you had some feeling of control over, giving hope and saving children and saving yourself too, having a meaning . . . because when the world screws with your reason for being . . . whatever we may see as our reason . . . it's very hard to. . . . I do know and I guess that's why I thought of my grandfather, maybe if they hadn't taken his casking away, he might have been kinder and I know when I lost Billy, how I felt . . . I had nothing to live for except the quest, and then . . .

"Well . . . putting pieces of a reason for being together I guess and also I was trying to absorb how it was possible that Jessie, someone I loved and thought loved me, no matter how puny the love was or flawed the person, that someone I'd cooked Thanksgiving for and whose head I'd held when he had food poisoning and whose fan I'd been and who I'd made a baby with, someone who *knew* me — knew what would be unbearable to me — that he did exactly that, the unbearable thing . . . so cruel or maybe he just didn't even see me or care about me enough to even be cruel, he just took what he wanted for whatever reason, which is even worse than if they do it to hurt you . . . do it in anger . . . if they do it with indifference to you as a human being, that's the hardest to bear.

"I was listening to you and I know this may sound really weird, but I envied you. I envied you loving your wife and child and being loved by them so much, and loving your mother so fully that you could mourn so completely, grieve their goodness so to speak, without the kind of shame I've always felt about my family and about marrying someone like Jessie and this sense that my life was tainted by people not really caring about one another . . . even losing Billy, but not being able to mourn him . . . until this week, until you helped me to accept. . . . Oh boy, I know I'm just evading like crazy here because . . .

"Shit! Poe!! It was Walter! Walter was part of this! Wasn't he? That's the thing Clarissa told me, that I swore I wouldn't tell the police, but you aren't the police, that's for sure! She heard the men who threw her overboard say something like, 'Dr. Worth didn't okay this.' Oh God! You did this with Walter! You *chose* Ian and Twinkle! She saw, them Poe! She fucking saw them with pieces cut off! Is it true?"

"Yes, it's true. Walter ran the medical part. He'd been working for the Israelis for several years before I got involved; when I started he had just gotten the retainer for the Empire lines, which seemed to all of us to be a perfect cover and a way to dispose of the, remains."

"No fucking way this is happening! Remains!!! He chose Clarissa's *friends*?"

"No, I chose them the night I met you. I had no idea who they were, I just watched them and studied their faces. The way it worked, no one knew too much. One of the ship's photographers would take pictures of whomever I pointed out and the pictures would be given to Nurse Peggy and . . ."

"I knew it! She was lying! That's what I saw in your face, that's why!"

"Yes. You were right. She was Walter's main support. She was perfect. Tough, amoral and with years of military training.

"She worked with two thugs who are on the maintenance staff and she was the liaison with local doctors. The photos were passed to Island hoodlums, who would waylay the chosen passengers with offers of drugs or partying or special deals on jewelry and then they would be kidnapped, coerced into sending text or cell phone messages to their families, and then chloroformed and taken to a local clinic where the operations were performed with Peggy surpervising.

"When you aren't trying to keep the patient alive, the skills of the surgeon do not need to be vast.

"The organs would be immediately transported by private jet or helicopter and then disseminated around the world. The bodies were put in supply containers and brought back onto the ship and stored in the morgue and then tossed overboard into the ocean during the night.

"No evidence, no trail. No island used more than once every 18 months or so. Everyone was paid in cash and no one had any interest in telling anyone.

"Walter made a great deal of money, but I don't think he planned on leaving when he did or telling his wife here on the ship. I do know when I told him this was my last job, he said it was his, too.

"And he was well aware of who I'd spotted. He said he detested them both and thought they were a terrible influence on Clarissa and I think he had other issues with Teddy Talbott, a lot of resentment and self-hate about having to pander to him, so that probably influenced him.

"I know he loved his daughter and even if he wasn't admitting the truth to himself, when she went missing, I'm sure on some level he was tormented by the thought she might have gotten tangled up in his mess and he couldn't face the possibility she'd been hurt or killed because of what he was doing. I think he just blew a fuse and took it out on his wife and ran away, but certainly not because he thought he might get caught. He had no thought Clarissa overheard anything or saw anything, but I think he panicked because he couldn't deal with the idea of his daughter being a victim."

Rory could feel her knees knocking together and her teeth chattering. Her entire body felt as if it had been electrocuted. All she was missing was a stick to bite on.

"You're sitting here and I'm sitting here and you're telling me all this and I'm responding to it and now I know all this stuff that will live in my head forever and you *know* I won't tell anyone because of you and Clarissa won't tell anyone because of her father and so we just la de da off of here tomorrow and whoops. . . . I guess at some point the Countess and the Talbotts what? Just have some kind of socialite memorial service or something and life goes on?

"I wish you *had* told me you were waiting for an organ transplant and I could at least have nursed you and let you go with all that Affair to Remember stuff in my heart but now . . . fuck this . . . Poe.

Prince Charming just morphed into the Hebrew Hannibal Lector. Life is really just full of surprises. . . . 'Trust me', you said. . . . 'Oh! but! there's just this one *teeny* thing I forgot to tell you . . .'

"I, wow, I, the thing is . . . I sort of truly do understand and I even sort of agree and could probably walk in your shoes, too but then again . . . I need another song, Poe. I do have to go find another song. . . ."

"Rory, please, not yet, please just stay for a . . ."

"Gotta go, Poe."

Wide awake, I can make my most fantastic dreams come true.
My Romance, doesn't need a thing, just you. . . .

Three Years Later: Where Are They Now?

ELONZITO STAYED on the ship. He never mailed the letters from that week to his wife, though he has kept all of them for his retirement.

Jo Jo returned safely to his family, bought his fishing boat and never spoke to anyone about what happened.

Derrick Doolittle stayed on board until the end of his contract and left with full benefits, after which he joined the Countess in New York, where they were married (her sixth and his first) and now live quite happily with their three long-haired Chihuahuas, Tou Three, Tou Four and Tou Five, Tou Two having become the favorite chew toy of the former. Ian's disappearance is still a mystery without closure.

Leah Worth, after a period of extreme self-doubt and depression, pulled herself together with the support of her daughter and an excellent plastic surgeon. She eventually met a widowed and recently retired pharmaceutical heir, who married her and whisked her off to Sarasota, Florida, where she is finally living the life she was supposed to have.

Uri Dayan, returned to his family a changed man, or so he said. There was a new almost macho confidence in his speech and his manner, which attracted new acolytes and fans. His book was published to much attention and all the publicity that ensued gave him the ballast he needed to raise the final funds to open his Center for Moral Mediation. He thinks of the cruise often, in moments when lust is necessary.

He also thinks of his nemesis Poe Evanoff, who seemed to vanish without a trace, leaving him with a strange form of melancholy. He sometimes conducts erudite one-way fantasy conversations with him, where he always wins his argument and yet, never feels satisfied with the victory.

Sissy and Teddy Talbott returned to New York with Nurse Peggy, who ministered to her for almost 6 months, before deciding not to push her luck. She left without notice taking only her medical bag crammed with a mother lode of valuable controlled substances.

Shortly thereafter, Sissy was transferred by private jet to a "Health Spa" in Arizona, from which she emerged three months later miraculously cured of her back pain.

Luckily for the Talbotts, none of their friends would ever be so tactless as to question the whereabouts of their daughter Twinkle. They never mention her, either, though her room is maintained and there is still the twitchy sense of unpleasant potential reality lightly tapping at their Park Avenue door.

Together with the Countess they did hire numerous private detectives after all attempts to find them by the island police and the F.B.I proved fruitless. Their antipathy to any tabloid attention being equal to their desire for the return of the miscreants, they never went public with their plea. No trace of Twinkle or Ian has been found.

Considering the unpleasantness of the memories, they no longer see the Countess and their lives go on much as before, though Teddy has divested himself of all interests in the Empire Cruise line and concentrates on his hobbies and golf and the study of History with ocassional excursions to certain private "men's" clubs.

Walter Worth and Flora Frampton are living quietly in a small coastal city in Brazil.

Clarissa Worth changed her major and applied to medical school, where she is thriving. She is engaged to her best friend and former classmate, Andre. Once a year she secretly boards a plane for South America. She never talks about this to anyone but Andre and never to her mother.

Collie O'Brian returned to her hometown to recover and after several months of fragility, she used her settlement to open a Day Spa, which has become quite successful, once again proving that good can come out of just about anything.

As for Heinrich Hensler, Teddy Talbott's last act as major stock-holder of the Empire Cruise Lines, was the recommendation of Mr. Hensler for the job of Chief Operating Officer. This was approved by the board, bringing much relief to the remaining crew of the *Palace of the Dolphins*.

Solly and Vera Russolini went home to Great Neck where they regaled their relatives with their adventures. Their dance trophy and framed photographs from every day of their trip have taken over two shelves in their family room. As expected Vera's sister was green and soon after planned her own *Palace* vacation.

The only detail they left out of their sea tales was the last night. Neither of them ever told anyone about Clarissa Worth; a promise is a promise, but sharing the secret and having gone through such a thing together has made them even closer. They have no plans for ever taking another cruise.

Rory Riley Saltz, did not see Poe Evanoff again before leaving the ship and picking her dog Herman up at the kennel. When she returned to her apartment, there was a message from her agent concerning some interest in her show from a producer who had been on board the ship and had heard some of the songs during rehearsal. Having absolutely nothing either to lose or, she felt, to live for, she followed up and spent the next two years preparing the show for a full production which it had, opening off-Broadway to mixed reviews and running for a respectable 390 performances.

Poe Evanoff went to the Azores and into his exile. One morning, as he was sitting on the terrace of his home, looking out at the sea, he heard footsteps, and dog steps most unlike the soft sandal shuffle of his housekeeper, Maria. He did not have to turn around to know who it was.

"Okay, Hannibal, I'm home," she said and they had a hearty breakfast.

⌒

PALACE OF THE DOLPHINS sails on, still number one, though that will soon change; bigger, more astonishing vessels are being readied. Nothing stays at the top of the pyramid for long; she will do her job and hold her secrets, journey by journey until her day is done.

But in the wee hours, Roy Rogers, still trolls the internet, haunted by the fates of the 30 disappeared passengers; he searches on, looking for links, unwilling to put the puzzle away.

THE END